HAZEL HOUSE

For my parents, with love and gratitude

"If you want to **keep a secret**,
You must also **hide it** from yourself..."

George Orwell, 1984

1

Since We Met

PHINA felt the cool September breeze across her face as she stepped out of Ophinas on Knightsbridge wearing a bright orange and red kimono. Strands of hair flew across her Gucci shades; some settling on the spare space between her lips. With one swift motion, she swept the hair from her forehead and tucked it behind her ear. As her bodyguard ushered her into the grey Mercedes Benz, she looked around the busy street, first to the left and then to the right. After the guard took his place in the front seat, she provided instructions to the chauffeur to head toward Luton where Patrick was arriving with a charter flight from Madrid. Patrick emerged through the automatic doors, and the guard made a dash for his luggage – a small carry-on, which he placed on the back seat.

"Hello darling," Patrick whispered as he grabbed Phina's shoulders, before taking her mouth with his.

"Goodness. It's only been two days, but it feels like a lifetime." She smiled at him with dewy eyes before kissing his right cheek. "I've been counting the hours since the moment you left. I can't stand the constant separation."

"I missed you, too," Patrick responded, almost choking on his words.

Whilst the van sped along the highway, he unstrapped her seatbelt and pulled her close. She repositioned her hips to leave no space between them while he took her left hand, first squeezing and then caressing it. During the fifty-minute drive to the city, they whispered into each other's ear, and kissed at intervals, completely ignoring the guard and the chauffeur in the front seat. Phina's full lips quivered whenever Patrick gazed into her pleading eyes with his piercing blue ones and delivered yet another kiss, each one more memorable than the last. Their attraction to each other had not faded, even after eight years of marriage.

As they approached their destination, Patrick nibbled her ear and whispered into it. Phina stared at him in shock and giggled.

"No!" she said, shifting uncomfortably in her seat and giving him the side eye.

"Why not? They don't care," Patrick said with a mischievous grin.

Phina glared at him and nodded fervently.

"Yes, they do. We'll provide a great show for them. Oh! That reminds me. I need to stop at the bakery on Duke Street to order bread for the dinner party tonight."

"Can't someone else take care of that?"

"And forgo the smell of freshly baked goods?" She inhaled deeply and shook her head.

"Try not to exhaust yourself," he said, smiling down at her.

"I know. It's going to be a long night."

From the bakery, they headed back to Ophinas, a five-storey stone and marble department store whose reconstruction was completed the year before. Phina and Patrick's top floor offices were side-by-side, both having direct access to the rooftop terrace with views for miles across London. The terrace was used on rare occasions when important guests came from out of town. Their offices were identical in size, but the décor was such that it suited their individual tastes. Phina's portrayed her status as an accomplished fashion designer and retail mogul. Hanging on one side of the wall were framed pictures she took with other famous designers. On the narrow end of the room were pictures from various award ceremonies, each telling a unique story — from when she won the best new designer award the year she launched her line to when she received the Fashion Idol Award in Milan the previous year. In the corner was a large table with a heap of fabrics, piled neatly and organized by texture. Finished pieces from the spring and summer collection were strewn on the right side of the table. These were awaiting her final approval before fashion week.

Patrick's office was a stark contrast to hers. Furnished with large Georgian furniture, antique lamps, and curtains that matched the dark brown and orange shade of the settee, it provided the feeling of a home away from home. Other than an imposing monk's bench in the corner near the fireplace, the room was snug and comfortable.

Patrick and Phina took the fifth-floor elevator and quickly dashed into Patrick's office. With the door shut behind them, he removed his jacket and pulled Phina close to his chest.

"It's been so long since I spent alone time with you," he said, grabbing her waist as she squealed in delight.

They kissed for almost a minute before he gave her head a gentle nudge.

"I need to complete something before we leave," he said as he transferred the papers on his desk to his suitcase. "Can you check on Brigitte? I'll need at least fifteen minutes to round up." His gaze was focused on the piece of paper in his hand

"Okay."

Phina hurried out of his office to the waiting room on the second floor. Inside, she found Brigitte fidgeting with a teddy bear. Pouting when she saw her mother, the little girl hid the teddy behind her.

"Where did she get that from?" Phina asked, shifting her gaze to the nanny.

"From Michael in Couture, Madam."

"No," Phina protested, shaking her head. "No more gifts from the staff. She'll be completely spoiled..." Brigitte's sulking caused Phina to stop mid-sentence. "Fine, you can keep it," Phina relented and covered Brigitte's hand with hers.

Brigitte stared at her with big round eyes and smiled. "Thank you, Mommy."

"You're welcome, my sweetheart," she said, running her hands playfully through Brigitte's long brown curly hair before giving her a hug.

After instructing the Chauffeur to take Brigitte home, Phina scurried back into Patrick's office.

"That was fast," he muttered, shutting his desk furtively as soon as she walked in. He turned the key in the lock, sat on a chair and patted his left thigh. Phina obliged him and sat on his laps.

Ignoring his awkward reaction when she entered the room, she asked, "How was your trip?"

"It went great. Production for 'Death is Me' will run smoother than all the other movies I've made in the past. By the way, there's already so much buzz about your new collection in the media. I'm not surprised though, after your performance last season."

"We're putting finishing touches on our upcoming shows," Phina said, stifling a yawn. "It'll be every bit as spectacular as fall's."

"Great! That should ease anxiety for your investors. The extent of growth these past few years must make them a bit nervous. You need to think twice before undertaking further expansions."

"Ophinas has not been a disappointment," Phina reminded him. "Rome was not built in a day."

—

Ophinas chain of stores had spread all over Europe – in Paris, Athens, Rome, Madrid, and Barcelona – before the big move to the new store in Knightsbridge. The individual stores, except for Madrid performed above expectations, breaking even within six months of their opening. When Phina – heiress to the Osoji real estate fortune in Portharcourt – received her massive inheritance after her father passed, it made sense for her to use the money and combine it with contributions from two investors to construct the new store. Her goal was to create a one-stop shop, not only for her designs but also for the two dozen designers that partnered with her. The edifice took four and a half years for the American construction company to complete. During its construction, visitors from all over the world would stop and marvel, which earned it a reputation as a tourist attraction.

—

Patrick and Phina met for the first time at a mutual friend's party. He was thirty-two at the time and she was twenty-six. Phina had spotted him from a distance – cool, sexy, with a hint of mystery – and ignored him as she usually did when she felt an instant attraction to a member of the opposite sex. To her amazement, Patrick called the following day. He too had noticed her and asked their host for her number.

Without hesitation, she agreed to a date and many years later; they were still completely enamored of each other. Brigitte was born four years after they were married.

During the first three years of their marriage, they globe-trotted and partied as they pleased, spending every waking moment together, and making love without inhibition in every corner of their home. Together, they made a splash in society, despite the prejudices they endured as an interracial couple. That Patrick was British and Phina, Nigerian, only strengthened their bond as the mesh of cultures ensured no boring moment passed between them.

Patrick's movie and television production projects took him to a different location every fortnight, but that didn't stop them. Phina spent whole production cycles with him. After Brigitte came, it became impossible for her to travel as much, if at all. Besides the need to stay home with a baby, the construction of Ophinas kept her busy.

Phina remembered with absolute clarity the night Brigitte was conceived. She had worn Patrick's favorite negligee, invited him to the room, and informed him that the purpose of their meeting that night was to make a baby. Patrick had stared at her in amusement and willingly obliged her request. When their lovemaking culminated into an orgasm, she sensed that something deeper and bigger than both of them had occurred. The thought had lasted for only one night, so it came to her as a shock when a visit to her doctor a month later revealed she was pregnant. The manner in which Brigitte was conceived coupled with her birthdate – the same as Patrick's Mother – convinced Phina that Brigitte's birth was predestined.

Brigitte's arrival brought a new wave of consciousness to the family. Patrick and Phina fell in love with the curly-haired, hazel eyed beauty that fell into their arms after ten hours of excruciating labor. Brigitte was a happy baby, tough but always smiling. She was Patrick's pride and joy. As she grew older, and her personality developed, she became even more strong-willed. The family moved to their new home right before her second birthday. Patrick tossed the old name that the house bore and renamed it Hazel House in honor of Brigitte.

-

By the time they were ready to head to Hazel House, Phina's head was ringing. There was so much left to do before the dinner party that evening – décor, seating, and presentation. Phina had survived major store openings but couldn't place a finger on why the frequent dinner parties at Hazel House always made her anxious.

"Iris is getting divorced," Patrick stated off-handedly after their car buzzed through the London traffic.

"What?" Phina cried out. "Will she still be at dinner? She seemed okay when I saw her a few days ago."

"Yes. She'll be at dinner. Alone, I presume. Where did you see her?"

"At Ophinas when you were away. She came to sign some papers. Oh no! She must be distraught. She acts so tough, but I know she's really soft inside."

"Remember, dear, not to mention this situation at dinner. In fact, we are to act as if we never heard."

"Okay. Now, this messes up my seating arrangement."

"That should be the least of your worries," Patrick scolded, nudging her playfully.

-

Lady Iris Thompson was one of the original investors in Ophinas. An old family friend of Patrick's, she had remained close to the family over the years. Talking about her had somehow drained their energy. They sat in silence, each escaping into a world of their own as the van roared past the city, and wound in spacious curves through affluent villages and fields. There was a sharp turn before striking the forest at a point where the view over the lake vanished and gave way to wooded streets. Phina looked out the window as the half-light of dusk peered through the evergreen trees that lined the streets for miles on the road to Hazel House.

"I wish we'd scheduled the dinner for a different night. I'm terribly exhausted," Phina said, breaking the silence.

"I know, but it's too late to cancel."

As soon as they got to the door, Phina dashed into the house, barely stopping to return the greetings from the butler. The housekeeper handed Patrick the mail while she continued toward the stairways that led to their room on the second floor. Safely inside the room, she heaved a huge sigh of relief, threw her bags on the bed and peeled off all the items of clothing she had on. She hummed a tune from "*How Deep Is Your Love*" and walked into the bathroom to draw herself a warm bath. She returned to the room seconds later and poured herself a glass of red wine before heading back to the bathroom and settling into the foamy tub. The bubbles popped and rearranged itself while she sat silently for a few minutes with her glass of wine and reflected about her day. Several thoughts flew through her head, with the top on her mind being the dinner party she was hosting that evening.

Still unable to relax after sitting for nearly seven minutes, she got out of the tub to grab the bottle of lavender oil she had left on her vanity table. She loved the smell, and it always helped curb her anxiety. To avoid slipping on the white marble floors, she tiptoed out of the bathroom. As she approached the bedroom, she heard the loud scraping of a chair and froze to the spot. When she heard Patrick speaking in a gruff tone and waving his hand in utmost annoyance, she couldn't imagine who was causing him to react that way. She wondered if the argument she heard had something to do with the mail scattered all over the table in front of him – the same mail he had picked up that evening. Clearing her voice to announce her entrance, he immediately darted around and glared at her.

"I'll call you back," Patrick whispered into the phone before placing the handset on the receiver and scanning her hastily as the remnants of a scowl slowly dissipated from his face. "Angel," he said. "We need to cover you up before you catch a cold. Come over here."

"I forgot my lavender on the dressing table…" Phina stuttered pointing at the dresser in the corner.

Patrick got up to look for the lavender oil and found it where she had kept it. After he handed it to her, he wrapped his arms around her body for a few seconds to transfer warmth before lifting her up and walking in the direction of the bathroom. Placing her on the edge of the tub, he checked the temperature.

"That works," he said and gently placed her inside.

After giving her a light kiss on the forehead, he left abruptly for the bedroom. Phina sat in silence for a few minutes and pondered the altercation she had just witnessed. It was reminiscent of the incident she observed earlier that afternoon at the office. She wondered who Patrick had been speaking with. As her mind wandered, she reached for the bottle of lavender and poured a generous quantity inside her bath water. She relaxed and almost drifted into sleep as the aroma filled her senses. Patrick's voice through the bathroom door alerted her.

"Honey, you've been in there far too long. What are you wearing tonight?

"One moment," she yelled. "Be out soon."

As Phina stepped out of the bathroom with her towel wrapped around her breasts, her heart skipped a beat the moment she set her eyes on Patrick. His bronze hair glowed in the light from the lantern and his midnight blue dinner suit hugged his perfect physique. Without hesitation, she walked towards him and ran her hand up his suit to feel the tight muscles in his back. Patrick planted his lips on hers and held her heaving chest against his before giving her a quick kiss.

"You smell divine," he said, looking into her eyes and running his hand slowly over her bare shoulders – the color of milk chocolate. "I have to get going, sweetheart, so quit tempting me right now."

"Wait!" Phina said and walked towards the closet. She retrieved her dress from the hanger and slipped it on. It was a long, fitted, one-shouldered, maroon colored number with a slit stopping at least ten inches above her knees. "Zip me up," she said, swinging her hips from side to side.

"Wow! I love it."

"It's a variation of one of our pieces from the pre-fall collection."

"It's sexy as hell. I can't help but marvel at your figure," he said. "You're even more beautiful than when I first set eyes on you."

"You're just as breathtaking and as good a lover as the first time," she responded. "I love you more every day and can't wait to have you all to myself after this damn dinner."

Patrick looked at her with raised brows. He imagined the beautiful girl he met many years ago, who refused to listen to a bad word, let alone speak it herself and shook his head.

"What?" Phina asked, smiling and revealing a dimple on one cheek as she searched his face for answers.

"I have to go," he said, frowning and looking at his watch.

Phina, stunned by his sudden change of mood, grimaced and eased back.

"Hurry sweetie. Don't be late," he continued, before springing up from the bed, patting her butt and heading out the door.

2

DINNER WITH MARTIN

HAZEL House was set on a hilltop with terraces, gardens, a lawn for tennis, one for badminton, and an orchard. A park sloped down a lake, and a series of greenhouses lay at the north end. The beautiful stone house dominated the entire landscape. The same splendidness reigned indoors. A large staircase divided the massive silhouette into two wings. The terrace side of the ground floor had a number of rooms reserved for entertaining guests, a large dining room, and several living rooms. Each room was adorned with a different theme. Moving from one to the other provided the illusion of traveling from one exotic culture to the next and then back to the familiar. The walls and the ceilings of one room were bedecked with African arts and crafts. The floor rugs were made with animal hide and the furniture was carved with ancient terracotta. Another room was Georgian while the adjacent one was Victorian. Despite their unique differences, the spaces worked cohesively, providing an immense level of luxury and comfort. On the second floor, a ballroom ran the entire length of the north wing. The south side had guest bedrooms and servants' quarters. The third floor was reserved for the family. Brigitte lived in an entire wing, complete with several playrooms and study rooms where she received private lessons on weekdays. Two nannies occupied the space with her.

Phina and Patrick loved entertaining at Hazel House. Their guests never seemed to want to leave after they've driven past the black sturdy wrought-iron gate that separated the front lawn from the street. That night's dinner was being held in honor of Patrick's new friends and business associates who came to London for a visit. At five minutes after seven, the first of the dinner guests – Lord Macpherson and his Lady, Debra Macpherson – arrived, followed by the Duke of Hampshire. His Lady had suffered a small mishap earlier that evening, and he didn't want to cancel or leave an empty space on the table, so he came with his brother, Blake Caldwell, a member of the House of Commons. Blake was striking and tall. He had jet black hair with flecks of premature gray and a physique that put most to shame. Several of the other guests arrived within minutes of each other. Cocktails and hors-d'oeuvres were passed around by four servers in black with red and blue striped bow ties. Patrick chatted with Lord Macpherson and his Lady before excusing himself to join Phina, who was deep in conversation with Blake Caldwell.

"I'm sorry about your sister-in-law," Phina was saying as Patrick slid his hand across her waist, startling her.

"Yeah," Blake said. "What a pity. I'm sure the Lady would have made better company tonight."

"No," Patrick responded, "Don't disparage yourself. You're welcome to our home. Your brother, the Duke has told us so much about you. I'm not at all surprised he brought you along."

As the two men got acquainted, Phina excused herself to chat with Lord Macpherson. Elsewhere, Patrick welcomed his business associates. He beckoned to Phina and introduced a middle-aged man of Middle Eastern origin as Mr. Yunus.

"Hello, Mr. Yunus," Phina said with outstretched hands.

"Hello, Madame. It's very nice to meet you. This is my wife Azra. She's full of admiration for you."

"Very nice to meet you too. Welcome to our home," Phina said with a warm smile.

"Thank you for having us," Azra responded, and surprised her by adding, "You are so beautiful."

"Thank you so much. You're gorgeous too," Phina said, falling in love with the attractive woman before her. She'd never quite mastered how to receive a compliment.

"I must introduce you to our other guests," Patrick said, taking Phina's hand.

"It was nice meeting you, Lady Campbell," Azra said.

"My pleasure, too."

As Patrick and Phina walked to the other end of the room, Patrick confided, "Yunus is the sole heir of the billion dollar Dynasty oil fortune."

"Really? He seems so humble. And his wife, I love her," she said casually.

"Wasn't that obvious," he said, raising his brows. Phina caught his stare and laughed.

Patrick introduced her to Mark Henshaw and his girlfriend Susan. Mark was a major investor in a new production Patrick was about to kick-off.

Just as Phina excused herself to check on the menu, Lady Thompson arrived in an elegant black evening gown, her long, silky, black hair cascading down her shoulders. An attractive middle-aged gentleman, who she introduced as Andrew was on her arm. Phina approached her and noticed the cool stare of her beautiful green eyes, set on a beautifully rounded face. The wry smile on her lips seemed to be daring anyone to question her choice of partner.

"Sorry I'm late," she said with one hand on her chest, as a few of the guests gathered around her. Her words had a musical tone that compelled her listener to hold on to every single syllable as they came out of her mouth. Phina always marveled at its impeccable quality.

"No problem," Patrick responded, stretching out his hands. "You're fashionably late. Cocktails?"

"Nothing too strong *mon cher*. I'll like to reserve my wits for later."

Several of the guests chuckled. Lady Thompson's arrival had created a change in atmosphere. She was not the most important person in the room by far, but she was a very impressive figure – the embodiment of class and style. Phina was indebted to her for providing support in her business ventures. Lady Thompson had acted as a mentor when Phina was still a budding fashion designer. It didn't stop there though. She provided the original capital needed for Phina's first collection and also contributed additional investment capital towards the new store. Being a savvy businesswoman, she had a rare ability to recognize raw talent. Her personal business, a renowned modeling agency, and a designer brand were not her only sources of income. She was also the heiress of a large shipping fortune.

While Phina made her acquaintance with Andrew, Patrick took Lady Thompson's hand and introduced her to a couple of the guests who had expressed an interest in meeting her.

"I can't help feeling that Lady Thompson is a little over the top tonight despite what you told me earlier," Phina whispered to Patrick after he returned to her side.

"Good for her. Just a few days ago, she was planning a divorce party. Well, you wouldn't be able to talk to her about all that."

"I understand, but I'm still a little miffed by her grand entrance despite being the last guest to arrive."

"Where is your compassion darling?" Patrick asked. "She's already offered an apology, so I think you should welcome her properly."

Phina took a quick glance around the room and found Lady Thompson chatting with some guests – an unusual occurrence because she typically kept to herself. Other than the slight change in personality, Lady Thompson didn't seem to have aged. She looked exactly like she did the first time Phina met her several years back and still carried the same air of mystery around her. Black was her signature color. Phina couldn't recall ever seeing her in any other shade.

-

By seven-thirty, the guests were already seated for the first course. Brigitte was settled in her room with the nanny; Phina never risked having her wander into their dinner parties. The parties usually started off classy and cool, but often ended with debates on the most grueling topics like war, crime, and dirty politics, as hard liquor settled into the system. That night was no exception.

"Our government has no clue, no plans," Lady Thompson grumbled. "The rioters just need their voices heard. You," she said, turning towards Blake, "spend so much of your time in the commons making ridiculous laws and pushing it to the populace. How can we get anywhere with such…" she concluded, throwing up her hands in a dramatic gesture.

"How else do you want us to approach things?" Blake replied, dodging Lady Thompson's attack with the slow smile spreading across his absurdly well-contoured face, a graceful slight turn bringing him face to face with her.

"That's not my call. After all, I am just a 'mere' woman, but something tells me the whole bunch of you could do better."

"My dear Iris, you are very confrontational today," Patrick chided playfully. "He is just a public servant who tries to do his duty of serving the queen. Strictly between us…," Patrick glanced around the table and paused for a second before saying, "I believe the house is doing the best they can for the masses, considering the circumstances."

"I agree with the Lady," Blake interjected. "We are mere figureheads. There is no statesmanship. A good proportion of our bills don't make it into law."

Phina was on the edge of her seat during the whole interaction. Impressed by the manner Blake had handled the sudden attack from Lady Thompson; she smiled and gave him a nod. He noticed and smiled back. As Blake continued to speak, Phina's mind drifted away to the next course. Having received a sign earlier from the butler, and asking him to wait a few minutes, she saw no way she could wait any longer without introducing the entrée – wild goose, savory kedgeree, ale pie, and roasted fish with steamed vegetables.

"May I interrupt," Phina finally said after she made a sign to the servers to bring the meal.

-

As entrée was served, the conversation changed to lighter topics. Azra wanted to know how Patrick got into the movie business. Patrick told the guests how a chance absence by an extra earned him his first role on a television set. He also told an abridged version of the immense challenges he faced to land his first movie role. Production came years later just before he met Phina and convinced her they were soul mates.

"In the end," Patrick said, pausing momentarily to rend importance to his last set of words. "We have been together and very much in love since then."

Phina chuckled lightly and the rest of the guests, starting with Lord Macpherson turned to look at her.

"What a beautiful account," Yunus announced. "Beautiful."

Patrick bent sideways and gave Phina a kiss on the cheek. She grabbed his chin with one hand and kissed him in return.

Azra wiped her eyes with the edge of her napkin. "This is embarrassing," she said in a slight whisper before she let out a giggle.

The gathering continued on the terrace, separated from a lawn by a stone banister. To the left was a cluster of trees that formed a woodland that led into an orchard. The grey stone and the green lawn were tinged with the glow of the full moon. A statue of a naked man and a woman in a tight embrace graced the center of a circular waterfall and a torrent of water spewed up at the point of embrace. Patrick had the statue built as a monument to commemorate their love. The location of their very first date had an identical statue on its grounds. It made a great conversation piece as the guests, who were now a little tipsy from the wine, chatted and flirted with one another.

Lord Macpherson excused himself for the second time that evening to use the bathroom. This time, he had no need for directions to navigate the halls of Hazel House. Apologizing yet again for his weak bladder, he walked stealthily away from the increasingly argumentative crowd, happy for an opportunity to get a moment alone. As he stumbled through the semi-lit walkways, he found the bathroom with ease. Within minutes, he was done but decided to examine the paintings on the wall in the main hallway leading to the formal dining room. Some minutes later, he struck up a conversation about the art, their history, and meaning with someone he thought was Blake. It was an interesting conversation free of the raucous he knew was going on at the terrace. He wasn't getting any younger and preferred his quiet sometimes.

"Hey, Blake," he said after at least twenty minutes had passed. "We'd better head back before our hosts start wondering where we are."

They continued their conversation as they walked in the direction of the terrace. Lord Macpherson was surprised by how much Blake knew and expressed that it never occurred to him that a statesman would have so much knowledge about ancient art. As he stepped onto the terrace, he saw Blake standing against the banister with his cigarette in one hand and a glass of vodka on the other, speaking with Lady Thompson. The moonlight framed his face as he puffed at his cigarette at intervals. Lord Macpherson looked behind him where he had expected Blake to be. Not finding him there, he stood in shock and pointed towards Blake, almost stumbling as he tried to navigate the last stair. Luckily, Patrick was on hand to catch him.

"I swear; I was just speaking with him. He was walking behind me," Lord Macpherson said, still pointing at Blake and taking another quick look behind him.

"Who?" Patrick asked.

Half of the guests gathered around them and looked in Blake's direction.

"B… B… Blake." Lord Macpherson stammered.

Patrick shook his head. "It wasn't Blake. He's been standing in that spot the whole time you were away. I wondered why you took so long. Luckily, I was heading up the stairs to look for you when you suddenly appeared. Thank goodness I was right here. You would have had a terrible fall."

"Then who was I talking to? I swear it was Blake."

Patrick and Phina looked at each other and smiled.

"It's possible you met Martin," Patrick said.

"Who the hell is Martin?" Lord Macpherson growled.

Patrick cleared his throat and tried to lead him to a seat. "Martin is our familiar ghost."

Everyone was now gathered around them.

Lord Macpherson edged his arm away from him. Stable enough to stand on his own and shaking his head to refuse a seat. "Are you saying I've been talking to a ghost for the past twenty minutes? How can that be? He even walked behind me as we came down the hallway…"

"Others have met Martin also," Phina said.

"How do you even know his name? Have you met him?"

Patrick and Phina shook their heads in unison.

"We learned his name from the servants and from the odd guest encounter," Patrick said. "This home was built in 1802 and from what we were told; Martin was a brilliant artist that painted portraits for kings and queens. After his reveal of a portrait of the Master and the Mistress of this home showed he had painted the master out, the Master flew into a rage and ordered him killed. But you needn't worry. So far, Martin has a reputation as a friendly ghost.

"That's a bunch of crap. It scares the living daylights out of people. Isn't that enough?" Lord Macpherson yelled, still severely agitated. "But why would he have wanted to upset the Master who was obviously a very powerful man?"

"Well," Phina cut in. "The story has a second version. Some say the Mistress, a very beautiful woman, bewitched him. To atone for his crime, Martin is condemned to roam the hallway for eternity."

As the conversation progressed, most of the ladies remained on edge. Lady Macpherson held her husband tightly, shaking like a leaf. She couldn't tell if Patrick and Phina believed the story or if they were merely teasing. Suddenly, a cool September breeze began to blow, and a chill filled the air. Lord Macpherson removed his jacket and placed it on his wife's shoulder. Lady Thompson seemed excited. She wasn't scared like the rest of the women. It was the sort of story she enjoyed, mysterious and enchanting. She wished she could meet Martin herself.

Soon enough, everyone relaxed and shared ghost stories. Lady Thompson told of when she was using her vanity in her parent's house and saw an image with a white face in the mirror. The image immediately disappeared when she cursed at it. Azra told about receiving phone calls from dead people asking her to do strange things.

The party went on till late with the butler and the kitchen staff serving wine and finger foods until the guests started leaving. After the final guest left, Patrick lifted Phina off the floor and carried her up the stairs to their bedroom while she squealed in delight. When the door shut behind them, he planted a big kiss on her lips, walked towards the vanity table and placed her gently on the chair before walking to the other side of the room to place a record on the music player. As she removed the pins from her chignon and allowed her long black permed hair to cascade down her shoulders, she spotted Patrick in the mirror with two glasses of wine.

"Cheers to another successful dinner," Patrick said, raising his glass.

"Cheers, darling. I was enjoying myself so much that I forgot how hectic my day was. I hope Lord Macpherson will be ok."

"Of course. In the end, he saw his meeting with Martin as some sort of adventure. I can't say the same about Lady Macpherson. She looked terribly shaken."

"Lady Macpherson?" Phina said, laughing. "Anything would have shaken her. She's such a…"

"Shh!" Patrick cautioned, placing his index finger on his mouth. "It's a bad idea to speak ill of our guests."

"Well, I don't think Lady Macpherson will ever honor another one of our invitations. Now, on the contrary, Lady Thompson was absolutely delighted. I'm positive she has fallen in love with Hazel House."

"Enough about the party guests. I want to devour you all night."
He took her glass and led her towards the bed.

"You naughty man," Phina whispered, her eyes droopy from her
long day and the drink.

"Yes darling," Patrick responded in a soothing tone.

He knelt before Phina and held her hips.

While she pushed the lone sleeve off her shoulder, he rested his
head on her stomach. Phina waited a few seconds for him to release
her so she could pull the rest of the dress off, but he refused to budge.
Convinced he had snoozed off, she nudged his head. "Patrick?" she
called.

"Yes?"

"Let go."

It took a few seconds before Patrick released her waist. She
caught a glimpse of sadness on his face even though he feigned a smile.

"Is everything okay love?" she asked.

"Sure. Why?"

Phina paused for a moment and eased back. "Does this have
something to do with your phone conversation before dinner?"

"What conversation?" Patrick asked, standing upright to meet
her gaze. "Oh… No. I'm just very exhausted. Why do you ask?"

An uncomfortable silence passed before he sighed and held her
hands.

"Honey," he said, "the call was from one of our investors. He
was concerned that our new production is guzzling more money than
our last three movies put together."

"But you were practically yelling at this person. I've never seen
you so mad."

"You see, this is the reason I try to shield you from certain
things. You worry about stuff you shouldn't bother your pretty head
about."

"I don't want to be shielded," Phina protested angrily. "We're partners. I should know when things aren't going right, especially if it's keeping you up at night and changing your mood like the weather."

Patrick leaned forward to kiss her, and she shook her head.

"Don't try to silence me," Phina said with a frown.

"Enough Phina! As the head of Ophinas, I don't dictate how you handle your affairs. Allow me to handle the issues in my organization my way." His tone was surprisingly calm. "I love you," he said in a whisper. "I want you to believe that always. Will you?"

Phina nodded.

"I need a verbal response," he said, looking deep in her eyes.

"There's no doubt in my mind that you love me," she said, melting into his arms.

Patrick placed his hand behind her back and unhooked her bra to reveal a pair of supple breasts. He kissed one after the other, causing her to moan and grab his shoulders for support. From her breasts, he moved to her mouth and then back again before gently placing her on the bed.

"You're such a turn on. I didn't think I had an atom of strength left after everything I've been through today."

With his thumb, he caressed her lips in the oval they formed with her half-open mouth before pressing his body against her and kissing her as she continued to moan.

"Tell me how much you missed this?"

"Like never before. I waited all night, two nights for you to come home."

"Really?" He groaned, driving once into her.

"Don't stop," he heard her plead when he took too long to repeat what he had just delivered.

The lights were off, but the moonlight provided some illumination. He could see her full quivering lips, the deep longing in her beautiful eyes, and her almost perfect face. The urgency with which they beckoned to him, forced the blood to his head and loins. Seeking her hands, their fingers locked into fists. He pressed his mouth on hers while her hips thrust like a string of bullets aiming for their target. There was nothing he wanted more at that moment than Phina's quivering body under his as the sensation mounted towards delirium for both of them. He drove hard and fast into her until she shrieked at the same time he released all the pent-up feelings he'd accumulated for days.

Several minutes later, they lay side by side panting. Phina was the first to recover, smiling as Elvis droned in the background.

"I love you," she heard him whisper.

He propped himself on his elbows and bent to kiss her mouth before grabbing her to intertwine their bodies and slowly drifting into sleep.

-

Patrick always knew how to make her feel loved but not enough for her to sleep soundly like him, breathe deeply like him. The sound of the clock was deafening, and she wondered when it will be daylight. While he lay there in peaceful slumber, Phina's mind wandered, not only to their conversation that evening but also to the events that led up to it. Her instinct told her something was wrong and those instincts never failed her. Their lovemaking that night had been sweet, but for the first time in their relationship, her mind was millions of miles away while her body yearned desperately for him.

3

WITHAM CAPITAL

PHINA awoke the next morning startled by the emptiness in her core as the sun streamed through the blinds and scorched her eyes.

"Patrick," she called. Her heart was beating furtively. She recalled being curled up in his arms the night before, desperately trying to fall asleep. After twirling and twisting in bed for a few seconds, she got up to look for him. With a white sheet wrapped around her naked frame, she headed towards the balcony. She found him fully dressed, with a tray of coffee and a pile of morning papers, too engrossed to see her standing in the doorway.

"Good morning," she muttered lazily, holding on loosely to the sheet that barely covered her breasts.

"Good morning love," Patrick greeted, standing to kiss her lips before pulling a chair for her. "I tried very hard not to wake you. Coffee?" He poured some in her cup and watched as she tilted her head and squinted a little. "You were awesome last night."

"Quit saying that," Phina shot back, giggling. "I'm not some bimbo you just met. I'm your wife."

"No doubt about that." Patrick laughed and stared at her in amusement.

Phina sipped her coffee as Patrick continued to pore through the papers. Suddenly a deep crease appeared on his forehead.

"What is it?" Phina asked. Her cup was midway between her mouth and the table.

Patrick kept his head down and shook his head. "Thatcher's monetary policies have done nothing but worsen the state of most businesses."

"But, I thought they were succeeding with curbing inflation."

"That's right, but business owners are struggling to find funds to operate. Things are going great for Ophinas and other luxury fashion brands, so you won't understand what it's like for most businesses out there."

"I understand," Phina mumbled. "It's a great thing we've diversified; our portfolio of assets should be enough to buffer the risk. You never know which direction the economy is heading. That reminds me; I received an invitation for the fifteenth annual Fashion Estes. I'm being honored with the Style Icon award. Apparently for my contribution to the world of fashion."

"Amazing! Congratulations," Patrick said, shifting his gaze from his papers to look in her direction. "I'm…"

The loud ringing of the phone cut him short. Phina ran into the room with the sheet trailing behind her.

"It's the chauffeur," she yelled to Patrick. "He wants to know when we'll be heading out."

Patrick walked into the room, grabbed Phina's waist with one hand and with the other took the handset from her.

"I'll be leaving now." He spoke directly into the mouthpiece as he caressed Phina's butt. "Pull the Rolls to the front right away."

Phina kissed his mouth. His touch had aroused something in her but she needed to stay focused.

"I won't be coming with you," she said.

"You're not?"

"I have a slight headache." She covered her mouth with the back of her hand to stifle a yawn.

"Darling, I'm so sorry to hear that. Go back to bed then."

She nodded. "I think I'll rest a bit."

"Well, I'll be late if I don't leave now. Take care of yourself. Okay?"

"Okay, my love."

As soon as Patrick's footsteps were out of earshot, Phina ran to the writing desk to search for the pieces of mail from the night before. She had lied about a headache. After barely sleeping, worrying all night about Patrick's unusual behavior, she wanted time alone to investigate and find out why he seemed so perturbed. Finding no trace of the mail on the desk, she walked to Patrick's side drawer and pulled the latch. To her surprise, it was locked. Exhausted after searching everywhere for the key, she decided that whatsoever the issue, it could be dealt with later. It was nine o'clock, and she needed to call her mother before leaving for the office for her first meeting of the day.

-

It had been a week since Phina last spoke to her mother in Nigeria, so she was delighted to hear her voice.

"How is my granddaughter?" her mother asked the second she picked up the phone.

"How come you didn't ask about me first?" Phina whined. "Is Brigitte the only person you care about?"

"Yes *now*," her mother teased. "Brigitte is my priority. When you have your own grandchild, you can do as you please,"

"Mom, that's not fair. Anyway, how is everything back home?"

"Everything is great my dear daughter. I'll be leaving for Lagos tomorrow to attend our governor's wedding anniversary – a big ceremony lasting a whole week."

"I thought things were hard in Nigeria. How can our leaders continue hosting these extravagant parties?"

"I don't know," her mother answered with a sense of indifference.

"Anyway, our people just sit and watch and take whatever they're dealt. I'm not surprised."

"*Eh heh*," her mother interjected, ignoring her rants. "Ezinne came home last weekend. She asked about you."

"How is her real estate business going? I feel so bad I wasn't there when she opened the offices in Lagos."

"The business is going excellently. The openings were grand. She said she spoke with you after the event. All your aunties, uncles and cousins attended. It was like the family reunion we had two years ago when she got married, with the exception you weren't there."

Phina caught the subtle accusation in her mother's tone. As she pondered her response, she heard, "Don't worry about it. There'll be other opportunities."

Ezinne was Phina's only sibling. Although she was younger than Phina, she was bright and downright unapologetic. For several years, she worked as a top lawyer in London. She later moved to Nigeria to resume a political position in the Ports Authority – a position their late father had detested. The real estate business was an additional feather to her cap. It allowed her to resign her position in the Ports and pursue her passion.

Phina felt instantly rejuvenated after speaking to her mother. Ready to take on the day, she put on a striped navy blue and white Ralph Lauren suit, pulled her hair into a high bun and dashed out of the door. As her chauffeur drove into the morning traffic, she reminisced about the dinner party. It seemed like ages ago. Slowly, her thoughts drifted to her issues with Patrick, and she sighed deeply. She thought about their lovemaking the night before. The feelings had been slightly awakened before Patrick left that morning and she had made every effort possible to prevent it from building into a crescendo, so she could carry out her plan to play detective. It was a wonder how she and Patrick were able to accomplish anything working next to each other. It helped that Patrick had to shuttle between three offices – Ophinas, the administrative offices for his sportswear line – Sportsmets, at the other end of town – and the production studios at Buckinghamshire.

With three businesses to juggle, Patrick was hardly ever at Ophinas. As a member of the Board of Directors, he attended meetings to influence the strategic direction of the company. Other than that, his focus was on Sportsmets and his movie production business. He had been in negotiations to divest a significant portion of Sportsmets through private equity investment. That alone, kept him occupied with new liaisons, interests, and opportunities.

-

Two weeks after the dinner party, Patrick walked to his car at the parking lot of Bright Street with a medium cup of coffee held loosely on one hand. It had been a week since he found out his entire portfolio had lost a third of its original value. Having put at least half of his fortune in stocks, he felt dejected knowing things had hit a new low. Phina had warned him against investing so much in the stock market, and now that everything had come crashing, he didn't know how he could face her. His private investment capital in Ophinas remained intact as the luxury fashion brands continued to maintain their momentum while the whole market took a tumble.

Upon arrival at Knightsbridge, he walked up the stairs to his office, careful to avoid the watching eyes of the staff and customers. He was relieved when he was told by the receptionist that Phina had left for her exercise class earlier than scheduled, so she could attend Brigitte's dance class. It gave him space to engage freely in his reverie. Besides, he didn't want Phina to catch him in his current state. Shortly after he rang for coffee, Gina – his secretary of many years – came in with a tray. He gestured for her to place it on the coffee table.

"Cancel the rest of my meetings for the day," he said.

Gina looked at him with a puzzled expression.

"But, Emilio – the lawyer from Witham Capital – is coming all the way from Milan…"

"Oh, I completely forgot. Make an exception for him. What time is the meeting?"

"Four."

Patrick shifted his gaze to the Georgian wall clock across the room.

"Excellent. This gives me at least twenty minutes."

Before shutting the door behind her, Gina shot a quick glance at Patrick. The sadness in his countenance troubled her. Thinking she had left, Patrick sighed, folded his hands together on the desk and laid his head down.

He was able to get a moment's rest before the loud ringing of his phone roused him from a snooze.

Two minutes later, his door opened and Gina walked in for the second time that afternoon with Emilio trailing behind her. She waited till the two men were seated before offering them something to drink.

Emilio shook his head and waved his hand. "Nothing, thanks."

"Let me know if you need anything," Gina said as she retreated from the room.

They waited for Gina to leave before they resumed their meeting.

"I have news for you," Emilio started

"What news?" Patrick said, straightening his back.

"The preliminary analysis we performed on your financials allowed us to approve the deal. However, our team performed a more detailed review and decided we will not be moving forward at this time."

Patrick shook his head as though to awaken from a nightmare. "What review? What aspect of our financials does your team have issues with?"

"We'll be sending a detailed report to you by the end of the week."

The news he just received hit Patrick like a ton of bricks. What he had thought was a simple visit from Emilio to finalize the terms of the deal for the private equity transaction, turned out to be an attempt to destroy everything they had been working on for months. He was counting on the private equity injection from Witham Capital to complete facilities for a factory that would reduce the need to outsource production for Sportsmets and therefore improve their bottom line. The terms of the agreement required him to forfeit a significant stake in the business. However, raising capital to inject into his project could help him escape filing for bankruptcy.

"When do they think they'll be ready?" Patrick asked.

"We are continuing to watch the market. We won't be able to provide any specific timelines to you right now. Besides, the report the team will be sending to you contains recommendations that, if you're able to execute, will improve your position greatly."

"Bull-shit." Patrick roared, standing and thumping his fist on the table.

Emilio looked at him in awe.

"We have gone too far for you to dump this on me," Patrick continued, his eyes glaring.

Emilio took the cue and stood up.

"I agree with you sir, but the assurance we gave you was only tentative. We stated that clearly during our meeting a month ago. Our letter also indicated that the results were preliminary."

"A cancellation without proper justification is not acceptable," Patrick said, shaking his head. "I'll do whatever it takes to recover every penny I have sunk into this deal."

"I'm sorry, sir…"

Patrick ignored his apology and dialed the phone. A few seconds later, Gina appeared.

"Please see him out," he instructed.

Emilio extended an arm to him. At first, it seemed as though Patrick would take it but he waved his hand to indicate his objection. Gina walked towards the door and beckoned to Emilio to follow her.

Patrick was devastated. His last chance of securing financing to grow Sportsmets had now been ruined. Already, he was in negotiations to sell his shares of Ophinas whose proceeds he would have used to finance the equity he was hell-bent on retaining in the private equity transaction, a fact he had hidden from Phina. Soon the transaction for the share sales would be finalized and he would have no choice but to let her know what had been going on behind her back. It burdened him to keep such a huge secret from her. A secret, now worsened by the distressing news he just received.

After Brigitte's class, Phina stepped into her office for a series of meetings. The first was with her managers to discuss the outcome of the fashion week. The success of the Ophinas brand that year was immense. It trumped all the previous years. Her managers laid out the results, and it showed that the brand had sold over a hundred percent more than it did the year before. This was a great win for Phina, who thought the past year alone had exceeded her expectations. She couldn't wait to share the good news with Patrick.

"Guess what," Phina announced right after she stepped into Patrick's office but stopped when she noticed Patrick was downcast. "Sorry for barging in. Is everything okay?"

"Whitham Capital backed down from their investment in Sportsmets."

"But Yunus gave his assurance," Phina said in an exasperated tone.

"Forget what Yunus gave. He's simply the majority investor. Witham will do what Witham wants even if Yunus wanted otherwise."

"I don't believe that," insisted Phina. "They can't back out after you've carried on for months with the hope of getting a brand new business. I don't give a damn that their original approval was provisional. What was their excuse?"

"Nothing tangible so far," Patrick said, shaking his head. "I'll get a report at the end of the week."

"I never trusted Yunus. I liked his wife though and thought I might really get along with her but now…"

"What did you want to discuss anyway?" Patrick asked.

Phina looked at him with arched brows. "Oh, never mind."

"No, no, no," Patrick protested. "It doesn't work like that."

"I honestly forgot," she lied.

--

Two weeks after the disappointment from Witham Capital, Phina stepped into the bedroom after a long day at the office.

"When were you going to tell me of this plan?" she heard Patrick say in a raspy voice.

She looked at him with wide-open eyes. The excitement she anticipated from sharing some important news with him slowly dissipated. That morning, she had been at a breakfast meeting at a café near Ophinas with a lawyer from Hartiers to plan her move into the US market – a goal she'd had since she started manufacturing some of her couture designs in New York. And one that many observers and customers had been asking her to consider. Her hope of spending a relaxing evening seemed like a foregone conclusion when Patrick placed one hand on his chin and fixed her with a hostile stare. It was rare for him to be that angry and when that happened, his naturally blue eyes tended to turn gray, like they were at that moment.

"What plan?" she asked, transfixed to the spot.

"How can you act like you don't know what I'm talking about?" he asked exasperatedly.

"Honey, I don't," Phina responded in a soothing tone, her chest heavy with trepidation.

"Okay, let me help you." He walked to the desk at the west end of the room, picked up the evening issue of the London Inquirer and flashed it before her. Phina stood wide-eyed and confused. The paper was folded on page six and in the middle of the page was a picture of her and the lawyer with whom she had met that morning. The lawyer was leaning towards her with a cup of coffee in her hand and a wide smile on her face. "Who did you meet for breakfast this morning and what did you discuss?"

Phina read the headline: *"Ophinas Making its Way to America,"* and looked up at Patrick. She redirected her gaze to the paper and read the whole article while Patrick stood and watched.

"Unbelievable," she finally said after she read the last word. "Darling, you knew I was exploring the possibility of going into business with Isabel. You also know I've always had the dream of expanding into America."

"I know, and I've always supported every dream you've had, from when you were a novice until now. Haven't I?"

"You have," she responded coolly, reluctant to match his tone. "Sorry. I've been so busy that I forgot to tell you how far we've progressed with the deal. This morning, a formula I suggested without any belief that it will be feasible was wholeheartedly accepted. I was looking forward to getting home and sharing the news with you." She paused as he unhinged from the menacing stance he'd assumed since he handed her the newspaper.

"Go on…"

"I'm sorry, love. I didn't mean to keep you in the dark. I admit I took for granted that we see almost every day and kept postponing the discussion with you. Besides, the newspaper report isn't accurate. The agreement I have with Isabel and her team is completely different from the rubbish they put in there."

"I understand, but we have a PR situation now. We need to involve your publicist. She needs to get the Inquirer to retract the news and re-report it in a more factual manner. Come here," he said, beckoning to her.

Reluctantly Phina walked into his outstretched hands. He kissed her forehead and placed it on his chest. She listened to his heartbeat. The smell of his cologne made her heady.

"I'm sorry, love," Patrick continued, "I didn't mean to sound so harsh. I was just so upset when I saw the paper this evening."

Phina loosened her grip and looked up at him as a frown spread across her face. "I wonder how they knew so much. Even though their report was inaccurate, they knew about my American liaisons and the meeting that morning. Doesn't that concern you?" she asked when she saw Patrick's face was blank.

"It does, but don't forget you're a public figure. Many people have an interest in what you're doing."

"No," Phina shot back. "There's something wrong about this one. These buffoons knew a lot more than they should and someone certainly followed me to breakfast. How else did they get those pictures? I could have been discussing anything... anything at all, but they were right on target about the topic of my discussion."

"Enough with the speculations. Can we discuss this later?"

Phina, too tired to continue, agreed to drop the matter of the tattle teller, but only for one night. Nothing would quench the rage she felt towards whoever was responsible for creating a messy situation for her business. She was certain someone was trying to embarrass her but was someone also following her around? She shuddered at the thought as she continued to reflect on how such sensitive information could have leaked so easily?

-

Right after Patrick fell asleep, Phina launched her own investigation. First, she called Isabel Hartier, her US partner and the owner of Hartiers, an American brand of fashion, jewelry, and leather goods.

"What nonsense," Isabel said in an angry tone after Phina relayed everything that transpired that day to her. "Who could have done this?"

"I don't know. It's twelve o'clock here. The store is not open for another ten hours. I won't be able to do anything about this until then."

"Well, let me know how it goes. Whoever is responsible should be weeded out and disposed of."

"Agreed."

"I don't know how things work over there in London, but here in New York, saboteurs are taken seriously," Isabel said.

-

When the shop opened in the morning, Phina called her Human Resources Manager and her Legal Secretary to launch a formal investigation into the issue.

In less than an hour, the legal secretary was back in Phina's office.

"So soon?" Phina asked. "Don't tell me you've found the culprit."

"Yes. We have." He said, a little hesitant.

"And?"

"It was Geoffrey. He passed the information to the Inquirer. We spoke to our contact there, and they gave us their source. They assumed he was reputable because he worked at Ophinas."

"How did he know so much?" Phina asked. "Is this the Geoffrey in accessories? The tall muscular gentleman... Baby-face... Ever pleasant. Who could have put him up to that?"

"We don't know. He resigned this morning."

"Really!" Phina exclaimed, raising her brows. "Did he leave a forwarding address? Find him and find out why he did this. Get Human Resources involved."

"I already did. Geoffrey left no valid address in his file and he sent his letter via courier."

Phina was taken aback. She immediately called Isabel when the Legal Secretary left her office. "He bailed before anyone had the chance to query him and find out who his accomplices were," Phina complained.

"Very strange," Isabel remarked. "Who could have put him up to that? It seems our poor Geoffrey was a pawn."

"I can't think of anyone who would want to sabotage me."

"Are you sure? Think very hard."

"I've tried."

"You'd mentioned that Patrick's company was having issues."

"Yes, but where is the connection? Oh, you don't think it could be him? That's impossible. Patrick would never do such a thing. Besides, I kept him in the loop about my plans for the US. He was always fully supportive. The report was a twisted version of the truth and he has nothing to gain by doing that. Nothing at all."

"I'm not suggesting that he's the guilty party, but a member of his team may have been involved." An awkward pause passed between them before Isabel spoke again. "You should be cautious though. Maybe not everyone around you is who you think they are."

"I also wouldn't rule out the possibility that Geoffrey was working with someone from Hartiers."

"That did occur to me," Isabel agreed.

"I'm completely spooked either way."

"I don't think you need to worry too much about it now. These things happen all the time. People get so caught up with their positions and go to extraordinary lengths to make sure those positions remain intact. Self-preservation, that's all it is. To cover all bases, I'll launch an investigation on my end to see if the problem originated from Hartiers."

Phina was more confused than ever, but she didn't want to argue with Isabel even though she sensed her reference to people close to her may have been targeted at Patrick or pretty much anyone else she trusted.

She realized the incident had occurred to achieve some hidden agenda, but she was oblivious to what that agenda was or who Geoffrey's accomplices were.

4

Montego Bay Tidings

THE night in January when Phina met Isabel was an especially magnificent one. Phina had been dining with some friends on the terrace of the sprawling Montego Bay Palace Hotel overlooking the ocean when a pleasant-looking waiter delivered a bottle of champagne to her table with four glasses for her and her guests. Her first instinct was to reject the offer before the waiter had the chance to say a word. However, as he struggled to open the bottle, an attractive, and curvy fair-haired woman, with shoulder length hair approached her with outstretched hands. Phina guessed her age at about mid-forties. She felt the woman looked familiar but couldn't recall where she had met her.

"Isabel," the woman said, "Isabel Hartier."

"That's right," Phina said with a nod, before shaking her hand. "Phina Campbell."

"I know who you are, Lady Campbell," Isabel purred. "I've been following your progress for years. I can't believe I finally get to meet you in person. Those magazines don't do you justice at all."

"Thank you, Isabel. Sorry, I didn't recognize you at first, I had no clue you were the same Isabel Hartier I've been reading about for almost two decades. What you and your husband do for those inner-city kids is amazing."

"Oh, thanks. Simon and I are staying in this hotel. Are you lodging here too?"

"Yes, I am. I leave the day after tomorrow. I'm here on a short visit. My husband forced me to take a break from my normal routine. Luckily I was able to find some friends to accompany me."

"What a nice husband you have. Simon and I are on vacation. We've visited Jamaica many times. We love it here." Isabel handed her a card on which she had scribbled her room number.

Phina wrote her room number on a napkin. "Let's meet for drinks tomorrow."

"Absolutely! I'm so happy to finally meet you. Oh, here comes Simon," Isabel said as a gentleman in his late forties, with the same shade of blond as Isabel, and about medium height, appeared right beside her.

Phina's heart skipped a beat when Simon Hartier of New York-based Hartier Group, a conglomerate of fashion, oil and gas, food and beverages and real estate smiled at her and shook her hand firmly.

"The indomitable Phina Campbell," Simon spoke in a baritone. "Isabel has been wondering all evening if she could walk up to you. You see," he said, turning to his wife, "it paid off."

Isabel chuckled.

"Well, it's nice meeting you. Hopefully, we can meet again before we leave," Simon concluded.

The next evening, the three of them met for dinner at the pulsating Rios Restaurant, located on a picturesque peninsula that overlooked the dock and the entire city of Montego Bay. They had set out together from the hotel and arrived at exactly five-forty-five, in time to see the sunset. They listened to the reggae music coming from the large stereos and chatted as they dined on an array of seafood dishes. Simon was expanding into Europe and its axis. His wife Isabel was a brilliant businesswoman. She ran their Hartiers chain of stores and was constantly on the lookout for phenomenal fashion designers to add to her repertoire of offerings. Isabel had admired Phina for years. How she built her empire from scratch and then grew it into one of the most admired fashion labels was a marvel to her. She couldn't believe her luck when she saw her that night.

"Would you consider partnering with Hartiers? We could open some signature stores – Hartiers-Ophinas… I don't know. We can find a suitable name. What do you think?" Isabel had asked Phina after they settled into their seats.

"That would have been such a great idea but my organization is stretched to the limits. The only way we can expand to the United States right now is by registering on the stock exchange and doing an initial public offering. I see no other way around it."

Isabel, disappointed, placed her hand on her forehead with a demure thespian quality.

"Surely we can find a way around this," she declared. "The exotic nature of your designs is exactly what I want in my store. Simon," she said turning to her husband, "Simon, what do you think?"

"Phina, say yes to her or she won't stop," Simon pleaded, looking deep into Phina's eyes.

Phina, amused by their persistence, chuckled and responded, "I'll discuss with my partners and get back to you."

-

After dinner, they had stopped at the restaurant bar and danced. Isabel and Phina moved seductively on the dance floor as '*Could You Be Loved*' blasted from the players. They slowed their pace as the music changed to '*No Woman No Cry*'. Phina, in her green jump-suit, and Isabel, in her tight black jeans and fitted top, danced until two in the morning. They laughed and spoke at the top of their voices so they could hear each other amidst the loud music.

The following day, they bid each other goodbye and promised to keep in touch. Phina had never experienced the bond she felt with Isabel with anyone else, especially at such a short time interval. Since their meeting, they talked on the phone on a near-daily basis. Mostly, the business took the back seat in their conversations, but it was always addressed sufficiently. Phina had kept Patrick in the loop about their discussions. It was not until a month before the Inquirer incident that Phina came up with the winning formula that would enable her to diversify her business to the United States without a huge investment or the complications of going public. She had called Isabel and laid out the terms. Ophinas Couture and ready-to-wear designs would be manufactured exclusively for Hartiers in the United States. The European design would be adapted for the US market. Hartiers would provide the wherewithal needed for design and manufacturing. Production would be carried out at the New York production center, limiting shipping costs to Hartiers Stores all over the United States.

Isabel had thought it was a brilliant idea and considered Phina a genius for coming up with it. It was a win-win for everyone involved and had the potential to boost both businesses, which perfectly complemented each other. For Phina, it was a way to test her European brand in the American market and make it a household name before she embarked on a public offering both in Europe and the US. Since Ophinas' clientele were women between the ages of twenty-five to seventy-five – the same range that Hartiers catered to, it made sense for them to collaborate in creating mature, classy designs that crossed multicultural barriers. Their partnership also suited their personalities – Isabel well traveled and versatile and Phina exotic and ubiquitous. They agreed to a two-year commitment, after which they could renegotiate or part ways if the arrangement no longer suited them. Isabel had already accepted Phina's terms, so the meeting with Hartiers' lawyer was merely to flesh out important details before formal contracts were signed.

The Inquirer issued an apology and retracted their story. To correct the impression that she was diversifying Ophinas without their knowledge, Phina called her investors, starting with Lady Thompson, to explain what had occurred.

"Do you plan to call everyone that's been affected to issue an apology? You really didn't have to explain," Lady Thompson said after Phina told her about the issue. "I've been in this business far longer than you and understand how these things work. It can happen from time to time. You just have to rise above it and keep moving."

Phina felt as though a heavy weight had been lifted off her shoulders.

"I appreciate your understanding," she said, "and I assure you, that I'm working to cleanup this mess."

"You've done a great job so far. I saw the retraction in the Inquirer. Thank goodness I didn't see the original story. I admit that would have upset me."

"I'm glad you didn't then."

Phina was elated by Lady Thompson's response. She never seized to surprise Phina and her response to that incident was no exception.

Next, she called Chief Gambo, who owned a significant portion of Ophinas. He, just like Lady Thompson and Patrick, had right of first offer in any future expansions. This entitled them to first-hand information whenever it became available.

Chief Gambo laughed after Phina related the issue to him.

"As long as my investment is secure, there's really nothing for me to worry about. Phina?"

"Sir?"

"My dear, you're free to do business in any country or region you want to. You don't need permission from anyone to do that. Are you not Phina Osoji?" Chief Gambo asked in a demanding tone.

Phina laughed. Chief Gambo always knew how to cheer her up. He was like a father to her.

"You're laughing now, but on a serious note, you shouldn't let these things wear you down." He drew the last three words for emphasis.

"Ok, sir. Thank you."

"Don't forget to let me know if you need investment in any new venture. You have never disappointed me. My investments in your companies have produced amazing returns."

Phina laughed.

"It's not a joke!" His voice reverberated over the phone.

"I'll think of you first, sir, if I need anything."

"Please do, especially now that Rashid has moved back to Nigeria from Dubai. He will start looking for stable businesses to invest in."

"Who is Rashid?"

"Rashid? My first son. I've told you about him several times. He keeps asking when he can meet you… Wait, he just walked in. Speak with him."

Before Phina could protest, Chief Gambo handed Rashid the phone.

"Hello," Phina heard Rashid say in an affected British accent.

"Hi, Rashid. How are you? It's really nice to meet you. Your dad has told me so much about you."

"Same here. He's full of praises for you as well. Phina, this, Phina, that. That's all we hear around here."

"He said you just moved back. What will happen to your business in Dubai?" Phina asked, suppressing a giggle.

"I have people managing it. I also have an office in the UK and the US. I visit now and then, but my managers do all the work."

"That's impressive."

"Thank you. I think you're pretty impressive as well. It was nice talking to you. Dad is pestering me to hand him the phone. Let's talk some other time."

"Oh! Nice speaking with you Ra..."

Before Phina could finish, she heard Chief Gambo on the other end.

"The guy refused to let go of the phone. I had to inform him you were married."

"You're funny, sir," Phina said, laughing.

"How is your mother?" Chief Gambo continued. "I hope she has gotten over your father's death. You mentioned last time that she was having a hard time coping with his passing."

"I spoke to her the other day. She's doing okay."

"Just okay? I'll try to visit her before I take a long vacation to Australia. I'm planning to expand my oil business there."

"I didn't realize you were into oil."

"Ahh. I'm into many things. You've not understood the full breadth of my work. I'm happy you talked to Rashid. Both of you have the same business sense and good heads on your shoulders. When you meet in person, you'll understand."

"I'm looking forward to meeting him when I come home for the holidays."

"Awesome."

-

Phina and Patrick met for dinner at their favorite Indian restaurant the following day. The report in the Inquirer had strained their relationship and Phina hoped a date night would help them unwind. Patrick, charming as usual, held her hands and stared into her eyes as soon as they were seated.

"I missed you," he said, causing Phina's cheeks to warm up.

"I missed you too, darling."

"This is just like old times. I never thought it was possible to love you more than I did then."

His words awakened something in her. All she could think about was finishing dinner, rushing home and making love to the beautiful man sitting right in front of her.

They fondled each other in the back seat until they got to a high point of arousal as the chauffeur drove them to Hazel House through the city. The snow created a romantic maze with the Christmas decorations that lined the streets. Patrick placed his right hand underneath her skirt and stroked her thighs causing her to gasp. Phina leaned on his shoulders to mask their behavior from the chauffeur who seemed completely oblivious.

-

When Phina and Patrick arrived at Hazel House, they headed straight for their bedroom. Patrick took Phina's purse, placed it on the table and then swiftly hoisted her over his left shoulder. In a rush to carry on from where they left off in the car, he pulled off her stockings with his right hand.

"Wait," Phina pleaded. "Let me…"

He ignored her weak pleas and walked swiftly toward the sprawling bed. Sitting on the edge, he placed her on his laps. Slowly, he removed her shoes and maneuvered her legs to remove her panties. Phina clung on to him for support, and as he peeled the panties off her left leg, he bent and kissed her on the lips. They remained in a lip-lock as he lifted her up and placed her on the bed.

He unbuttoned his shirt as he devoured her with his eyes.

"Wait, I'll undress you," she heard him whisper as she tried to pull her dress over her head.

She obeyed and laid back in the exact position he had placed her. The wait was agonizing, but in her mind, it was worth it. As he leaned over to kiss her with one hand between her thighs, she felt ecstasy course through her. Grabbing his head with both hands, she pulled him towards her. Slowly, he pulled her dress over her head and unstrapped her bra. He sighed when he saw her full taut breasts peeking at him. Breathing erratically, he took one in his mouth while his hand caressed the other. "You never cease to amaze me," he said, his words barely decipherable.

Before she could come up with a response, he pressed hard against her and lunged desperately. When they finally collapsed in each other's arms, Phina found her voice.

"I'm sorry for all the stress."

"I love you my darling," Patrick responded. "I'm so sorry for everything," he said, his voice choked with emotion.

Phina's heart skipped a beat. She was stunned by the way he said 'everything'. Afraid to discover the dreary meaning behind his words, she decided to ignore his comment, but fear filled the pit of her stomach. Of recent, she felt Patrick was hiding something from her. He seemed lost in thought most times and even though she had attributed it to the state of the economy, sometimes she felt there was much more going on with him. There was nothing tangible she could rely on. It was just a gut feeling.

5

OSTRICH PLUMES

IT was Christmas Eve, 1982. People, noise, music, and the smell of baking and delicious food filled Hazel House. Phina had forgotten what it felt like to have so many people spending time together in one place. There were so many demands and so many options. It reminded her of the Christmases in her parents' home when all her cousins came to visit. Fully recovered from her initial shock, she settled down to enjoy Patrick's family. His Mother Irene, his sister Victoria, her husband Jorge and their two children Samson and Benetta had come to spend the day at Hazel House. Phina cherished moments like that because it provided an opportunity for her to spend time with Victoria, also her best friend.

"Looking at Brigitte and Benetta reminds me of how we used to be," Victoria chirped as they watched the children argue while they played a game of monopoly.

Phina nodded in agreement. "Friends one day and enemies the next and then best friends again. How I miss those days."

"I'd rather not go back though. We were so green behind the ears."

"Green is an understatement," Phina agreed, smiling as she caught Patrick's blue eyes looking longingly at her from the distance.

Victoria turned a fraction to see what had distracted her. "You two should get a room," she said mischievously.

Phina recalled how she and Victoria met several years back when she was still dating Patrick. They had become fast friends. Over the years, they had both grown into successful businesswomen. Phina couldn't fathom how Victoria was able to manage two active children and a busy career as the Creative Director in a fashion house she had co-created. Jorge's career as a stockbroker didn't complement hers, but none of that seemed to bother her.

After a heavy lunch of Welsh cawl, roast turkey, minced meat pies, and a delicious toad in the hole, the children ran off to the library to play while the adults converged in the Georgian room. Irene relaxed with a book in the corner and soon dozed off. Patrick and Jorge became engrossed in deep conversation while Victoria and Phina continued their discussion.

"I can't believe you chopped off your hair," Phina scolded, holding Victoria's jaw to examine her face. "Anyway, it showcases all your angles, and it looks great on you."

"Thank you. Jorge loves it too. It's grown a few inches since I cut it. Sorry, I couldn't make it to your show, but I saw the collection in your showroom. You're so full of surprises."

"Thank you, sweetie, I missed you at the event but assumed you would be too busy. How is your collaboration with Lady Thompson going?"

"Oh! That!" Victoria sighed. "If you hadn't been so preoccupied, you would have known I haven't worked with Lady Thompson in three whole months."

"Wow!" Phina exclaimed, staring at her in disbelief.

"Yeah, I needed to spend time with the children and I'm planning to start my brand for young adults. I'm surprised Patrick didn't tell you."

Phina grimaced and shook her head. "No, he didn't."

"Lady Thompson and I parted on great terms though."

Phina sensed Victoria wasn't being entirely truthful with the terms of her parting with Lady Thompson, but she let her save face.

"You know," Phina said, leaning towards Victoria and lowering her voice. "Patrick has been a little withdrawn these days. I have a feeling there's something wrong but I can't place my finger on it."

Victoria paused for a second before responding. "It's the general state of the economy. The men feel it more than us. Jorge is acting out too. I catch him brooding at times. Patrick is more heavily invested so I can only imagine."

Phina sighed, and, she noticed Victoria's demeanor change. A worried frown had clouded her face, but she immediately replaced it with what Phina sensed was a forced smile.

-

By the time the family left and Brigitte settled with the nanny, Phina cuddled up with Patrick on the sofa in their bedroom. They were both exhausted but excited for the season. Outside, the pelting snow provided every indication they needed to know it would be a white Christmas. Phina was delighted when 'Feliz Navidad' came through the stereo. That night, they talked about her trip to New York and concluded it would be a great opportunity for her to garner inspiration for the fall-winter collection. Their talk lasted until late into the night before they finally fell asleep until Christmas morning.

-

Phina headed to New York in the middle of January 1983. She hated to leave Brigitte and Patrick all by themselves, so she planned to spend only a week. Isabel insisted she stayed at their estate in Long Island instead of a hotel. The estate was a luxurious twenty-thousand-square-foot complex complete with three swimming pools, a sauna, a spa, a gym, and a tennis court. It was identical in size and splendor to Hazel House but compared to the latter, looked completely unlived in. Phina was shown into a large room as soon as she alighted from the limousine that picked her up from the airport. Other than a set of low and narrow sofas and a few large paintings on the walls, the room was bare. Before she had time to look around, the heavily molded door at the other end of the room swung open and Isabel, with Simon trailing behind her, walked in with a smile on her face and her arms outstretched. They advanced towards Phina, and Isabel kissed her several times on both cheeks.

"When will I get a chance to hug the princess?" Simon, who had been waiting for the initial excitement between the ladies to subside, asked with a touch of sarcasm.

"So sorry!" exclaimed Phina, freeing herself from Isabel's embrace. "Simon," she said, shaking her head adoringly. "It's so lovely to see you."

"Lovely to see you too, my dear," Simon responded as he embraced her. "I hope you had a smooth trip."

"I did. Thank you for having me in your beautiful home."

"Our pleasure dear."

-

Phina was escorted up a flight of stairs and shown into a large guest room, almost as large as her bedroom in Hazel house. Left alone in her room, she took stock of her surroundings. The windows overlooked a swimming pool surrounded by a flower path. On one end was a bar with a thatched roof and a row of stools. There was something striking about the hue in the pool from the setting sun that took her breath away. Everything about the room was completely in keeping with Phina's taste, except for the bathroom which took on a completely modern twist – whitish gray and simplistic, with geometric patterns on the tiles. It felt too serious. She didn't see how it could be comfortable.

Memories of home flashed through her mind as she sat on the vanity table and freshened her makeup for dinner. She missed Patrick and wished he had come with her. The Style Icon award from the Fashion Estes was the most prestigious award since the Remas. Patrick had wanted to come with her, but he couldn't forgo his work at the studio that weekend. After dinner, too tired for anything else, she headed straight to bed and slept till morning.

-

Phina woke up very early the following morning confused about her surroundings. The sun streamed through the gaps in the muslin curtains and shone in her eyes. It was already nine, and she had promised Isabel she would join her for swimming at nine-thirty. With no time to spare she hurried into the shower and changed into her blue sequined one-piece swimsuit with side cutouts that gave the illusion of a two-piece. When she got to the poolside, Isabel was already there waiting for her in a sexy red bikini that flaunted her bosom. By her side was a tray with delicious fruit juices and desserts.

They rested in between laps as their skin glistened from the natural sunlight, through the glass ceiling of the indoor swimming pool.

"One more lap and I'm done," Phina announced. She was getting tired and Isabel looked like she hadn't even started.

"What a shame. I was hoping we could do five more," Isabel responded.

"Go ahead. I'll watch you from the pool deck," Phina promised as she sipped her drink.

Isabel took three more laps down the entire length of the pool while Phina watched her and reminisced about the day. She could not imagine what a partnership with Hartiers would be like. For her, the adventure into newer and even bigger territories had just begun.

Isabel swam by the edge and playfully splashed water on Phina, waking her up from her reverie. Phina tried to retaliate but was too late as Isabel had sped to the far end of the pool.

Sneaking in beside her a few moments later, Isabel asked, "Ready to take on the day?"

"Absolutely. I feel overwhelmed just thinking about what we have to accomplish, but I trust you have taken care of everything."

Isabel giggled.

"No need to feel overwhelmed. I'm a stickler for schedules. I know that's how you operate too and that's why I'm certain we're soul mates."

"No doubt," Phina agreed. "I pray our new business venture knocks everything out of the park."

"We'll do the best we can."

"We'd better leave for breakfast. Simon will be waiting for us."

Simon had already eaten by the time Phina and Isabel arrived at the breakfast room.

"I apologize for being late, *bon*," Isabel said, kissing him on the cheek.

"No problem, darling, I perfectly understand. Hello, Phina. Not sure why Patrick didn't come with you. I would have really loved to meet him. It's not every day we get to have royalty with us in this part of the world."

Phina grinned. "He's just like everybody else you'll ever meet. In fact, he doesn't even use his title, Marquis. He feels it's…" Phina stopped mid-sentence as Simon squinted his eyes and raised both hands.

"He thinks it's pretentious? Why?" Simon asked, shaking his head.

"Well, in his opinion it's all rubbish. Believe me, he's the only person who sees it that way. Everyone bows and curtseys around him."

"I'd love to make his acquaintance."

"I'll try to bring him next time," Phina said before devouring the vegetable omelet before her.

-

After breakfast, Phina and Isabel headed out for the three-hour drive from Long Island to New Jersey. Their first stop was the New Jersey factory. The thirty-thousand-square-foot complex was situated on an old farmland. From the distance, Phina could see steam escaping from four concrete chimneys. Inside, the sound of machinery whirled and a line of workers focused squarely on their tasks. Not one looked up to greet them except for the line Manager who offered to give them a tour. They spoke at the top of their voices.

Thirty minutes later, the chauffeur turned the car back in the direction of New York. The snow-filled road glistened as the sun shone on it.

"I wish I could still skate like I did back in the day," Isabel complained when they saw a group of skaters as they drove by Central Park.

"Why can't you? I say we challenge ourselves to that one day."

"No, no, no. Our schedules are too full and Simon will think I'm crazy since I haven't skated in ten years. You must be hungry. Don't worry, I've arranged for us to get some food. I thought I'd pay homage to your husband's origin by treating you to some English food in New York."

"Thoughtful of you but you know, even Patrick doesn't eat English food as much. He'd rather eat Nigerian which has become a staple in our home. His favorite is *jollof rice* and fried plantain."

"How does he handle the spice?"

"Spice?" Phina asked, arching her brows. "Really well. He's never complained about it."

"Impressive."

The two women treated themselves to lunch at a restaurant in Tribeca and from there visited Hartiers in Manhattan. Phina thought the store was magnificent. It glistened and shone with bright lights and sparkling chandeliers. The high ceilings looked imposing with the colorful larger-than-life artistry that covered its entire square footage.

"We better head home now," Isabel said before Phina completed viewing the entire store. "Need to save some of our strength for the awards tonight. Tomorrow we can tour a little more. I have two more stores to show you. You'll love the one on Long Island."

"That's the one I'll really need to see."

"I guess we've saved the best for last," Isabel concluded before they parted ways to get dressed for the award ceremony at nine o'clock.

-

The Fashion Estes – a set of awards provided to deserving individuals for merit in the world of fashion – was the highest fashion award institution in the US. The organization was run through charitable donations received from large sponsors and was held every two years. Award recipients were selected through recommendation and voting by members. Isabel and Simon recommended Phina, and through the voting process, campaigned heavily for her to win the most prestigious of the awards. The Style Icon award was reserved for the fashion designer that made the most contribution to the world of fashion while catering for various humanitarian causes. The award recognized innovation, brilliance, and a sense of community. Phina had been nominated each year for the past two years but was finally chosen as the recipient that year.

The hairdresser and makeup artist Phina hired to get her ready for the evening were waiting for her at Isabel's home when she arrived. Her outfit had been selected months in advance — an item from her winter collection. It was an elegant, wine-red, velvet evening gown, cut low in the back. The neck and back hems were lined with red crystals and the hem on the hands and at the bottom were lined with ostrich plumes. The dress fit Phina like a glove. Her hips swayed with such fluid-like motion as she walked up the stage to receive her award, it was difficult to distinguish the woman from the dress.

Cheers of admiration ran down the hall when her name was announced. Blinded by the photographers and the light on the stage, Phina used her hand to shield her face. She was happy she had practiced her speech, or she would have been completely lost amidst the chaos. Isabel was sitting right in front cheering the loudest as Phina walked up to receive her award. On the stage, Phina waited for the noise to die down before she cleared her throat.

"I am astounded," she said, looking at the crowd.

Her words were further drowned by continued clapping. Everyone was mesmerized by her unique, but elegant outfit. She waited a moment for the sound to die down before she continued.

Holding up her award — a platinum androgynous sculpture in one hand, she put one leg slightly over the other and placed her other hand loosely on her left thigh.

"Good evening everyone," she said, speaking directly into the microphone. "I am honored to receive this award today. Not in a million years could I have imagined this honor being bestowed upon me. When I joined this business, close to a decade ago, I had no idea where I was headed. All I knew was that I loved and breathed fashion. That motivated me to leave my family and everything I knew behind in

Nigeria and move to London to pursue my dream. Fast forward a decade plus later, I have achieved even greater success than I could ever have dreamed.

"I'll like to let all young women out there know that they too can achieve their dreams." She paused for a second before raising up the award. "I owe this to my family, my wonderful husband and all the people that walk in and out on a daily basis from Ophinas stores all over Europe. Friends like you..." She pointed to the crowd in Isabel's direction.

Phina placed her left hand on her chest and bowed when it was over. The speech had won her a standing ovation. A few people in the crowd were drawn to tears. She caught Isabel wiping the corner of her eyes with a handkerchief. With one hand holding the award and the other tugging at her gown, she walked down the stairs, with help from an usher and maneuvered her way back to her seat next to Isabel and Simon.

Isabel continued to cheer with a happy smile on her face as Phina sat down.

"That was such a moving speech, darling. We're so proud of you. Congratulations!" Isabel said, holding Phina's hand in hers.

"Congratulations." Simon echoed, with a broad smile on his face.

The rest of the night was a blur to Phina. After the award segment, guests were served a sumptuous dinner. In between courses, people walked around and mingled. After barely taking two bites of her meal, a server presented Phina with a business card on a small silver tray. The name on the card read Nduka Eze M.D.

"Madam, there's a note at the back," the usher muttered as Phina angled her body to see if she could spot anyone in the distance.

She turned the card on its back. On it was written, in a rather scraggly manner,

"Congratulations! You're still a stunner. I'll come by after dinner."

Phina was astonished. She hadn't seen Nduka in almost fifteen years. Recalling their last encounter – kissing at his parent's home right before she left for London in the sixties – she exhaled deeply. She remembered it all too well like it was yesterday. Marveling at the possibility of meeting him any second, her heart pounded in her chest as she wondered what he looked like now. Several thoughts crossed her mind. Was he married? Did he have children? The thought of finding answers to all those questions both excited and alarmed her. She took one more bite of her food and gently pushed her plate away as the fluttering in her stomach increased.

Various award attendees came by to congratulate her and ask for an autograph. Isabel excused herself to address some guests. Just as Isabel was leaving, Phina spotted someone she was sure was Nduka heading towards her direction. His physique, his tux, his extremely dark handsome face, and the manner in which he advanced took her breath away.

"Phina Osoji," he said with his right hand outstretched.

Phina stood up and gave him her hand.

"Hello Nduka," she responded in a low tone. "If you hadn't sent that note, I wouldn't have recognized you."

"I recognized you when you walked in with your friends. Isn't it funny that I only saw your back and knew it was you?"

"How could you have known it was me then? That's preposterous," Phina said with a chuckle.

"Anyone would have recognized you from behind. You have a unique and amazing figure."

"Well, I'm glad you didn't approach me then. I would have been nervous as hell making my speech. It's hard enough doing it in a room full of strangers; it's even worse in full view of someone you haven't spoken to in a hundred years."

Nduka laughed and grabbed his chin with his left hand. Phina remembered that gesture as she had witnessed it several times in the past.

"Wow! You haven't changed," she whispered.

"Phina, you look a hundred times more beautiful than the last time I saw you."

"Stop," Phina said, struggling to contain a chuckle. "Why are you here? I thought you were a big shot doctor. I didn't know doctors attended these kinds of events."

"Apparently we do. My colleague's wife received an award. Dr. Bashir. What have you been up to? I know a bit from the news. I tried to reach out a couple of times but got no word back. Now I've seen you I won't let you go until you promise you'll keep in touch."

"I didn't know you tried to reach me. The last I heard you had moved to America to study Medicine. I thought that was amazing. What else have you been up to? Are you married? Do you have children?"

"No, and no, but I have a girlfriend. That's a gorgeous ring," he said, pointing at her rose-gold twenty-carat diamond ring which caught the full glare of the light from the chandelier above. As she glided her hand in admiration of the ring as though she was just noticing it for the first time, Isabel and Simon returned to their seats.

"Isabel, meet Nduka. He's an old friend of mine."

"So nice to meet you, Nduka," Isabel said, stretching her hand.

"My pleasure, too," Nduka responded and gave her hand a little kiss causing Isabel to blush.

"You should invite him for dinner tomorrow," Isabel said, looking at Phina. "We're hosting a formal dinner for the honorees. That would be a perfect opportunity for you two to catch up on old times."

"Can you come?" Phina asked Nduka.

"Sure, I'm honored. How could I refuse an invitation from the amazing Isabel Hartier?"

Isabel smiled coyly.

"Well then, that's sorted," Phina concluded with a smile. "It was nice seeing you after so long. Bring your girlfriend tomorrow. I'd love to meet her."

"Will do," Nduka said with a small bow.

-

After dinner, a lineup of speeches left Phina yearning for her bed. She'd practically had no rest since she arrived. Work was dragging her down and her body was beginning to show telltale signs. The next day, she and Isabel were expected at two Hartier stores before ten. There was also a meeting at eleven and the formal dinner at the end of the day. The schedule was a lot to stomach and the only remedy, Phina thought, was to retire early that night. She was thrilled when Simon announced they would call it a day.

Settled in her room, Phina called Patrick to recant the events of the evening. "It was splendid," she said. "I wish you could have made it."

"I wished so too, but the work at home will not take care of itself. I miss you and I'm so proud of you. I'll always be proud of you. Try to get some rest now. I imagine you have a busy day tomorrow."

"Absolutely. I love you and I'm proud of you, too," she said, sounding exhausted.

After they hung up, Phina realized she had omitted Nduka in their conversation. It had completely slipped her mind. Shrugging it off, she grabbed the extra pillow and hugged it tightly as she reminisced about her trip. So far, it had been exciting, so exciting she had found no time to think or even worry about the issues she left behind at home. Her meeting with Nduka was the most exciting part of her trip so far, and she looked forward to seeing him the following day.

-

After a few hours of sleep, Phina succeeded in getting dressed in time to leave for her morning meetings. Isabel was outside in the driveway waiting for her.

"We're headed to the largest of our stores. You're gonna love it." Isabel declared while Phina admired the scenery.

When they arrived thirty minutes later, Phina was stunned by the magnificence of Hartiers. It was reminiscent of the Ophinas on Knightsbridge, but more translucent, with stained glass windows covering most of the architecture from the second floor up.

"Beautiful!" Phina exclaimed when she laid eyes on it. "The pictures don't do it justice. One definitely has to see this in person."

"That is the beauty of American architecture."

Phina smiled. All she could think of was how she would be proud to do business with Isabel's team – they were capable of elevating every effort to a new level of magnificence.

"I love what I've seen so far, and I hope this new business venture will be profitable for all concerned," Phina said, extending her arm to Isabel.

Isabel chuckled. "It will, my dear friend. It will." Pausing momentarily, Isabel asked, "How is Patrick? How does he feel about all of this?"

Phina hesitated before responding. "He's fully supportive, and he's gotten over the incident with the Inquirer. I think he felt left out when he found out that way. Later, when he realized no harm was intended, he relaxed and accepted that was the nature of the business."

Isabel nodded in silence.

"Well," Phina continued, "he has so much else to fret about, anyway. His business ventures keep him very busy. These days he's preoccupied with worrying."

"That reminds me. It seems your guy… what's his name?"

"Which guy?"

"The one that leaked the news to the inquirer."

"Oh. Geoffrey?"

"Yeah. Have you heard anything about him lately?"

"No," Phina said, shaking her head. "Since coming to New York, I've been completely worry free without even trying."

"Well, Geoffrey was working with someone from our end. My staff discovered that a fax machine in our office building was used to transfer pages of the contracts we drew up for our venture to an unknown number in Sussex."

Phina listened in amazement. "Who would care so much about our little transaction?" she asked, pulling hard on her temples and creating a squinted look in her eyes.

"I don't know. I don't understand the interest. We're not hurting anyone. Someone was definitely snooping and providing confidential information to someone in England. I've asked my staff to look into it."

"I'm amazed."

Their discussion slowly progressed to the event the night before.

"Who was that handsome gentleman?" Isabel asked.

"Which one?" Phina responded, feigning ignorance.

Isabel grimaced.

"You know which one I'm talking about."

"Nduka?" Phina kept a straight face. "He's an old, old friend of mine from way-way back in the day."

"Okay," Isabel said through pursed lips. "He's quite attractive. It would have been impossible to guess he was a doctor."

Phina laughed and purposely omitted telling her that Nduka was her first kiss and that she had crushed on him for years before life and distance drove them apart.

6

THE CONFESSION

THE large formal dining room was set up with linens and crystals long before Isabel and Phina returned from their tour. Simon arrived minutes before them. The sun had disappeared from the sky but the last rays of light still illuminated the grounds. Through the bay windows in the dining room, the pine trees in the garden looked lush and green and whistled slightly in the wind.

Phina snuck to her room to apply finishing touches to her makeup and later joined the crowd that had already congregated on the balcony on the second floor. The servers handed out cocktails. Nduka was there with Bimpe, his girlfriend, and so were fourteen other guests – award recipients from the night before and their dates.

"Happy to meet you," Phina said to Bimpe.

"Pleasure, too," Bimpe responded and curtsied.

Bimpe had impeccable makeup and a voluptuous figure that was incredible to look at. She was about the same height as Phina, but her high towering heels made her seem much taller. Her deep, dark skin glistened in the light from the chandeliers and created an illusion of water on glass.

Phina, feeling the need to reciprocate returned her curtsy. She wasn't sure if she was older than Bimpe since the gesture was usually reserved for elders as a show of respect in the Yoruba culture.

"Nduka told me about you when we met yesterday," Phina said.

"Did he? I'm a little stunned because all he did was talk about you last night," Bimpe responded, smiling.

"I haven't seen Phina in at least two decades," Nduka said, looking at Bimpe defensively.

"Hey. I was just stating the facts," Bimpe responded, raising her hand mid-air while Phina chuckled over their exchange.

-

After dinner, the guests hung out in the large living room with their cocktails. Isabel and Simon were the perfect hosts, so no one seemed in a hurry to leave. Light music played from the ceiling and raucous laughter reverberated in the room.

As the waiters tidied the dishes, people banded up in little groups. Phina saw Nduka approaching her at the bar. She scanned the room furtively for Bimpe and saw her deep in conversation with Simon. They were laughing and gesticulating like old friends. When Nduka got close, he took Phina's hand and guided her to the balcony.

Phina smiled and hugged him. "It looks like Dr. Bashir couldn't make it," she said.

Nduka grimaced and shook his head. "He couldn't. Hey, how are you? I'm amazed by how much you've transformed. When you took the stage yesterday, I couldn't believe it was the same girl I knew many years ago."

"You didn't expect me to remain the same, did you?" Phina teased, chuckling a little.

"Not at all. How long have you been married?"

"Almost a decade."

"A decade?" Nduka asked, wide-eyed.

"Almost… What about you? Why aren't you married yet?" Phina arched her brows and awaited an answer.

"No tangible reason. My girlfriend and I have dated for nine years."

"Really? Do you have something against marriage?" she asked with a grimace.

"Absolutely not! I'm constantly being hounded by my family to get married. It's agonizing."

"Then why the delay?" Phina asked, shaking her head. "You're definitely old enough and you're a successful surgeon." She tactfully omitted that he was also well built, sexy and handsome, and smelt like heaven.

"Trust me, I want to," he responded. "The pressure from my family to perpetuate the next generation would have forced me to marry the first girl I set my eyes on, but it didn't work out that way for me. By the way, I would never have imagined you'd be an advocate for marriage. You never struck me as someone that cared."

"I do care. I believe in the marriage institution. I've always believed in it. However, I have never appreciated the pressure our people put us under to get married."

"I agree." Nduka nodded fervently. "On a different note, your outfit is stunning," he said, gazing admiringly at her black, off-the-shoulder gown, further cinched at the waist with a gold-plated belt.

"Thanks," Phina responded with a smile. "You look great too. Your girlfriend Bimpe is lovely. Nine… Long… Years... Hmm…"

"Our families... They're giving us a hard time. The last time we broached the subject with her mother, I remember her saying 'over my dead body will my daughter marry anyone that is not Yoruba'."

Phina rolled her eyes. She wondered why Bimpe's beauty didn't invoke Nduka to defy all odds and marry her.

"My parents insist that I bring home an Igbo girl," Nduka continued as though he'd read her mind.

"Ridiculous," Phina said, shaking her head.

"I agree. Once, Bimpe even suggested we go our separate ways since, according to her, her biological clock was ticking."

Phina laughed. Nduka chuckled and lifted both hands to gesture his bewilderment.

"Enough about me. I can't believe you're leaving tomorrow," he said. "I wish you could stay a little longer."

"I wish I could too, but I have lots of responsibilities."

"I come to London often so if the mountain can't come to Mohammed, then Mohammed will have to go to the mountain."

Phina saw Bimpe approaching from the corner of her eye. "Your girlfriend is on her way here," Phina whispered.

Nduka ignored her comment. "What do you say about my coming to London?"

"No problem. Just let me know whenever you're there."

Soon the guests left one after the other. When it got to Nduka and Bimpe's turn, Phina escorted them to the porch. As their chauffeur opened the door of their car, she waved goodbye to them and rejoined the party.

After all the guests had left, Isabel and Simon presented Phina with a beautiful diamond encrusted Cartier watch, made from eighteen-carat gold.

"Wow! I couldn't possibly take this," Phina responded. "It's too much."

"You must. It's against the law to return a gift in America," Simon said, looking at her mischievously.

"This is beautiful!" Phina exclaimed and hugged Isabel and Simon one after the other.

"We love you," Isabel said, wiping a tear from her eye.

"I love you, too."

The following day, Phina received the result of the due diligence carried out by her team on Hartiers, and the results were satisfactory. Patrick had directed the team that carried out the exercise, so she knew the results were thorough. Combined with the result of her tour of Hartiers, Phina knew it was time to approve the deal. Isabel and Phina celebrated over a glass of wine and agreed to finalize the remaining steps after Phina returned to London.

-

In her luxurious first-class cabin, Phina heaved a huge sigh of relief and reminisced about everything that happened in New York. It didn't take long for her to resume worrying about the issues at home. She and Patrick still loved each other but his business troubles seemed to have taken a huge toll on their relationship. The failed transaction with Witham Capital bothered him more than he was willing to admit.

As the plane touched down at Heathrow, she awoke from a deep slumber. She had been dreaming and the last one was both weird and scary. When she got to Hazel House, the door was wide open, and the butler stood on the stairs to welcome her. Brigitte ran to hug her after she stepped inside. Phina lifted her up and kissed her on both cheeks. Patrick was not home, so she headed straight to their bedroom. Other than the ticking of the wall clock, everywhere was silent. A fresh bouquet sat on the writing desk and the vase stood empty beside it. It seemed like Patrick had been in earlier and left abruptly. She took a shower and laid in bed quietly waiting for him.

Patrick came into the bedroom at around eleven o'clock.

"Where is my beautiful girl?"

"I'm in here," Phina responded, rising to lock her body in his. "I thought you'd be here when I returned."

"I had to rush out for a quick meeting. I hope you achieved everything you set out to do in New York."

"Yes. Isabel and Simon are great. Their home is a tropical paradise. I wish you had come."

"I didn't think you cared if I was there or not," Patrick said matter-of-factly.

Phina eased back and looked up at him.

"How? What do you mean?"

"I tried several times to call you last night and the night before. You didn't pick up. When you finally called, it seemed like an afterthought."

"Oh! Is that the reason you weren't here to welcome me? When you said you couldn't pick me up at the airport, I thought you'd at least be home waiting for me. I wanted you in New York with me. There was no one I wanted more by my side."

Disappointed by Patrick's reception after what seemed to her a long time away, she went to bed without saying so much as another word to him. She was disillusioned and hurt, and he seemed to have his mind elsewhere.

The following day, they scarcely spoke to each other before heading out for work. Phina phoned Isabel and Simon to let them know she had arrived home safely. They agreed to launch their new line during her next trip to New York. With so much work to do to get up to speed with the businesses at home, the euphoria she felt from her trip wore out faster than she'd expected but returned as soon as she received a call from Nduka.

"I'm surprised to hear from you," she said cheerily when she heard his voice. How are you? How is Bimpe?"

"She's doing fine. I wanted to hear your voice. It was so nice to see you after so many years."

"Same here. It was quite a surprise."

"You promised to keep in touch."

"I will. Why not?"

Nduka and Phina maintained their friendship while her relationship with Patrick continued to dwindle. Their fights increased and as she grew apart from him, she began to look forward to the respite Nduka's frequent calls provided.

-

Two weeks after she returned from New York, the phone rang as Phina was about to make her way up the stairs in Hazel House. When the butler handed her the handset, she heard Isabel's voice on the other end.

"Phina, what will Iris Thompson need information from Hartiers for?" Isabel blurted. Before Phina could respond, Isabel continued, "Our internal investigation revealed that our saboteur was working for Lady Thompson."

"Are you sure?"

"Geoffrey had to have been working for her."

The news Phina just received worsened the tension in her head. After hanging up, she headed straight to her bedroom.

"Let me draw you a bath darling," she heard Patrick say the moment she walked in.

"Sure," Phina responded, relieved that they were on speaking terms once more, but still thoroughly disturbed by the news she just received.

"I'd love to join you if you don't mind."

Phina paused for a second to consider his request. "You've never needed my permission before. What's different now?" she asked when she finally responded.

Patrick ignored her question and drew a bath. Rather than join her in the tub, he sat by the side – loofah in hand – and scrubbed her back. He remained silent as he went through the motions. Phina looked up at him and saw sorrow, so deep, her heart skipped a beat and she had to struggle to catch her breath.

"What is it, love?" she asked, choking on her words.

Patrick woke from his daydream and looked down at her. They held a gaze for at least two seconds before he dropped the loofah on his hand and bent to kiss her, first on her lips, then all over her cheeks, forehead, and chin.

"I love you so much," he said, almost sobbing. "Let no one or anything convince you otherwise."

Phina looked at him in dismay and sighed.

"What are you saying?" she asked. His demeanor, coupled with her disappointment from the news she received from Isabel, got her so overwhelmed that tears rolled down her cheeks. Getting the sense that something was wrong she asked again, "What is it, love?"

"I'll tell you. Just get out of the bath before you catch a cold." He pulled the faucet and as the water ran, he picked up the loofah and squeezed it onto her back before allowing it to fill with water again. He then let the water from the loofah drip on her right breast, causing her to sigh. He repeated the action with her other breast, so she grabbed his wrist and turned to face him, only to find his mouth barely an inch from hers. With their mouths locked in a kiss, he squeezed her breasts in slow successive movements, pinching her nipple as he got to the peak. He then carried her out of the tub and dabbed her hair with a towel before wrapping her body with another one and carrying her straight to bed. Running his fingers through her hair, he kissed her passionately. She glanced at his face at one point and found a distant look in his eyes. Soon after, they slept in each other's arms.

Patrick awoke long before Phina and paced the room, stopping at intervals to stare at her beautiful face as she smiled intermittently in her sleep. Watching as her chest heaved, he thought about how much he loved her. She was the most amazing person he'd ever met, and he doubted anyone could ever be above her. While he waited patiently for her to wake up, he took a bath and threw on some slacks. It was Sunday, and he hoped to spend the whole day indoors. The butler had brought up a plate of food – an omelet, some fruits, nuts, and yoghurt – which Patrick placed carefully by Phina's bedside. She woke up soon after and ate slowly while he watched in silence.

"What is it you wanted to tell me, *hon*?" Phina asked, looking him directly in the eyes with her fork midway to her mouth.

Patrick walked to the window and stared out for a few minutes.

"You never asked me about the equity transaction."

"What about it?"

"I got the report from Witham Capital and they refused to go on with the deal."

"What was their reason?" she asked.

"Something to do with the extent of our obligations." He sighed and shook his head. "There's something I need to tell you."

"What?" Phina asked, swallowing hard.

"I'm in the final phase of selling my shares of Ophinas."

Phina was dazed. She sat silently, waiting for what he said to sink in. "What do you mean?" she asked.

"I'm sorry. I've wanted to tell you for a while about the transaction but there never seemed to be a good time."

"A good time? No, no, no!" Phina cried. "That is our legacy. It's not yours to sell." She placed both hands on her head. "Do you realize what you've done? You've diluted our interest in Ophinas and put us in jeopardy."

"I had no other choice. The money was supposed to pay to retain my interest in Sportsmets."

Phina's eyes brimmed with tears as she pushed the tray away from her legs causing the food to splatter all over the bed. "You do realize that when you act carelessly with other people's interests you bring ruin unto yours, right?"

Patrick stared at her in bewilderment.

"Patrick, please explain!" she yelled. "How could you do something like this? You know how much I sweated to get this company to where it is today. Who did you sell the shares to? Who did you sell it to?" she repeated when he didn't answer fast enough.

"Iris Thompson."

"Lady Thompson?" Phina blurted, panting heavily. "Is that why she was spying on us?"

"What do you mean?"

"You know what I mean. Isabel found out that Geoffrey was working for Lady Thompson. So, that's what this was all about. Were you part of that plan?" Phina asked exasperatedly.

"Absolutely not. Why would you even ask?"

"Why not?" she asked, laughing derisively. "Anything is possible at this point," she concluded, throwing her hands in the air. "I will use the powers inherent in me as the majority shareholder to overrule this."

"You can't."

"Why not?"

"Because the company's constitution does not give you the authority to overrule such a decision."

"You must halt this process now!" Phina yelled. She was sitting at the edge of the bed, breathing hard with her hands pressing down the mattress.

"It's too late," Patrick murmured, avoiding her gaze and letting out a deep sigh. "The valuation is done. The Share Purchase Agreement has been signed and sealed."

"When did this happen?" she shrieked as she stood up from the bed and walked towards Patrick. Tears welled up in her eyes.

"Right before your trip to New York."

Phina burst into tears and hit Patrick's chest with both fists. He grabbed them with his hands and pulled her forcefully towards him.

"Darling, stop," he said, his voice laden with emotion.

She continued to hit him and when he succeeded in locking her hands in his; she looked up at him, her chest beating wildly as streams of water rolled down her face.

"I'm sorry. I'm so sorry," Patrick pleaded.

Phina shook her head.

"You've hurt me. I never dreamt you would ever hurt me," she said, sobbing uncontrollably.

-

Patrick resigned his position on the board of Ophinas the following day. Selling his twenty percent ownership of shares to Lady Thompson, guaranteed her a thirty percent stake of Ophinas. Chief Gambo held ten percent of the shares. Phina remained the majority shareholder with a sixty percent stake.

Phina called Chief Gambo to explain the state of affairs to him.

"I am sorely disappointed," he said. "I liked Patrick. Who could have thought he would do such a thing? I also like Thompson, but they shouldn't have done this without consulting you," he concluded with a long drawl.

"I know you could never pull the rug under my feet like that," Phina assured him.

"Let me tell you something," Chief Gambo said after a long pause. "I will never do a thing like that. I keep telling people that integrity is very important. One should always be consistent and tell the truth at all times. I don't know how you'll cope with Lady Thompson on the board but you'll have to try. Such is life!"

"I don't blame Lady Thompson for any of this, although I do a little. The entire blame lies with my husband. He's the one that owed me loyalty."

"I agree. When all this settles down, find it in your heart to forgive him and move on."

"Oh no," Phina responded, shaking her head. "I have already forgiven him. The only thing left to happen is for him to understand that there is something he needs to be forgiven for. That's when he'll be able to receive the forgiveness and be free himself."

"Good girl. Don't worry. He'll always be there to support you. Even though he may not be physically a part of the company, he'll support you like he always has. Think of it this way, he may have needed the money for something important. He's not stupid, you know."

-

From then on, Phina viewed Patrick differently. She had trusted him completely with her life and he had never given her any reason not to until then. She realized she needed to sharpen her wits and rely less on him. To take back the reins, she set out to weed out anyone who may have been involved in executing the transaction and felt the need to keep her in the dark about it. The process started with the accountant who performed the valuation and then to the company secretary who drew up all the papers. They had failed her miserably and there was zero tolerance for their actions – or lack of thereof. The firings kept the mood at Ophinas dreary for a while. Phina waited for a month to pass before she hired a consulting firm to fill the vacant positions, but not before she thoroughly interviewed the top candidates to ensure that their values and vision were aligned with hers. It was of utmost importance that they understood they had to maintain loyalty to her.

To get over Patrick's betrayal she relied on her friends to keep her head above water. She spoke to Isabel nearly every day, but she wasn't due to see her until her next visit to New York in the spring. Traveling always helped her heal, and she needed to heal desperately. She tried several times to reach out to Victoria but always ended up not following through. She hoped Victoria would make the first move to avoid creating an awkward situation.

-

Victoria did call, but only after Phina had given up on her.

"Hello," Victoria said after Phina settled down for lemonade with Brigitte right before bedtime. "I haven't heard from you in a long time. How are you?"

"Fine," was all Phina could say.

"Don't lie. You don't sound fine. Where is Patrick?"

"He's still at the office."

"This late?"

"He has to complete some work."

Phina couldn't bring herself to tell her best friend that her marriage was on the rocks. Worse still, she dreaded telling her that Patrick was keeping late nights and on a couple of occasions didn't come home until morning. And when she found the courage to ask him where he'd been, he had provided a lame excuse about how he had stayed overnight at the office to get some work done.

7

BITE THE BIG APPLE

PHINA returned to New York in the spring. Flowers had started to bloom, and the trees were beginning to regain their colors and former glory. The official launching of her designs in Hartiers was approaching. The work they'd done in the past six months was finally paying off and her efforts were coming to fruition. Not only did she have the Ophinas brand to cater to, but she also had to create a whole new set of designs to launch in the American market. She had never worked so hard in her life. Although she hired six designers to help her accomplish her vision, each item in both collections always had to pass her scrutiny.

Isabel and Simon were waiting for her at JFK when she arrived. The moment she entered the posh limousine, the sound of a champagne cork popping, startled her.

"Welcome to the Big Apple," Simon greeted in a deep voice.

Phina laughed with her hand on her chest as she recovered from the shock. "Thank you, Simon." She gave him a hug and then hugged Isabel before taking her position across from them.

"Happy Easter," Isabel greeted. "Glad you get to spend it with us."

"Happy Easter to you both," Phina responded with glee.

"How is Patrick?" Simon asked. "The last time we spoke it sounded like things were getting a lot better."

"Oh yeah. That was the biggest fight we ever had and hopefully the last."

"I'm happy to hear that," said Simon. "If not for the sake of Brigitte then for the sake of the love you have for each other."

"Simon always sees the best in people," Isabel remarked before Phina could respond. "This time around I agree with him. Patrick is your soul mate."

Phina nodded in agreement. They sat in silence for a while and gazed out of the window, admiring the scenery. New York was warm, the skies were a clear blue and the promise of beautiful weather for the Easter Parade going on at Fifth Avenue held true for most of the day. Phina was awoken from deep thought when Isabel touched her lightly on the knee. "I looked at the collection. Every piece was as incredible as the next. It was quite the assortment," Isabel said.

"I'm glad you loved it," Phina responded.

"Our investors will love us for bringing you on board."

-

The mansion was gleaming with lights when they arrived. The front door was open, and the butler stood on the stairs just as the chauffeur pulled to a stop. Phina took a whiff of the delicious smells and marveled at the splash of colors delivered by the tulips, daffodils and winter aconites that filled the flower garden.

"I could live here forever. I wish I had brought Brigitte with me though," Phina whined the moment they stepped onto the stairs.

"I asked you to bring her," Isabel chirped. "You would have been more relaxed and not feel the need to leave so soon."

"No," Phina said, shaking her head. "I wouldn't have been able to focus. Besides, I can't stay in New York for too long. There's still so much to accomplish at home. I have to start creating the next collection."

"New York will give you the inspiration you need. Don't worry about that. Even though it's going to be a roller coaster week, I have everything arranged," Isabel assured her.

"I hope so."

"See you at dinner," Isabel said as they parted ways on the stairs and Phina headed to her room.

Her room was warm when she entered, and fluffy slippers and a bathrobe had been put out. A shiny red vase with fresh spring flowers stood on the writing desk and a fresh undecipherable smell lay in the air. Phina had hardly had time to take in the luxury and beauty of her bedroom when she heard a knock on the door and the butler announced that dinner was ready.

-

"Ohh, what's that I smell?" Phina asked as she walked into the dining room where Isabel and Simon were already seated.

The table was set with identical burgundy ceramic dishes with white rims. Steam oozed out of the bowls and a large Atlantic salmon garnished with scallions, beets, asparaguses, and carrots, sat in the middle of it all. For their first course, the cook served mushroom soup with house biscuits. The soup was so delicious; Phina had to caution herself to quit eating to leave room for the entrée. The trio talked while they ate and by the time dessert was served, Phina was too full to take another bite.

"You've got to try it," Simon urged her.

Phina obliged and took a bite of the blueberry pie. One bite turned into two, and then three, and before she knew it, she had finished the whole plate. It was the most delicious blueberry pie she'd ever tasted. "At this rate," she said, "You'll have to wheel me out of here when I leave in a week."

"That won't be necessary," Isabel teased, "we have so much to do that every calorie you eat will be burned two-fold."

"I hope so," Phina said, giggling lightly. "Thank you, my dears. I wonder how I would have coped without you two."

The following day, Isabel and Phina drove around to review the placement of the Ophinas brand of clothes in each of the Hartiers' stores. At the main store in Long Island, Ophinas collection was beautifully placed with mirrors, lights, and chandeliers and the clothes were already selling in amazing numbers.

By four o'clock in the afternoon, the ladies realized they had forgotten to have lunch and stopped at Reno's – a small restaurant in mid-town Manhattan to grab a bite. After settling at a corner by the window, they resumed their favorite sport – people watching.

"What a day," Isabel said, sighing and arching her brows.

"We still have so much to do before the D-day though," Phina responded, as she pointed out her selection to the waiter.

"How about your friends, Nduka and Bimpe? Any plan to see them?"

"Oh," Phina hit her forehead with her palm. "I completely forgot. I promised Nduka I would call when I arrived. I've been in over my head. I'll call him when I get back this evening. He may still be at work."

"I spoke with him today."

"I didn't know you guys talked," Phina said, staring at Isabel in amazement.

"He and Simon have become good friends. They play golf sometimes."

"Oh, wow. What about his girlfriend Bimpe? Do you speak to her? She seems quite reticent."

"No. I haven't seen her since the day Nduka brought her to dinner. I was surprised to learn she was a pediatrician?"

"Nduka never mentioned that," Phina muttered.

"He seems successful," Isabel continued. "I didn't know doctors made that much money. His home in Manhattan is magnificent. Simon visited him once."

"Apparently doctors make a lot of money."

–

After lunch, they headed back to the office and worked until they were both exhausted. Getting home around eight, Phina spotted a Rolls Royce parked in the driveway.

"Isn't that Nduka's car?" she asked Isabel.

"That's right," Isabel said. "I'm sure he's with Simon. He probably came to see you."

As soon as they stepped into the opulent living room, they heard laughter on the balcony and headed in that direction.

"Here you are," Simon said in a raucous tone. "Hello sweetie," he said, planting a kiss on Isabel's lips and leading her into the living room.

Nduka hugged Phina and kissed her cheeks before he announced that he needed to take his leave.

"So soon?" Isabel asked. "I assumed you'd stay for dinner."

"Not tonight," He said with a deep drawl. "I'm on call. I wish I could stay. It feels like ages since I saw Phina."

"I'm around the whole week so maybe we can see some other time," Phina said. "Hey, come for the brand launch on Friday. I'll be leaving the following day."

"I already entered that in my calendar. Isabel sent me an invitation a while ago," Nduka said with a smile. "Walk me to my car let's catch up a little bit."

"Okay," Phina responded.

She stepped outside with Nduka and they talked for a while until a chilly wind started to blow. Nduka reached in his car for a jacket and wrapped it around her.

"I had no idea New York would be so cold in April," Phina said, her teeth chattering.

"Let's get in the car and finish our discussion. I don't want you to get sick before your launch. Isabel would kill me," he said jokingly before opening the door for her and waiting for her to get in. He went behind the car to the other side and first instructed the driver to wait inside the lobby before he got in. "Finally, I get to talk to you alone. How have you been?"

"Even though it's been work, work, work, since I arrived in New York, Isabel and Simon still find opportunities to give me a good time. I wish I could relax though and enjoy every bit of it, instead, I find myself worrying so much. How are you? How is Bimpe?"

"I'm doing great. Bimpe is fine. You know the nature of long-term relationships. They can be difficult at times. You're in one, so you understand."

"Mine was fine until I got the rug pulled from underneath me. Even though we're working through things, I don't think I'll ever truly trust him again, but time will tell. With Bimpe on the other hand, you have your whole life ahead of you."

"My issue with Bimpe is a different ball game."

Phina shrugged "You're still hung up on that tribal nonsense."

"No. not that," Nduka said, shaking his head. "It's just that after you and I reconnected, I can't stop thinking about the passionate kisses we used to share."

"Don't be ridiculous," Phina said, staring at him in shock.

"I'm not trying to be. After I saw you the last time, I've not been able to get you off my mind. You can call it ridiculous if you want, but that is my truth."

"Don't even think about it. Patrick and I are solid. Yes, we've had a few bumps along the road, but nothing significant enough for me to betray him. I still have faith we'll be able to resolve our issues," Phina concluded, looking away.

After a momentary silence, Nduka blurted, "I don't think that guy is good for you. He doesn't respect you as he should."

"He does respect me!" Phina retorted, easing back to glare at him.

Nduka looked at her intently. "He doesn't. If he did, he wouldn't have treated you the way he did with regards to that transaction."

"Hey!" Phina warned. "I told you that in confidence."

"Yes, and it's held in the strictest confidence. You're a gem. He doesn't know that.

Phina was shaken. She looked down to hide her eyes, which were almost clouded with tears. Nduka had succeeded in reminding her about her issues with Patrick. Although their problems made her miserable at times, they were not significant enough for her to leave him. She loved him with every fiber of her being. Besides, she had Brigitte to consider. Even though she still shuddered whenever she remembered how Patrick had betrayed her, she still believed that time could heal all wounds. Nduka was not to blame for expecting otherwise as she had relied heavily on him to get by in the past months.

"I better leave for my call," Nduka said, interrupting the cozy silence that fell between them as they listened to the sound of each other's soft breathing.

"That's true. You shouldn't be late. Go save a life."

Nduka chuckled and bent towards her. Phina, assuming it was for a kiss on the cheek, came close only to find her mouth engulfed in a kiss with his. The lip-lock lasted for only a brief moment before she pulled away, her heart racing uncontrollably. Nduka put his arm slowly around her waist and stared at her affectionately while she tried her best to avert her eyes. With nowhere else to look, Phina returned his gaze. Something in his eyes sent her heart aflutter. The longing in it changed everything for her.

"Excuse me," Phina said, wriggling out of his arms and struggling to fight back tears.

"Wait," Nduka said, swallowing hard. "I'll get the door for you."

He stepped out of the car and opened the door for Phina. He was only gone for a couple of seconds, but she felt a rush of emotions coursing through her body. When she got out of the car, Nduka planted another kiss on her lips with both hands firmly placed on her back, causing her head to swoon. It was nothing like the kisses they stole from each other behind the cherry bushes in her father's compound back in the day. The kiss was a mature, deeply affectionate and terribly addictive one.

"I need to go," she said breathlessly, pulling away from him.

"I'll call you tomorrow," he muttered.

Phina could not believe what had just transpired. Her head was spinning when she got into the living room, so she asked to take her dinner in the bedroom. Isabel and Simon quickly obliged her, but not without first looking at each other in surprise.

In the privacy of her room, Phina ran her thumb over her lips to check if she had really kissed another man. Her lips were soft and supple, and the lip gloss she applied earlier had disappeared completely so there was no doubt that the kiss had occurred. As she lay in her bed that night, she thought desperately about how she would dig herself out of the mess she'd created. There was no chance in hell she would reveal the incident to Patrick as it would only drive them further apart. She would have to deal with the consequences herself and the only way, she thought, was to avoid Nduka completely.

-

The day of the launch, Phina and Isabel started at the mansion with stylists and makeup artists as well as photographers. Phina was nervous about how the day would go. She had hosted several launches for her stores in the past, but this one was different. Everything was planned and prearranged for her. She just had to show up, make her speech, and be graceful. Her outfit was an elegant, fitted, black Zalia design, and she paired it with a diamond choker and bracelets with matching earrings. Her hair cascaded down her shoulders. Her shoes were red; Phina had thought that would contrast too much with her dress, but it turned out to be a great choice.

Simon was the first to step out of the limousine, followed by Isabel, and then Phina. A horde of press and photographers surrounded her. It took a lot of maneuvering by the three bodyguards hired to accompany her to the event before she could make her way through the crowd to get into the store. Safely in, she was ushered into the VIP section. The store buzzed with shoppers looking for an opportunity to catch a glimpse of her, have a word with her, or get her to sign an autograph. Isabel brought every single celebrity in attendance to meet her. She met almost a dozen music artists and movie stars, many of whom she recognized from television. When it was time for her speech, she felt a little winded and opted for the short version. Nduka walked in while she was rounding off. Her heart skipped a beat when she first set eyes on him. As her eyes darted from corner to corner to find out where he was at each moment, she realized the extent of her infatuation. Her heart beat furtively when she looked up after signing an autograph for a fan and realized Nduka was standing there waiting for his turn to speak with her.

"Congratulations," Nduka said, extending his hand for a handshake.

Phina's knees buckled the moment she took his hand, and he caught her by the waist. She felt his breath on her face and his heart beating loudly as he guided her to a seat. Even though it was a moment's occurrence, the incident caused Phina to recall their kiss.

"I don't understand why you need to leave tomorrow," Nduka said after they took a seat in the VIP section.

"Is that the biggest issue we have right now?"

"I'm not implying that. I just wish you could stay a little longer."

"That won't be possible, but I need you to promise something," Phina said, looking at him expectantly.

"I'll do anything you want."

"Not to say a word about what happened between us to a single soul."

"I promise," Nduka said, crossing his arms over his chest.

-

Phina kept her appointment with the airline and left for London the following day. She continued to speak with Nduka every other day. Once, he offered to visit her in London but she declined. Several months passed before Nduka relocated to the UK for work. By that time, Phina's relationship with Patrick had stabilized, although they both realized it needed a lot of work to get it to how it used to be.

8

GLOOM

THE phone in her hotel room rang at 2 AM.

Still groggy from sleep, Phina slammed it when she tried to pick it up and accidentally displaced it.

It rang again and this time she successfully grasped it.

"Patrick?"

"It's me," the butler said in a tight, mellow voice.

"How is Brigitte?"

"She is fine, Madam."

"Then?"

"Senior Superintendent Claudio from the Metropolitan Police is here. You must come home immediately, madam. The Marquis… Something happened to the Marquis."

"Pass the phone to the Superintendent," Phina demanded.

It was at least five seconds before Phina heard the policeman's voice.

"Madam," she heard Senior Superintendent Claudio say. "Your husband is in St Margaret's Hospital. He's in a very critical condition."

Phina paused for a second to absorb what she'd just heard. Her heart dropped and her vision clouded. She wasn't sure the policeman had the right person. Patrick had traveled to Barcelona on Tuesday; two days after she went to Florence for business. He was scheduled to return the following day, and she wasn't due back until Friday.

"Sorry, I don't understand," she finally said. "He was supposed to be in Barcelona. What happened to him?" she asked in a raised tone. "What happened?" She bent forward and clenched her stomach as she waited for a response.

"I don't have all the details. We were notified after he was transferred to London. Please, Madam, come home as soon as you can. I'll leave my number with your staff should you need to reach me."

"Can you at least tell me what happened to my husband?" she cried at the top of her voice.

"He was found unresponsive in his hotel room."

"By whom?" She asked frantically.

The superintendent hesitated at first. "I don't have all the details. I'm assuming hotel staff."

Terror gripped Phina as she got up from the bed and paced the room.

"I'll leave for London first thing in the morning."

"I'm sorry, madam. I wish I could have delivered better news."

-

Victoria and Jorge stood amongst the small crowd that gathered in the front porch at Hazel House when Phina returned at 10 AM. As her car pulled closer, the crowd dispersed, and she caught sight of the distraught face of the butler who came close on Victoria's heels. Confused, Phina opened her door before the chauffeur pulled to a stop, forcing him to halt abruptly.

From the look on Victoria's face, it was obvious she'd been crying heavily and Jorge looked distressed. A little group of servants hovered sympathetically. Phina immediately knew something was wrong.

"What's going on?" She screamed from a distance. "Where is Patrick?"

Tears streamed down Victoria's face. Jorge tried to console her, but she continued to sob uncontrollably.

"He's gone," Jorge muttered.

Phina froze. Panic overcame her. Her heart lurched, and blood rushed to her head. Almost stumbling, she leaned on the Limousine and placed both hands at the top before slipping unexpectedly to the ground.

"Call 999!" she heard Victoria scream.

Jorge picked her up and took her into her private living room. When she regained her senses and found herself in Jorge's arms, she wept uncontrollably. He placed her gently on the sofa and sat next to her, gently forcing her to stay down whenever she tried to move. After two attempts to get up, she finally gave up.

"What happened to Patrick?" she asked through shoulder wracking sobs.

"We don't know yet. He was gone by the time they brought him to London." Jorge was choking on his words.

"When did this happen?" Phina asked, clutching her stomach and breathing heavily.

"Last night."

"But the Senior Superintendent told me…"

"I know. He wasn't supposed to tell you the whole story over the phone. We heard you weren't due back from Florence for another two days so we had to find a way to lure you back."

"Where is Brigitte?" Phina asked, glancing around in terror.

"In her room," Jorge answered. "With the nanny."

"I must see her now," she said, sitting up abruptly. "Does she know?"

"No," Jorge replied, shaking his head. "We didn't think it was our place to tell her. It's also not a good idea for you to tell her in your current state."

"I need to see her," Phina insisted and rose forcefully.

"Take it easy. We'll take you to her room. She's been asking for you all morning."

-

Brigitte was playing with her toys in a corner when Phina, Victoria, and Jorge got to her room. The nanny was seated in a different corner reading a book.

"Mommy, Mommy," Brigitte screamed, eagerly running to her mother's side.

As hard as she tried, Phina was unable to mask the sullen look on her face as she bent down to kiss Brigitte.

"Why are you sad?" Brigitte asked when she noticed Phina's tear-stained cheeks.

"Do I look sad?" Phina asked, wiping the tears from her eyes. "Oh, my eyes just hurt, sweetie."

"Why is Vicky here? Where is teacher? Where is Daddy?"

"Oh, Brigitte, so many questions."

Phina beckoned to the nanny.

"I'll tell you everything," she whispered to Brigitte. "Go with your nanny. I need to speak to the fine people waiting for me downstairs. I'll be back soon."

"Okay," Brigitte responded, looking around in confusion.

After they left Brigitte with the nanny, Victoria and Jorge followed Phina to her room.

"The coroner pronounced him dead last night," Victoria stated off-handedly after they sat on the bed. "Did they tell you how he was found?"

Phina shook her head and looked away. She was afraid to look Victoria in the eyes for fear of what they might reveal.

"He was lying face down on the floor in his hotel room," Victoria continued, her shoulders wracking as she started to sob again.

Phina, too weak to handle the emotions, stretched out her hand and hugged Victoria. Efforts to get her to stop sobbing were to no avail. Soon, she was sobbing with her.

"Come and spend the night at our place," Jorge said to Phina. "Bring Brigitte with you. I don't feel comfortable leaving you both by yourselves."

Phina pondered his request for a second and then shook her head. "I think we're better off keeping Brigitte in familiar surroundings. Yanking her away from her home would only increase her anxiety."

"That makes sense," Jorge agreed. "Don't hesitate to call if you need anything though. I'll check on you tomorrow."

"Thank you."

-

After everyone had left, Phina sat alone in her room, terribly agitated. She ignored the blaring sound of her phone for a few minutes before she decided she couldn't bear its ringing anymore. When she picked it up, she was surprised to hear Nduka's voice.

"I saw the news," Nduka said, while Phina sobbed silently.

"Hello... Hello," Nduka repeated when he heard nothing.

"Yes, hello," Phina finally responded, choking on her words.

"Can I come over?"

"That's probably not a good idea. Right now, it wouldn't be appropriate."

"When can I see you then?"

"I'm not sure. I…"

"I'm sorry about what happened."

"Thanks, I'll call you back tomorrow."

Phina hung up and called Lady Thompson. Her phone rang many times before a steward picked it up and confirmed his mistress was on a business trip. The steward provided Lady Thompson's hotel phone number which Phina tried a few times before giving up. Too tired to make any more calls she cried herself to sleep.

-

She woke up the following morning with Brigitte by her side. The nanny had brought Brigitte to her room early in the morning as the child had been restless the whole night. To avoid waking her, Phina sobbed quietly as she spoke to her mother on the phone.

"Have you told Brigitte?" her mother asked.

"No, I haven't. I'll tell her later today, but I'll have to figure out the best way to do it."

"You should tell her soon before she hears it from someone else."

"Definitely."

Before Phina could say another word, Brigitte shot up from the bed.

"Mummy, when is Daddy coming back?" she asked, rubbing her eyes with the back of her hands.

Phina said goodbye to her mother and hung up the phone.

Shaken by Brigitte's words, Phina was immediately struck by a flood of emotions. Her shoulders convulsed as she tried to control her sobs. She let out a whimper and when she looked up; she saw Brigitte staring at her, perplexed.

"Come here," Phina said to her.

Brigitte curled into her mother's arms.

"I don't think he's coming back, baby. He's in heaven now."

"How? Is he dead?" Brigitte asked wide-eyed, tears forming in her eyes.

"He's with God now."

Brigitte broke down and cried uncontrollably, her shoulders rocked and her chest heaved. Phina didn't think telling Brigitte about her father's death would be an easy feat. But nothing had prepared her for the pain she saw in the little girl's eyes. It hadn't occurred to her that Brigitte at five years old would understand the full impact of the message.

She held Brigitte against her chest for a few minutes before she heard her say in a whisper, "Mummy, does that mean Daddy is watching us now?"

Before her mother could respond, Brigitte broke their embrace, threw her head back and gazed at the ceiling, while moving her head from one side to the next.

Phina gasped in relief. "You're such a smart girl. Your daddy will be so proud of you,"

"But I want Daddy," Brigitte squealed, shocking her mother and causing her already swollen eyes to throb. To calm her, Phina pulled her close and rocked back and forth until shoulder wracking sobs became an occasional whimper before she finally fell asleep.

-

Phina roused from her stupor shortly after the nanny took Brigitte away. Ruffling through her purse, she found the piece of paper she had written Senior Superintendent Claudio's number on. She dialed the number and was directed to a voicemail. Still on edge after leaving him a message to request details of what happened to Patrick, she got up to look through Patrick's belongings. She recalled doing this often when they were first married as it always made her feel closer to him, especially when he was away for a few days. This time, it was different – strange even; this time he wasn't coming back. At first, she went through the neat pile of papers on his writing desk where he worked most nights before bedtime. Then she ransacked his shirt closet and the armoire that held his ties. Everything was neatly arranged in his usual style. When she picked up the striped silvery grey Armani tie he had worn at the last event they attended together, her emotions surged, and she sobbed again. Unable to carry the weight of her own body, she dragged herself to his side of the bed and laid on her back. She gasped for breath as her heart pounded uncontrollably. Her vision was blurry from non-stop crying, so she shut her eyes, but the images she saw in her mind's eye jolted her. Shooting upright on the bed, she grabbed her hurting head with both hands. A thought crossed her mind, so she tugged at his bedside drawer and to her utmost surprise, not only was it open, it looked disheveled. Inside, she saw his old passport, a couple of ID's, a business card holder with almost a dozen business cards stuffed in it and a letter written on crisp cream paper, lined with blue ink.

She picked up the letter and after reading the first word; she bolted upright and squinted her puffy eyes to adjust her now blurry vision. The writing was somewhat scraggly, so she struggled to get through the rest of it.

Darling,

Our last time together was phenomenal. I still cherish that moment till this day and look forward to our next meeting. Remember that you're never alone...

The handwriting was not Patrick's, but there was no indication of who the letter was from. Phina wondered who may have written it to him. The other thing that puzzled her was the manner in which he had left his drawer – untidy – which was uncharacteristic of him. His trip to Barcelona had been impromptu, and he was expected home at least two days before her, so it made sense that he hadn't tried to be discrete about the letter. The letter was short but impactful, and the more Phina thought about it, the more she felt her muscles stiffen. Her skin tingled, and a heavyweight landed at the pit of her stomach. She wanted to scream as another surge of emotions swept through her, but the sounds could not form in her oral cavity. Searching for further clues, she knelt in front of the drawer and opened the bottom layer to see if she could find an envelope or anything that could give her an indication of who the note was from. Discovering none, she furiously yanked the top drawer from the slides. The bottom one was harder to get off, so she pulled until she was panting heavily. Exhausted, she slipped her right arm behind and groped the bottom with her fingers. Her eyes were dry and sore. She gasped as she felt something cold to the touch. A closer look at her find revealed a silver charm bracelet. The charms included a combination of Roman numerals, letters of the alphabet, and a few objects she couldn't decipher through her tired eyes. The combination of numbers and letters made no sense to her. Confused, she slid the drawers in place, dragged herself back into the bed and studied the bracelet for markings. Finding none, she placed the note back where she had found it and threw the bracelet into her own drawer.

After pondering for a few minutes how the letter could have come about, Phina decided to accept the obvious fact that it was sent by someone with a romantic connection to Patrick. But from whom, she couldn't tell. Her eyes were now completely dried of tears as she glared into the distance, hoping for the answers she so desperately needed to come out of thin air. As for the bracelet, there was no way for her to tell if one had something to do with the other. She couldn't recall ever owning one like that.

Shocked and devastated at the knowledge that Patrick may have been cheating on her, Phina placed her head under her pillow and let out a loud heart-wrenching scream. Fainting from exhaustion, she sat upright and folded her arms around her chest as though to shield her entire being from the ills that had befallen her. She peered lazily around the room and sobbed again till her eyes protruded from their sockets.

Shortly after she fell asleep, she was jolted by a chilling nightmare. She felt traumatized and sick from the memories of what she had dreamt but fell asleep again as she was rationalizing why she found the scenes so terrifying. When she awoke the second time and recalled her current situation, a feeling of dread, worse than the one she experienced when she first heard Patrick died, filled her chest and almost busted her insides. She could never have imagined that she could endure so much. The pain was so intense that she feared she would never recover. Not only that, she felt ashamed; how long had Patrick been cheating on her and with whom? She wondered if it was with one person, multiple people at the same time, or numerous lovers at different points in time.

-

For several weeks after she found the letter, Phina moped around, unsure of everything and everyone around her. The nightmares kept her awake every night and her business suffered greatly. She had loved Patrick with every fiber of her being and had believed he had loved her tremendously as well. Even in recent times when they'd had problems in their marriage, she had hoped that things would turn around after the economy got back to normal and his outlook changed. Eating became a foregone conclusion for her. Breathing was achieved through great effort. In her mind, if she died with the pain she was carrying around, it wouldn't make any difference since her life no longer held any meaning. The respite she imagined she would get from dying led her to smile for the first time in weeks, but even that lasted only a few moments before the pain consumed her again.

Phina spoke to her mother and sister often and discovered meditation through her mother's persistence. She prayed whenever she could – on her drive to work, during the day when her mind began to wander, and in the middle of the night when she was awoken by the nightmares. Her depressive state slowly dissipated as a result. Having marginally recovered, she found some needed strength to estimate when Patrick's meandering could have started. Their first year of marriage had been romantic and full of bliss. The following year, after Brigitte came, they had maintained the momentum with which they first started. In the years that followed, they had placed a lot of focus on their careers but still were able to make time for each other. Things had begun to change between them only in the past couple of years. She had continued to grow her business and his movies had done marvelously at the box office, but his other ventures suffered unprecedented damage during the financial downturn. Before she knew it, he had begun to resent her success and her offers to help him had fallen on deaf ears. An emotional divide gradually grew between them, which worsened when his portfolio lost most of its value.

His betrayal with the Ophinas share sale was one thing and dreadful as it was, the cheating tipped the scales. Slowly, everything she'd observed in the past months gradually came back to her. The packet of unopened condoms and lubricating gel – both which she had assumed were meant for her were now red flags. His restlessness and the need to leave the room anytime an important discussion came up were every bit as indicative of a double life.

Unable to make sense of it all, she decided to give Victoria a call.

Victoria responded only in monosyllables. Phina imagined that she was still despondent over her brother's death.

"I'm not sure what you mean by who he was cheating with," she had answered when Phina asked if she knew about Patrick's affair.

"I saw a note in his drawer. It seemed he had a lover."

"I don't want to get involved," Victoria answered coldly.

Phina felt her stomach lurch.

"Victoria. Do you know something then?"

"I had my suspicions but can't say for sure."

"So are you saying you don't know about any extramarital affairs?"

"No. I don't," she said categorically.

Phina's conversation with Victoria left her even more confused. For the first time in her life, she began to question herself and the way she judged the people and the circumstances around her. She had trusted Patrick, Victoria, Irene – his entire family. She hadn't expected such an atrocity to be committed against her and her child. Worse was that no one found it necessary to tell her so she could choose; whether to leave, stay and accept the behavior, or stay and demand boundaries. Whoever knew of his affair and failed to inform her, she concluded, colluded in keeping her in bondage. Her presumptions led her to view everyone as culprits and accessories to what by now she concluded was soul rape. In her mind, Patrick had raped her soul by bringing other beings into her space without her approval and forcing her to sleep with them. She wondered how he would have felt if the tables were turned. The thought made her smile for the first time in weeks because she knew it would have killed him.

Patrick's funeral was held on an unexpectedly chilly day in the middle of October. Phina looked beaten down walking behind the casket as the pallbearers, six of Patrick's closest friends marched slowly to the sound of trumpets on the way to his burial site. Ezinne walked behind her and on a couple of occasions had to reach out to support her when she started to lose her balance. All color left her expressionless face as she scanned the faces at the funeral wondering who knew about Patrick's infidelity and didn't warn her. "They must think I'm a fool," she thought, as her heart filled with resentment. She sighed when she imagined what everyone thought her grief was really about. If only they knew she was grieving a far bigger loss – the loss of her memory of him.

During the reception at Hazel House, sunrays flooded through tall glazed windows illuminating the drapes in the hallway. Flower garlands flanked family photos of Patrick, Phina, and Brigitte. Patrick's mother, Irene, had been especially close to her son. She sat on a long bench in a black dress and veiled hat; her face poignant, and a symbol of profound grief. Blake Caldwell, whom over the years became a close friend of Phina and Patrick, looked at Phina from a distance and saw the pain that enveloped her. It showed in her eyes, her movements and even in the tone of her skin, the bit that showed through her black long-sleeved dress. He wondered how someone that beautiful could be so aggrieved. Finally, he got his chance to speak to her amidst the throng of people that had come to offer their condolences.

"I'll need you to pick yourself back up again," he said.

"I am... I will," she stuttered as the pain surged through her heart again and she fought back tears.

"Hey, Phina, you have to be strong."

Phina looked at him and then shook her head.

"Did you know?" she found the strength to ask.

"Know what?" Blake asked, easing back, his face puckered a little.

Phina shifted her gaze to the floor and sighed. "I'm sorry. This is not the place."

-

Two days after the funeral, Phina walked into Hazel House to find Blake standing in the foyer holding a glass of whiskey.

"What a surprise!" she said. "What were you doing out in this storm?" she asked when she noticed the dripping umbrella – one of theirs – on his other hand.

"I decided to take a look at the garden. I realized I never really had a good look at the grounds. It's amazing how ubiquitous it is."

"But it's raining cat and dogs out there."

"It was nothing. Just a small drizzle when I was out. I was so sure you'd be home considering how distressed you were at the funeral. But I'm happy you're able to get around and do other stuff."

"I have to. I can't keep myself locked in forever."

"Did I catch you at a bad time?"

"No," Phina said, shaking her head. "Now is a good a time as any."

Blake flashed a wide smile and placed the now empty glass of whiskey on the table beside him before following Phina to the living room.

"You were saying something at the funeral. Do you mind letting me know what that was all about?"

Phina looked away in embarrassment, sighed and returned her gaze to him. "I found out Patrick was having an affair." She looked intently at Blake, hoping to get her answer even before he opened his mouth. His expression was hard to read. She squinted as he raised his brows. "Did you know?"

"It's not possible," Blake responded, shaking his head. "Who told you such a thing? Patrick worshipped the ground you walk on."

"That's what I thought, and that's why this hurts even more. I found a letter from his lover."

"Who?"

"There was no name on the note."

"How could that be?" Blake asked after he'd hesitated for a second. "Can I see it?"

"Sure." Phina roused from her seat. "Give me a minute," she said as she headed out the door.

In her room, she searched for the note in her side drawer until she remembered she had placed it back with Patrick's stuff. She opened Patrick's drawer, but the note had disappeared. She asked the housekeeper and the butler on the intercom, and neither one of them had seen the note or knew what could have happened to it. Thirty minutes after she left Blake in the living room on the main floor, she ran to him, confused.

"I couldn't find it," she said exasperatedly. "Someone must have taken it."

"Someone like whom? Martin, the ghost?"

Phina glared at him. No one had mentioned Martin in months and with a recent death and the anxiety she felt with regards to Patrick's demise, it was the last thing she needed to be reminded of. It would make her jump at every touch and crumble whenever someone called her name in the dark.

"I'm sorry," Blake said, realizing he had touched a sore spot. "That was in poor taste. You probably left it in between some sheets of paper. You can look for it later. What did it say?"

"Something about their last meeting and how she would want to meet him again to continue from where they stopped. It was indicative of an affair."

"Could it have been something else and not necessarily an affair?" Blake asked with raised brows.

"No, it was an affair. The tone and the greeting told me everything I needed to know," Phina said in an exasperated tone.

"That doesn't make any sense. I'd like to see the note as soon as you find it. I may be able to help you decode it. Was there an envelope?"

Phina raised her brows and shook her head.

"No, there wasn't any. It's been devastating. I've cried about it for weeks and the more I've tried to analyze it, the more it's eluded me."

9

THE PROPOSAL

IT was freezing, even for February, and it had begun to snow at the first light of dawn. Shivering, Phina pulled the lapels of her camel fur coat over her green cashmere sweater with one hand. With the other hand, she grabbed Nduka's waiting palm and used it to steady herself as she stepped out of her car in front of his Chelsea apartment building.

"Hello, sweetheart. How are you doing?"

"Good, these days. I never thought I'd ever feel like myself again. Time is an awesome healer." She gave him a faint smile and a hug.

"Come inside."

Hand in hand, they walked into the lobby and headed straight for the elevator.

When he shut the door of his flat behind them, he took her purse and set it on the table.

"Nice place," Phina said, scanning the room on all sides while dangling her car key on her index finger.

"It's only a temporary solution till my house is completed. I can't raise a family in this hole," he smirked.

Phina smiled and raised her brows. "It sounds like you've got it all figured out. Haven't you?"

Nduka smiled at her in return.

"I'll need a little help from you though. Why do you think I moved thousands of miles?"

"I assumed it was better for your work and more so, better for going back and forth to Nigeria. What better reason is there?"

"You."

"Me?" Phina asked, with a puzzled look.

"I wanted to be closer to you, but it's been so rough since the incident. To be honest, we talked more when Patrick was alive than we do now almost six months after his passing. The other day at Claridge's you left me yearning for more," he said, sighing audibly.

Phina looked up at Nduka with a blank expression on her face before she closed her eyes. She remembered the day in question like it was yesterday. Nduka had invited her for afternoon tea at Claridge's, where he was staying while his flat got renovated. Shortly after they were seated in the foyer, she had felt a piercing pain in the pit of her stomach and asked the waiter to send their order to his room. She had felt better soon after and they had spent a glorious afternoon reminiscing about old times and laughing till their sides hurt. At some point, Nduka had brought up the issue of marriage, which Phina despised. During an emotionally charged argument, they had both found themselves in each other's arms. Nduka had caressed her thighs; bringing her to such a high point of arousal that it took every ounce of willpower she had left to pry herself off his arms. Since that day, barely a fortnight ago, she had thought about him every day yet rejected his invitations to visit him at his new flat until then.

"Don't you think it's time for you to move on dear," Nduka continued, jolting Phina from her reverie.

She opened her eyes and took a slow breath. "I don't think so," she said, shaking her head slowly. "Besides, I've been burned severely. There's no way I'm getting into anything serious. Not in the near future."

"Your issue with Patrick should be a thing of the past. He's no longer here."

"No," Phina said, continuing to shake her head. "If you think I'm referring to the share sale issue, then you're mistaking. It's a lot more than that."

"I know the share sale is the least of your problems right now. You and Patrick were really close, so his passing must feel unbearable. I've never lost anyone that close, so I'm in no position to judge you. But it's been six months. You should find a way to get yourself out of this funk."

Phina was too embarrassed to tell Nduka why she'd been incommunicado. The emotional turmoil she suffered over the discovery of Patrick's affair trumped the one she experienced over losing him.

"Let me take care of you," Nduka said, holding her hand. "Would you like something to eat?"

"Yes, please. I'm starving. My appetite has suddenly returned. Something nutritious if you don't mind."

"I know just what to make for you."

Nduka headed in the direction of the kitchen after he handed Phina the remote for the television and emerged fifteen minutes later with a bowl of breadfruit and fried fish on a silver tray. He placed the tray on the dining table and beckoned to her.

He sat beside her at the dining and watched while she slowly nibbled at her food. The sad look in her eyes confirmed his belief that her road to recovery was still a long one even though she claimed to be doing better.

After her meal, Phina snuggled into his arms on the sofa and let out a quiet sigh. She found comfort in her position and stayed still to avoid disrupting the balance. After two episodes of *Magnum, P.I*, she dozed off and was accidentally awoken by Nduka when he moved slightly.

"Whew. It's so late," Phina said, glancing at her watch. "I had no idea so much time had passed."

"I was hoping you'd spend the night," Nduka said expectantly.

"Ah, no," Phina objected, shaking her head. "I have to go home."

"Can't the nanny take care of Brigitte for one night? She's asleep most times when you get home, anyway. You said so yourself."

"Yeah, but I'm trying to put a stop to all that, especially now."

"Can't you make an exception for tonight? Please."

"No," Phina hesitated, shaking her head. Brigitte is most definitely asleep now, but I need to get home. There's so much I have to do in the morning.

"Please, I'll make it worth your while."

"I know you will," Phina responded. She stood up sluggishly and walked towards the window. "I can't believe what I'm seeing!"

"What?" Nduka asked, walking towards her. When he realized she was referring to the snowstorm outside, a slow smile spread across his face. "On a serious note, you can't possibly drive into this storm," he said in a stern voice.

"Why not?"

"Well then, but you'll have to let me drive you. Then you can send your chauffeur to pick your car in the morning."

Phina looked at him and sighed.

"Okay. It's only a few hours till daylight. I'll stay till morning."

Her decision to spend the night was an easy one. For some months now, she had been struggling and fending for herself. The aspects of her life that Patrick naturally took care of became an additional burden. Things she had considered inconsequential in the past – such as Patrick pulling the sheet over her shoulder before she fell asleep or helping take off her shoes and giving her feet a little massage were now missing from her life. She realized how much she missed those little pleasures and Patrick himself. That evening with Nduka had been comforting. While they held each other on the sofa, it felt so strangely reassuring that when he asked her to stay; it took a lot of determination for her to reject his offer.

"Come with me," Nduka said, grabbing her hand and pulling her away from the window. He led her to the bedroom and opened an armoire full of shirts in mostly earth colors – grays, mauves, beiges and browns.

"Pick one," he said in a husky voice.

"No, you pick one for me," Phina pleaded with a sultry look.

"This one," Nduka said, pulling a beige cotton shirt from the lineup.

She took the shirt from him, immediately held it to her face and took a whiff. It smelt of a combination of cinnamon and spice. A second whiff later, her head swirled. She couldn't tell which was to blame, the scent from his shirt, or the two glasses of wine she consumed over dinner. After she handed the shirt to Nduka, who had watched her entire performance with amusement, he unbuttoned it and placed it back on her hand.

"Will you like a bath?" he asked.

"I'll take a shower. I'm too tired to sit in a tub."

"Take your time. I'll join you later," Nduka said as he made his way out of the room.

"Wait a minute," Phina said, pulling his hand and bringing him face-to-face with her. She tiptoed and kissed him full on the lips, her eyes half-closed.

"Phina," Nduka said in an accusatory tone.

"Ye…"

Before the word fully formed in her mouth, Nduka grabbed her waist and kissed her until she could feel her insides erupting. She melted in his arms. Losing all inhibition, she let him slip her dress off her shoulders and take her bulging breasts in both hands as he continued to kiss her. Had he not supported her with one hand while he continued to caress her with the other, she would have slumped on the floor. She had lost all feeling in her legs and her senses seemed to have eluded her. Without warning, Nduka released her.

"Oh my God," she said. "I'm so sorry."

He shook his head and chuckled. "What exactly are you sorry about? Assaulting me?"

Phina laughed, grateful that her senses had cleared a bit. "Stop it!" she said.

"Now do you still want to take that shower and let me go tidy up?"

"Go," she said, smiling and waving her hand.

Immediately after Nduka shut the door behind him, Phina sat on the bed and sighed. Had Nduka not stopped her, she believed she would have had sex with him right there and then. That would have been a recipe for disaster, she thought. Even though she knew he liked her, she couldn't imagine a position as his rebound woman. The reason he provided for his breakup from Bimpe that day at Claridge's wasn't satisfactory to her. Also, he hadn't given her sufficient explanation as to why he abandoned his successful practice in the US and moved to the UK. His declaration that he had moved to be near her, wasn't convincing enough. Despite that, she was terrified of jumping into a new relationship before she had a chance to retrace her steps and heal completely from her marriage.

-

Nduka hovered outside the bedroom door for a few seconds. Hearing only silence from the other end, he opened it gently and walked inside. Phina was sleeping, curled up like a baby, wearing the beige shirt. It covered the whole of her upper body but left her legs, thighs and half her bum exposed. Nduka swallowed hard and headed in the direction of the bathroom. When he emerged, he threw on a pair of pajama pants and a t-shirt, grabbed an extra blanket from the hamper and lay with his legs sticking out on the settee. Shortly after he closed his eyes to sleep, he felt a soft breeze blowing across his face. When he opened his eyes, he saw Phina kneeling in front of the couch, smiling mischievously at him.

"I thought you were sleeping," Nduka said, his voice deep and husky as he struggled to control his heartbeat.

"I tried to, but all these thoughts keep flying through my mind. I heard when you came in, but I pretended to be fast asleep."

"Come here," he said, grabbing her waist and pulling her on top of him.

Phina giggled as she struggled to position her body properly. Nduka ran his hand down her back, his heart beating in a mad rush when he felt her warm body and succulent butt. She wriggled on top of him, grabbed his head with both hands and kissed him fervently.

"I love you," he said after she withdrew her lips for a second to stare into his eyes.

Phina felt her body stiffen.

"How? What about Bimpe?"

"Didn't I tell you we broke up?"

"Yes, but I didn't think it was final," she retorted. "She's the person you're in love with."

Nduka shook his head slowly and pointed his finger at her chest. "You're the one I love."

His declaration sent a warm sensation down Phina's spine. And, for some reason she couldn't fathom, it terrified her. She knew what it felt like to love someone and to feel that they loved you in return. She knew it could all turn out to be a lie. She knew what it was like to have loved and lost. Her feelings for Nduka were strong. Branding those feelings was something she neither had the ability or willpower to do and certainly not after what she'd been through with Patrick. Love did not make sense if the one you loved could betray you in the most inexplicable way. Had Patrick been alive, would she still classify her feelings for him as love?

Nduka stared at her as she seemed to have been transported to another realm – one which produced lines on her face.

"What's the matter?" he asked.

"Nothing," she said despondently. "I don't think I can love anymore."

"I love you," he said, placing her on his laps. "You shouldn't say things like that."

"I can't help it. I'm wired that way now. Why do you love me?" she asked, squinting her eyes.

"I can't believe you'd ask me such a question," Nduka responded in a wounded tone.

"Then?" she demanded.

"I've always loved you. You were so elusive, and then you disappeared for years. Next thing I knew you were married. I could never catch you which is why I can't believe I'm carrying all one hundred and forty pounds of you right now about to..." he let out a deep sigh.

"About to what?"

"Ravish you."

Phina threw her head back and laughed but before she knew it, Nduka lifted her up and positioned her on the bed before slowly lifting her shirt. Then he ran his hand down the entire length of her body while she wriggled from the pleasure of his touch.

"You are so beautiful," he whispered, shaking his head.

She made no move to cover herself but let out a deep sigh as he pulled off his shirt to reveal perfectly contoured pectorals. A clear-cut six-pack made it obvious that he spent several hours at the gym. Her anticipation grew when he placed his left hand beside her breast as he pulled at his boxers with his right. The sultry look on her face and her heaving chest drove him to his peak. He pressed his weight on her and found her soft middle with his bulging penis and as he alternated between kissing her breasts and her mouth; he stopped at intervals to watch her display her insatiable need for him. She moaned as he moved, first in slow successive movements, then in an erratic mode before he lunged non-stop like a torpedo. Her piercing scream would have been heard from outside the flat if not for the superior acoustics in the building.

-

Very early in the morning, before sunrise, Phina skidded away from Nduka's street towards Hazel House. She looked through the window of her car at the freshly fallen snow on the streets. It was reminiscent of the fresh start she knew was inevitable for her. Safely in her bed, she immediately fell into a deep slumber, free of nightmares. The trauma she suffered as a result of Patrick's betrayal suddenly dissipated and she finally was able to dream — sweet dreams — something she thought had eluded her for good.

When the sun rays hit her face right before noon, she found it difficult to get up from the bed. For a second she forgot about her escapades the night before. When she regained her senses, she understood why her body felt so numb. She and Nduka had made love not once, not twice, but three times. She touched her insides to recall the experience before her phone rang. Startled, she forced herself out of bed to pick it up. Delighted to hear Nduka's voice over the phone she forgot her numbness.

"Hello," she said in a whisper.

"I'd like to see you again today. Brunch?"

"I just woke up. Lunch maybe. A late one."

"I know where we can get the best steak in town."

A long pause followed before she responded. "Can we send the steak to your flat? It won't be good to be seen in public at this time. The media will rip me apart."

"Why do you care what they think?" Nduka asked abruptly.

Phina sighed deeply, loud enough for Nduka to hear. "Patrick has been gone for less than a year. I don't want the attention and the rumors that could result from us being seen together. I also have Brigitte to consider." She sounded frustrated.

"Sorry, I didn't mean to be insensitive. We can stay at my place."

-

Instead of steak, Phina and Nduka devoured each other's bodies for lunch. Their lovemaking the night before had been debaucherous and this time around it was mind-blowing. When it was time for Phina to leave, she found herself in a state of inertia.

Nduka, completely enamored of her blurted, "Marry me."

Phina shut her eyes, unsettled by the uncomfortable silence that followed Nduka's request.

"Did you hear me?" Nduka asked.

"I heard you," she said, finally breaking the silence. "Can't we just have fun?" she pleaded, with both hands spread in front of her.

"No," Nduka responded, shaking his head. "I've had enough fun. Marriage could be fun too."

Phina was quiet again. "What am I to say to him?" she thought. "He'd never been married so how could he understand."

"If you marry me, I'll make you the luckiest woman in the world," Nduka said, interrupting her reverie.

"I know you will," she responded.

"Then why won't you at least consider it?"

Phina raised her hand to gesture her frustration. "Will you stop? I can't bear to talk about such things," she said in a taut tone.

Nduka paused and looked at her. The hurt in his eyes broke her heart. Phina knew she could never tell him she was never marrying again even though she loved him. Her situation was worsened by the fact that she couldn't reveal her true feelings for fear that he could pester her into submission and cause further emotional turmoil if she ever needed to rescind her decision. Her boundary lines had become so clear as a result of her experiences, and with its ease of penetration, she would most certainly have the need to flee at the drop of a hat, emotionally or otherwise.

Nduka had looked away when she sank into her reverie but returned his gaze when he heard her blurt out, "Patrick was having an affair."

"Are you sure?" he asked, easing back in disbelief.

"Of course I'm sure. I have adequate proof."

"Well, I'm shocked to hear that. From what I've heard of him, he was completely in love with you."

"I doubt it very much now," Phina responded sadly.

"What did you expect? You married a stud, and that comes with consequences." He chuckled to release some of the tension that had built earlier.

Phina looked at him with puckered lips. "You're making a terrible case for yourself," she said.

Nduka placed his right index finger on his lips. "I'm sorry, but jokes aside, will you ever forgive him?"

"What choice do I have?"

"Let's put it this way, if he were alive, would you have forgiven him?"

"I would have left him. No doubt about that."

Nduka sighed in disbelief. "I think that's the option you would have preferred but the only problem with that choice is that he would never have let you go."

Phina looked at him forlornly and suddenly felt a pang in her chest. She knew Nduka was right.

"Please take me home," she pleaded.

"Already?"

"Yes. Talking about Patrick brings back old memories and I can't deal with it right now. I need more time..."

"Common, don't tell me he still has this much effect on you. I'm a little pissed."

"It's not that," Phina mumbled. "You wouldn't understand."

"Ok. Give me a minute to get my jacket."

-

Getting to Hazel House, Phina checked her answering machine and saw a missed call from Blake and called him immediately. During their hour-long conversation, he listened intently when she told him Nduka had proposed to her.

"Did you say yes?" he asked.

Phina could hear his heart beating in the background.

"No! I could never marry again."

Blake let out a deep sigh.

"You don't seem to like the idea," she said after a moment had passed.

"It's not that I don't like the idea," he said after a long pause. "I'm in no position to pass any judgment. I don't know this guy. He could be good for you, and on the contrary, he could be bad news. I can't tell."

"I made it clear to him I was never marrying again," she assured him.

No matter how Blake skirted around the issue, Phina sensed that he hated Nduka's presence in her life. His reason, though valid, was packed with mixed messages. If he didn't know Nduka as he said, then why did he feel too strongly about the proposal?

10

THE AFTERMATH

FROM the name Lombardi and his stance when she spoke to him on the phone, Phina pictured a short, balding policeman in his sixties with a bit of a potbelly and a shiny well-groomed mustache. When he walked through the front door at Hazel House, she was surprised to see that he was at least eight inches taller than her five-foot-six and well toned. There was no trace of a mustache or a potbelly and he reminded her of the main character in a television series she used to watch in the seventies.

"Lady Campbell?" he said with arms outstretched.

"Detective Superintendent Lombardi?"

"Yes, and this is my assistant Inspector Dawson."

Phina quickly assessed Inspector Dawson. He fit more of the image she had expected of Lombardi, only much younger – mid-thirties at least. Everything about him – his shoes, mustache, and his snazzy blue suit showed a police detective that was wound too tight.

"Good evening," Phina said, nodding in their direction before leading both men to the drawing room.

"Sorry about your late husband," Lombardi said.

"Thank you."

"I never met him but from what I hear, he was an active member of the society and one of the best movie producers in these parts."

"Yes. He was a great man, and talented too. You mentioned when we spoke yesterday that you wanted to discuss something important."

"Oh! Yes. My partner Dawson and I have been assigned to take over Lord Campbell's case after a new discovery led us to believe that his death was not due to natural causes as we originally thought. We are now treating it as suspicious and launching a new investigation to find out what really happened that night."

"Suspicious?" Phina asked, staring at Lombardi in disbelief.

"Our initial investigation revealed that he died of heart failure but since post-mortem examination found no ruptures or scarring we soon dismissed those results. Our pathologist ruled his cause of death as asphyxiation."

Phina, who had been listening intently and hunched over in an abnormal position, bolted upright when she heard Lombardi utter the last word.

"What does that mean?" she asked with furrowed brows.

"He gave up breathing."

"Okay. Isn't that an indication of natural death?"

"No." Lombardi shook his head fervently. "Not really. Not when he hadn't presented other symptoms. He could have been smothered, but there were no contusions on his face or neck to indicate that was the case. His real cause of death remains a mystery."

"So, how did you come to the conclusion that he was murdered?" Phina asked, perplexed.

"Since the new investigation," Lombardi continued, "we have received further tips from his hotel in Barcelona. A hotel staff saw an unidentified person leave his hotel room in the middle of the night – hours before he was found. The hotel cameras caught a glimpse of this person although it revealed no identifiable facial features."

Phina placed her hands under her chin and stooped forward.

"This unidentified person, was it a man or a woman?" she asked in an undertone.

"Interestingly, it was a woman. But we're not certain this person is directly tied to the case. We're collecting all the clues we need to help us determine with absolute certainty what occurred that night. Based on the evidence we have so far, there is a high probability that he was murdered. However," Lombardi said, raising his left index finger, "until we can produce valid suspects in the case, we will not be able to make any progress in our investigation."

Phina sat frozen to the spot as she considered all she had just learned.

"Who would want to kill Patrick?" she asked, looking at Lombardi with curiosity.

"That's something we were hoping you could help us with. Do you know anyone that would want him dead? Anyone, he may have offended?"

Phina shook her head slowly.

"I can't think of anyone."

"Your husband was a successful businessman. He would definitely have crossed one or two people along the way, don't you think? If you don't mind, we'll need your help in getting the names of the people that were closest to him."

"Patrick was straightforward in his dealings. I can't think of anyone that would want to kill him, but yes I can give you the names you want."

Reluctantly, Phina provided Lombardi with the names of Patrick's closest friends and associates and then told him about Patrick's hobbies and habits but purposely left out her discovery of infidelity. Her only evidence – the letter – was missing, and her other evidence – the bracelet would only cause them to start digging around for a lover. It was bad enough that she found herself in that mess, but creating a public relations nightmare was the last thing she needed.

The moment Lombardi stood up to leave, Dawson, who had been meticulously taking notes and shifting his gaze like a clockwork mouse from person to person, stood up as well.

"Please let me know if you remember anything or learn any new information that will help us with this investigation," Lombardi said before handing Phina his card.

She took it reluctantly.

"I will. Let me know if you make any progress," she said, sighing audibly.

"We will." Lombardi turned on his heel and turned back immediately. "With the possibility of a killer out there, I'm inclined to suggest that you make sure you have adequate security around you at all times until we can make a break in this case."

Phina nodded in agreement. "We will have to increase security. I feel apprehensive about this news."

"I can only imagine."

-

As soon as the police car drove off the driveway, Phina instructed the servants to lock the doors and windows and to remain on high alert from then on. Visitors were required to call ahead of time and they weren't allowed to hang around the house unless she was home to receive them. In her room, she sat in front of the vanity mirror and stared at her own image for thirty minutes, asking herself so many questions. Could the woman Lombardi talked about be the same person that wrote the letter to Patrick? If so, what was she doing in his hotel room that night? Could she be responsible for his death? When it occurred to her that by hiding Patrick's affair she was impeding the progress of the investigation, she woke from her stupor and walked to the writing desk to grab the business card Lombardi had given her. She dialed his number. After two rings, she decided it could be a terrible mistake pointing the police in the direction of Patrick's affair, so she hung up.

Back in front of the mirror, she placed her hand on her face, and continued to stare at herself. Sadness clouded her features as the realities of Patrick's demise dawned on her. She realized that he had been unable to protect himself, so would not have been qualified to provide the protection she and Brigitte needed so badly at that moment. As she fought back tears, she reminded herself that she'd decided a while back not to cry over the issue anymore. Desperately needing to speak to someone, she called Nduka.

"What exactly did they ask you?" Nduka asked after she rambled a few words.

"They wanted to know if anyone would have any reason to kill Patrick."

"I hope you didn't answer that question."

"I did. I said I didn't know of any reason anyone would want Patrick dead."

"Perfect answer."

"Why do you say that?"

"Well, from my experience with these kinds of issues it's very easy for the police to twist one's words and later use it against them."

Phina shrugged her shoulders.

"I have nothing to hide so…"

"It doesn't matter. Once you find yourself being questioned by the police, you've got to be extremely careful."

Phina felt even more disoriented than she was before she picked up the phone to call Nduka. Their discussion didn't bring her the calm she'd hoped for, so she slept fitfully that night trying to make sense of everything that was happening around her.

-

The following day at the office, she received a barrage of phone calls. Most were from credit companies who wanted to negotiate the terms of their outstanding debts with Patrick. A number of the calls were from some of the friends whose names she had provided to Lombardi. They wanted to keep her informed about what was going on.

Of all the calls she received that day, a particular one disturbed her the most. It was an anonymous call from a mysterious woman who refused to leave a name. She wanted to meet with Phina to discuss 'something' she claimed was too personal to discuss over the phone. According to her, she had tried to reach Phina several times since Patrick died but was turned away by her staff. Phina suggested a location she was comfortable with for their meeting, but the woman disagreed and insisted Phina meet her alone at a small café near Loughborough Junction. Before Phina could respond, the woman hung up, causing Phina to stare at her handset for a few seconds as she wondered what to do next. The call sent chills down her spine. She was convinced of the necessity of the meeting with the mysterious caller as it might help her make sense of what happened to Patrick. Her safety was also of paramount concern, so she called Lombardi immediately to notify him of her intentions.

"No. It's a bad idea," Lombardi insisted after she told him her plan to meet with the woman the following day. "If Lord Campbell was murdered in cold blood, then your lives — that of you and your child — are at risk until the killer is found. I think it's foolhardy to meet her alone."

"What if she has important information about Patrick?"

"Have you considered why she insists on seeing you in secret?" he asked in a discordant tone. "She could be armed and dangerous. She may even be the killer we're looking for. Are you going to walk right into her trap?"

"What would you have me do?"

Lombardi paused for a few seconds.

"This person could provide us with the clues we need so I think it's important you meet with her but not alone. I can't let you go to that meeting unaccompanied. There will be at least six plain-clothed policemen stationed in and around the café to ensure you don't get into any danger."

"Will I be able to identify these policemen?"

"No. They will blend into the crowd. You won't notice anything."

-

The chauffeur dropped Phina at a quiet little side street barely wide enough for her SUV to pass through. Turning to the right, she walked a dreary distance to the block where the café she was supposed to meet the woman was located. At that hour, the quaint café looked miniature sitting in the middle of two large, old buildings that crowded it on both sides. A waiter ushered her to a seat as she walked in. She took a quick glance at the place and chose a seat that would provide her with a proper view of the exit. Everyone in the café was minding their business. No one seemed to recognize her in the camouflage she had on. Her disguise included a scarf over her head and a large pair of reading glasses – sans prescriptions. It did a great job of masking her identity.

Phina ordered an espresso while she waited for the phone at the counter to ring twice – a signal that the woman was ten minutes away. After what seemed like an hour, she ordered a muffin to pass time and avoid the constant badgering by the waiters. She was startled when the phone rang. However, it only rang once and stopped. Thirty minutes later, after another espresso, she left a tip and headed straight in the direction of her car, walking briskly without breaking stride to avoid any encounter in the already darkening street. Her heart beat profusely after she got in the car, and she chided herself for putting her life at risk. No amount of plain-clothed policemen was sufficient, in her mind, to warrant the reckless situation she had just put herself in. What if someone had put a gun to her head in that café as she walked in? What if she'd been kidnapped? Would Lombardi's men have been able to save her?

Feeling terribly agitated, she instructed her chauffeur to bypass the office and drive to Hazel House. When the car screeched to a stop on the porch, she immediately ran in, ignoring greetings from the butler. Lombardi, who had been waiting for her call, rang the moment she stepped into her room, robbing her of the only wish she had that evening – to hug her daughter and settle in for the night.

"Maybe she changed her mind." Phina declared after Lombardi queried her about her meeting.

"Changed her mind…" he said glumly. "Did you get her phone number the day she called?"

"No. She wouldn't even say her name or why she was calling. How on earth would she have given me her number?"

"I'll ask the phone company to retrieve the number so we can try to trace this woman. So far, she's the only lead we've had in this case."

"Feel free to do that. I really need a conclusion to this issue. It's been so disruptive to our lives – mine and Brigitte's."

"We're doing everything in our power, Lady Campbell."

-

Phina awoke the following morning, worn-out, after a night of tossing and turning. She had wanted to call her mother as soon as she hung up the phone the night before but realized it would be past her bedtime.

One look outside her window promised another sunny but cold day, so she sprung out of bed and took a quick shower. She put on a black three-quarter skirt and a turquoise silk and chiffon shirt to add some color to what she thought was tired looking skin. Satisfied with the way she looked in the mirror, she practiced her dialogue for her meeting with the board of Ophinas. That morning, she had the uphill task of convincing the six-member board that it was time to take their company public and raise the funds required to diversify into foreign markets. So far, she had managed to convince Chief Gambo and Lady Thompson that it was a great idea. It was time to get the executive board members and officers to buy the idea too.

Lady Thompson was there in time and stopped by Phina's office. She had been a great source of support for Phina since Patrick passed, calling almost every week to inquire about progress on the case and her welfare. Phina began to let go of some of her resentment from when she learned Patrick had sold his entire stock of Ophinas to her. In retrospect, she realized she had transferred her aggression to the wrong person. Lady Thompson's role had been to offload stock from a friend who needed money, so it had been a waste of time labeling her as the enemy.

Their meeting that morning went as expected. A committee was nominated to champion the daunting process required to get the process of going public in motion. The first step, everyone agreed, was to work to ensure that the company structure, processes, human resources, and reputation would allow Ophinas qualify for an Initial Public Offering – IPO. The company's balance sheet was solid, projections for future performance were great, and they could boast of top talent in the senior roles. It was the job of the committee to identify a sponsor to help raise the funds needed for the expansion.

As work for the IPO progressed, Phina, exhausted from everything that had occurred in the past year, craved to leave England for Jamaica. This time, she planned on taking Brigitte with her. Nduka pleaded with her not to leave but his pleas fell on deaf ears.

"I have to," she insisted. "Come with us."

"I can't."

"Why not?"

"Too busy with work. Stay. We can go next month. I'll be a bit freer then. I promise."

Phina had no intention of succumbing. She wished she could take him along but her need for a breather was stronger at that moment than her need for romance. Having spread herself so thin, she didn't have much to give of anything let alone romance.

"I'm sorry, love. I've already told Brigitte, and she's so excited. It's the only break she and I have had since Patrick died. This trip is important."

"Ok. When do you plan to leave?"

"In three weeks."

"Three weeks? There's still time."

"I know."

-

Phina counted the days and the nights before she was to leave for Jamaica. Isabel and Simon were excited they would see her soon as they planned to vacation together on a private island. The two of them had supported her during the Patrick ordeal and provided her weekly updates on the performance of her brand at Hartiers. Phina continued to work day and night with the IPO committee to complete all the internal elements needed for submitting their prospectus. The legal steps mounted additional pressure on her. However, having recently endured not only Patrick's death but the mystery that surrounded it — the letter, the mysterious woman seen leaving the hotel and now the mysterious caller – she developed amazing strength and resilience; so much that she felt nothing in the world could stop her from achieving anything she set her mind to. Everything else paled in comparison to what she had just been through. She pursued the IPO process with rigor to make sure no stone was left unturned. In her quiet moments, she pondered Homicide Detective Lombardi's recent theory about Patrick's death being suspicious.

11

ANYWHERE BUT HERE

PHINA began to get used to Policemen swarming Hazel House. Between her upcoming trip to Jamaica and the IPO, she had barely found time to discuss with her lawyer before Lombardi and Dawson appeared at her doorstep again.

"We need to clarify a few things," Lombardi said. "Can we come in?"

"This is a bad time but sure. What do you need?" Phina asked.

"Is there somewhere private we could talk?" Lombardi said, shifting his gaze to the butler who had remained standing next to Phina after he let them in.

Phina led them to the private study she shared with Patrick.

The room was freezing. It reflected the frigid temperatures outside, which was uncharacteristic of that time of year. Spring was approaching, yet it felt like the middle of winter. Phina hoped the weather would improve until at least she was far away in Jamaica where she'd only have to hear about it in the news. After she ushered Lombardi and Dawson to their seats, she called the butler to build a fire. It flared at first and then simmered low, adding needed warmth to the study with its view of the vegetable garden.

"Beautiful home," Dawson commented. "I read about it in the annual issue of Indoors & Outdoors. The pictures can't compare. It must take a great deal of effort to maintain."

"Thank you," Phina responded eager for the meeting to be over.

An awkward silence followed before Lombardi eased forward in his seat and placed his arm on his thigh. "I appreciate your time Lady Campbell. The last time we were here we informed you that your husband's death was considered suspicious even though it was originally ruled by the coroner to be as a result of natural causes."

"Yes," Phina said, nodding impatiently. "Since then, have you been able to confirm or refute your hypothesis?"

"Well, now we're treating his death as a homicide. We'll like to know where you were the night Lord Campbell died."

Sitting upright, Phina squinted her eyes at Lombardi, and then shifted her gaze to Dawson before returning it to Lombardi.

"I was in Florence that day," she said, glaring at him.

"Can anyone testify to that?" Dawson asked in a flat tone.

"Testify? Am I a suspect?" she asked, raising her brows.

"Just standard questioning," Dawson responded, easing back in his chair and throwing open his overcoat.

"If you're asking if I have an alibi, I spoke to Senior Superintendent Claudio the night Patrick died. I'm shocked by the direction of your questioning."

Dawson looked at the notepad on his hand and shook his head.

"No, you spoke to Superintendent Claudio the day after the attack that led to his death."

Phina chuckled lightly and hissed.

"Are you saying that I left my mission in Florence on Thursday where the entire town council saw me, flew to Barcelona, murdered my husband and then flew back to Florence in time enough for Senior Superintendent Claudio to call me at my hotel room?"

"I'm not making any such assumptions."

"I shouldn't be speaking with you when your superior is here." She shifted her gaze to Lombardi. "I'll not be having any further discussions with you without my lawyer present. Your entire team should be ashamed of your progress on this case. Instead of using the resources at your disposal to find the person who murdered my husband, you're spending it on harassing a poor widow."

She stood up to leave.

"We're just doing our job madam," Lombardi rejoined. "We never intended to harass you and we're sorry if you feel that way. Please sit down so we can finish our discussion."

Phina ignored his request.

"The steward will show you out," she retorted and turned on her heel.

She stopped in her tracks when she heard Lombardi announce off-handedly, "We would like your permission to search the premises."

"Why?" she asked. "What do you hope to find?"

"Anything that could help our investigation."

"You really do think I killed him?" She glared at Lombardi for a second and shook her head before pointing in the direction of the door. "Please leave my house."

"You mean Lord Campbell's house?" Dawson added in an undertone.

Phina clenched and glared at Dawson.

"Oh yes. That's exactly it. I want you to leave the home I shared with my late husband until he passed. And you know what else, never come back here without a search warrant and we all know you can't get one without probable cause."

"We'll get one," Dawson retorted, smiling sheepishly.

"Lady Campbell," Lombardi said, straightening his tie and giving Dawson a side-eye. "I apologize if you feel hounded."

Phina laughed so loudly that her voice reverberated across the library.

"Oh? Do you have any idea what I've been through since my husband died? You think I may be feeling hounded right now? You'll need to speak to my lawyer from now on."

She walked in between the two men and held the door open with one hand. With the other hand, she waved to gesture their exit.

"Thank you for your time," said Lombardi.

"Excellent, because you won't be getting any more of it."

She walked ahead of them into the hallway and watched as they drove away. As soon as they were out of sight, she called Blake.

"You need a good lawyer," Blake said after she recanted her ordeal that afternoon.

"That's ridiculous."

"I know, but it's unwise for you to answer any more questions unless you have a lawyer present. McCracken is an excellent criminal defense lawyer. She's handled several high-profile cases and wins almost every time. Take her number and call her right away."

Phina called the number Blake had given her and was immediately transferred to McCracken.

"I was expecting your call," McCracken said.

Knowing her reputation for cracking cases for her clients, Phina had expected someone with a tough demeanor, so she was surprised by the gentle tone of the woman she spoke to on the phone. She provided her with the history of the case as well as details of her encounter with Lombardi and Dawson that afternoon.

"I hope this issue will not affect my plans because I've reached my breaking point," Phina enquired, dreading the possibility of having to cancel her planned trip to Jamaica.

"I don't see why it should. You're not officially a suspect. They had merely asked you the same questions they would ask anyone who was close to your late husband. I won't be surprised if they addressed your staff as well."

"I don't think so, or they would have told me."

"Not necessarily. This is a murder case. Listen, my advice to you is to not speak another word to anybody about it and just keep to yourself. Keep my number handy in case those men bother you again"

-

The morning Phina was to leave for Jamaica, she was confronted by Lombardi and Dawson on the front porch. Lombardi pulled her aside.

"You've been officially named a suspect in Lord Campbell's murder," he said.

"That is ridiculous," Phina announced in an exasperated tone. "You people can't give your fellow human a break."

"On the contrary Lady Campbell, I've done all that's in my power to avoid making this trip today, but everything seems to point in one direction."

"Really!" Phina cried, gritting her teeth. "It doesn't appear you've done everything in your power. I've been waiting to hear from you about the identity of the mysterious caller. Have you even checked with the phone company?"

"There's no indication that call was ever made at the time you specified."

"Oh, so you're saying I cooked up the story. Why? For what reason?" Phina was glaring at him.

"Look, Lady Campbell…" Lombardi began to say before Phina interrupted him.

"The other day, you and your partner acted like I was guilty of the crime. You barged into my house asking the *stupidest* of questions…" She stopped the moment she remembered McCracken's advice. Her heart raced and her stomach boiled as she buckled under the strain. Lombardi tried to support her by grabbing her arm but she slapped it off and straightened her skirt, the whole time avoiding looking at him.

"We have a search warrant," he continued, pulling out a sheet of paper and presenting it to her, "and we will need you to come with us to the station for questioning."

"Did you just tell a joke?" Phina asked, her eyes scorching his. "I'll not answer any further questions without my lawyer present."

"Feel free to call your lawyer but they'll have to meet you at the station. We have enough evidence to make an arrest, but out of respect, we will not handcuff you because I'm certain you're not a flight risk."

"What evidence?"

"We can discuss that at the station."

-

At the police station, Lombardi took Phina into a tiny room with two chairs on either side of a square table – the rest of the room was bare.

"We know you have a motive," Lombardi said after he sat across from her.

"What motive do I have for killing my husband?" Phina asked, shaking her head as she watched Dawson pace the room. The sight of him made her skin crawl. "Assuming I had a motive, how could I have killed him? I was in Florence when he…"

Before the last words came out of her mouth, Lombardi pulled out a sheet of paper from his folder. Phina immediately recognized the letter she had found in Patrick's drawer soon after she heard news about his death.

"How did you get that?" Phina asked.

"It seems you recognize this."

"Yes, I do. It went missing from my house a few months ago."

"Months?" Lombardi asked, glaring at her in contempt. "We gave you every opportunity to tell us what you knew when we visited you. Why didn't you mention the existence of this letter?"

"And tell the whole world my husband was seeing a whore?"

Lombardi was taken aback. "Wow! Didn't you think it was worth mentioning that you thought Lord Campbell was cheating on you?"

"It was none of your business," Phina responded, glaring at him.

"This is a homicide case. It is our business. You should not withhold pertinent information," Lombardi reminded her.

Phina placed her elbows on the table. "Why don't you arrest me since you think I did it?" she said, tilting her head, and glaring viciously at him.

"No," he said. "We think you're an accessory. Your boyfriend is the real culprit."

"What boyfriend?" Phina asked with a puzzled look on her face.

Lombardi and Dawson looked at each other.

"You mean Nduka?" she asked.

"Not another word," McCracken said, barging into the room. "Hello, I'm Judy McCracken."

It was Phina's first meeting with McCracken. She was shocked by the authority the beautiful, dark-haired, five-foot-three woman wielded in the presence of what she now perceived as ogres.

"Is she charged with any crime?" McCracken directed her question at Lombardi. "If not, I'll suggest you let her go about her business now."

While she waited for Lombardi to respond, McCracken took a quick look at Phina and nodded.

"Not yet, but she may be charged for the murder of Lord Campbell," Lombardi responded.

"On what grounds?" McCracken asked.

"First," Lombardi said, hesitating a bit. "She had reason to believe her husband was cheating on her. Jealousy is a strong motive."

"And what proof do you have?"

"We are aware that she found the proof herself…" he said, waving the letter.

"What nonsense. I found that letter after Patrick died," Phina retorted.

McCracken shot a quick look at her, a signal for her to be silent.

"Secondly," Lombardi continued, "We have evidence that she was seeing another man while her husband was still alive."

Phina bolted upright. McCracken placed a hand firmly on her shoulder.

"Which man?" McCracken asked, before raising both hands in the air.

"She knows who we're implying," Lombardi said. "She just admitted to knowing him. She called his name as you stepped in."

Phina shrugged and shook her head. She glanced at McCracken, her heart pounding heavily.

"Never mind. It doesn't matter because it doesn't make any sense," McCracken shot back. "Your case will be thrown out by the judge. We all know jealousy can only work as a motive if love was involved." She paused and crossed both hands below her waist. "Tell me. If she was seeing another man while she was married to Lord Campbell, how can you prove to the judge or any jury that she was in love with her husband – the only basis for one to commit a crime of passion?"

Lombardi shifted in his seat. Dawson sighed and averted his gaze to the floor.

"Well," Lombardi grunted, "We don't think she acted alone. Her boyfriend is the prime suspect. She's only an accessory."

"It seems you have already convicted my client before trial. Whatever happened to innocent until proven guilty? If you think her 'boyfriend'," McCracken said, pointing her finger in Lombardi's direction and nodding her head with authority, "is the real culprit, why aren't you speaking with him? Why are you harassing my client?"

"We have him in custody."

Phina's heart raced as she glared at Lombardi.

"You have the wrong person," she said, unable to keep silent any longer. "Nduka and I were not seeing each other before Patrick died and the two men never crossed paths."

McCracken looked at her disapprovingly.

"We have reason to believe otherwise," Lombardi hinted.

McCracken scoffed. "Then arrest her and present the reason to the judge or let her go."

"She's free to go for now, but she cannot leave the UK until our investigation is complete."

"Very well," McCracken added, signaling to Phina to follow her lead.

-

As soon as they stepped out of the room, Phina pleaded with McCracken. "You've got to help Nduka?"

"I would love to, but your case is best served if you separate your legal representation from his."

"Everything they said in there was a lie. These accusations are preposterous."

"It makes no difference if you were seeing him. Do you understand? My job is to defend you even if you're guilty. And if that is the case, all I have to do is make it impossible for the prosecutor to prove that you committed the crime. Right now, there's not enough evidence to convince a judge or jury to convict and the only proof they have contradicts itself."

"Thank you," Phina said, taking a deep breath. "Nduka's case is still connected though. If he gets implicated, I will be too. Don't you think?"

"I don't know this man. Can you vouch for him?"

"I can," Phina said, nodding slowly.

McCracken, unconvinced, pursed her lips and shook her head. "I can recommend a good lawyer to handle his case. That's the best I can do. I'd hate to see your case worsen because of your association with Nduka. Promise me you'll stay as far away as possible from him until this blows over."

"What choice do I have?" Phina asked, perplexed.

"Good!"

12

REVELATIONS

"HAVE you checked your messages?" Blake asked the moment Phina picked up her phone.

"No, I just stepped into my room. I was at the police station all day."

"I know. I asked McCracken to meet you there after I received a call from your housekeeper."

"She arrived at the perfect time. Thank you."

"I hope they didn't harass you."

"They didn't, but I'm completely overwhelmed by the accusation Lombardi and his men have laid against me. How could they believe I killed Patrick? They're messing with my life and my reputation. Not only that, I really needed an escape but now they won't let me leave the country until this issue is sorted out."

"You'll have to exercise patience. Don't worry. McCracken is the best there is. It will be all over soon. As for Nduka, I'm not so sure what his role was."

"Oh, so McCracken already told you."

"Turn on channel five."

Blake waited patiently for Phina to find the remote and turn on the television.

"Oh my God!" Phina exclaimed. Amidst all the chaos, she had forgotten what could happen if the media got hold of the news of her detention. She listened as the newscaster rambled on about a deadly love triangle and how she and Nduka were arrested that day.

"I wasn't arrested. They just held me for interrogation. I'm so embarrassed. I only found out Nduka was implicated in the matter when I got there."

"The raucous started this morning. My advice to you is to stay away from him."

"Don't you think that's unfair?" Phina shot back.

"Well… it may seem unfair now, but this is a matter of life and death. I'm not suggesting you never see him. Just wait until your name is cleared in this mess."

"According to McCracken, the evidence they have against me is circumstantial. No jury will convict based on that. Apparently, the proof I found that Patrick was cheating on me gives me a motive for a crime of passion, but it's all lies. I found that letter two nights after Patrick died."

"They have no way of proving that ridiculous motive. If you could find a way to convince them that you found the letter after the fact, it will help your case a lot, but there's the small matter of the affair. That gives Nduka a motive. As for you, that gives you a potential second motive."

"There was no affair!" Phina screamed.

"Well, can you prove it?"

"No," she responded after a moment's pause. "I've known Nduka for ages, and we met recently when I visited New York. Shouldn't they be the ones to prove that an accusation such as the one they're acting upon is true?"

"Either way, it doesn't look good. If you're able to prove you were not having an affair, it would strengthen the motive of jealousy. So, the only way to clear your name is to prove both, not one or the other."

"So either way I'm royally screwed. What about my alibi? I was nowhere near the scene of the crime."

"So far, with your alibi, the only thing you can prove is that you didn't commit the act yourself. However, since they only view you as an accessory I don't see any use for your alibi."

Phina's heart skipped two beats, and she felt faint. "This is too much for me," she said, choking on her words.

"I know."

"I can take a lie detector test. I know I'm innocent."

"I'll be careful with that if I were you. It could be a death sentence if the equipment malfunctions and produces an undesirable effect."

"There's another way out of this."

"I'm listening," said Blake.

"Nduka."

"What about him?"

"I'm sure he didn't kill Patrick and if it's proven that he didn't, I couldn't be an accessory then. Nduka was not even near Patrick when this happened."

"How do you know?"

"He was out of town."

"Where was he?"

"Traveling."

"Exactly. He didn't have an alibi. He claimed he was sleeping in his hotel room. Travel records show he was in Spain. He could quite easily have been in Barcelona that night."

"How do you know all this?"

"I made a few enquiries before I called you. The point is, you weren't with him and he could have been anywhere."

"I don't believe he could kill anybody. I'm sure he's innocent."

Blake laughed. "Despite what you believe, please stay away from him to avoid implicating yourself further. You must not allow him anywhere near you to avoid getting further entangled in this mess."

Phina avoided gritting her teeth. "I'm already in so deep."

"But I'm on it. I'm working to get you out of whatever it is. I have called the attorney general's office. He seems to know you and thinks the accusations are ridiculous. Like I said, stay calm. Don't do anything drastic."

"I'll try my best. Thank you so much. I don't know what I would have done if McCracken hadn't come in when she did. Thank you."

"My pleasure dear. Avoid having any conversations regarding this case over the phone. They could be tapped."

"Tapped?" Phina yelled.

"Just precautions."

After they hung up, Phina played her answering machine. It was full and there were a dozen messages from Isabel who had been expecting her in Jamaica that evening.

"I saw the news my darling. I was calling to see if you were all right. Simon and I have been so worried," Isabel said before Phina could render an apology.

The tension and the stress from her activities that day rattled her in that instant and she started to sob. "I can't take it anymore. There's so much going on. I wouldn't even dream of the things I'm being accused of."

"I know that. I know you're not capable of killing anyone. Simon and I were really upset about the news. It's just wicked to go after you like that on top of the burden of losing your husband. What do they have on you?"

"A letter that proved Patrick was cheating on me. It mysteriously disappeared from my room a few days after I found it. They presented it as evidence at the police station. They also claim I was cheating on Patrick with Nduka."

"That does not make any sense. There's no way they can prove you were cheating with Nduka. That's an outrageous thing for them to say. Don't worry. You'll soon be absolved of all this nonsense. I'll discuss with Simon. If you can't come to us, then we're gonna have to come to you."

After Phina hung up, she drew herself a hot bath and tried to clear her mind. Patrick – the only person she could rely on – was gone and left a trail of destruction behind. As her mind drifted to the letter, she said out loud, "How on earth did it leave my room?" It was obvious someone had been through her stuff and she was determined to find out who that person was. The only people allowed access to her room were the two housekeepers that had been with the family since they moved into Hazel House. As she tried to conjure up the best way to sedate the situation, she scrubbed her skin with the loofah until it was raw and almost bleeding.

-

A few days after the arrest, McCracken called Phina with even more distressing news.

"Nduka," she said, "is a member of a drug syndicate with a secret code. In America, he and his cohorts ripped the government of hundreds of millions, writing fake prescription drugs. He had lost his license to practice Medicine in the United States and was lucky to avoid prosecution there. His move to the UK was a necessity. Are you there?" McCracken asked after an uncomfortably long silence.

"Yes," Phina answered sullenly. She was breathing hard, lost for words.

"What reason did he give you for moving here?"

"I'm embarrassed to say this, but he claimed he did it to be near me. He moved some months before Patrick passed. I feel used," Phina concluded, trying hard not to let McCracken hear the ache in her voice.

"That is a bold-faced lie. He left America because he had no choice. He was about to be prosecuted, but his cohorts fought tooth and nail to abort the charges against him. With the help of some members of their syndicate here in the UK, he was able to carry on practicing medicine as though nothing had happened."

Phina panted heavily.

"Are you okay?" McCracken asked in an uneasy tone.

"Yes, I am," she lied. "I wonder what else he's hiding from me."

"Do you now see why you can't trust him?"

"I'm dumbfounded. That's all I can say."

Phina was beyond dumbfounded. She was gripped with fear. Not just because someone she'd known so intimately had turned out to be a totally different person than what she'd expected, but she feared what else he was capable of. Could he have murdered Patrick, stolen the letter and tried to implicate her? She shivered as a chill ran down her spine.

–

Hard as it was, Phina went about her business. On her first day back at Ophinas since her visit to the police station, her staff stole glances, so she gently walked by the throngs of people and locked herself in her office. She lay on the settee to think, but the numerous calls she had to deal with throughout the day didn't give her much space to do so. The public relations nightmare resulting from the issue caused her partners, Lady Thompson and Chief Gambo to worry.

Lady Thompson was the first to call her.

"This is killing our plan," she said in a firm tone. "It will make a mockery of our valuations and if that happens we can say goodbye to the IPO."

"I understand," Phina said in a soothing voice hoping to calm her down. "This case will soon be resolved. I'm trying my best to cooperate with the police and have them take their tethers off me so we can resume a normal existence…"

"You may have to do more," Lady Thompson said, stopping her mid-sentence. We did really well last quarter, but this quarter, with the way things are going, if the public believes you did what you're being accused of, sales could plummet. That alone could get our application denied."

Phina tried her best to reassure her. "I've looked at the sales figures. They are fine. I've also talked to our finance team. The valuation looks good. Projections show that our sales for the next two quarters will surpass that for the previous quarters."

There was a momentary silence before Lady Thompson finally spoke. "Okay," she said. "We have to monitor it closely."

When Phina hung up, she felt an excruciating pain at the pit of her stomach. She'd always seen Lady Thompson as cold, but it never really bothered her. But with Patrick gone, she now saw everyone's faults glaringly. Lady Thompson had seemed to be insinuating for her to step down from her role as the head of the retail empire she had built with her sweat and tears. She had been more concerned about her reputation and bottom-line than the fate of the woman she'd had a close relationship with her family for years.

Chief Gambo's call was less threatening. Even though his concerns were similar to those of Lady Thompson's, unlike Lady

Thompson, he listened attentively, accepted her explanations and was sympathetic to her struggle with the police. He assured her that everyone back home was on her side. Rashid sent his regards and swore he would do all he can to absolve her. No one believed she was capable of doing what she was being accused of. Everyone felt that in a matter of time the real culprit would be caught and her name would be cleared.

13

DOOM

THE trial lasted only three months. Phina was allowed to sit with Nduka at the back of the truck as they traveled from the remand center to the court. She wanted to cry, but he nudged her and searched her face just as she searched his, looking for clues. With her eyes, she told him everything she had been unable to say to him all these months; I love you; I miss you; save me. The trial was harrowing. They were led out of the gallery, through the bar and asked to stand as hundreds of eyes pierced through them. Their gazes penetrated her skin. She heard hissing and commenting. Even though she couldn't make out what they were saying, she knew they were cursing her, calling her names and wishing she would hang for the crime she was accused of. She ignored the crowd for a moment and looked at Nduka. He was calm, even calculated. His face looked sympathetic enough for a jury. McCracken had taught her the expressions to wear, how to position her body, how to speak to achieve the look she so clearly saw on Nduka's face.

As she listened to Senior Superintendent Claudio go on and on about the night Patrick was found lying face down in his hotel room, she wondered why he completely avoided looking in her direction. Lombardi was next. Wearing a grey suit that made him constantly tug at his sleeves, he called an expert to explain the intricacies of DNA testing. He muttered obscenities whenever McCracken cut him off to explain to the judge that he and his cronies were covering up their incompetence.

After one particularly harrowing exchange between him and McCracken, Lombardi brandished a large caliber revolver.

"Duck!" she heard Nduka screech. Her gut instinct kicked in and she leaped under the table, crawled to the farthest end, pressing her hands against her ears before she heard a loud bang and a piercing scream. She jumped upright and assumed a sitting position on her bed, still screaming at the top of her voice. She covered her mouth with both hands and heaved a huge sigh of relief when she realized it had only been a dream. Her cheeks were caked with tears and her nose ran. She had been crying in her sleep. "Thank God," she said, placing both hands on her chest to calm her breathing down.

The nightmare, scary as it was, woke Phina to the realities of her situation. With Patrick gone, Victoria cold, and Lady Thompson, passive-aggressive, she knew she had to step up to the plate and do more to clear her name. Even though she and Nduka were released the same day they were detained for questioning since the police could not produce definitive evidence to tie them to the crime, they remained the prime suspects in Patrick's murder. She could no longer rely on the police to solve the case for as long as their lens was focused on her. Even though McCracken had warned her to stay away from Nduka, she felt that the best way to take her fate into her own hands was to hear directly from him, so she arranged for them to meet.

Wearing a disguise, she sneaked into the lobby of his building, up the elevator and to his flat on the sixth floor. At first, Nduka did not recognize her. Before he let her in, he glanced at both sides of the hallway to make sure no one was watching. After the door was closed behind them, Phina confronted him with the question at the top of her mind.

"Did you do it?"

"If you mean, kill Patrick, why would I kill him? You of all people should know that," Nduka said defensively. "You're well aware we weren't dating by the time he died."

"Well, the police seem to think you killed him so you can be with me. You were in love with me." She studied his face for a reaction after she made the allegation and saw none.

"Does that automatically make me guilty? You and I weren't even intimate at the time."

"Well..." Phina shrugged her shoulders. "I know, but no one else knows that. What did the police want from you?"

"They asked about my alibi and when we started dating," Nduka responded.

"That's all?"

"Also, they wanted to know if..." he paused.

"If?" Phina asked impatiently.

"They wanted to know if you were in love with me."

"What did you tell them?" She was curt.

"I'm not stupid. I told them we hadn't gotten to that stage in our relationship and that you're a traditional girl and because of that, you take your time," he said dejectedly. "I'm so upset that you haven't agreed to see me. I miss you. When this raucous is over, I want you to seriously consider my proposal."

"Did they believe you?" Phina asked, ignoring his poorly timed comment.

Nduka, dejected from the possibility of another rejection, sighed and eased back in his seat before whispering, "They have no choice."

Phina sensed his hurt but was surprised he could think beyond their present predicament. She reckoned that the condition of their relationship should have been the last thing on his mind.

"Why didn't you tell me about your issue in America?"

"Which issue," he asked, feigning ignorance.

"You know what issue I'm referring to. It's public knowledge at this point."

"I was too ashamed to tell you," he said, exhaling deeply. "It's not something I'm proud of. Moving to the UK gave me a new lease on life and I was going to make amends in any way I could."

"Is that all?" Phina asked, frowning and shaking her head. "You lied to me. You made me believe you moved to be near me."

Nduka walked towards her and took her hand, but she slapped it off.

"Okay, let's leave my needs aside for a moment and focus on the situation at hand," she continued. "What could have incited you to take this route? Back home, you attended the best schools, and moving to America you went to an Ivy League. You're intelligent, your parents are rich, I don't understand. Does your family know? What do they think?"

Nduka bent his head forward for a second. "They don't know. In fact, my biggest fear is that my 'old man' will find…"

He paused when Phina stood up to walk around.

"Continue. I'm listening," she said.

"I was going to say that my father might collapse and die if he finds out."

"So how do you hope to keep this from him?"

"I don't know," Nduka whispered. "When I first came to America, I was young and naïve. I sort of mingled with the wrong crowd. They had friends in 'high places' and before I knew it, I was being jetted to private islands, hosted in luxurious homes and provided with expensive gifts. By the time I graduated, they offered me a job."

"Who are they?" Phina interrupted, struggling to suppress her annoyance.

"My Associates. I can't tell you more than that," Nduka said as he stood up and walked towards her.

"You mean your former associates," Phina said, glaring at him. "How does Bimpe fit into this? Oh, is that why you and Bimpe are no longer together? Did she dump you when you ran into problems?"

"Bimpe knew I was leading a double life. How could she not have known? We lived in a fifteen-million-dollar mansion in Manhattan. She had a private chef, a chauffeur, stewards, and two luxury cars. She was very much aware the money wasn't from my doctor's salary."

"Then why aren't you together anymore?"

"Our relationship fizzled naturally when my legal troubles began and I had to move. Also, she knew I was in love with you." He bent forward to kiss her, but she blocked him with her hand.

"No," she said, shaking her head in annoyance. "Even though I've taken all these precautions to see you, we may still be under surveillance."

Sighing, Nduka withdrew from her.

"I'm hoping when all of this dies down, we'll be able to resume our relationship," he remarked in a solemn tone.

"First pray all of this dies down."

When Phina headed towards the door, Nduka reached out to grab her hand a second time, but she swiped it from him. On her drive home, she marveled at his nonchalance regarding their predicament. In her mind, he was either guilty or too confident that the system would absolve him if he was innocent. Her feelings for him were still strong, but she resolved not to meet him again. Her freedom was more important than any residual feelings. She was not taking matters lightly herself and was becoming terrified of her situation. Her nightmare reminded her not to take any chances as there was no telling how far the police would go to further implicate her in the matter.

-

As hard as it was, Phina tried to fit the pieces of the puzzle together. Her first step was to call the Metropolitan Police and enquire about the hard evidence they had against Nduka and herself. The person she spoke to made it clear that as the suspect in the case, she was not entitled to more than the public had access to. The privilege that would have allowed her to access the information she needed was lost the moment she was named a suspect. Determined to get to the bottom of the case with or without their help, she began her search for a good private investigator. She sought the help of her trusted friends who were able to provide her with a couple of contacts who she planned to meet discreetly over the following week. In her private time, she reviewed the different angles of the case and jotted down her thoughts on a drawing board in her study. Her best assumption was that Patrick had really died from natural causes as originally speculated by the coroner since she could not think of any valid reasons why anyone would have wanted to kill him. The theory that Nduka could be the killer did not sit well with her. He didn't have a valid motive in her opinion. The third possibility, that someone Patrick had dealt deceitfully with wanted him dead did not seem plausible enough to her, because as far as she knew, Patrick had been fair in his dealings. However, when she recalled his behavior months before his death – the late nights and the strange reactions whenever she walked into the room, she concluded that the third option could very well be a valid one.

-

Despite his efforts to keep out of the way that dreary spring of 1984, Blake couldn't stop thinking about Phina, who he had become close to since Patrick's passing. The weather was particularly cold that year. One Saturday evening, he visited her at Hazel House. Phina had decided to take matters into her own hands and do some digging herself with the help of a private investigator. The intensity of her efforts to solve the case kept her away from social interactions and behind closed doors. Since the issue with the missing letter, she resolved to not tell a single soul what was going on. It was a matter of life and death for her since she didn't know who she could trust. Blake arrived in a midnight blue shirt and matching pants in a slightly darker shade. Phina was in awe of his unique quality to remain simple and inconspicuous yet still able to emit an impression of accomplished refinement. His pitch-black hair shone in the lights from the lamps. The sky was growing dark through the windows in the drawing room where he came to meet her. They held each other in a long hug which neither one of them wanted to break. When she felt a cold chill run through her spine, Phina eventually let go. She wasn't sure what made her body react that way, the fright she had earlier from a thunderstorm or Blake's intense masculinity which was in full display for her to savor.

"I'm sorry," Blake said after what seemed like ten minutes. "I should have come to see you before now. The elections tied me down even though I tried my best to see how I could help from a distance. Now that we're done, I have more time to devote to the case."

"Congratulations on your re-election," Phina said, grabbing his arm and smiling up at him.

"Thank you," he responded, bending to kiss her forehead.

The smell of his cologne made her heady. His lean muscular body fit so perfectly with hers, and she realized she missed his embrace. He provided her comfort, and she liked him in a safe, innocent and trusting way. Blake always ran to her side, like a brother and friend all in one.

They sat a few centimeters from each other on the settee. Without a moment's notice, Phina sobbed quietly. Blake leaned towards her and wiped the tear falling from a corner of her eye. He couldn't fathom what could have triggered the episode. As the intensity of her sobs increased, he stood up and grabbed a box of tissues from the cabinet filled with old books.

"Here you go," he said, dabbing her eyes with a tissue.

Phina chuckled quietly. "I'm so sorry for all the trouble I've caused."

"It's okay. I'm here now," he said, touching her hand lightly.

She mustered some courage and looked in his direction. He had his gaze on her with his head cocked to one side.

Phina smiled at him.

Blake smiled in return. "I'll get us something to drink," he said before leaving her side to bring a bottle of bourbon and two glasses from the bar. After a few sips, her head began to reel.

"The drink was a bad idea," she said, looking at the nearly empty glass on her hand.

"It feels good though."

"Yes. I haven't felt better in weeks."

"You look a lot calmer than you did when I first stepped in," he said, sitting next to her and holding her hand. "I have to take my leave. First, let me help you up."

"I'd appreciate that."

Wrapping his arm around her waist, Blake helped Phina to her feet. Hand in hand, they walked to the foyer.

"Will you be okay when I leave?" he asked.

"Yes," Phina said with a nod. "It's all right. I'll be fine. Thank you."

Blake left around midnight. His head reeled from the activities of the day. He could not keep his mind off the beautiful tortured woman he'd known for a few years. He always thought Patrick wasn't right for her. Now he had hurt her. Not only that, now that she was free to be with whoever she liked she had fallen yet again for someone, who he thought, was the wrong guy. Her relationship with Nduka bothered him. He hoped that would soon become a thing of the past with the revelation of Nduka's illegal dealings. Before he fell asleep, he counted the hours until he could see Phina at the office the following day. They still had a lot to discuss. The night had been ineffective since Phina had been too distraught to function.

When they met at Ophinas in the morning, he broached the subject of Patrick's murder with her.

"Who do you think could have done it?" he asked, placing his hand across his mouth.

"I've asked myself the same question several times. Could be one of the business partners he had dealings with," Phina responded, staring blankly at him.

"Did you confirm Nduka's alibi?"

"I'm not sure," Phina said, shrugging her shoulders. "He said he was at a business meeting with his partners in Madrid."

"Do you know these partners?"

Phina shook her head. "No."

"Then how are you sure he was in Madrid?"

"I'm not sure where you're going with this," Phina said, looking at him quizzically.

Blake stood up and walked towards the window.

"Wouldn't you like to know exactly what happened to Patrick? I would have thought you would like to be absolutely sure it isn't Nduka who killed him."

"I'm sure," she responded in a whisper.

"Can you vouch for him? The prime suspect?"

Phina looked up at Blake. The morning sun was blinding her eyes, so she shielded her face with her hand.

"The only thing the police have on Nduka is a motive. One, I for certain know isn't credible. Remember that I'm the person he was supposed to be seeing. That they haven't been able to confirm his alibi doesn't make him guilty."

"Agreed. But that doesn't mean he's innocent either. All I'm asking is that you keep an open mind and cooperate with the police when and if they ask for it. Make sure you don't stick out for him. That could jeopardize your case."

Phina's mind went to her last meeting with Nduka. He had seemed unperturbed by what happened to Patrick and the fact that they were both prime suspects in the case. "Could he be trying to ride on her to absolve himself?" she asked herself. They had spoken the weekend before Patrick died and he'd failed to mention any upcoming trips. That he was in Madrid, though not a mystery, presented a red flag. She made a mental note to discuss her doubts with her private investigator but did her best to remain neutral with Blake as she didn't want to implicate Nduka any further.

"I'll keep an open mind," Phina finally responded, grateful that she had the luxury to reflect.

"Thank you. That's all I need from you."

–

The issues Blake raised during their discussion awoke a new consciousness in Phina. When she got to Hazel House that evening, she began to search for anything that might tie Nduka to the case. The police had refused to reveal details of their investigation to her so there was no way she could tell if they had gathered additional evidence on him. Just as she was trying to settle into bed, McCracken called.

"I have some news for you," McCracken said.

"Good or bad?" Phina asked in an agitated tone.

"Good and bad, depending on which way you see it. I got wind that the police have confirmed Nduka's whereabouts when Patrick was murdered."

"Go on," Phina said impatiently.

"Well, police cameras spotted him in Barcelona the same period Patrick was there."

Phina's heart raced uncontrollably.

"My Goodness," Phina gasped.

"Are you okay?" McCracken asked.

"Yes, I am. Go on."

"He was invited for questioning at the police station but was later released. Just questioning, nothing more. I don't think there was sufficient evidence to arrest him."

Phina sighed in relief. "Why did he lie about being in Madrid?"

"I don't know. You see why you can't trust anyone, especially not now."

"I see now."

"Did you tell any of your friends about the letter?"

"No. I never mentioned it," Phina lied. "Why do you ask?"

"Till this day, I still wonder how the police got that letter in their possession. I have tried to find out from Lombardi, but he wouldn't reveal their informant. Could their men have broken in and searched your room when you weren't there? Have you asked the servants if they saw anyone?"

"I have and they denied seeing anything. I'm terribly confused," Phina mumbled.

"Is it possible someone you know gave the note to the police? Someone with access to your room!"

"I can't imagine who would do such a thing. I was so embarrassed when I found the letter that I basically kept it to myself. It's not something you tell another person. What's worse is that I didn't know who it was from. It wasn't signed."

"Well, I'll like you to retrace your steps."

Phina couldn't bring herself to admit to McCracken that she had discussed the letter with three of her closest friends – Victoria, Blake, and Isabel. And since she was certain neither one of them could have taken it, she saw no reason to reveal that detail to McCracken even though she still wondered how the letter had disappeared right under her nose. Part of her wondered if Martin could have moved it, but she quickly dismissed the theory and shuddered at the thought.

14

THE LETTER

"I knew this would happen," Phina heard Lady Thompson gripe in reaction to the news that the underwriters had backed down on their agreement for listing on the London Stock Exchange. "You should have stepped down when the road was clear."

Phina regretted picking up the phone. "Nothing on earth will make me step down from the company I've worked so hard to build," she said defensively.

"Don't you care that we lost our guarantor for the IPO? I thought making Ophinas public was your dream."

"The scandal, as hard as it may try to ruin my life, will not ruin our business. We were doing fine before I got the idea to go public and we will continue to do fine."

"No, no, no. We're not doing as fine as you say. Sales have plummeted. The scandal is impacting the way the public think about the brand. I'm worried that it may get worse if nothing is done to curtail it."

"Iris…, let me remind you that I started this company with my own blood, sweat, and tears and I'll never step down to please anyone. I'm innocent of the crimes I'm being accused of and soon I'll be able to prove it."

"Let's hope it's not too late by the time you do," Lady Thompson said sarcastically.

"Come what may, I'm not wavering on this decision," Phina retorted.

"Don't you have the future of your daughter to consider in case you're found guilty? Let me rephrase. Would you rather let the company die than relinquish power?"

"I'm not sure what you're getting at, but I have to go now."

Phina furiously hung up before Lady Thompson could respond. "What baloney," she muttered under her breath. "That woman has a lot of guts and I'm starting to lose respect for her."

It was still early morning and a light April snow was pelting the window frames, forming different patterns every few seconds. Still stunned by Lady Thompson's lack of decorum, Phina rushed her morning routine and arrived at Ophinas an hour earlier than she was accustomed to. It was time, she thought, to set things straight. She invited her top personnel to an impromptu meeting in the boardroom. Several anxious looks were exchanged the moment the invitees walked in since Phina hadn't mentioned why she wanted to see them.

"Questions for me?" she asked, looking from one end of the table to the other.

Everyone looked on with raised brows until the Head of Human Resources spoke up.

"There's one thing I know has been on most people's minds because I've received tons of questions from the staff regarding it."

"What is it?" Phina asked, sitting upright.

"We would like to know what the rejection by our underwriter means for the future of the company."

Phina grimaced a little. "Our plans are very much still in place. Be rest assured that we're working very hard to find a new underwriter. Until then, it's business as usual. Any more questions?"

After she addressed a couple more requests, she volunteered the answer to the question she knew had been plaguing everyone's mind – even though they dared not ask.

"I regret that I took so long to address this issue. Some of you have known me for many years and you know it's impossible for me to commit the crimes I've been accused of." She paused as a murmur spread across the room. Several members of her staff nodded and fixed their stares on her, waiting anxiously for her to continue. "I loved my late husband Patrick very much. I was just as shocked as anyone about the news of his death and have been unable to make sense of the accusations. Notwithstanding the state of my personal life, I am fully committed to resolving the IPO in no time." Some staff members raised their hands to speak. "Just a moment," Phina said, raising her left index finger. "I'll address all your questions but first I wanted to commend you all for standing firm and moving things along when I wasn't there to guide you. Together, we will continue to move our company in a positive direction and repair our reputation."

Looks and nods followed.

At the end of the meeting, after answering a dozen questions and listening to concerns related to the fate of the employees, Ophinas bottom-line, and even Patrick's former role, Phina mustered all the strength she could find and headed back to her office. It took all afternoon for her to finally go through all the paperwork on her desk. Her assistant Gina ran up and down to get her everything and every person she needed to complete her work. By the end of the day, she was satisfied with the results and confident she was on track to take back the reins at Ophinas.

-

Back at Hazel House, she poured herself a glass of champagne and sat on the settee with her legs outstretched. Patrick occupied her thoughts and as hard as she tried to shake it off, it remained. She still struggled with forgiveness and hoped the drink would drown the negative thoughts that constantly cropped up in her head and forced her to hate his memory. That night, she dreamt she was in her late twenties, living in the Caribbean, and as she passed bare-footed by a river, she saw her friends sailing on a yacht. She waved to them, but they just looked on without waving back. Realizing they hadn't recognized her, she continued walking and used the pieces of colored wool she left along the path to retrace her steps. When she spotted the bicycle she had docked at her starting point, it was all the confirmation she needed to know that she was in the right spot. Much to her dismay, she realized that the entrance had been blocked by an overgrowth of wisteria with venomous snakes. Desperate to leave, she ran around seeking a different entrance and saw the friends she had waved to earlier on. They were getting in through a different route. The new way in was adjacent to hers and was delightful and smooth sailing.

Still feeling contented when she woke up, Phina found herself smiling and pondering her dream for several minutes. The dream was reminiscent of how she had lived her life, taking care to keep her path straight and secure, only to reach a crossroads and find that after all that care, the actions of others could make her fear and stumble. But a look around could show her a way to follow that was free and fun and devoid of pain.

Phina's choices from that day on led her on a mission to forgive Patrick. Drawing a parallel to her dream, she knew if she didn't let go of what she thought was her original source, she would have to deal with the vines and the snakes. Both were destructive elements that played a crucial role in hindering her dreams as well as her ability to move on.

-

In her new found quest to forgive and resume her life as normal while keeping her vision on discovering who killed Patrick, Phina headed out into the London traffic the weekend before Easter to meet Victoria and two of their friends – Marion and Deena. Their meeting was at a trendy restaurant in Soho. Marion and Deena were already seated when she arrived. They ordered a bottle of champagne while Phina looked furtively at the door.

"Victoria canceled at the last minute," Deena blurted out.

Phina's heart sank. She had been looking forward to meeting Victoria who she hadn't seen in months. Their separation had begun to concern her. At first, she had figured that Victoria was just too busy to meet, but she had soon dismissed the thought as a figment of her imagination. It was now clear to her that Victoria was purposely avoiding her.

"Cheer up." Phina heard Marion say amidst the loud music playing in the background.

"Oh!" Phina responded, sitting up as she realized she had fallen into a dark mood. "I'm fine."

"No, you're not," Marion said, putting an arm around her. "I can't imagine what I would do if I were in your shoes, so I'm not trying to underestimate the trauma you've been through but try to have fun tonight okay?"

Phina looked at Marion with glossed over eyes while Deena looked on. They ordered their meals and chatted while they waited.

"Does anyone know why Victoria canceled?" Phina finally asked when she couldn't bear to ignore the situation anymore. She was hoping to smooth things over with Victoria that evening.

Deena looked straight ahead. Marion looked down for a second and then transferred her gaze to Phina.

Surprised at their reaction, Phina asked with a slight shake of her head, "Am I missing something?"

"I'm not sure," Marion finally spoke up. "I honestly believed she would show up."

-

Phina left before she could finish her meal to respond to an urgent call from Detective Derek Sommers – the Private Detective she hired to investigate Patrick's murder. Sommers was a former military investigator turned PI who was known amongst his peers to have a keen eye to detail and the ability to solve the most difficult of cases. He had asked Phina to meet him at his office in south London to discuss something of utmost importance. When she arrived, Detective Sommers came downstairs to meet her at the lobby and together, they walked to the second floor of the four-storey building that also housed the General Insurance Company. Detective Sommers and his partner occupied the smallest flat in the building. Although their tiny unit did not provide much of a view as it overlooked a mechanic's workshop, it was effective as a discreet location for their clients. They passed a tiny hallway and an empty reception area before they got to Detective Sommers' office. A slim well-dressed woman in her late thirties stood and greeted them when they walked in before settling back in her chair at the end of a large table. Detective Sommers pulled a chair for Phina to sit and walked towards a wooden cabinet to retrieve a file.

"My partner, Arnold isn't here today. Kara is my secretary," he said, waving his hand in the woman's direction.

Phina placed Kara's age at about mid-thirties and Detective Sommers at late forties. With their slim stature and angular jaws, she thought they could pass as siblings.

"How close are you to Victoria?" Detective Sommers asked after he took his seat across from Phina

"Patrick's sister? She's my best friend, but these days I don't see much of her. She was supposed to be at the dinner with some friends tonight but she didn't show up. Why do you ask?"

Detective Sommers placed two sheets of paper in front of her. "Look at this," he said, pointing to the middle of the page. The text was in faded ink.

Phina sighed. "I've had a really long and somewhat depressing day," she said, raising her hand mid-air. "Just summarize for me, please."

"Okay. I thought you might want to see for yourself. Victoria told the police you were cheating on her brother with your 'boyfriend'." He waited for what he said to sink in before adding, "Did you know?"

Phina first gaped at Detective Sommers and then squinted to decipher the text on the sheets in front of her.

"What?" she gasped. "Where did she get that nonsense from?"

"You need to tell me everything that's transpired," Detective Sommers continued as Phina hurriedly scanned the contents of the sheets. "Please don't leave anything out this time. Things are already as bad as they could be. According to Victoria, her brother found a letter addressed to you. It was sent to Hazel House while you were in Florence the same week he died. This is the main case the police have against you and Nduka. They think the two of you killed Patrick and will probably do everything conceivable to nail you for it."

Phina stared at Detective Sommers in amazement.

"I'm confused. What exactly did the letter in question say?" Phina asked, adjusting herself on the seat.

"I don't have the full details but it said something like, '*I had so much fun the other night … can't wait to see you when you return*' Look, it's all in that excerpt."

Phina dragged her chair back as the space in the room suddenly became too small for her. The loud scraping noise startled Detective Sommers.

"My goodness! The letter was for me?" she asked, wide-eyed, with her right hand on her chest to control the heaving.

"You knew about it?"

"It's the same letter the police were hounding me about. The one I told you I found in Patrick's drawer after he died. Remember?"

Detective Sommers nodded. "I do."

Phina shook her head as though to unclog it. "It was not addressed to anyone in particular, so I concluded another woman had sent it to Patrick."

"Apparently it was meant for you. At least, that's what the excerpt says. I don't mean to pry, but why didn't you immediately go to the police and explain everything to them when you first saw the letter?"

Phina looked at him and sighed. "I didn't think the letter had any significance. Besides, the original assumption was that Patrick had died from natural causes. At the time, I thought the letter was evidence that he was having an affair."

"But you should have alerted the police when the case was upgraded to a homicide."

"I know, but they got the letter before I could decide what to do with it.

"The police knew all along the letter was written by Nduka. They marked it as evidence of your affair. They think you colluded to kill Lord Campbell to pursue your relationship with Nduka."

"I see that now. It's sad that they held my original assumption about the letter against me as a motive for a crime of passion when all along they thought it was proof of an affair."

"True. They were hoping to catch you unawares. Those men were working your psych, hoping one charge would stick and there you were unknowingly helping them prove another."

Phina shook her head in disbelief. "And digging a deeper hole for myself from every angle. I'm glad I sought professional help. What should I do now? I'm totally at a loss."

"There's only one way to approach this. We need to bring to the attention of the police every proof that places the timing of your relationship with Nduka to after Patrick's demise. I need these in my office before Friday. It will be foolhardy for them to keep pursuing you after we present all the facts to them. I'll see to it that they scrap the case against you and focus their energy on finding the real culprit."

Phina trembled in her seat. "Wow, I can't believe I let them mess with my head for so long. I wonder if Victoria knew what the police were up to. No wonder she's been keeping her distance. She thinks I was having an affair and that I killed her brother."

"Well. She thinks Nduka had a hand in it. At least that's what the police think."

"I was in deeper trouble than I thought. How on earth can I prove to the entire world that I wasn't cheating on Patrick? Worse still, how can I prove that I didn't kill him?" she concluded, shaking her head.

"Isn't that the reason you hired me?" Detective Sommers added in a soothing tone.

"I guess so."

"Something still baffles me though. Why did Nduka write that letter? What was his intention? To ruin your marriage? I have pondered this for several hours and I still can't make any sense of it."

"How are the police sure Nduka wrote the letter? He didn't sign his name, and the envelope was never produced as evidence."

"The details are in the excerpt," Detective Sommers said, pointing at the sheets. "He was asked to fill some forms during his detention. With the information he entered, the police handwriting expert was able to match the scribbles on the letter to Nduka. Before then, they relied on Victoria's claim that her brother figured out that information from the envelope."

Silence fell in the room as Phina fought back tears. "How did you get this excerpt?"

Detective Sommers hesitated a little before responding. "One of the tricks of our trade. What's more important is what we do with it."

Phina felt as though she had lost Patrick all over again. If everything she discovered that night was true, and she saw no reason it shouldn't be, then she had wrongfully accused him.

Detective Sommers watched as her mood went from sullen to almost depressive. "It's going to be all right," he said in a soothing tone. "I'll do everything humanly possible to find out who the killer is. I hope you're ready for the ride because I don't promise it'll be smooth sailing."

Everything Detective Sommers said landed on deaf ears.

"I can't believe that rather than mourn Patrick, I have hated him all these months, believing he was cheating on me with an imaginary woman. I should have trusted that he wouldn't do such a thing. Even worse was that he thought I'd been cheating on him. Can you believe that?" Phina asked, fixing sad eyes on Detective Sommers. "And Victoria… she must hate me. I need to speak to her now."

"I believe that's a great place to start, but why don't you wait until tomorrow when you're a little calmer."

-

Phina ignored Detective Sommer's advice and called Victoria the moment she arrived at Hazel House.

"I now know why you've been avoiding me." Phina blurted. "I never, ever, even once, cheated on Patrick and I loved him from the bottom of my heart,"

Victoria was shocked by her tone and how late in the night it was. She looked to Jorge, who was lying next to her for approval and he gave it with a wave of the hand. It was obvious to him that whatever Phina wanted to discuss could not wait because it was unlike her to call that late.

"Why are you telling me all this stuff?" Victoria asked, sounding indifferent.

"I believe you know why. Pay attention, Victoria, this is a serious matter. I could go to jail if you don't listen." Phina's voice cracked up.

"I'm listening."

Phina told Victoria what she found out, leaving out no details. She was sobbing by the time she was done.

"Stop!" Phina heard Victoria say amidst her own sobs. "When Patrick told me about the letter, I didn't know what to believe. The content was quite incriminating. It devastated him."

Phina sighed audibly.

"If the letter is from whom I imagine, then he was just saying how much he enjoyed my company. We met at Isabel's the night in question, nothing more." Phina recalled the night Nduka kissed her in his car at Isabel's. But, since she put a stop to his advances before it could progress, she felt no need to admit their indiscretion. "I never cheated on Patrick. You told the police I did?"

"I had to report the facts as I knew it. Patrick told me you were having an affair, and he had proof. What did you expect me to do?"

"You could have talked to me," Phina said, choking on her words. "Do you know how they got the letter?"

"No," Victoria responded curtly. "Did you think it was through me?"

"I don't know what to think. When I told you about the letter you never mentioned that it was meant for me. You allowed Lombardi and his men to lord two motives over my head."

"What two motives?"

Phina recanted her struggle with Lombardi to Victoria.

"I didn't think you were referring to the same letter," Victoria denied after Phina was done speaking. "In fact, I don't think I gave it any thought at all. I was so distraught by Patrick's death that when you called to ask me if he had been cheating, I didn't really want to listen to you. Patrick told me about the letter the week you were in Florence – the same week he died so you can imagine how I felt. As for taking the letter from Hazel House, I haven't been there in ages. How could I have taken it?"

"Do you believe my innocence now?" Phina asked.

"I don't know what to believe because you were seeing Nduka soon after Patrick died. I don't believe you killed Patrick, but I'm not sure Nduka is blame free. It was forward of him to send such an incriminating note to your marital home. What did he plan to achieve?"

"I'm still pondering that."

"My advice to you will be to stay away from him. When I told Lady Thompson about his letter…"

"Wait! You told Lady Thompson?" Phina asked incredulously.

Victoria gasped for a moment and steadied her voice. "I needed to talk to someone close to Patrick. I couldn't talk to you then. I was so angry. If you say you weren't cheating on Patrick, then I have no choice but to believe you. Other than the letter, he had no other proof you were cheating. He told me he was completely devastated because he loved you so much."

"I loved him, too. More than anything in the world and I can't believe he died thinking I didn't."

"And I can't believe... Never mind," Victoria said, choking on her words.

Phina could hear Victoria sobbing in the background. A bittersweet feeling enveloped her. Pain from all she had missed since Patrick died and then relief from the pain, all occurring simultaneously.

"I can't imagine what he thinks when he watches us," Victoria continued after she regained control of her emotions.

Phina wasn't sure if Victoria really believed Patrick could see them. Martin crossed her mind, and she was immediately reminded that the possibility existed. On second thought, she realized she had no real proof of her own of his existence except second-hand account from others. She hadn't really met Martin herself.

-

Victoria arrived at Hazel House the following morning just as Phina was setting up the breakfast table. When Phina heard the doorbell ring, she placed the napkins on the table and ran to meet her. It was still too soon to hug, but both women held hands and gave sullen looks to each other.

"I've missed you," Victoria said with a sigh.

"I missed you, too."

Both had lost the person they loved the most in the world and failed to be there for each other. They sat in silence for a few minutes.

"I talked to Superintendent Lombardi," Victoria finally said after their breakfast was served. "I told him it wasn't possible you killed my brother. You had an alibi and their case against you is only circumstantial and can't be proven even with that stupid letter. He agreed to review the new evidence."

Phina hugged her. "Thank you. This should help the argument Detective Sommers is putting together for my case. I can't believe we ignored each other for so long. How did we get here?"

Victoria shook her head. "I don't know."

"What about Nduka? Do you know if they'll take their hooks off him?" Phina asked.

"That, I can't say. His case is a little more complex. He wrote that letter, and his handwriting was matched when he was brought to the police station."

"But that doesn't make him guilty."

"It also doesn't make him innocent. He could have been obsessed with you to the point of mischief."

"That's ridiculous."

"Hmm... I'll tell you what I think. He should hope and pray his lawyer is good because there's more to him than meets the eye. For instance, they've not been able to establish his alibi. One day he says he's in Madrid and another day he's in Barcelona," Victoria concluded, raising both hands mid-air.

"How do you know so much?" Phina asked with a puzzled look.

Victoria grimaced before letting out a deep sigh. "I've kept my nose to the ground. Mother... She thinks the only reason you weren't arrested is because of your status."

Phina sighed and desperately fought to suppress her annoyance.

"Hmm... Just because the world thrives on scandal especially where money, sex, and celebrity is concerned doesn't mean I'm not innocent. She just assumed I was guilty. Neither one of you thought to give me a chance to tell my own side of the story."

"When Patrick's death was ruled a homicide, I went ballistic. It was hard for me to separate truth from fiction. I'm sorry; we all believed you were guilty."

"I'm sorry too."

They ate breakfast mostly in silence. It was impossible to imagine that they had been best friends for years. Phina was hopeful she would soon be cleared of any involvement in Patrick's homicide. The months she suffered thinking he was cheating had battered her psychological wellbeing. Afterward, being accused of his murder further ripped her entire world apart. She still felt the numbing pain of the two incidents in her chest. It was comforting to know that she only needed to deal with one thing now – his demise – the only incident she had neglected up until that day. Had he been there, she thought as she fought back tears, he would have been sitting at the head of the table, possibly with Brigitte on his lap. And, he would have been serving them jokes to get their day started.

"Patrick would be happy we've resolved this issue," Victoria said, cutting through Phina's reverie.

"He would also have been so sorry he created the mess in the first place," Phina responded.

They headed out together into the cold morning, Victoria, in the direction of her home and Phina, towards Ophinas where she held a closed-circuit meeting with representatives of her investors to discuss a resumption of their plans to go public. Several calls were made to Ophinas' attorneys, bankers, accountants, and the London Stock Exchange, after which it was agreed that they needed to file a new application for the IPO. Several more hours were spent discussing and documenting the new strategy. Lunch was non-existent – cold sandwiches from a café close by sufficed. Meeting participants were cross-eyed by the time they exited Phina's penthouse office later that evening.

15

BRACELETS AND CROWNS

ONE month after Ophinas IPO lost its underwriter, a syndicate of three investment banks banded together to act as guarantors for the offering. With the lens off Phina as a suspect in Patrick's murder, investor confidence increased and with the added publicity, sales doubled two quarters in a row. The results of the IPO were staggering – seven billion pounds was raised, shattering existing records. The day Phina received the news, she pranced around her office with her hands in the air and a huge smile on her face. For the first time in months, she felt like herself again, and happy that she hadn't let her team down. As she was about to enter her English White Rolls-Royce, she took a look at her surroundings and sighed. The sweet May air worked wonders on her nerves as she breathed in.

To her surprise, Lady Thompson was the first to call to congratulate her.

"I'm in shock," Lady Thompson said. "I can't believe we pulled this off."

Phina, ignoring that they hadn't really spoken in months, responded with excitement, "Our IPO committee worked unbelievably hard. At times I thought we were going to shatter into pieces. We were all stretched beyond our limits."

"You'd have to find a way to reward them," Lady Thompson suggested.

"I was planning to take the key players for a spa weekend. Would you like to join?"

"I would love to, but I've got piles of work after my trip to America, so I'll pass. And you, it's time you finally take that trip you've been craving. I'm sure the work will still go on in your absence."

Phina hadn't been on a trip in almost a year and had begun to get used to being stuck in one place.

"Yes, a trip would be wonderful," she said. "No one would be able to stop me now since all suspicion of my involvement in Patrick's murder has been cleared."

"Oh, really? What about Nduka?"

"Well, the theories flying around about our affair has been put to rest so I'll assume he's in the clear too. Thanks for asking."

Nduka's situation was still hanging in the balance but so far, charges had not been laid. He hoped the police would find a new target since Phina had convinced them there was nothing romantic between them at the time Patrick was murdered. The letter had only expressed Nduka's interest in a relationship and had been a tad bit affectionate. Other than that, it could not hold up in a court of law as proof of an affair even though his alibi was yet to be established. Phina had ruled him out as a suspect, but the question still remained as to who the actual murderer was.

-

As Phina continued to work on finalizing all aspects of the company transition, Detective Sommers worked behind the scenes searching for any vital clues they may have overlooked. After months of investigations revealed nothing new, he began to question if Patrick was really murdered.

"What if Patrick took matters into his own hands?" he asked Phina, startling her as soon as he stepped into the drawing room at Hazel House where Phina had been waiting to meet with him.

"It's impossible," she said, shaking her head fervently. "I've known Patrick for years. It's unlikely he'll resort to that."

"But, what about the times you claimed he was distracted? Did you find out what got him in that state?"

Phina shook her head again. "No, but now I assume it was a combination of the financial crisis and the fact that he'd sold his shares of Ophinas behind my back."

"So far it seems that we've been on the wrong trail," Detective Sommers said after scribbling something on a tiny notepad. "Every clue we've received so far has led to a dead-end. I'm going to apply a new approach. This time around, everyone will be under my radar and I promise to leave no stone unturned."

"That's what I expected all along, so I'm pleased to hear that. It's very important that the culprit is found and punished to the fullest extent of the law."

-

Detective Sommers cast his net wide in search of Patrick's killer, while Lombardi and his team refocused their investigation on the mystery woman that was seen leaving Patrick's room that fateful night. Other than the fact that the image was that of a woman, as determined by the attire, a long robe with a unique structure to the lapel, the cameras did not capture a clear image of a face or any other identifying feature. The hotel employee who saw the woman as she was leaving the hotel had provided a composite that Lombardi and his team shared with several news sources. That move had only yielded false leads. A reward was announced for anyone who could provide information about the woman in the blurry video footage. Lombardi was under extreme pressure from his superiors to find a resolution to the case, so he mustered enough courage to call Phina to seek her help. Patrick was a high profile figure and the situation had started to embarrass the police department, especially as no valid arrests had been made in almost a year since Patrick was killed. Phina and Nduka's detention and the public relations nightmare that ensued afterward was a big source of that embarrassment.

When Phina heard Lombardi's voice on the phone, she regretted picking it up and almost hung up in panic. She couldn't fathom why he wanted to speak with her as she thought her business with him was finished. The sloppy manner in which his team handled Patrick's case still caused her to resent him.

"Hello," she said, her voice void of any emotion.

"Sorry to bother you," Lombardi said in a tremulous voice before clearing his throat. "How have you been?"

Phina sighed in frustration. She couldn't fathom why Lombardi always had to start with pleasantries. Trying her best not to sound hostile, she responded, "I've been great." In her mind she was screaming, "Can we cut to the chase?"

It was as though he read her mind because he went straight to the point. "The reason I called is to ask about the woman that contacted you right after Patrick died. The one you went to meet at Loughborough Junction?"

"Yes…"

"Did you ever hear from her again?"

For a few seconds, Phina contemplated how to respond to Lombardi. He and his men had insinuated she was lying about the mystery caller when they arrested her at Hazel House, so she pondered his renewed interest in the case.

"Why do you ask?" she said when she finally spoke.

"Just covering all bases," Lombardi responded.

"Hmm… I wonder if I should respond to you without my lawyer present. I thought you didn't believe the mysterious caller existed. I remember you specifically saying that I made her up. What changed your mind?"

"I'm sorry Lady Campbell, but I can't reveal that information to you."

"Okay. I never heard back from her."

"Any clue who it might be?"

Phina derived no pleasure in helping Lombardi with his investigation after he'd wasted months following the wrong leads and harassing her and Nduka. Yet, she didn't want to be charged with withholding critical information in a murder investigation, so she chose her words carefully. "No. She never called back and till today, I have no clue what she so desperately wanted to discuss with me. I suspect she got cold feet, or maybe she got hurt by the same person who killed Patrick."

Lombardi sighed. He sounded more relaxed when he said, "Thank you for your help. Please keep me informed of any new developments."

"I will."

Phina neither called nor heard from Lombardi for months after that and despite the occasional debrief from Detective Sommers, she focused her energy on her business. The results of the feasibility studies completed before the IPO were now being reviewed for proper execution of their plan for expansion into the American and Caribbean markets.

She had come a long way since she received that dreadful call in her Florence hotel room. Forgiveness had transformed her life, miraculously revealed the truth and brought her on the path of healing. That year would mark her thirteenth year in the retail business and she couldn't be prouder of what she'd achieved so far. So much had happened to derail her – the demise of her right-hand man, being implicated in that demise and almost losing control of the business she'd worked so hard to build.

-

After an excruciatingly long day at Ophinas, exactly two weeks after she spoke with Lombardi, Phina immediately headed for Brigitte's room with the hope of catching her awake. Brigitte was already tucked under her blanket ready to go to sleep. The nanny was sitting beside her, pushing locks of hair away from her face. As Phina approached, Brigitte flashed a toothless grin. Amused, Phina chuckled and poked her chin with her index finger. When Brigitte pulled her left hand from under the blanket to reciprocate her mother's gesture, Phina saw dangling on her wrist the same charm bracelet she found in Patrick's drawer after he died.

"Wait a minute," Phina said, grabbing Brigitte's arm to get a closer look. "What's this?" she asked, shifting her gaze between the nanny and Brigitte.

The nanny shrugged while Brigitte tugged to free her arm from her mother's grip.

"I saw it in your drawer. I thought you bought it for me," Brigitte whined, and successfully restored her arm.

"I'm sorry, honey," Phina said, sighing and shaking her head. "Give it back. It's not yours. How long have you had it?"

"I took it yesterday when I was in your room."

The bracelet was too big for the little girl, so she slipped it easily off her arm and handed it to her mother.

"Thank you," Phina said and kissed her on the forehead.

Phina looked at the bracelet. Silver, or white gold, she wasn't sure what precious metal was used in its manufacture. The combination of alphabets and Roman numerals still didn't make any sense to her. "You shouldn't have taken it without asking me," she reprimanded Brigitte. "Now go to sleep and I'll see you tomorrow."

When Phina shut Brigitte's door behind her, she leaned against the wall in the hallway and examined the bracelet again. Out of frustration, she smacked her forehead with her arm and muttered, "How did I forget all about this?" In the dim light, she could see that the bracelet was handcrafted, which increased its value. It was made from platinum, not silver like she originally assumed. The Roman numerals comprised of the numbers six, eight, and two. The alphabets were simply A, B, and C and provided no more clues than the numbers did. In between the letters and the numbers were six beautiful teardrop faceted cut diamonds, a magnifying glass, and three crowns.

-

Her thoughts drifted as she walked to her room. At first, she thought the bracelet could be the missing clue she was looking for to break the case of Patrick's murder, but on second thoughts, she reminded herself why she had tossed it in her drawer several months back and forgotten about it. When she found the letter after Patrick died, she had immediately thought it was linked to the bracelet and even though the letter got missing in her care; the bracelet had been carefully tucked away. Things had changed significantly since then. The letter mishap had been resolved and Patrick cleared of adultery, so she saw no reason to share information about the bracelet with Lombardi or even Detective Sommers.

She tossed the bracelet in her bag and decided to sleep over her decision. Right then, she had no doubt in her mind that Patrick loved her, so the bracelet did not elicit the same feeling it did when he first died. Then, she had thought he was cheating on her because of the letter. Since she'd been proven wrong, her only concern now was to make sure she wasn't holding anything back in the investigation. She slept fitfully, pondering her approach to the issue and woke up, still groggy from lack of sleep.

16

IF YOU WILL

PHINA was surprised when the Managing Partner from Radny and Associates, a firm comprised of the finest estate executors in England informed her that Patrick had left a will. With their extremely busy lives, it hardly occurred to her they needed to create wills. She became emotional when the executor insinuated that her involvement with the prime suspect in Patrick's murder was the reason it took too long for the will to go through probate. Since she'd been cleared of any involvement in his murder, it had seemed appropriate to gather Patrick's closest family together for a reading.

The entire family – Victoria, Jorge, their two children, and Patrick's parents – arrived within minutes of each other. They first gathered in the small dining room for a light lunch and spoke quietly in appreciation of the solemn purpose of their meeting.

"I commend how you've been able to take care of Brigitte on your own." Patrick's Mother, Irene, said to Phina with a drawl.

Phina was frozen to the spot on hearing her compliment. She held on firmly to her cutlery and looked down for a few seconds before looking up again to fix her gaze on Irene and mouthing, "Thank you."

Irene had been by Phina's side when Patrick had first passed, but when his death was ruled a homicide and Phina named as a suspect, Irene turned her back on her. When Phina called to tell her side of the story, Irene had completely ignored her calls.

After lunch, the adults gathered around the meeting table in the large study where Patrick worked most nights. The bespectacled lawyer's balding head shone from the overhead light bulb as he read the will to them. They listened intently as he went through the fifteen-page document. Patrick had provided sufficiently for his parents, who he left two homes and a substantial amount of money. The money was to be placed in a trust to be used for their care when they became unable to fend for themselves. The rest of what he owned, including two houses in London, a home in Nice, one each in Paris and Milan as well as shares and money in the bank, he left for Phina and Brigitte.

"Any objections?" the lawyer asked when he finally read the last line.

No one raised any, and no one dared look at another for fear of revealing what they were thinking. Victoria was not mentioned in the will and this came as no surprise. As Patrick's only sibling, she was bound to inherit everything their parents owned, at their passing.

"If you have any, give me a call as soon as possible at my office so we can discuss it," the lawyer said after an uncomfortable silence.

"Thank you," Patrick's Mother said. "We're a peaceful family. I doubt there will be any."

The lawyer nodded once and stood up from his seat. Before he left, he thanked everyone for gathering together and wished them the best of luck.

The activity gave Phina a sense of finality even though she still missed Patrick. She wished she could have discussed the outcome of the reading with his family, but the gathering was soon dispersed without as much as a word to one another. Being read Patrick's will reminded everyone that he had thought about his death as far back as two years before he died. After everyone had left, she retreated to her room and tried to take her mind off the experience by doing some work on the personal computer Patrick had installed in their bedroom a few months before his passing. She still found it hard maneuvering the equipment and soon her mind was wandering again. Since the attempt to use work to get her mind off things had failed, she decided to call Blake. Blake had been close to Patrick, and she felt he would understand what she was going through.

"We just had the will read to us," she said when she heard his voice.

"How do you feel?"

"Disillusioned, to say the least."

"Why? Were there surprises?"

"Not in my opinion. I guess I just never imagined I would go through that sort of thing, at least not at this stage in my life. His mother was there, and I felt so sad. You could have heard a pin drop whenever the lawyer paused."

"It's never an easy process. How are you doing now though?"

"Okay. Just okay," she said in a solemn tone. "I'm doing much better than when I was considered an accomplice to the prime suspect. Keeping my fingers crossed and hoping they find the real culprit. All our lives could be in danger. Do you understand?"

"I do. You never know what or who may be lurking in the background. Make sure you have your bodyguard with you at all times."

"It sounds terrible when you put it that way," she said, gritting her teeth.

"I don't mean to scare you, but it's the nature of things."

After Blake hung up, Phina reflected over his words. She dug both hands into her hair. Her heart raced as she wondered if she had done enough for the security in Hazel House. Too scared to sleep alone that night, she asked the nanny to bring Brigitte to her room. She fell asleep soon after. When she woke up in the middle of the night to use the bathroom, every shadow seemed to resemble Patrick's ghost or even Martin's. After she returned from the bathroom, she gazed at Brigitte's face. It was slightly illuminated by the bedside lamp. "My poor child," Phina muttered under her breath.

Brigitte had been very close to her father. Phina had not minced words with her when Patrick passed. She had let her know he was never coming back, and that he was in a better place. Phina recalled the day Brigitte finally came to the full realization of what she was told. She had bawled uncontrollably, and it had taken hours to console her. After Phina placed her on Patrick's side of the bed, Brigitte had curled up like one seeking protection from something ominous, causing Phina to ponder if there was a hidden meaning in her posture.

Phina began to look into Patrick's finances after access to his accounts were released to her. With his shares in Ophinas completely gone, she focused on his shares in Sportsmets, his real estate investments and his stock in various companies. She scheduled a meeting in his plush corner office with his lawyer and accountants to discuss the state of his affairs.

"Welcome all," Phina said after everyone sat down to address the issue at hand.

They started with his investment in Sportsmets and moved the discussion to Patrick's ranch in Essex and then to his jewelry business.

Lastly, they reviewed his stock holdings. These made up a majority of his fortune, at least fifty percent. Even though they had lost significant value during the financial crisis, they still constituted a massive fortune.

"Here you go," the lawyer said, handing Phina the folder containing details of Patrick's investments.

Phina looked at the pages for a few seconds. "I'm not sure how to interpret this. Please... some assistance," she said, beckoning to the lawyer to come and stand beside her.

"These are the remainder of his holdings," the lawyer said.

"I need further clarification. My husband had hundred thousand shares in Mico Corporation, and almost a million in Sanders. I see zero on the sheet here. Not to talk of the meager amounts I see right here." She pointed at the bottom of the page.

"As far I know, he transferred all his shares in these companies a few months before his death."

"To whom?" Phina asked, turning her head to look directly at the lawyer.

"The documentation does not show who or where he made the transfers to."

"What do you mean?" Phina asked, glaring at him.

The lawyer shifted uncomfortably and looked at the puzzled faces at the table. Phina, realizing that the entire room was staring at them, followed his gaze and addressed the accountants.

"Thank you, everyone," she said. "Please excuse us. I'll get back to each one of you to conclude this business."

She waited for everyone but the lawyer to leave the room before she pulled the seat beside hers and invited him to sit.

"I don't understand," Phina began. "Please explain."

"The documentation does not leave any clue as to where the shares were transferred. This number," The lawyer said, pointing to the bottom of the page where a number was scribbled in black ballpoint ink, "may provide an answer."

"I recognize Patrick's handwriting," Phina said, nodding slowly.

"That proves he was aware of it and most likely gave his approval."

"That proves nothing," Phina retorted.

Breathing heavily, Phina sat and stared into the distance for a few seconds as she regained her composure. She was stunned beyond belief by all the things Patrick's passing had unraveled. There had been so many mysteries, and she hoped this one would not trump them all. He had been distant before his passing, and she was now beginning to put two and two together. Each day, she discovered something new, and she didn't like the look of this one.

"Can you find out what this company is, where it is and who it belongs to?"

"I'll do my best."

"Please, please keep this matter between us. You must not discuss your findings with anyone, not even the people on your team. A lot depends on that."

"I understand."

"One more thing. I know it's not my place to ask, but are you aware of any dealings Patrick may have been engaged in?"

"What kind of dealings?" the lawyer asked, perplexed.

"Never mind," Phina said, waving her hand. She had never involved her staff in her private business as it was bound to complicate matters and result in a slippery slope. "I'm sorry. Just help me find out those details as soon as possible. It's very important. I'm sure you understand."

"I understand," the lawyer confirmed, nodding his head.

-

As Phina left for Hazel House that evening, she made a note to call Detective Sommers and provide him with the new information. She could not wait for the lawyer to get back to her with his findings as time was of the essence. It was clear to her then that Patrick was murdered and with each day the murderer was allowed to roam around; she felt increasingly unsafe. The motive was up in the air, and with Patrick's business dealings in shambles, it seemed to her his business and his murder were connected. If her assumptions were right, then she, Brigitte and the rest of the family were in severe danger.

-

On arriving at Hazel House, Phina asked the butler to lock all the doors and windows. In her room, she kicked off her shoes, walked into the adjoining study she had shared with Patrick and pored through folders and folders of papers. When it became too tiring to sit up, she moved to the floor and continued to search for anything that could help with tracing the stocks in the pile of papers she had dumped on the floor. A loud ringing woke her up after she fell asleep, and she dragged herself off the floor and staggered to the writing desk to pick up the phone. The ringing had stopped by the time she got close. "I wonder who that was," she muttered under her breath, before looking at her watch and realizing it was eleven o'clock. She had been lying on that floor for almost two hours.

"Oh my God!" she exclaimed, placing both hands on her face. "I've missed everything." She had missed dinner and an opportunity to spend time with Brigitte. It was a wonder they didn't break down the door as she expected the nanny would have tried several times to reach her. It was too late to call for the child who she was sure would be fast asleep, so she got up and walked to the phone. There was no message on the answering machine. "Who could that be?" she said aloud. Convinced it was Nduka, she dialed his number.

"Did you try to call me?" Phina asked after she heard Nduka on the other end.

"That wasn't me. How are you, darling?"

"I wonder who it was then," Phina said apprehensively, ignoring his greeting. "I fell asleep in the study... on the floor."

"Why on the floor?" Nduka chuckled. "That could make you sick. Should I come over?"

"No, not at all."

"Why?"

"I don't know," she responded defensively. "Put yourself in my shoes, and stop acting like you live in a vacuum."

"I have considered how you may feel, but I see things differently. I could come over and we could just talk for a while. Your happiness is my priority and it will always be."

Phina smiled. Nduka always had a way of making her forget her troubles even though he was responsible for creating a big portion of it for her. He'd had so many of his own recently, but still, he never ceased to put her first.

"No. Let's just talk over the phone."

They talked about everything, from the home goods line, to pop culture, and then to their plans for summer. He thought the home goods line would be a great addition to Ophinas.

"Try to come back in one piece," Nduka told Phina, regarding her upcoming trip to Nigeria.

"I will."

"Is Brigitte going with you?"

"No, not this time, although I feel some trepidation leaving her behind. I'm not sure how safe we all are."

"You should consider taking her then," he said in a taut tone.

"No, she'll be fine. I don't think anyone will hurt her."

It saddened Nduka that he could not see Phina whenever he wanted to. After news of his dealings got to her, she'd maintained a physical distance from him and he tried his best to maintain a friendship as he could not bear to lose her entirely. It was getting increasingly hard for him to pretend that he could carry on like that for good but was happy whenever he got a chance to speak with her.

-

The results of Patrick's business dealings came in two days later. The lawyer walked into Phina's office with results of the investigation and shut the door behind him. Phina eased back in her chair and waited anxiously.

"I still don't know who owns these shares," he announced.

"What do you mean?" Phina asked, glancing at him for a second before taking the folder he had just handed her. "What is this?"

"These," the lawyer said, pointing at the center of the page, "are dummy companies, not one or two but three in total."

"Go on," Phina said when the lawyer paused a little.

"Patrick had transferred all his stock to these corporations at least six months before his death. As you can see, it was done in chunks of tens of thousands until he completed the transfers. Sander's is the only exception. There are still ten thousand shares left in your late husband's name."

"None of this makes any sense," Phina said, shaking her head and ramming the folder on her desk.

"I tried to find out who owns these companies and I have not been able to make headway."

"You need to keep looking."

"I've looked everywhere. I even called the registry."

"What did they say?"

"They'll get back to me."

"I'll need you to follow up on your sources. I hate to say this, but it seems that he went to great lengths to hide these transactions from me."

The lawyer shook his head in sympathy.

"I don't think he meant it for your hurt. Lord Campbell loved you very much."

Phina looked at him for a split second and looked away. She opened her mouth to speak, but shut it immediately and shook her head. How could she explain to him that love shouldn't hurt, it should feel sweet and safe? All she had felt since Patrick's passing had been the opposite. It had been one traumatic discovery after another. Even though one – the letter had turned out to be a mistake – the stock transfers had cropped up to rob her peace. Then again, she thought, until Patrick's killer was found she had to brace herself for whatever else laid beneath the surface.

"Let me know when you hear back from your sources. We can't afford any delays," she finally said.

"I'll do my best."

No matter how hard she tried, Phina couldn't figure out what Patrick did with the stocks. The sale of his shares of Ophinas to Lady Thompson had been for the sole purpose of raising funds to revive his interest in Sportsmets. The reason for the recent transfers was a complete mystery, and she was hell-bent on finding out who those dummy companies belonged to. As the clock struck four, she gathered her things to leave for a meeting with Ophinas licensees.

17

LASGIDI

THE moment Phina's plane touched down in Lagos, she felt a surge of emotions rise from within her as she imagined the tastes, sights, and sounds she was about to encounter. The humid air hit her face and brought her to the realization that she was home. About to disembark from the plane, she observed as the coach passengers scrambled to unload their bags. They stepped over one another as bags fell haphazardly out of the overhead compartments. She wondered why everyone was in a massive hurry, especially as they ultimately ended up in the customs queue. And no matter how hard they tried, could not go faster than the customs agents could process their entry.

At the customs area, a short pleasant looking gentleman in a tightly fitted suit approached her.

"Good day Madam Phina," he said to Phina in an overly joyful tone. He had a big smile on his face that had no likelihood of waning soon.

"Good day," Phina responded, smiling in return. "How did you recognize me?"

"Ah ah. I know you *now*." He dragged the last word. "Our MD also told me what you were wearing. It's easy," he concluded, chuckling uncontrollably.

Phina resisted the urge to laugh, so she shrugged her shoulders and smiled. Too tired to engage after the six-hour flight, she simply mouthed, "Thank you," and followed him behind to the customs counter reserved for VIPs. This counter had a short queue and as the guide pulled up the bar that separated the counter from the others, a throng of travelers scuttled to pass through. A uniformed customs agent sprang to action immediately and dispersed the trespassers before hurriedly hooking the straps in place. Phina could hear grumbling as the crowd expressed their displeasure at the preferential treatment they felt she was receiving. A male traveler in his late thirties said loud enough for everyone in the crowded area to hear, "Are we not all the same?" in a fierce Igbo accent.

The woman standing next to him smacked one hand over the other and then repeated the same movement with the alternate hand before declaring, "I don't know o o…" the whole time rumpling her lips. Others looked on in amusement.

"What is your name," Phina asked her guide.

"Usman. My name is Usman. I thought I told you earlier Ma."

"Usman, thank you for all your help."

"No problem, Ma."

Within a few seconds, Phina presented her passport to the customs official who stamped it and returned to her.

"How many bags do you have?" Usman asked when they arrived at the baggage area.

"Five. I checked in five."

Usman looked at Phina in amazement as she described her luggage. He dutifully picked them up from the carousel and placed on a trolley before he led her outside. In a matter of seconds, she was ushered into a black limousine and taken straight to her hotel. When she opened the door to her suite, a beautiful platter of macaroons and chocolate dipped strawberries teased her senses. Without hesitation, she devoured the macaroons — all eight of them, as well as the strawberries. Then she poured herself a glass of Dom Perignon and walked into the bathroom for a quick shower before dressing up to attend a welcome dinner Chief Gambo was hosting for her.

-

When Phina arrived at Chief's house, the uniformed gateman peeked into the chauffeur's window to verify the occupants of the Limo.

"I'm bringing Madam," the chauffeur said, pointing to the back seat.

The gateman looked at the back.

"Good Evening Ma," he said to Phina who grew impatient by the excessive protocol.

"Good evening," she responded with a forced smile.

The gateman ran back joyfully with a spring in his step and opened one side of the large cast-iron gate while he yelled at his partner to open the other side. As the car drove in, the two gatemen bowed and saluted.

The driver circled through the large compound, driving by a beautiful waterfall, a flower garden and a fleet of luxury cars. He finally stopped at a porch leading to an unreasonably long flight of stairs and up to a large crafted door with gold intricate sculpting and a large knocker. He stepped out of the driver's seat and held the door for Phina, who let out a small gasp the moment she saw the magnificence of Chief Gambo's compound. It towered over the horizon as though attempting to consume it. Phina could spot four tennis players — two men and two women hitting a ball back and forth at the tennis court in the far corner. The women wore short white tennis skirts and sleeveless low-cut tops that left most of their bosom hanging out. A large swimming pool glistened on the north-east side with ripples spreading endlessly from the light wind as it blew. As Phina stood, absorbing the beauty of her surroundings, she felt a light tap on her shoulder and turned around to see a gentleman, just over six feet tall, light-skinned, strong jawline, smoldering eyes and the most enchanting smile she'd ever seen on any human. She was transfixed to the spot and her mouth formed a small oval as she searched for the right words to curb her embarrassment.

"I see you love the outdoors." He spoke slowly and with something Phina detected to be a slight British accent – a voice she thought she recognized from somewhere.

The allure in his voice caused her heart to pound heavily in her chest. She opened her mouth to speak but still couldn't find the right words, so she closed it, took a deep breath and smiled to avoid making a fool of herself.

"Forgive my bad manners," the gentleman said, offering his right hand. "I'm Rashid."

"Phina," she said in her sing-song voice as she moved her clutch from her right hand to the left and offered him her hand in return. "I should have known it was you. I recognized your voice from the times we spoke on the phone."

Rashid smiled, revealing perfect teeth.

"We've all been waiting for you. Please come with me."

Phina felt shockwaves as she took his hand and walked up the flight of stairs. The door swung open just as they approached it. They walked through the foyer and into a grand living room with about sixty guests, who were chatting, laughing and performing slow dances with cocktails in their hands. *Joromi* was blasting in the background. The women moved their hips slowly from side to side with sultry expressions on their faces as the men danced to the rhythm with their hands on the wriggling hips of their female counterparts. Phina was taken aback when she saw a life-size portrait of Chief in all his resplendence on the sprawling white wall of the magnificent living room. The DJ lowered the volume of the music the moment she stepped in causing the guests to look in the direction of the raucous caused by Chief and his wife. Chief was shouting, "hello, hello," as they headed towards her. Chief was in a long purple and silver robe and his wife wore an '*iro*' and '*buba*' in a fabric that matched his. Her *gele* accentuated her hair beautifully, and her silver purse and shoes were from a rare designer brand. Phina scanned the room for Rashid but he was nowhere nearby. He had disappeared from her side the moment they stepped in. Chief and his wife took turns hugging and kissing her on both cheeks.

"Our guest of honor is here," Chief announced in a booming voice loud enough for the whole room to hear, his face brimming with a wide smile.

Phina smiled, momentarily shifting her gaze from one person to the next.

"Welcome to Nigeria," Chief continued, looping his arm around hers and walking towards the center of the room. "I hope you enjoyed your flight."

"Yes, it was great. The services at the airport have really improved since the last time I was here. Oh and thank you for the driver and the bottle of Dom in my suite. I know that was your handiwork."

Chief laughed a long throaty laugh, easing back to achieve the dramatic effect needed to express his pleasure.

"I was hoping you would notice, but anyway, I'd like you to meet my first son. He cut his trip to Dubai short so he could be here today to meet you." Before Phina could utter a word, Chief excused his wife, twisted his neck and scanned the room with his eyes for a few seconds before announcing, "Here he is."

Taking Phina's hand, he dragged her halfway to a crowded corner of the room. "My son Rashid," he said in a haughty tone.

Rashid gave Phina his hand for the third time that evening. "We've already met," he said, looking into her eyes. "I found her when she first arrived. Lovely to finally meet you in person, Phina. My father talks so much about you. One would think you were his first daughter."

Chief laughed in his usual manner. "Phina is a gem. I love all my children, but I wish she was my child," he reiterated, still laughing.

Phina, touched by Chief's proclamations, placed her left hand on her chest and purred, "Ohh. Thank you so much, sir. You've been wonderful to me since we've met and always treated me like your own. God bless you."

"Come, there are people I'd like you to meet," Rashid said to her, cutting their theatrics short. He held Phina loosely around the waist and led her to two gentlemen, about the same age as him, in their late thirties. "These are my business partners. We've known each other since we were kids and started our business when we were only twenty…"

"Sorry," Phina cut in, "what business are you in?"

"Telecoms. Didn't father tell you? He's always bragging about his children, so I assumed you knew."

"Oh, he mentioned that. Hello," Phina said to the two men."

"Hi," they responded in unison and took turns shaking her hand.

"I and these two fellows," Rashid said, patting his friend's backs one after the other, "are the founders of Vano Communications."

"Is that so?" Phina raised her brows in admiration. She took another look at the two men in front of her. Both were unassuming and handsome in their own right. "You guys have really broken boundaries with your invention of the Vano marketing software. When I heard the company behind it was indigenous, I was impressed."

The three men chuckled. "Thank you," Rashid said.

"What new inventions are you guys working on these days?"

"We have a hospital app that will change the face of hospital administration, in the works," the friend in the blue shirt responded.

"Amazing! I know someone that'll be really interested in your app," Phina said with a slight nod.

"Let me introduce you to the rest of the party before they think I'm hogging you," Rashid said, interrupting their conversation.

"By all means, it was nice meeting you guys," Phina said before she got whisked off again by Rashid.

-

The party continued for hours with guests making their best effort to have a chat with Phina. She took several photographs and exchanged business cards with almost everyone in the room. The guests were treated to a variety of soup and rice dishes as well as pounded yam and a range of delicious desserts that tickled the most delicate of senses. Phina was forced to watch her portions, but she didn't hesitate to help herself to the free-flowing champagne and the abundance of testosterone that surrounded her. After meals were served and all the guests had eaten, the floor was set for dancing. Sade was playing softly in the background when Rashid led Phina to the terrace where a good portion of the party had moved.

"When father told me you were coming, I cleared my schedule to make sure I could be here for this one in a lifetime opportunity. You are the most beautiful thing I've ever set my eyes on," Rashid said as they settled into a corner.

Phina laughed hysterically.

"I'm being serious," Rashid continued, looking down at her with a wide smile on his face.

"I know you are. Sorry, I laughed so much. It's just that this is not the first time I've heard that."

"Damn!" he swore. "And I thought I had the perfect pickup line."

"Oh. Were you trying to pick me up?" she teased.

"Of course. Why not? Have you looked at yourself in the mirror? Any man with blood in his veins would want to pick you up."

Phina rolled her eyes before laughing again. This time around, it was a sensuous laughter, one she could only ever emit after her senses had been dulled sufficiently with champagne.

"Stop the flattering," she mumbled afterwards. "It's giving me a headache."

"Ever think of moving back to Nigeria?"

"Definitely. I'd like to move back with my daughter at some point. She needs to learn about our culture. I try to teach her, but there's no better way than living it."

"Yeah. Father told me you had a four-year-old..."

"Six. She turned six in July."

"Wow. How are you coping with raising her on your own?"

"She's a great kid, and she doesn't give much trouble. How about you? Any kids?"

"Nope," he responded, shaking his head. "Never been married."

"Why? You've never met anyone that's good enough for you?"

"Actually I have. I just met her tonight." His eyes were staring into hers with so much intensity. As they spoke, the physical distance between the two of them slowly disappeared leaving only a little over an inch to work with.

Phina smiled to disarm him.

"Interesting... Who?" she asked, slanting her head to the right.

He looked into her eyes for five whole seconds before wrapping his hand around her waist while managing to maintain the miniature distance that was left between them. Phina saw something in his eyes that made it difficult to control the rhythm of her heartbeat. He looked down to the cleavage created by her red V-necked dress. The dress hugged her tightly and showcased her hour-glass figure despite the dimness of the lighting on the terrace. She felt the desire exuding from his entire being and cleared her throat to break the uncomfortable silence.

"I hope you're not referring to me," she said in a whisper.

"Isn't it obvious?" he responded, backing off a little to create more space between them before taking her hands. "If you're free, I'd like to take you to dinner tomorrow night."

"I'll have to check my schedule."

"Do that and let me know."

"And if tomorrow doesn't work, we can try a different time," Phina suggested.

They were interrupted by Chief's voice over a microphone asking everyone to gather for a toast. The guests converged from all corners – the terrace, the adjoining living rooms, and the staircase to meet in the center of the grand living room. Chief cleared his throat and made a short speech after which he toasted to Phina and everyone of the guests that had come to welcome her. After the toast, the D.J continued to play soft music.

Phina danced to 'Sweetest Taboo' with Rashid. His body was warm and firm as he enveloped her in his arms. There was something strange about their two bodies melded together on the dance floor. She felt safe and protected for the first time in a whole year. This man, whom she'd just met, had the strangest effect on her. She became convinced it wasn't the champagne alone. When the track was over, she excused herself to go to the washroom. After she locked the door behind her, she gazed at herself in the mirror. Her makeup was still intact, but she saw something else – joy. It radiated from her pores and shone in her eyes, which had a twinkle once again. There were bags underneath them from the many sleepless nights she'd spent worrying, but the twinkle overshadowed them now. Exhaling deeply, she said, "Goodness gracious! What is going on with me?" She stared at herself for a few more minutes before reapplying her lipstick and stepping out the door.

Phina left the party shortly after but not before thanking her hosts. It was past midnight and Rashid accompanied her to the limousine and kissed her hand before he let her in. She wound down her window after strapping her seatbelt.

"I'll call you tomorrow to confirm dinner," she said.

"I'd love that. Have a wonderful night."

As Phina's car approached the exit, the two gatemen sprang to their feet and positioned themselves to open the gate.

"Goodnight ma," they said in unison, waving frantically at her.

"Goodnight," Phina said and chuckled to herself.

-

Phina awoke with the sun piercing her eyes and white sheets tangled around her naked frame. She had been too tired when she returned to her suite the night before that she jumped right into bed after peeling off her clothes. Adeyinka, her assistant was arriving in only a few minutes to whisk her off to the lineup of meetings for the day, so she hurried to take a bath and get dressed before she arrived. With only two weeks to spend in Nigeria and two months' worth of work to accomplish in that time, she had no time to waste.

Adeyinka arrived on time. She knocked on the door and waited for Phina to answer. Within a few minutes, Phina, fresh out of the shower with a towel wrapped around her, opened the door.

"Come in," she said, rushing back into the bedroom to put on some clothes. "How have you been, Ade? It's been a long time." Phina talked loudly so Adeyinka could hear her from the living room.

"I'm doing fine. Welcome to *Lasgidi*. How are you finding it so far?"

"Lagos is still as spectacular as ever. Nothing beats that oceanic smell that hits your nasal passage as soon as you approach the Island."

"How is business in London?"

"I thank God. I was out till late last night at Chief's. That's why you found me in this state."

"I thought as much because I was knocking for a while. How was the party?"

"Interesting," Phina said as she stepped out in a fitted, navy, midi skirt with a silk top in a matching color and a camel-colored belt that complemented her shoe and handbag. Her hair was pulled into a tight ponytail that accentuated her face and created a doe-eyed look.

"That was fast," Adeyinka muttered.

"Sorry I didn't welcome you properly when you first came in. I was undressed."

"No problem. Our first meeting is at the Vicko Plaza. We're meeting with their MD to discuss taking one of their store rentals."

"Please remind me. How large are the available spaces?"

"Some are two thousand square feet. One is four thousand square feet."

"Let's try to secure the four thousand one. It will be impossible for us to cram all our wares into two thousand square feet."

"That's okay. I assumed that's what you'd prefer, so I asked them to keep that one for sure. You'll make the final decision after you see it. After the plaza, we'll head to the orphanage."

"Will it be possible for me to hold that one here at the hotel, later in the day?" Phina interjected. "That way I can cover more ground and have a minute to take a break."

Adeyinka hummed, looking in the direction of the ceiling as though urging an answer to drop from it. "I had thought of that, but I also reckoned you might want to meet the proprietors in their surroundings just to see how they're keeping the place. That way you can kill two birds with one stone – tour the premises and meet the officials."

"That's a good idea. Well done Ade. I just remembered that I might be meeting Rashid this evening. It's not confirmed yet."

"Which Rashid? Gambo?" Adeyinka asked in a hushed tone.

"Yes. Chief's son. I met him last night. He's quite a charming gentleman."

"And Africa's most eligible bachelor," Adeyinka chirped and batted her eyes.

"How is that of any concern to me?" Phina asked, giggling softly. "I hardly know the guy. I'm just meeting him because I'm in business with his father. It's not a date if that's what you're thinking," she said sardonically.

"Well, you're unattached so…"

"So what?" Phina chuckled.

"Never mind. Let's go. We can't afford to be late for this meeting."

-

The meeting at the plaza was with its owner – a former senator that used the loot from his position – funds stolen from government coffers – to build a state-of-the-art shopping plaza in Victoria Island. His second Senate run had been a disastrous one but luckily for him, he had amassed enough wealth for himself and generations to come. The plaza was complete with a small amusement park and movie theater, making it a tourist attraction and a favorite hangout for the locals. He welcomed Phina with zeal, answered all her questions and promised she wouldn't find a better location for her store in Lagos. Phina believed him. He had the capital to build the edifice, a feat that could only be accomplished with the kind of funds at his disposal. At the end of what Phina considered a successful meeting, both parties agreed to have their lawyers meet and sign the required contracts as soon as the paperwork was sorted out.

During the long drive to Badagry to visit the orphanage, Phina thought about her encounter with Rashid the night before. "Oh, my!" she said aloud. "I was supposed to call Rashid to confirm if I could have dinner with him tonight."

"You can call him when you get back to the hotel. Will it be too late?" Adeyinka asked.

"No," Phina responded.

When they arrived at the orphanage, they were provided with a tour of the premises by the Head Proprietor, who also provided Phina with a breakdown of their achievements so far. The tour gave Phina the assurance that the funds she frequently sent to the establishment were used for the right purposes.

-

By five o'clock, after a couple more meetings on the mainland, Phina headed back to her hotel. She had decided to meet Rashid for dinner that night. With only a few days to spend in Lagos, she didn't want to miss the opportunity of getting to know him better. She dialed his number and was made to wait a few minutes by the assistant who then passed her to his special assistant. By the time Rashid got on the phone, Phina was annoyed and prepared to hang up.

"I have been expecting your call all day?" Rashid said in a warm tone that made Phina immediately let go of her annoyance.

Her heart skipped a beat upon hearing his voice.

"I couldn't call earlier. It was a really busy day. You know how it is with the Lagos traffic."

"I was incredibly busy as well," he said. "It's fascinating how slowly things run in this country. Stuff that would typically take me one day to complete in the UK takes about five days here. There's just too much bureaucracy. Everyone acts like a big man."

Phina rolled her eyes and was glad he couldn't see the irritation on her face. She wanted to tell him that his phone protocol was every bit a reflection of the '*big manism*' he complained about. Having his phone passed from assistant to assistant before she could speak with him was quite frustrating, but she dared not tell him that. Instead, she said, "I completely agree with you."

"Anyway," Rashid responded with a sigh. "There's a new restaurant in Ikoyi that I'll like us to try out. It's called Nubu. What do you think?"

"Sure. Why not?" Phina said in a high-pitched tone.

"Great! I'll pick you around eight. That gives me time to finish my work here."

"Eight's fine."

-

Right after she hung up the phone, Phina looked through her belongings for the perfect dinner outfit. After trying on five different items, she settled for a mid-length, off-white, fitted skirt that accentuated her hips and a fitted navy-blue top. She accessorized with gold stud earrings and a necklace with a cross pendant. The cross rested in between the curves of her breasts while her luscious hair cascaded down her shoulders. A glance at her image in the mirror produced a smile on her face. She was pleased with her creation – a perfect balance between being carefully dressed and yet not having tried too hard.

At eight o'clock on the dot, she heard a rap on her door. Rashid smiled and nodded when he saw her.

"I thought you looked stunning the night we met but now you look so delectable." His eyes devoured her and he resisted the urge to scoop her up in his arms and kiss her passionately.

Phina surveyed his Adonis-like looks. He looked striking in white linen pants and a fitted blue golf shirt that highlighted his perfectly toned shoulders and biceps. The tightness of his abdominal muscles and the way the shirt hugged him, took her breath away. To mask her intense admiration, she faked a chuckle and muttered, "Identical outfits."

"Telepathy. That's it," he said, waving his hands in the air. "Our date is heading off to a good start already."

Phina smiled as she grabbed her purse from the table.

"Let's go," she said before shutting the door behind her.

18

IN SHINING ARMOR

RASHID'S chauffeur drove to the front in the black SUV the moment he sighted them coming out of the revolving doors. As they drove out of the hotel, on their way to the Nubu eatery, they were immediately greeted with a stunning view of Adigun Arts Center and the intriguing signs of life on the spectacular tourist attraction. They chatted like old friends while music from the FM radio blasted through the car speakers as it cruised into the dense Lagos traffic.

"Hope you had fun at the party last night," Rashid said, turning to face her.

It was hard to hear him over the loud music so she cupped her right ear with her hand and bent towards him.

"Turn that thing down," Rashid ordered the driver, before repeating to Phina. "Did you have fun yesterday?"

"I did. Thank you. Your dad is such an excellent host."

"He'll be flattered if he hears that. How is Lagos treating you so far?"

"Oh. I'm still trying to get my bearings. Having not been around in three years, it's taking me a little while. Things change so fast in this city."

"How long will you be staying?"

"Two weeks. I'll be traveling to Portharcourt for a few days though."

"I don't know what you plan to accomplish, but two weeks is too short."

"I know," Phina shrugged. "But I have no choice. I can't stay longer. Running a business and a family can be extremely demanding."

"I can only imagine... I mean, I can't imagine," he corrected himself. "Business and the demands of the extended family are tough enough as it is. When you add a six-year-old to the mix, that's one area I can't claim to have experience in. How do you handle it though?"

Phina paused for a second before responding.

"Well, I can't take all the credit because my nannies and chauffeurs pick up most of the slack. I have absolutely nothing to complain about."

As she spoke, Rashid turned a fraction to look at her. She looked up and met his gaze. A sensuous smile spread across his face and remained. Phina sighed as a familiar feeling crept up in her stomach. She felt as though he was undressing her with his eyes. The music from the radio drowned the sound of her heartbeat. She couldn't remember the last time she felt that nervous. To her relief, the driver pulled to a stop in front of the restaurant before she could fall apart.

"I'll get the door for you," Rashid said, pulling his door latch and stepping out of the car.

A second later, he held the door open for Phina with one hand, and with the other took her right hand.

"Thank you," Phina whispered. "This is beautiful," she said, looking at the surroundings of the eatery. The tall palm trees that lined the pathways were wrapped with luminescent lights, and a row of beautifully trimmed hedges flanked an exterior lounge that overlooked the ocean. Her mouth watered when she caught a whiff of the barbecue roasting on an open fire at the north end of the grounds.

-

"Hi," a young curvaceous, dark-skinned beauty with enviable hips and a bright smile said, as soon as they were seated indoors. "Can I take your order?"

"A glass of Bailey's for the lady," Rashid responded, smiling at the waitress who slowly tucked her hair behind her ears. "And a beer for me," he said, returning his gaze to Phina.

"I'll be right back," the waitress responded.

She returned minutes later and set a small ceramic bowl filled with roasted groundnuts on the center of the table and passed hot towels with prongs from a silver bowl to them. Shortly after, a different waiter brought their drinks and took their meal orders.

"Great choice; by the way, Bailey's is one of my favorite drinks," Phina said after the waiter left their table. "Do you always order for ladies?"

Rashid smiled and shook his head, averting his eyes a little. "No, I just thought you wouldn't mind."

"Am I making you blush?" Phina asked with a chuckle, the whole time staring at his face.

"Not a chance," he countered, sitting upright and staring back at her. "If you must know, you're one-of-a-kind. That's why I ordered for you."

It was Phina's turn to blush and look away. She felt naked as his eyes pierced through her, sharp as a knife; all traces of bashfulness diminished. Before she could decide what to say to him, he continued, "You should relax and let me take care of you."

"Okay. My knight in shining armor," she said, giggling softly.

-

They talked throughout their meal of *jollof rice*, fried soft *dodo*, salad and peppered snails. Phina was unabashed to tell Rashid how Patrick's death over a year ago had turned her life upside down – a life that only really started after she met him. She also told him how she had been implicated in his death and how by a stroke of luck she had managed to divert the attention of the police to enable them to focus on finding the real killer.

Rashid listened with keen interest and shook his head in wonder.

"The whole incident must have been traumatic for you," he said. "Father told me about you and Patrick. It sounded like you were very much in love."

Phina nodded once.

"We were. But since his passing, I haven't felt the bond I had with him when he was alive. I thought I'd be able to feel his presence around me but with everything I've been through, who knows why that hasn't happened." She shrugged her shoulders before concluding, "My senses must have completely numbed."

"It will feel normal, eventually. Time works wonders. How would you rate dinner?"

"Fantastic," Phina responded, happy for the change of topic. "I'd love to visit this restaurant again before I leave."

"You liked it that much? There are still tons of places we could visit."

"Yes," she said, nodding. "I'll be back here if I need a good meal. I see no point in reinventing the wheel. Do you?"

"Interesting," Rashid agreed, nodding slowly.

After the driver pulled up in front of Phina's hotel, Rashid stepped out of the car and gave her a quick hug.

"I'll call you tomorrow," he said after he released her. "We could go dancing at this new club in Victoria Island."

"I'm so sorry. I'm actually going clubbing with my sister and my friends tomorrow night," Phina said with an apologetic look. "They'll never forgive me if I ditch them."

"Ok. What about lunch?"

"I wish I could but I'll be working during lunch. I have two meetings to power through and I'll be traveling to Portharcourt the following day, which rules out next-tomorrow too. We can go dancing when I come back," she said half questioningly. "I'll be spending only two days in PH."

"Here's a better idea. I could take you somewhere for the weekend when you return."

Phina looked up and her eyes met his piercing gaze. Her heart fluttered when she noticed the somber look on his handsome face. She smiled and immediately returned her gaze to the path in front of her as so many thoughts, including the complicated status of her past relationships raced through her mind. Spending a night with Rashid, let alone, a weekend would turn her into his entrée. The chemistry between them was intense. A weekend with him would present a problem and she knew that with absolute certainty.

"That could be a problem," she stated, interrupting her own reverie.

"Why?" Rashid asked with both hands in mid-air. "No strings attached, and I promise you'll love every minute of it."

"No strings? Okay, I'll let you know as soon as possible if I can make it."

"It's an exclusive resort. I thought you might like to see the other side of Lagos."

"Let me think about it. Okay?"

-

Phina met Adeyinka, Ezinne, her childhood friend, Bolanle, and a couple of their friends at the Veer nightclub in Ikoyi at eleven o'clock the next day. The dance floor was jammed, causing patrons to bump and grind against one another. Phina had been desperate to escape the hustle and bustle of her work day for hours, so when she was led to the VIP section, she settled in as fast as she could, ordered some champagne and watched the couples on the dance floor. The women were the most fun to watch. Phina was amused by how their butts did all the dancing, causing the men to drool and hyperventilate as they watched their rounded behinds.

The waitresses were decked in matching black miniskirts with fitted shirts and thigh-high boots. Phina wondered why they wore boots in thirty-degree weather even though the temperature inside the club was much cooler. Bolanle took the floor and beckoned to Phina with both hands to join her, but she politely declined. As soon as the music from the live band changed from afrobeat to afrofunk, Phina lost her inhibitions and joined her on the dance floor. They swayed their hips from side to side but were soon separated by two gentlemen who held their waists from behind. Phina's bodyguard approached to disperse the men but Phina waved to gesture her disapproval.

The ladies danced until they could barely feel their legs. By the time Phina got to her hotel room, it was almost three o'clock in the morning. She was happy she didn't need to wake up early to catch a flight since her trip to Portharcourt was by road. Before she slept, she thought of Rashid. She had missed him at the club and regretted not inviting him to join her. Then again, she was glad she hadn't as it was necessary for her to maintain some distance since there was no telling what their instant attraction could lead to. She wasn't ready to jump into any new relationship; she was confused about the state of her life at the moment.

–

Phina spent most of her time in Portharcourt taking walks around her parent's palatial compound and enjoying the beautiful weather. Ezinne didn't join her on the trip as her busy life in Lagos couldn't allow her. With so much to accomplish in Nigeria before she returned to London, she counted the days until her departure. Finding Patrick's killer and clearing her name for good remained her top priority.

In the two days she spent in Portharcourt, her mother and aunt constantly reminded her that her biological clock was ticking. On the second day, having undergone immense pressure from their excessive badgering, she locked herself in her room and refused to speak to either one of them until they calmed.

To her surprise, her mother came to her door and banged on it several times. "Come out of there," she shrieked. "You're not too big to listen to your mother."

Phina knew her mother too well. If she didn't respond and step out of the room at that moment, all hell would break loose and she didn't want to be held responsible for that, so she opened her door slowly and came out smiling.

"Mom, I don't understand why one child is not enough for you," Phina said as respectfully as she could muster.

"One child is not enough *noow...*" her mother said with both hands folded over her chest.

Phina responded with equal fervor. "Babies don't grow on trees you know, Mother?"

"You need to marry as soon as possible so you can provide me with a second grandchild – a male one if possible."

Phina decided to ignore her allusion that not only was she required to manufacture a baby; she was also expected to control its gender. "Anyway, I met Chief's son, Rashid," she said off-handedly after they resumed their seats in the living room.

Her mother hummed in response.

"Is that all? Won't you say something?"

"How is Nduka doing?" she responded, pointing her chin downwards and easing back slowly in her chair.

"Nduka is in London. Rashid and I sort of like each other. Honestly, I'm not sure what we're doing."

"You're not sure what you're doing?" her mother asked, wide-eyed. "You should be thinking about settling down with a successful Igbo boy like Nduka. You went too far with your first marriage. You should not make the same mistake again."

Phina had not told her mother about Nduka's past and with her mother's tendency to overreact, she was sure she would demand she dump him and move in with Chief Gambo's son right away.

"Who's talking about marriage?" Phina blurted, hoping that would change the trajectory of their conversation.

"Are you not?" Her mother stared at her with a surprised look on her face.

"No, Ma. My main concern right now is to clear my name. As long as Patrick's killer is still out there, everyone will keep wondering if I did it.

"I thought you'd been cleared," Phina's aunt stated after she got tired of sitting silently. She had been watching their theatrics for almost an hour.

"Yes, but for a while now, I've been feeling like someone is following me around. Some man I suspect to be a private investigator called me to request an interview and when I insisted he reveal who he was working for, he hung up right away."

"What rubbish?" Phina's Mother declared. "You need to keep fighting so these people won't make you their target." She hissed before snapping her fingers in derision.

"I'm fighting very hard. I even hired a PI to do some digging for me. No one – not even my lawyer – knows this."

"And you should keep it that way. I don't feel too good about someone following you around. I don't."

She looked visibly sick.

–

Rashid was waiting at Phina's hotel when she returned from Portharcourt to whisk her off to a private beach resort. He had managed to convince her that time away, would provide her with the rest and relaxation she needed before she returned to London. In her room, she unpacked the clothes she took to Portharcourt and then packed for an overnight stay. She had agreed to spend the night and watch as the sun sank beneath the horizon.

From the hotel, they drove to the harbor and climbed aboard his luxury yacht. They cruised for forty minutes as their dinner of pasta in a creamy white wine sauce was served by all white-uniformed waiters. While they drank from tall champagne glasses Rashid provided the entertainment by regaling Phina with creepy tales of the Denge people on whose land the resort was situated. Phina had told him outright that she didn't believe the tales as they sounded ridiculous. Rashid had insisted the stories were true and the diligence with which he approached the rest of it left her no choice but to believe him.

"Enough!" Phina pleaded as Rashid was about to tell her yet another tale while she clung to his sides for fear that the cannibals from his last story would spring out of the ocean and attack their yacht. "No more stories please," she said, shivering.

Rashid wrapped his arms around her. "You're scared?"

"Yes, I definitely am. Didn't anything fun and glamorous happen to these people?"

"Of course. This was hundreds of years ago. Long before Christianity came. Rumor had it that the first set of Christian missionaries were sacrificed by the Denge people and driven into the ocean on rafts to pacify the sea gods."

Phina covered her ears with both hands. Rashid laughed mischievously. He was satisfied he had provided her with enough history to get her excited about their date that evening. Just as they were finishing dinner, their yacht pulled to a slow stop at the corner of the pier. Four hosts with bristling muscles, wearing batique pants, and with white and red chalk painted on their faces helped Phina alight. Seconds later Rashid landed and lifted her with one hand. With the other hand, he dispersed the hosts as they laughed at his heroics. It was long past sunset, but the entire resort was lit for miles on end with beautiful street lights in varying colors.

As soon as they got off the pier, Rashid gently placed her on the sand and guided her to the beach car that was waiting to drive them to their accommodation. They rode for a little over five minutes past a row of coconut trees that created a pathway which now culminated into the beautiful entrance of a large duplex on a secluded part of the beach.

"This is huge," Phina cried when she entered the building.

"It's a guest house. I sometimes rent it out for parties or weekend getaways. Not many people know about it and we like it that way."

"Well, I'm happy you shared it with me. It's the perfect getaway," she said with a smile.

"Wait till I show you all I have planned for tomorrow. Tonight, we should just relax and maybe go for a drink at the pub. A live band plays there every evening."

"I'd love that."

-

Phina took a shower and changed into a short, flared, flowery dress that accentuated her figure and made her look like a breath of fresh air. She and Rashid set out for the pub shortly after and sat on the deck overlooking the ocean and the starlit night. At Phina's request, Rashid tried a *shandy* for the first time and loved it. With their drinks on their hand, they joined the other guests and danced as the soft ocean breeze blew across their faces. When the music changed to a soft tune, they placed their drinks on the table and held each other in a warm embrace as they moved from side to side, with their cheeks pressed together.

"I like you," Rashid whispered into Phina's ear.

Phina hummed in response, closing her eyes briefly and sighing deeply.

"You haven't mentioned your trip to Portharcourt even once. I hope it went well."

"Oh. Sorry about that. It was okay…"

"Just okay? Did you miss me?"

"Umm… let me think…" She stopped mid-sentence and laughed hysterically as Rashid tickled her sides.

"So did you miss me?" he asked again.

"I wish I found the time to miss you," Phina admitted. "But I was mostly preoccupied with the situation at home."

"What situation?"

"You know…" She stopped and shrugged her shoulders.

Rashid took her hand, and they returned to their seat.

"Something is bothering you."

"Yeah. The police have still not found Patrick's killer. Even though I'm no longer officially a suspect, life is still not easy for me as some people still think I'm guilty. Don't you wonder if I did what I was once accused of? Aren't you afraid I could be a murderer?" she asked, staring intently at him.

"I know you're innocent," Rashid responded with a wide grin.

"How do you know? They thought I had a strong motive and even though I was in Florence that night, I still had the opportunity. Besides, no one could verify my alibi since I was alone in my hotel room."

"I just know you couldn't do a thing like that."

"Well, that's very trusting of you," Phina stuttered. "Thank you."

"Is there anything else you'd like me to address?" he asked, peering into her eyes.

"No," she whispered, a bit embarrassed for always pouring her heart out so easily to him.

"Good. Then let's get out of here. We'll talk some more when we get to the house."

Phina felt certain that Rashid would be less interested in her life story now they'd shared a few drinks and danced so closely with their bodies rubbing against each other. But, when they arrived in their lodgings, she discovered that she had been too presumptuous as he turned out to be a complete gentleman. After they shared a bottle of wine and a plate of desserts in the parlor, he led her to a plush room fit for a princess, kissed her forehead and wished her goodnight.

The following day, after a fun and exciting time, spent lounging around, playing beach volleyball, and riding horses with a half-dozen of his friends that sneaked into the resort very early in the morning, they boarded the yacht and headed back to the city.

—

Phina visited Chief Gambo her last night in Lagos, not only to bid him farewell and thank him for being a great host but to discuss certain aspects of their business. She had picked him as a partner because he had been a good friend of her father's, was dependable, and showed particular interest in her.

"You and Rashid will make a great match," Chief said in a hoarse voice. "I've never seen two people more perfect for each other than the two of you."

Phina was about to burst into laughter when she spotted the sincerity in his facial expression. Not only did he not seem amused, from his posture, she could tell he was expecting a befitting response from her.

"Look," he continued, crouching forward in his chair, "Rashid is handsome, intelligent, and rich and… I don't know about love but he seems to like you very much. That's a good place to start. Don't you see?"

Phina giggled. "I like him too." She gave Chief Gambo a hesitant smile.

"So what are you waiting for?" He eased back and waited for her to respond.

"You're serious sir?"

Chief Gambo pressed his chin forward and peered at her through his glasses. "Of course, I'm serious. I wouldn't joke about a thing like this."

"I don't know what to say," Phina sighed. "I honestly haven't considered dating anyone seriously since…" She stopped mid-sentence when she realized she hadn't been completely honest. Although her relationship with Nduka had been fraught with challenges, he had still technically been her boyfriend.

"That's okay. You'll heal sufficiently from that. You can't mourn Patrick forever. Soon men will be seeking your hand in marriage, and you'll have to move on. I won't be surprised if they aren't already. You've got to move on," he said with finality.

"No problem. Everyone will know when I'm ready," Phina responded, happy she didn't need to bring up Nduka and disappoint Chief.

Soon, Rashid arrived at his father's house. He knew Phina was meeting with him that evening and had agreed to meet her there.

"It's so nice out. Let's move this discussion to the terrace," Rashid requested, after exchanging pleasantries.

"I have been itching to, but your Dad is holding me hostage in here," Phina said with a grin.

Chief Gambo laughed and got up from his seat.

"You're free to go with him. Enjoy the natural breeze. Air-conditioning can feel stuffy at times. I'll go to bed now. Have a safe flight tomorrow, my dear."

"Thank you, sir."

Rashid took Phina's hand and helped her rise from her seat. He walked towards the door leading to the terrace and unlatched it before stepping out with her. Once out, he raised his head to the sky and took in a breath of fresh air.

"What a difference the natural air makes."

Phina nodded and looked into the horizon. She heard a squeaking sound in the bushes. "Did you hear that?" she said, sounding a bit scared.

"It's the aviary. Look," he said, pointing in the distance. "Can you see the building on the other side of the compound with the lights, the one in the shape of a pyramid? That's where my father keeps his collection of exotic birds."

"Can we see the birds?" Phina said excitedly.

"I can't believe you were scared a few minutes ago and now you want to abandon everything and go off in that direction. It's too late in the day. Maybe when next you come."

Other than the sound of the birds in the distance, there was complete silence. Phina stared into the beautiful evening sky as velvet clouds sifted across the surface of the moon.

"Don't stare too long. You'll strain your neck," she heard Rashid say as he pulled her down to sit on his lap. He placed his hand around her waist, and her eyes darted to the door.

"Am I crushing your knees?" Phina asked with a mischievous look on her face.

"Impossible," he said. "You're light as a feather. Tell me, what were you and father discussing all evening?"

"Business," she lied. They had discussed a little bit of business but for the most part they talked about him.

"Are you sure?"

"What do you suppose we were talking about?"

"Did he tell you I'll be in London in a few weeks?"

"No," Phina responded, shaking her head. "He never mentioned that. It must have slipped his mind."

"Where are you going?" he asked as Phina wriggled on his laps trying to get up. She was anxious someone would come on the terrace and catch her in that position. "Don't worry, no one will bother us." When she calmed, he held her shoulders and gave her a light kiss on the lips. "I'll miss you. I'm so happy we met. You make me feel like a teenager all over again."

"I'll miss you too," Phina sighed. The kiss had sent shockwaves down her spine and her words were merely a whisper. She rose from his laps and rested her hand on the banister. Rashid rose and hugged her tightly from behind creating a feeling of déjà vu in her mind. When she turned to face him, she felt her mouth lock perfectly into his as her entire body dissolved into his tight frame. Her racing heart was the only indication she was still alive, but a look into his eyes revealed an intense, almost frightening expression.

For a moment, Phina thought she had done something to offend him.

"I can't ever let you go," Rashid muttered.

Phina looked away and chuckled. It was then she understood what that look meant – immense and unquenchable desire.

"Stop! You're making me nervous," she pleaded.

"I think we passed that stage five minutes ago." He grabbed her waist and kissed her again.

Phina quivered in his arms, this time returning his kisses with as much passion and intensity as he delivered his. They remained locked in an embrace as he caressed her back, her waist and her hips. She moaned in response and pressed her body against his while running her hands through the muscles of his back.

"Let's go to my place."

"No," Phina responded, shaking her head. "I want it as much as you do, but I have so much to deal with right now, it could only be detrimental."

"When then?" Rashid asked.

Phina could feel his heart pounding heavily against her hand.

"I don't know," she whispered.

–

After the chauffeur pulled up in front of Phina's hotel, she ran straight to her room, took a bath, and patted herself on the back for having acted responsibly. Being able to resist Rashid's overtures while her body yearned desperately for him was enough reason for her to feel triumphant. As soon as she crawled into bed, she heard a knock on her door. Before she could decide whether to climb down and look through the peephole or ignore the knock, she heard, "Phina open. It's me," in a drawn out husky voice.

Phina, heart pounding, juices flowing, snuck out of bed in her black, lace, satin negligee and opened the door. Rashid, rousing, smoldering from head to toe in a kaftan, lifted her and took her mouth hungrily with his as her legs wrapped around him. He positioned her gently on the bed and in one swift motion pulled his kaftan over his head to reveal a six-pack and a thick bulge beneath his white underwear.

Phina, mouth agape, was unable to contain herself, so she sat upright and pulled his shoulders forward. "Take me," she moaned. "Please…"

He obeyed and did as she asked. It was nothing like she'd ever experienced before. After she came, her mind flashed to Nduka, Patrick, and the only guy in all her years in Cambridge that had ever managed to get her into bed. None of them had ever satisfied her the way Rashid had. As she pondered why this time was so different, she reckoned it must just be the chemistry they shared or perhaps because it'd been months since she experienced pleasure.

"Do you mind my staying?" he asked after his heart settled.

"I don't mind."

"Great. I can accompany you to the airport in the morning."

"I'd like that," she answered, still struggling to catch her breath.

19

RUINED ALIBIS

DETECTIVE Sommers pulled out his notepad and surveyed the list of suspects with dissatisfaction. He ticked off Nduka's name and along with it went Phina's. His note entries in order of likelihood were:

Nduka Eze – confirm alibi

Phina Campbell – complicit

Patrick Campbell – suicide

Dummy account owner – blackmail?

The mystery female caller – ?

The mysterious woman at the hotel – last person to see him alive?

No one was above suspicion and the case against Phina and Nduka were not mutually exclusive of each other. Nduka's innocence meant Phina was completely in the clear. Detective Sommers imagined what Phina would have done if she knew he had her on that list for months; she would have fired him on the spot and asked for a refund. His military background trained him to leave no stone unturned. He had told Phina his approach, but he guessed she wouldn't have imagined that she too would also be under his radar. Phina's alibi, although not thoroughly verified, was plausible enough. She had been in Florence that night and even though it was possible for her to have flown to Barcelona and back; it was Nduka's alibi that needed complete and thorough verification since he had been in Barcelona at the time Patrick was murdered. But, since he marked Phina as complicit, clearing Nduka's alibi automatically cleared her. In the two weeks Phina was in Nigeria, in addition to trying to trace the source of the dummy accounts, Detective Sommers focused his energy on Nduka.

The effort paid off as he successfully tracked Nduka's whereabouts at the time of Patrick's murder. He discovered that Nduka's reluctance to be upfront with his whereabouts the night Patrick was murdered had little to do with his guilt over the dastardly crime but rather with his need to conceal the nature of his dealings at the time. The FBI confirmed to have in their possession surveillance tapes that placed Nduka at a different location from the scene of the crime. He had been in secretive closed-door meetings with four senior members of a notorious drug cartel. The same group he'd been associating with in America. Revealing his exact location would have provided him a foolproof alibi. But it would have exposed his associates with whom he had been discretely meeting at the same location for months. Their clandestine activities in Barcelona were exposed by the FBI who prevented a successful operation by the largest drug syndicate in history. Unknown to Nduka, he had remained under surveillance after he left the United States. Even though this finding gave his legal trouble an international dimension, it completely absolved him of any involvement in Patrick's murder.

Phina was unable to utter a word when Detective Sommers first reviewed his findings with her. She recollected her thoughts for a few moments before muttering, "No wonder, I didn't get a single call from him the week Patrick was murdered. Where is he now?" she asked.

"Out on bail, but under federal protection. He's been given two choices – to testify against the cartel and be allowed to stay in the UK or be deported to America where he would be tried. Either way, he will never be allowed to practice medicine in any country in the world."

"So, his career is doomed?" Phina asked.

"That would be the least of his problems. He'll be lucky if he doesn't end up rotting in jail. Will you be okay?"

"I'll be fine," Phina said, unsure of herself. "What about the share issue? Any new information about who they were transferred to?"

"I've been working hard to find out," Detective Sommers said, knowing it was far from the truth since he had spent most of the entire two weeks Phina was in Nigeria searching for clues on Nduka. Now that Nduka and Phina's involvement had been cleared without reasonable doubt, he thought he could relax and focus on the other suspects. Patrick remained on the list. The possibility that he committed suicide was still a plausible explanation to Detective Sommers. To validate the suicide theory, he needed to work closely with his client to discover the truth.

"I'd like to discuss the other possibilities in this case."

He quickly created a new list without Phina and Nduka's name and handed it to her. "We're still looking for any leads on these suspects and in this order of priority."

Phina looked at the list and shook her head.

"Patrick didn't commit suicide. I'm certain of that so you might as well strike him off your list."

Detective Sommers slanted his head. "I wouldn't rule it out completely. There could always be a possibility. What if we just keep an open mind about it while we continue to follow other leads?"

"Okay, but of top priority right now is finding the owners of those dummy accounts. They reek of blackmail. Don't you think? I won't feel safe until I know who may have been blackmailing Patrick and for what reason."

"I agree."

Detective Sommers thought Phina made an excellent point, but he also considered the other suspects on the list every bit as important as the dummy account owner. It was also possible that they were all connected, and could be one and the same person.

That same summer of eighty-four which saw the appointment of Blake Caldwell to the Upper House, also saw Nduka's legal situation deteriorate. Phina reviewed the case against him and discovered that it was worse than Detective Sommers knew or had let on. Whichever option Nduka chose – to expose his accomplices or be repatriated to the United States, he was required to serve some jail term. With Blake's position in the house, Phina had hoped he could help Nduka. When she spoke to him, he confirmed that meddling with a federal case could jeopardize his appointment. Instead, he solicited the help of Lord Macpherson, who had remained a close friend of both him and Phina, and asked him to leverage his connections in government. With his help, Nduka was able to avoid prosecution after several weeks of negotiation with federal agents but lost his medical license in the UK and was forced to move to Nigeria.

Two days before Nduka was scheduled to leave, he pleaded with Phina over the phone to consider his marriage proposal. He swore he would change and get things back to the way they were.

"That's not possible," Phina responded kindly even though she was stunned by his request.

"I completely understand, but promise this won't change anything between us."

"If by anything, you mean friendship, sure, but I can't promise anything else. You let me down with your lies and secrets. You destroyed any chance we had to be together yet you don't have the decency to apologize for your role in the matter. How could you repeat the same mistake over and over again?"

"I'm sorry," Nduka said after a long pause. "I promise it will never happen again."

"I'm curious, what will you do without a license?"

"I'll be fine."

"Okay. I'm sure you have enough money stored up to last a lifetime. Did you even ever practice medicine?" Phina asked in an exasperated tone.

"Hey! Stop. Are you going to consider my request? I can give you heaven on earth. You can move with me to Nigeria and we'll find people to run your business while you're away. Brigitte will be well taken care of. I'll love her like my own. I already do."

"Are we talking about your ill-gotten wealth?" Phina scoffed, unable to maintain a kind tone any longer.

"It's practically legitimate," Nduka countered and tried to educate her on the details of his dealings with the cartel. "We weren't hurting anyone."

"Really?" Disgust was written all over her voice.

Phina marveled at Nduka's nonchalance regarding the harm his actions had done not only to their relationship but to his future prospects. She wasn't surprised he thought she could just pack her bags and follow him to the ends of the earth. The fact that she had forgiven him in the past and remained friends, made him feel that the option of forgiveness would always be available to him. This time around, she was utterly disappointed in him. It was not entirely a loss because Nduka had made things easy for her now that a new love interest occupied her dreams and waking thoughts. He had paved the way for her to pursue her relationship with Rashid without feelings of remorse.

-

Blake's appointment had put him in the upper echelon of society. With his new position, he began to have increased demands on his time even though he always made effort to see Phina every once in a while. She was grateful that he had helped Nduka without resorting to an "I told you so," since he'd warned her severally about him. "He is a ticking time bomb," he had said once, and she had pretended not to hear him. To show her appreciation, she hosted a dinner in his honor at a restaurant in the trendy Park Lane neighborhood which got rumors swirling that they were an item. In the past, she would have brushed off this strange new development as she'd found herself in similar situations with almost every successful man she'd ever taken a photograph with. Now, she was concerned that this piece of news could put her new romance with Rashid on a delicate balance and it was the last thing she wanted.

-

At Ophinas, the management team had underestimated the rigorous process required of a company listed on a public exchange. As they prepared for the upcoming quarter, they found a whole new set of compliance requirements needed to ensure 'investor confidence'. There was also talk about succession. Phina had thought she never needed to worry about such issues as she had built the company from the ground up with the help of her partners. She imagined that when she became incapacitated and unable to handle the decision making for Ophinas, Brigitte could take over the reins from her. In the new regime, that type of thinking was not enough. The board requested that she create a succession plan that was robust enough to account for every aspect of her business should anything happen to her or any of her principal officers. She found the request sinister and irritating but had to succumb as that was what she signed up for when she decided to list the company on a public exchange.

The team sent out an emergency RFP for the task of creating a robust succession plan. Within a few weeks, after several hours of work by the supply management team, and nine interviews, some of which Phina took part in, they selected the consultancy firm of Sylvern to do the job. With that task completed, Phina felt freer to take care of her other affairs – creating her line at Hartiers, managing her interests in Nigeria, raising Brigitte, finding who killed Patrick, and navigating her ever exhilarating love life.

–

In July, Phina pitched her idea for the home goods business to the board of directors. Lady Thompson was absent, but her male representative was at the meeting. "It will dilute the nature of the brand," he said after listening to the ecstatic nature in which the others received the proposal.

"I have thought of it," Phina responded, "But in reality, it shouldn't because we plan to sustain the level of luxury we have for our existing products. Our goal is to be the sought after place in the future for the most luxurious home goods. The product marketing and all what not will be done separately. We may even decide to create a different brand name for the unit." She paused as she saw nods of approval across the table. "The beauty of adding the home goods," Phina continued, "is that it would attract a new set of customers, like Hartiers in the United States and Simones right here in the UK. These stores are driving customers through their doors with the same strategy."

"Are there statistics that substantiate that?" Lady Thompson's representative asked.

"I don't have any hard proof, but my gut instinct tells me it's the right thing to do. Those instincts have never failed me"

Everyone laughed.

The representative tried to speak but another member of the board interrupted him. "We should proceed without further ado."

"Agreed," a few voices echoed across the table.

Phina felt exhilarated and liberated even though the attack by Lady Thompson's representative caused her to yearn for Patrick's protection. She thought of calling Nduka to vent the moment she left the room, but she recalled that Nduka was no longer an option even though he would have been the perfect sounding board. In retrospect, although they were still friends, she thought it was best she distanced herself from him to make room for her budding relationship with Rashid.

—

Phina was relieved when Rashid called the moment she got back to her office. Delighted by the sound of his voice, she blurted out, "You've really assumed the role of a knight."

"What did I rescue you from this time?" he asked.

"I just had a hectic day trying to convince the board that we should diversify into home goods. Not all of them thought it was a good idea. One of them, Lady Thompson's representative, grilled me to no end."

"So sorry, dear. I wish I was there to protect you like a real knight."

Phina chuckled. "I'm sorry for ranting."

"That's what friends are for, even though I don't consider us to be friends."

"Why not?" Phina asked in a curious tone.

"Aren't we more than friends?" Rashid asked playfully. "How is Blake?"

"What?" Phina was shocked he had asked about Blake. "He's fine. Do you know him?"

"The tabloids had a picture of you and him and the report is that you're dating."

"We're just friends. You shouldn't believe everything you read in the tabloids. I'm sure you know that by now."

"Remember, you're on a mission to clear your name for good," Rashid scolded.

Phina sighed. She wanted to tell him that was no longer an issue, but that would mean bringing in the Nduka connection. Instead, she said, "Noted."

Rashid continued offering his advice like a protective parent. "People will be watching your every move. Someone could try blackmailing you."

"Absolutely. I know I need to be careful. That reminds me. When I came back from Nigeria, I was told by my secretary that a man in plain clothes who sounded like a policeman came around asking for information about me. I didn't take it seriously because I had so much on my plate. In retrospect, I should have probed further."

"Any idea who sent him?"

"I would have thought Patrick's family, but then, their suspicions have been cleared. I suspect this might be the insurance investigator looking for a way to avoid paying the fifty-million-pound settlement Brigitte and I were supposed to receive. They had been there, in the beginning, pretending to be on our side. What I didn't realize is that they'd hoped it was suicide so they wouldn't have to pay."

"That might explain it."

"Whatever it is, I'm fed up. I'll talk to my staff to get more details on what information this person was asking for."

-

Phina knew only one way to fight the harassment for good and get the prying investigator off her back. Her only recourse was to intensify her efforts to find who killed Patrick. When she got home, she called Detective Sommers. He revealed that he had a few leads but would need a couple more days to tie up the loose ends before meeting with her.

Two days later, they met at Hazel House. Detective Sommers arrived with his partner and Phina ushered them into the library. She looked at him with expectation as he slowly pulled a folder out of his suitcase with a sullen look on his face. The usually outspoken detective was unusually silent.

"Have you heard about Ashley?" Detective Sommers finally spoke up.

"No," Phina responded, shaking her head. "Who is she?"

Detective Sommers shook his head slowly. "Ashley is male."

"Should I know him?" Phina asked with a quizzical look on her face.

"I didn't expect you to know him. He's only two years old…"

"Go on…" Phina said, circling her hands to gesture her impatience.

Detective Sommers continued.

"From what we found, Ashley is Patrick's child."

Phina squinted and sat still for a few seconds staring at him in shock.

"I'm sorry, Lady Campbell," Detective Sommers continued. "I wish I wasn't the person to deliver such awful news to you."

"No problem," Phina responded in an icy tone as she struggled to keep her cool. "Who is the mother?"

"That's where the difficulty lies. We don't know yet. The child lives with affluent guardians in Notting Hill. They claim they don't know who the mother is. They had agreed to take care of the child as they have none of their own."

"Do you know for certain that this is Patrick's child?" Phina asked in a surprisingly calm tone.

"The only way to know for certain is through a DNA test and we're working on a strategy to accomplish that."

"How did you come about this new piece of information?"

"Our investigation revealed that Patrick had wired large sums of money to the guardians over a one-year period. When we tracked them down to their home, they confirmed the child was Patrick's. Here is a picture," he said, handing Phina a passport photo.

Phina, who had tried to stay calm until that moment, took a look at the photo and felt the blood drain from her face.

"I can't believe I have to go through this again," she said, shaking her head, her right hand cupping her mouth as tears streamed down her face onto her beige silk pants.

Detective Sommers swallowed hard as the emotion coursed through him while he watched her sob.

"I'm sorry Lady Campbell."

"I know he was distracted in the last couple of years of our marriage but nothing could have prepared me for this."

"Now that you know the truth, do you think Patrick's murder may have been linked to this secret he kept from you?"

Phina ignored him and retreated into a world of her own. "And here I was suspecting everyone around me as his killer," she said. "Little did I know that Patrick was leading a double life right under my nose. I refuse to mourn him any longer," she concluded, punching her fists on the chair and standing abruptly.

"Lady Campbell," Detective Sommers called.

"Yes?" she responded and walked towards the window. "Now," she continued, shaking her head slowly. "His list of potential killers includes every whore that ever existed on this planet earth. I thought he was a great husband but decent husbands don't have adulterous affairs and then hide the child conceived from that affair."

"What a mess," Detective Sommers blurted while his partner took notes. "I'm sorry. I didn't mean to say that aloud."

"He deserves the disrespect. No need to apologize."

"You're right. Our new list of suspects now includes every woman of childbearing age that Patrick ever came in contact with. The risk is still very high that the killer may strike again."

Phina turned to look at him, fear written all over her face.

Detective Sommers continued. "We're trying our best to get to the bottom of this matter. It's very important that you don't tell a soul what we found until we're assured of your safety. This information could turn out to be dangerous in the wrong hands. That is, assuming we're on the right trail."

Phina looked at the photo of the child in the picture again. "This kid looks nothing like Patrick," she said. "Who are these guardians, anyway?"

Detective Sommers glanced at the folder on his hand. "Evans. Paul and Melissa."

Facing both Detective Sommers and his partner squarely, Phina provided them with her final instruction. "Get a DNA test to prove that Patrick actually fathered that child and then find his killer." She stood from her seat and paused for a minute. "Do you suppose we're getting closer to catching her? Could the mother of the baby be the person we've been looking for all along?"

"That's possible but we can't draw any conclusions now as we don't have enough information," Detective Sommers said with a little hesitation.

After Detective Sommers and his partner left, Phina's anguish rose like a thick black cloud. Standing in front of her vanity mirror, she stripped off all her clothes. Then she cried until her tear ducts declined to produce further tears. The surrounding air was stuffy. Certain it would help her ability to breathe, she screamed at the top of her voice before letting out a deep sigh. She dragged herself to the bathroom and filled the tub with hot water before settling gently inside. Her entire life with Patrick flashed through her eyes and she felt as though she was dying. The feeling was worse than when she found the letter that convinced her he was cheating. The relief she felt after she realized the letter was really meant for her, was shattered with this new revelation. From the tub, she crawled into her bed, still wet. The secrecy required to conduct a vital investigation had isolated her, so she could call no one to ease her mind. As a last resort, she said a prayer and almost instantly fell asleep. She was lethargic when she woke up, her heart still heavy when she realized she could no longer recognize her loving husband. Her memory of him had vanished – like a ghost – like Martin.

20

THE VISIT

SATURDAY, exactly eight days after Phina received news about Patrick's secret baby, Rashid arrived in London. Phina had offered to pick him up from the airport, but he had vehemently declined.

"I don't want to inconvenience you," he'd said to her.

"It's no inconvenience," Phina had insisted. "The chauffeur will be driving and I'll usually have some paperwork to look over while I wait."

"No, no. A gentleman never makes a lady wait. Besides a friend will be picking me up," he concluded.

"Ok," Phina agreed, although reluctantly.

After Rashid checked into the Ritz where he planned to spend the entire week he was to be in London, he called Phina.

"Hello," she said when she heard his voice.

"Hi, Sweetheart."

"I can't believe you're just a driving distance away from me. How was your flight?"

"Great. The limousine driver was very courteous."

"I thought your friend was picking you up?"

"Oh, that… I changed my mind. I saw no reason in having him drive all the way from Kent."

"You act so British – so polite," she teased.

"No," he responded shaking his head. "I'm a proper *Naija* man."

"You're welcome to London, *Naija* man."

"Thank you, my darling."

Phina felt a tingle in her core.

"I'm hosting a welcome dinner for you tomorrow."

"Who will be there?"

"Just a few friends. There's Azra, Lady Thompson…"

"Iris Thompson?"

"Yes, do you know her?"

"I know her through father. Will my rival be there?" he said half-jokingly.

"Who?"

"The Statesman."

"Blake? There's nothing going on between us. I sent him an invitation but I'm yet to get an answer. Let's just assume he's coming. Don't worry; he's not a bad guy."

"I'm not worried. Just being protective of what's mine. That's all."

Phina chuckled. "You're really possessive aren't you?" Phina said, secretly excited that he had called her 'mine'. Even though they had been intimate once and their relationship hadn't been fully defined, she found herself thinking about him at all hours of the day and night.

Rashid laughed.

"Any man, who has you and doesn't feel the need to protect what he has, really needs to have his head checked. What time is dinner?"

"Seven."

"I would have loved to see you tonight but I have a couple of meetings to attend and by the time I'm done, it may be too late to come over. Will you be okay to wait until tomorrow?"

"I'll try. Come at least an hour early so I can take you on a tour of Hazel House before the other guests arrive."

"I'm looking forward to that."

-

The sun was out and a soft breeze was blowing when Phina stepped into the garden to pick a bunch of flowers for the dinner party that evening. She took her time as she listened to the blackbirds singing. Rashid's visit had provided the perfect antidote for her grief. She couldn't remember the last time she was that happy. It made her wonder why she had been so sad when the world held so much promise. Her recent experiences had been traumatic and since nothing had prepared her for them, she cut herself some slack. There in the garden, she reminded herself to always celebrate whenever and however an occasion called for it. It was only then she could achieve the balance she so desperately sought for. Luckily, she'd taken time to deliberate on what had occurred, and the aspects that were within and outside her control. Deliberating had brought the issues out of the dark and exposed them to the light, which smoldered her hurt and turned it to ashes.

Rashid's visit provided a very good reason to celebrate. After she placed the flowers in the vase, she went to her room and dialed his number.

"What time is it?" Rashid asked in a panic after she said, "Hello."

"One o'clock."

"Thank God. I thought I was late for dinner. I plan to be at your place early… sixish. I can't believe I slept this long. Anyway, I was in meetings till 3 AM yesterday, I meant to get up early and call you."

"No worries. It's still a long way until six."

"Okay, love. I miss you."

"I miss you too and can't wait to see you."

Phina was disappointed Rashid had to work so hard on the trip. She knew his visit to London was mostly for business but she hadn't expected him to spend so much time working and so little time with her.

-

Before heading to Hazel House, Rashid stopped at a florist and bought a bouquet of fresh roses for Phina. When he arrived, he first scanned the elaborate surroundings before the butler met him at the doorstep.

"Lady Campbell is expecting you," the butler announced.

"Yes, of course," Rashid said and walked right behind him.

Phina met Rashid in the foyer at five-thirty on the dot. He looked striking in a black dinner suit, white shirt, and a black bow tie. The disappointment she felt earlier in the day disappeared the moment she set her eyes on him. She hugged and kissed him right there, not minding that the butler was watching. The other guests were slated to arrive an hour later, which gave her enough time to savor his company. Rashid handed her the bouquet and a little black box.

"What is this?" she squealed.

"Open it."

Phina complied even though all she wanted to do was continue hugging and kissing him. She was stunned when she opened the box and saw a pair of dazzling grey diamond earrings with a radiance so pure it was impossible to imagine they weren't lit by an internal flame. Her heart skipped a beat. Mouth agape, she looked up at him and shook her head gently from side to side to gesture her bewilderment.

"I saw it at Connor's and thought you might like it."

"Thank you," she said, almost choking on her words. "I love them."

Rashid's eyes had a glint of satisfaction in them. Phina leaned forward to plant a kiss on his lips, and with his hands on her waist, he drew her in between his thighs. The delicious spiciness of his cologne, the hardness of his body and the sensuous manner in which he kissed her, all combined to create an illusion that she was floating. The butler had since left, but as she slowly recovered her senses, it occurred to her that he could return any second, so she pulled back a few inches.

"I have to show you around Hazel House before the other guests arrive?"

Rashid smiled. "I'm guessing it'll take hours for us to get through this mansion."

"Not really. I'll show you the important sections only."

She took him down the hallway and nudged him ahead of her while she gazed at his back which was now in full view with his jacket thrown over one shoulder. Marveling at how his black pants hugged his butt, she resisted the urge to squeeze them. It was as though Rashid read her thoughts because he immediately turned and slid his hand around her waist while she giggled mischievously. He bent down to kiss her cheek and in one swift motion placed one hand on her breast.

"Stop it," she whispered,

"There's no one here," he protested.

"Yeah, but you never know what's lurking around."

He ignored her and squeezed tighter. She moaned and grabbed his butt with both hands.

"Are you satisfied now," he asked eyeing her critically. "I felt you staring at my glutes earlier."

"That's not true," Phina responded, chuckling. "There's no way you could have known that. You don't have eyes at the back of your head."

"You might be surprised to find out that I do," Rashid said and lifted her off the floor.

"Put me down," Phina pleaded in a whisper.

Rashid ignored her. She was still trying to persuade him to put her down when they heard the doorbell. He put her down gently and together they turned around and walked towards the entrance to welcome the first guests – Yunus and Azra. Both had remained friends with Phina since she met them a while back and had been supportive of her since then. Phina introduced them to Rashid as her partner's son. Blake arrived soon after. Contrary to what Phina had expected, Rashid responded graciously after she introduced them. The men shook hands like old friends – no hint of rivalry between them. They took their camaraderie further by retreating to a corner to chat. Phina was puzzled by how they laughed easily at each other's jokes.

As usual, Lady Thompson was the last to arrive. Phina didn't need to introduce her to Rashid. She found Lady Thompson and Rashid chatting freely when she came by to meet her.

"I see you both have met," Phina commented, pleased with the enthusiasm all her guests showed at seeing one another.

The Iris Thompson she knew rarely opened up easily, so Phina was relieved that she didn't need to perform any special rites to break the ice. Had Lady Thompson not been at least ten years Rashid's senior, Phina would have assumed she was secretly attracted to him. It seemed evident by the way the Lady touched her hair seductively in his presence.

It was the first party Phina had hosted at Hazel House since Patrick's passing, almost a year back. Their usual party guests had wondered when they'd receive another invitation to the stately mansion. When they finally sat down to eat, the trajectory of their conversation as they devoured the mixture of African and European cuisine revealed that half of the guests were already tipsy from their cocktails.

"Is the ghost still in the hallway?" Lady Thompson asked Phina.

Phina smiled slowly and stared at her in surprise. "I don't presume it has anywhere to go."

"Ghosts are known to stay put," Azra suggested. "Isn't that so darling?" she said turning to Yunus.

"I believe so," Yunus responded, then continued to immerse himself in his meal.

"Why didn't I get a tour of the hallway?" Rashid demanded playfully.

"I only take guests when we have to use the grand dining room which has some of the best artwork in the entire house. Besides, you don't strike me as someone that believes in ghosts," Phina, scolded playfully.

Rashid shook his head. "I don't... I didn't. It's just that it sounds so surreal the way you talk about him."

"It is real," Phina added. "A few of our guests have encountered him."

"Have you?"

"No. And I hope I never will." She shuddered at the thought.

Phina, who never believed in the supernatural, developed a fear of ghosts soon after Patrick passed. Martin became real for her then. She avoided that hallway like a plague and hated Lady Thompson for bringing it up. Convinced she would be unable to get any sleep that night, she glanced at Rashid across the table, making extreme effort to repress her irritation. He took the cue and changed the topic. "Great meal. Any chance we get to hang out on the terrace later on?" he asked.

"It's a bit too warm out today. I've set up board games in the study. I hope we don't bore you to death," Phina responded.

"It sounds like fun."

-

They played board games until midnight before the guests started to leave one after the other. When Yunus was about to leave, he pulled Phina aside.

"I think you deserve to know why Witham Capital withdrew their offer to Sportsmets," he said.

Phina stared at him for a moment or two before responding. "I've always wondered," she said in a quizzical tone.

"Witham withdrew their offer when they discovered that Patrick's company had thirty-five million pounds in undisclosed liabilities over and above the forty million in debt Witham had agreed to take on as part of the sixty million acquisition deal."

Phina placed her hand over her mouth and stared at Yunus. After she recovered from her initial shock, she muttered, "Thank you for telling me. Patrick hid so many things from me."

"I'm surprised he didn't tell you. Anyway, men act like that sometimes."

"No," Phina said, shaking her head. "He's a liar. If a woman were to act that irresponsibly, would the same consideration be given?"

Yunus smiled at the obvious rejoinder.

"I didn't mean that," he apologized.

"I know, Yunus. I'm sorry I took my anger out on you."

"I understand. Azra and I are here for you. Let us know if you need anything."

-

Rashid waited until the last set of guests left before returning to his hotel. At sunrise, he called Phina while she was still in bed.

"Thank you for dinner," he said, still barely awake.

"The pleasure is mine. I hope you slept well."

"I slept like a baby," he lied. He had slept on the futon, having stayed up late into the night to catch up on his work. "How about you?"

"Oh! I thought about ghosts all night. I've started to feel terror once more with all this talk about ghosts. I jump when I hear echoes in the hallway. Even the sound of birds now give me the chills."

"I'm so sorry, love. This is why you need a strong man by your side. I wish I could be there with you right now. Anyway, I was thinking of coming to your office? How does two o'clock sound?"

"Great. We can catch a late lunch."

-

Rashid arrived at Ophinas at two. He was impressed by the empire Phina had built and was even more impressed that his father had the vision to buy into such a successful operation. In Phina's office, he grabbed her waist and kissed her passionately.

"I can't believe we haven't had a moment alone since I arrived."

Phina giggled.

"I would have come to see you the night you came in, but you had to go for those meetings."

"I'm sorry. That was bad planning on my part. Tonight is clear though. I expect you in my hotel wearing the same lingerie you wore that night in Lagos."

Phina – embarrassed – smiled a little. It seemed to her Rashid took their intimate moment together as something to tease her about. As she scrambled to come up with an appropriate response, she found the respite she needed with the loud ringing of the phone. She walked to her desk to pick it up. When she heard Lombardi's hello on the other end of the line, she realized she had got out of the frying pan to jump into the fire.

"Hello, can I help you?" Phina responded grudgingly.

"I'm sorry to bother you Lady Campbell, but something came to our attention about the state of your late husband's financial affairs. Ten million pounds was recently transferred from his account to an unknown recipient in an offshore account. Are you aware of this transaction?"

"Did you say ten?"

"Yes."

"I am not aware of this amount but some other transfers were made recently. It's probably something to do with Ashley or anything else for that matter. I don't know who Patrick is anymore."

"Who is Ashley?"

At that moment, Phina realized she had revealed too much. The fact that Ashley existed was privileged information between her and Detective Sommers. Struggling to find an answer, she glanced around the room. Realizing it was too late to retract, she whispered into the phone, "Patrick's illegitimate child."

Rashid, who had been waiting for her at the other side of the room, caught her eye and immediately turned his attention to the fashion magazine he'd picked from her pile.

"I wasn't aware such a person existed," Lombardi protested.

"This is new information I just received from my P.I. Hope you don't mind. I'll call you back a little later. I have someone in my office."

"Who was that?" Rashid asked the moment she hung up the phone.

"Police detective," Phina responded. "I don't appreciate how they've handled the case so far, so I don't feel like corroborating with them. For a while, I was their prime suspect, and they wasted so much time harassing me instead of looking into important leads, like the call I received from the mystery woman at the beginning of their investigation. My private investigator has done so much more in the few months since I hired him than they've done in almost a year."

Rashid listened with keen interest.

"Which mystery woman?"

"It's a long story. I'll tell you another day."

"You realize this is a police case right? Should you be snooping around with a PI?" His eyes met hers and she shook her head. "For your own good, and for the good of this investigation, I think you should let the police do their work. You could get into serious danger. Who is this PI by the way?"

Phina felt she had revealed too much already with her whining.

"I'm sorry," she said. "I shouldn't burden you with my problems."

"As you wish. Just know that you can't conquer life's challenges alone," he responded coldly.

Phina stole a quick glance at Rashid. He had never spoken to her in such an aloof manner and she was aware she had hurt his feelings. Having not treated him like her protector in that instance had left him with a bruised ego. As her thoughts deviated from what Rashid might be feeling, she marveled at the power whoever was blackmailing Patrick was able to wield. First, was the shares transferred to the dummy accounts; now, was the ten million pounds? She was certain that if she could find the mother of the baby Patrick was supposed to have fathered, then she would find the blackmailer and possibly the killer.

21

DNA

PHINA called Detective Sommers the moment she got home to brief him about the ten million pounds transfer.

"Where is this account?" he asked.

"Offshore… Switzerland."

"I'll look into it right away."

"Just to give you a heads up, I told Lombardi about Ashley."

"I thought we agreed to keep our investigation separate," Detective Sommers asked after pausing for a few seconds to consider the implication of the news he just received.

"Sorry. He caught me unawares and for a moment I thought a little collaboration could help us get faster results."

"No. It will most likely have the opposite effect. I'm concerned it could slow down the progress we've made so far. Now, we'll be forced to cooperate and share the results of our investigation."

"I'm sorry. This whole business has been so exhausting I don't know what I'm doing anymore."

"We'll find a workaround for it."

"Thanks. Have you been able to find out who the mother of the baby is?"

"No. We're still on it. I tried to reach the Evans' for further questioning, but they haven't picked up my call since that day. I have a feeling they're lying about not knowing who Ashley's Mother is."

"I believe so too. If this person is the killer, then they're probably being threatened or paid to shut up. Can the police force the Evans' to talk?" Phina asked.

"No," Detective Sommers responded. "Except if they're charged with a crime. In that case, the court can subpoena them. We're working on finding the hospital where the baby was born. That will most definitely lead us to the mother, even though it could turn out to be a long, convoluted route."

"Were you able to confirm if the baby is really Patrick's?"

"Again, if they're charged with a crime, then a subpoena can get us the specimen we need to subject Ashley to a DNA test."

"It looks like we've reached a dead-end," Phina said, perturbed.

"Not at all. We're still trying to follow the trail of the stock transfers. We will start following the trail of the ten million also. I believe those could lead us to the killer or at least shed more light into the case. Right now we have more to work with. Please be patient."

"Okay."

"I have a pertinent question for you," Detective Sommers said.

"Go ahead," Phina urged him.

"How is your relationship with Patrick's family?"

"Why do you ask?"

"We found out his mother hired a private investigator of her own."

"Really?" Phina asked, wide-eyed. "We haven't been on the best of terms since Patrick died, but she apologized the day the will was read."

"From what we know," Detective Sommers said, "She has you under her radar. Her investigators are constantly watching you."

Phina was stunned. "How do you know all this?" she asked.

Detective Sommers waited for a moment or two before responding. "The investigator that interrogated your staff was working for her. He's also the same person that's been following you. We followed the trail and after a little underground work, he revealed to one of my agents that Irene Campbell hired him. Nothing a little alcohol and a hot lady won't do to a horny male."

"What does she still want from me?" Phina said exasperatedly, ignoring his last comment.

Detective Sommers cleared his throat. "The same thing everyone is trying to figure out. If Patrick was murdered and if so by whom."

"She's such a hypocrite. Her apology was just a scam to get me to loosen my reins. I wonder if Victoria knew…" Phina's voice trailed off.

Detective Sommers hesitated a bit. "That wouldn't have changed anything."

"I was so sure the P.I was sent by the Life Insurance Company. So, has he found anything useful?"

"Oh, no! Not even close," Detective Sommers said with slight amusement. "His sole focus has been on the wrong person – you – so he has come to a dead-end. He just doesn't know that yet. We need to be very careful about who we talk to from now on though. As far as I know, you and Nduka are off the police radar, but the slightest mistake could put you on again."

-

246 - OBY ALIGWEKWE

Rashid, with only a few days left of his visit, invited Phina for a walk in Hyde Park. The weather was warm, and the sky was clear. Phina could not refuse the invitation. It was Saturday, and she had nowhere she needed to be. She met him at a cafe nearby and together they walked across to the park.

After strolling side by side for a few minutes, beneath lush trees, and taking in breathtaking views, they sat silently on a wooden bench, looking out across the lake. They watched the ripple created by a soft breeze on the lake surface as geese and swans pecked around the edges. Cautious of being labeled an item, Rashid discreetly took her hand and said as courteously as he could muster, "You're one of the best things that's ever happened to me."

Phina turned her head a fraction to look at him and then returned her gaze to the lake. She sighed deeply as she pondered what he'd just said.

"What do you say?" Rashid asked after waiting a whole minute for her to respond.

She returned her gaze to him. "Are you serious?"

Rashid retrieved his hand and laughed softly. "Of course, I am. Why would you think otherwise?" He took her hand again, firmly this time. "I have to have you," he said, looking into her eyes. His expression was so intense that he startled Phina and caused her to look away abruptly.

As she struggled to catch her breath, Rashid bent sideways and pressed his mouth into her slightly open one. She moaned quietly and when her voice rose above two decibels; they knew it was time to leave.

Phina was lost in thought after Rashid offered his hand to help her up the bench.

"Sorry," she finally responded. "There's so much on my mind. I can't seem to get a break."

He stooped to face her and held both her hands. "Marry me. That will give you the break you need. I'll make you very happy. We'll have children of our own, and I'll help you grow your business beyond anything you can imagine."

Phina looked into his eyes. The sincerity she saw in them caused her head to swoon. She looked down and shook her head.

"Give me time. I'll need to think about it."

"Take all the time you need. The only thing," he said, pausing to run his hand seductively behind her back, "that I care about is for you to recover your peace of mind."

Phina was touched by his words. She glanced up at him with big round eyes before following him to his car where his chauffeur was waiting to take them to his hotel.

In his room, they made love like their life depended on it.

"Where's the ring?" Phina teased later at lunch. "Proposing without a ring? You must have known it was bad timing."

"I had to be sensitive to the situation. Wanted to first gauge where your mind's at. If I pull one out now, will you say yes?" He pulled his right hand from hers and searched through his drawer."

"Oh no," Phina exclaimed, covering her mouth with both hands while she waited.

Rashid laughed and pulled out a pen.

"Don't worry. When I formally propose, it will be special."

Phina sighed in relief.

"My heart almost jumped out of my mouth. Don't ever do that again." She laughed till tears filled her eyes.

"I love you."

"I love you too."

22

WE SHOULD HAVE ASKED EVANS

THE weather would have been perfect if not for the slight drizzle that came with the early morning light. "Rashid should be in Lagos by now," Phina said to herself. She missed him terribly and tried to occupy her thoughts with the work that had piled up on her desk. When her phone rang, she thought it was due to some sort of telepathic influence when she heard his voice on the other end.

"I missed you," he said, "so I thought I'd call before I head to work for what I'm sure will be a very crazy day. How are you?"

"I missed you too," she said, chuckling slightly. "I was just thinking about you."

"You were?" Rashid asked abruptly.

Rashid's response drew a chuckle from Phina

"Yes, I was! How's Lagos?"

"A bit terrifying for everyone concerned because of the rumors that another coup d'état is imminent."

"That might be a good thing since the present government has failed on its promises."

"Good for whom?" Rashid enunciated his words. "We businessmen suffer the most consequences with these sudden shifts in power. It takes years to build networks and alliances only to have them shattered in one day, and then we have to build a different set again. It's expensive doing business that way."

"When will that country ever return to civilian rule? I don't understand why these people will not give democracy a chance," Phina said coldly.

"The military feels justified to stay indefinitely since the issues that caused them to take over are still prevalent."

"Don't tell me you're in support of the military staying on," Phina said in an exasperated tone. "Indiscipline will exist, regardless. Human beings by nature are undisciplined. A great democratic institution can have structures and systems in place to block the loopholes that create room for disorderliness."

"I'm on your side Phina. You should really come home to Nigeria and contest for an elected office when we get over this military rule nonsense. You're smarter than most of our leaders and you have a lot more integrity. You'll be great as the first female president."

"Did you just crack a joke?"

"Does it sound like one? We need fresh blood in Nigeria. I've always known that. The alternative is for things to remain as they are. We keep repeating the same mistakes over and over again. Now, let's focus on the issues we can solve. Have you thought about my proposal?"

An awkward silence passed between them. Rashid was only two years older than her, but he related with her as though the gap between them was twenty years. Somehow, he reminded her of Patrick when the going was good. The thought made her sigh deeply enough for him to hear.

"Look," he said. "I don't want you to feel stressed. Think about it. I have to go now to provide father the lowdown on the trip. I have to report on the business I did for him while I was away, particularly on how Ophinas is faring. He's awfully busy these days and can't fly in and out like he used to."

"Yeah. It's quite flattering that he's willing to entrust the business to us despite his large investment."

"It's easy. You're an excellent businesswoman, that's why. Have a great day. I love you."

-

Nduka walked into his massive office in Ikeja with its smooth mahogany furniture. Several plaques with his accomplishments graced the main wall. He stood and looked at the inscriptions on all four plaques and thought aloud. "But all I want is Phina." Over the weekend, he had read from the gossip column of a popular magazine that she was dating Chief Gambo's first son. The news filled him with trepidation. Since then, he'd been unable to function. He had tried to call her many times – both at home and the office – but could not reach her. After phoning Isabel to help him make the connection and still not achieving the desired goal, he promised himself that if attempts to reach her by the end of the day failed, he'd take a morning flight to London.

Painful thoughts swirled around his head that afternoon. "I don't believe it," he kept muttering to himself. "How can she be with me one day and then with a different man the next?" In his fury, he pounded his fist a bit too hard on his desk and winced in pain. Phina had rejected his proposal, but he still had hopes she would change her mind. He wondered how far she'd gone with Rashid and if there was any hope left for them to be together.

Since his return to Nigeria, he'd set up a large medical practice in Ikeja and hired local doctors while he dabbled in other businesses. With the excess funds at his disposal, he was able to acquire some oil wells through contacts he established long ago. He had spoken to Phina sparsely – not for lack of trying – but because she always seemed to be unavailable. On his twentieth attempt that day, he was finally able to reach her.

"I thought I'd never get to speak with you," Nduka said, trying his best to contain his anger.

"Sorry, I've been in meetings all day," Phina responded. "You won't believe how crazy it's been around here."

"What about all the days before? I called several times today. Your phone was ringing engaged," he complained.

"I was on a long distance call."

"For hours? I tried a couple of times and finally gave up. Who were you speaking with for so long? Was it Rashid Gambo?"

"Why Rashid?" Phina asked coldly.

"Everybody knows about you and Rashid," Nduka responded sarcastically. "I was probably the last person to know."

Phina, trying her best to remain calm, responded, "Rashid is a friend of mine."

"A friend you sleep with?"

"I'll hang up if you have nothing important to say," Phina said, unable to tolerate his sense of entitlement any longer. She reckoned there was no way he would have known she'd slept with Rashid. He had to have speculated and hoped he would hit the mark with his comments.

Nduka regretted the words the moment they were uttered. "I'm sorry," he said. "I hope I haven't blown our chance of ever being together."

"But Nduka, I don't see how we can be together ever again. I thought I made it clear the last three times we spoke."

Although she still had feelings for him, she had decided to distance herself emotionally even before she solidified her relationship with Rashid. She blamed herself for having not made her position clear enough. Her relationship with Nduka had suffered a serious blow when news of his crimes in America surfaced. With the repeat offense exposed, she couldn't imagine how Nduka would expect her to take him seriously, let alone move to Nigeria with him. She thought his request was ridiculous at the time but dealt kindly with him as she saw no reason to kick him when he was already down.

"I just wanted to touch base to see how you're doing," he said after a short silence. "Thank you for not hanging up. You and I have known each other for a long time. We've been through a lot together, what with being accused of Patrick's murder. Most of all, you're the best lover I've ever had."

"Yes, but we need to move on from that now."

"I want us to remain friends no matter what."

"I would love that," Phina said, heaving a sigh of relief.

"How is the investigation going?"

"New things are coming up every day." Phina felt they had a safe enough distance between them so she bared her heart to him. She told him about the progress she had made. "Finding the killer is dependent on finding the mother of Patrick's baby," she concluded.

Nduka was puzzled by the theory. "There's a deep flaw in that conclusion," he said. "Why would the mother of Patrick's baby want to kill him? Doesn't she have more to gain from Patrick being alive than dead?"

"That's a valid point. Detective Sommers had said something similar, but in my opinion, she may want to kill him if he threatened to expose their secret, or if he failed to deliver on a promise."

"What promise?"

"Perhaps, to divorce me and marry her," she responded with ease. "She may have killed him out of jealousy. Hotel cameras saw a woman leaving that night. I can't help but think sometimes that it's the same person."

"It could be… What I'm about to say now might upset you, but I think you need to hear it. Have you considered the possibility that Patrick was having multiple affairs?"

"Don't worry. That doesn't upset me. It's crossed my mind a few times but I always dismiss it. Just consider it as my way of helping him retain some dignity. Yes, it's very possible."

"So, if that's the case," Nduka continued, "Solving this case could be extremely difficult because you're not looking for anyone in particular."

"I'll leave that to my investigators to worry about."

"I wish you the best of luck."

-

Detective Sommers was waiting in the driveway when Phina got to Hazel House a little after seven in the evening. He had called her at the office to let her know he had some important news. They walked to the house, entered the study, and shut the door behind them.

"What's going on?" Phina asked, sitting down and placing her purse on the desk beside her.

"Paul Evans was found dead in his home sometime last night."

"What?" Phina screeched as she looked at Detective Sommers with terror.

"Yes. His wife contacted me. She found him lying face down in their bedroom after she returned home from an event."

"Let me take a wild guess. Lombardi and his team are all over the case now."

"That's correct. They got there first."

"Why did Melissa Evans call you then?"

"That's what I'm here to discuss with you. I provided the results of our investigation to Lombardi and his team after you told me you'd revealed some of the details to him. It's a good thing we did that. With Paul Evans dead, we… or I would have been in deep shit had they found we were hiding details of a murder investigation from the police. Paul Evans was found in pretty much the same position as Patrick. The only difference between the two cases is that Paul seemed to have left a suicide note."

"Why would he kill himself?" Phina asked, wide-eyed.

"Good point. I don't think it was suicide. The two deaths are connected, but I don't know how. The coroner's reports for both are eerily similar though; no contusions to indicate strangling yet both men somehow gave up air and stopped breathing. In Paul's case, something doesn't seem right. The suicide note…" Detective Sommers stopped mid-sentence and shook his head.

"What are you thinking?"

"If the cases are connected, then the suicide note in Paul Evans' case was an attempt to deter the investigators."

"Makes sense," Phina said. "I'll be curious to know if Lombardi and his team buy the suicide gimmick."

"We have to change our technique. Killing one man is one thing; two proves that we have a dangerous killer on our hands."

"Have they queried his wife?" Phina asked. "She was the last to see him alive, and she found his body. I don't trust her – a woman who would have another's baby in her care and claim not to know who the mother is – could be capable of anything."

"Definitely, the case will take its due course. I won't be surprised if Lombardi starts poking around Hazel House again, asking you questions. Be prepared for that, and refuse to answer any questions without your lawyer present."

"McCracken," Phina said, raising her tone. "I haven't spoken to McCracken in a long time. I'll call her as soon as we're done and give her a heads up. I don't want her to be caught unawares."

"We have no choice but to bring everything to the open now. It's dangerous for us to hide the results of our investigation at this point. In my books, this case is now classified a double homicide. If Lombardi and his team are not treating it as such then there's something wrong with them."

"Where is the baby now?" Phina asked.

"It's with Melissa. She seemed overwhelmed taking care of it all by herself. Apparently, Paul was the main caregiver, and she only helped when Paul traveled."

"They have to take it from her then. It's not her biological child, and the situation seems very dangerous. Next thing you know, you'll hear Ashley has been kidnapped."

"Careful not to speak that way to Lombardi's hearing. They'll automatically label you a prime suspect."

"Nonsense... When everything calms down, I'll like to see Melissa. Can you arrange a meeting for us?"

Detective Sommers hesitated for a second. "I don't think she'll agree to that. I know for sure because I'd asked her. In retrospect, I don't think it's a good idea. I wouldn't want you entangled in this mess any more than you are, not with your position in society."

Phina nodded in agreement and waved her hand. "Never mind. I'm not sure what my meeting her will achieve, anyway. The mother of this baby is probably still alive and a psycho murderer. It's best for me to stay as far away as possible."

"Best if you can," Detective Sommers agreed.

Phina walked outside with him to his car.

"Make sure the doors are locked all the time and always have security with you. I believe that to get to the root of Patrick's case, I may have to solve Paul's. It may be the only valid lead we have right now. The ones we have followed so far have led us to an actual dead end – another murder occurred right under our noses."

-

Detective Sommers headed back to his office and immersed himself in his work. He thought again with regret how much time he'd wasted with the investigation. If he had focused his time investigating other likely suspects, rather than fixating on Nduka and Phina, he may have found the killer by then. Even after FBI tapes of Nduka's whereabouts surfaced, and Lombardi and his team cleared him as a suspect, Detective Sommers still felt there was a slight chance Nduka could be the culprit as the letter provided a strong motive. But, compared to the potential motives on the table, the letter now seemed like child's play. Paul Evans' case removed any lingering doubt about Nduka's innocence since Nduka was out of the country when Paul Evans was killed.

He pulled out the notepad with his old list.

Nduka Eze – confirm alibi

Phina Campbell – complicit

Patrick Campbell – suicide

Dummy account owner – blackmail?

The mystery female caller – ?

The mysterious woman at the hotel – last person to see him alive?

The first two names on the list had already been struck out but were still visible. He used a black marker and etched them out in its entirety. Next, he etched out Patrick's name. He no longer considered his death a suicide. Paul's death made that clear to him. He'd reckoned that the culprit must have wanted both deaths to look like suicides but in Patrick's case may have left in a hurry and not been able to execute effectively. Having narrowed his list to the last three items, he added as number four '*every woman Patrick ever came in contact with*'. He knew he could get that information from Phina and any contacts she could provide. As he was about to place his notepad back in his bag, he stopped and included *Melissa Evans* as a bullet point below his last entry. Below Melissa's name, he added *Ashley's Mother* and sighed deeply.

23

SOMETHING IN THE CORNER

THE end of August was beautiful. Every single day, the sky shone a clear blue – azure blue – with no clouds in sight. The gardens were bursting with carnations, lilies, roses, honeysuckle and the star of Bethlehem. Insects hissed, buzzed, and chirped. There could not have been a more perfect time for Isabel and Simon to visit Hazel House. For days, Phina prepared the house for their visit. She repainted the best room in the house a stylish gray and hung ivory and lace curtains to match the Victorian furniture set that came with the room. When she was done, she was overwhelmed by the sheer beauty of it and thought it was a shame they would be spending so little time in there as Hazel House had a lot to offer.

Isabel and Simon spent the first day touring the city and ended at Ophinas at mid-day.

"I'm still stunned by the architectural details of this store. It's no wonder it took so many years to complete."

"Several years and several million pounds," Phina added, as she stepped in front of Isabel to open the door to her office after they came out of the elevator. "We're still paying for it till this day."

"Some of the capital you raised during the IPO can be used to pay off existing debt. I don't think that is much of a problem," Simon countered.

"Not with the IPO. Maybe with a new offer… Here you go," Phina said as she gestured to a settee when they walked into the room. "Welcome to my office."

"I have a feeling of déjà vu because I've spoken to you countless times while you were sitting right there," Isabel said, pointing in the direction of Phina's desk. "I never imagined it to be this modern."

Phina laughed. "Patrick's office will be more your style then. It's just around the corner."

"Can we see it?" Isabel asked, wide-eyed.

"Yes, by all means. Come with me."

They walked into Patrick's office, with Isabel acting like a kid about to enter a candy shop. The office had a musky old scent like a place that was unlived in. Phina couldn't remember the last time she came in there. She had combed through it when Patrick first passed looking for leads. Of recent, she had settled into a more nonchalant existence. His actions didn't bother her any longer. Lombardi and his team had also been there a few times – with a search warrant but not before she had the chance to go through his things herself. A scan through convinced her that everything was still intact. The large Georgian clock that stood in the corner was his favorite piece of furniture. As she wondered if she should take it to Hazel House and create a memorial for him, Isabel yanked her out of her reverie.

"Patrick had great taste," Isabel gushed.

Phina nodded in agreement. "The best."

"Such a pity we didn't get to meet him," Simon added, walking around the room, and slowly taking his time to appreciate the details and arrangements. "His life was cut short so soon."

Phina caught Isabel as she gave signs to Simon to change the topic. Simon, completely oblivious, continued. "What is the state of the investigation? Have they made any headway?"

"Isabel, it's okay," Phina said, causing Simon to pause and look at her. "I'm over his death and betrayal. I have only one goal which is to solve the case and move on with my life. I would have moved on earlier but since the police are convinced he was murdered, I cannot rest until the culprit is found."

"I know," Isabel said, waving her right hand to gesture understanding, "but I wanted this trip to be one where we're able to bring you comfort rather than dig up old wounds."

"Thank you, sweetie. One thing I've learned in my thirty-six years on earth is that we never truly heal until we've deliberated enough on those things that have caused us heartbreak. For as long as this topic brings me pain, that's how long I need to discuss it and eventually find a way to rise above the situation. Only then will I be completely healed."

"That's an excellent approach you've described there my dear," Simon said as he continued pacing the room. "Your Patrick was a wonderful man. I pray the people responsible for this will be found and dealt with,"

"I pray so," Phina managed to say.

Through Patrick's office, they accessed the rooftop terrace, another spot Phina hardly visited anymore. Isabel was impressed by the views and the décor.

"I'd like to have lunch here sometime," she said. "This has got to be the most beautiful spot in this entire city."

"Maybe tomorrow," Phina suggested.

"Tomorrow, I'll be meeting with the Lourdes remember?" Simon interjected. "I'm having lunch with them."

"I don't want to mess up any of your plans," Isabel said. "I can come alone with Phina. We only have a few days here and I'd like to make the most of every moment."

"Will you be back before sunset though?" Phina asked Simon. "I invited Blake Caldwell for dinner tomorrow and I want you both to meet him. He's a very conscious statesman. You'll like him."

"I would love very much to meet him."

"I'm sure he'd be delighted to meet you both."

-

The following day, Phina and Isabel had their afternoon tea on the terrace at Ophinas, with the sky still as clear as the day before.

"It's been a while since I let my hair down," Phina said.

"Why? You shouldn't shut yourself in. There's no reason to."

"I know. I just can't find any time to breathe these days," she said, a slow smile spreading across her face.

Isabel grinned and shuffled her feet on the ground.

"How is Nduka?" she asked. "We haven't heard from him in such a long time. Simon misses him in New York. They became such great friends."

"I believe he's fine. For a while, we were romantically involved, but he refused to quit his life of crime. How could you trust somebody like that?"

"I heard about his troubles. Yes, I always wondered how a doctor could earn so much," Isabel said through pursed lips. "You were married to Patrick for how long?"

"Nine years."

"After a while, dear you need to choose one from the legions of men I'm sure are chasing after you." Isabel gave her a mischievous wink before continuing, "Don't write off a chance at happiness just because Patrick failed you. If you do, then he's won in keeping you stuck forever."

"I don't foresee that being my lot though." Phina continued to smile. "I'm grateful the disappointments didn't make me lose my zest for life."

"Are you dating anyone now?"

Phina slanted her head. "Yes… and no."

"You're either seeing someone or you're not. Which is it?"

Phina paused for a moment.

"Yes," she said when she eventually responded. "Something serious could be developing." She stopped, uncrossed her legs and leaned forward to look Isabel directly in the eyes. "This person is different. I never knew I could ever feel this way. I know it may sound cliché, but he makes me want to stop and smell the roses. He's a calming presence in the chaotic situation I find myself in. Even when he's not there, I feel his presence. I loved Patrick but nothing like this. This man keeps my mind afloat; he gives me balance; he's giving me everything I need to finally breathe again."

Isabel's heart was beating rapidly as Phina was speaking. She shook her head slightly; a tender look spread across her face. "This could be love," she muttered, sighing deeply.

"Possibly," Phina whispered, a feeling of euphoria sweeping through her.

Too engrossed in their discussion, they failed to notice the person standing before them with a tray of sandwiches and colorful desserts. After waiting for nearly thirty seconds, the server, a stout man in his sixties, cleared his throat to get their attention.

"Oh!" Phina exclaimed and pointed at the table.

"Anything else, Lady Campbell?"

"No, thank you."

After the man left, they both got lost in thought and nibbled on their sandwiches in silence for a few minutes.

"Does this person you're seeing have a name?" Isabel asked, breaking the silence. "Is his name Blake Caldwell? The same person you invited to dinner."

Phina burst into laughter, almost spilling her tea. "Oh, no!" she exclaimed. "Not Blake. Rashid. Chief Gambo's son."

"Rashid? You talk about him all the time, but I never knew you were… you know."

"That's because I wasn't quite sure how to define the relationship. It's still in the early phases even though he's already pushing for a commitment…" Before the next word could form in her mouth, Phina heard a low rumble. "Is that what I think it is?" she asked, looking at Isabel in panic.

"Yes," Isabel said, pointing at the sky which had turned a dark gray with a bunch of curly clouds floating around. It had been like that for a while but they hardly noticed it. When the ladies saw a flash of lightning and heard a loud cracking sound, they ran frantically to the stairs and back to the safety of Patrick's office before it started pouring.

"Let's get out of here," Phina said, shivering and folding her hands to her chest. "It's time to go home."

-

The party of two was in full swing when Isabel and Phina walked into the Georgian living room in Hazel House. The huge burnished brass and silver chandelier glowed over the ceiling and the center table created a warm and welcoming ambiance. Simon was speaking at the top of his voice and Blake was nodding and laughing at every word that came out of Simon's mouth. The two men were standing in front of the fireplace nursing their drinks.

"I see you both have met," Phina announced as she stepped in.

"Hello darlings," Simon greeted his wife with a kiss on the lips and for Phina he reserved a kiss on both cheeks.

"Isabel, this is Blake Caldwell of the House of Lords."

"Hello Blake," Isabel said with outstretched hands. "I have heard so much about you. Thank you for looking out for my friend."

"I feel as though I know you already just by the number of times she's spoken to me about you," Blake said, taking Isabel's hand and kissing them tenderly.

Blake was wearing a dark grey pant and a grey shirt that hugged his chest and shoulders and revealed his contours in massive detail.

"Hello dear," he said as he kissed Phina on both cheeks.

"Hi," Phina responded, shivering from the cold. "How long have you been waiting?" she asked in a raised tone.

"Not too long. I met Simon on the driveway an hour ago. We've been discussing politics since then. I think I've found my soul-mate," he said cheerfully.

Phina rolled her eyes. "I can see that."

"We really hit it off," Blake continued. "I got an invitation to visit him in New York and I'm seriously considering it."

"I don't doubt that," Phina responded, smiling.

Blake glanced across the room and when he saw Simon deep in conversation with Isabel at one end, he found an opportunity to have a moment alone with Phina, so he pulled her to a secluded corner.

"Phina, what is this I hear about you and Rashid?"

"What about?" she muttered, in the manner of an errant child.

At that moment, Isabel walked behind the two of them.

"Sorry for interrupting," Isabel pleaded. "I was wondering if I could excuse myself for a few minutes before dinner."

"By all means," Phina said. "Dinner will be ready in fifteen minutes. Take your time."

Phina and Blake joined Simon in the center of the room. Shortly after, Isabel returned, and they moved to the dining room where a sumptuous meal of steak, cob salad, lasagna, and apple pie was waiting for them.

"This smells superb," Isabel sighed.

"I bet it tastes delicious too," Simon added.

During dinner, Phina joined in the conversation whenever she could but mostly went in and out of reverie as she tried to make sense of what Blake had been trying to ask her. She'd had two proposals in the past year – Nduka's, which Blake knew about but which he'd rejected vehemently and Rashid's – which she had never discussed with Blake and was still hanging in the balance. There was also the need to reconcile both proposals with the experience she had being married to Patrick. Still deep in thought, she felt a light tap on her wrist. It was Isabel.

"Blake just told me all about Martin. How come you never mentioned him?" Isabel asked excitedly.

"Martin?" Phina said, raising her brows. "Oh… That. What is there to tell?"

"What is there not to tell?" Isabel whined.

"I'm sorry. I've forgotten all about Martin. I've had so much to deal with these days. He used to scare the living daylights out of me but now I just avoid taking that hallway."

–

Someone was tailing Phina and she could feel it in her soul. She quickened her pace, but the person walking behind her along the barely lit hallway mimicked every move she made. Afraid to look back, she called out to Isabel, hoping to get an answer. Receiving no response got her adrenaline pumping, so she shrieked, "Stop Isabel." Still, no response. She continued but could sense that there was undoubtedly a being behind her. This being was determined to catch up with her and do her harm. Knowing this convinced her it wasn't Isabel she had to contend with. Gripped with fear and unable to find her voice again, she took a quick look behind but saw no one. A second later, she hastened and felt the person following her do the same. With her heart pounding, she decided to run the entire length of the hallway which ended with the Victorian living room on the right. Hopefully, there she could call for help, or better still her assailant would give up pursuing her. As she started to make a break for it, she felt a heavy hand grab her shoulder. She let out a piercing scream, but a hand went across her mouth muffling her cries of agony. When she felt a tight grip on her neck, she kicked and flailed her hands in every direction before she drifted out of consciousness.

Later, when she opened her eyes, she saw Isabel looking down at her. With her head cradled on Isabel's lap, she looked around in confusion. Simon was standing nearby and beside him were the butler and the housekeeper.

Isabel was the first to speak.

"We have notified the police."

"Why? What happened?" Phina asked, trying to recover her senses.

"You were attacked," Simon answered, helping her to the chair provided by the housekeeper.

"By whom?" she asked exasperatedly.

"We were hoping you'd know," Isabel responded, shaking her head. "Did you see anyone? Do you remember anything?"

Phina squinted her eyes and looked from left to right.

"No. The last thing I remember was someone grabbing me from behind. At first, when I heard the person following me, I thought you were pretending to be Martin just to give me a fright," she said pointing at Isabel, "but next thing I knew, I was getting choked. I didn't get the chance to see the person."

Two policemen barged in before she could continue. They took a statement from her, Simon, and Isabel. Phina could not remember anything after she fainted.

"My head hurts," she said.

"Let me see." The first policeman bent down to examine her head. "Nothing that needs emergency attention. Does any other part of your body hurt?"

Phina sat upright, turned her body from the left to the right and shook her head. "No."

"Should we call the paramedics?"

"No," Phina insisted. "I'm ok."

"Do you know anyone that could have a reason to attack you?" the second policeman asked, note in hand."

Phina shifted her gaze from one person to the other hoping for some help.

"Ok. Did any of you see the person who might have done this?" the second policeman asked, shifting his gaze from Isabel to Simon and then back again to Phina.

Simon spoke up.

"No," he said. "We were having a relaxing evening, and the girls decided to go down the 'famous' hallway to explore. Soon after they were separated, we heard her scream. That was when we all came running and saw her sprawled on the floor, unconscious."

-

As Simon spoke Phina tried to recall the events of the evening. After Blake left, Isabel had pestered her to go down the hallway. They had chatted as they walked, stopping at intervals to admire the century-old artwork that lined the walls of the adjoining rooms. Isabel had said to her, "We should have come to England a long time ago, but we just couldn't find a perfect time when Simon and I could come together," and Phina had responded, "I feel that all is well with my world with you both here. I didn't realize how much I missed you." Their conversation had turned to Martin and Phina pleaded with Isabel to change the subject. She had obliged but soon they were separated because Isabel had insisted on stopping in one of the rooms to look at a gothic painting. Phina was in a hurry to complete the tour and scurried ahead of Isabel. It was a few seconds after they were separated that she felt someone behind her. She'd never encountered Martin and wasn't even sure if she believed in his existence. When she ran, it wasn't so much for fear of a ghost than it was from a realization that there was a murderer on the prowl.

Phina's final thought jolted her, and she raised her hand for a chance to speak.

"I'm not sure if you're aware, but my husband was murdered almost a year ago, and the killer hasn't been apprehended."

"Yes," the first policeman said, nodding. "We're aware of the investigation. We'll look into this new development to see if there's any connection."

"I don't think your department is going to achieve anything until we're all murdered," Phina responded, glaring at the two policemen one after the other.

"Lady Campbell, let me assure you that we're doing everything we can to solve this case. Now, it is our understanding that you have also retained a private detective for the same purpose. I'll implore you to remind your team to share any valuable information that could help us move forward as quickly as possible."

-

Later in her room, after the policemen left, Phina shuddered at the realization that she could be a target. She was sure someone wanted her dead and that the attack was connected to Patrick's murder. What she couldn't fathom was what the attacker hoped to achieve by going after her. She started to rethink her earlier blackmail hypothesis as she realized she was most likely in someone's way. Could it be that she was getting close to the truth, and the murderer became uncomfortable? Could it be why Paul Evans was also murdered? She became terribly agitated and was happy that the police department sent a couple of policemen to camp around Hazel House after that night's attack. It provided her a temporary sense of security.

24

FULL DISCLOSURE

PHINA woke up the following morning feeling worn out after a whole night of tossing and turning with sweat dripping down her forehead onto her silk pillowcase. She looked outside the window and the sun was beginning to appear behind the bright orange and gray clouds that streaked the horizon. Under better circumstances, that would get her excited for her day, but that morning she was weighed down by memories of the attack. It was seven o'clock, and she'd wanted to call Detective Sommers as soon as she woke up. Rather, she got up and walked towards her window and saw two policemen different from the ones from the night before patrolling the grounds.

Detective Sommers called right after she came out of the shower. Sprinting to reach the phone before it stopped ringing, she was panting by the time she picked it up.

"I'm so happy to hear from you," she said with trepidation. "You won't believe what happened yesterday."

"I heard. Lombardi told me as soon as it happened. I insisted they provide police protection for you until this case is finally resolved. Last night I called Melissa Evans and told her what happened to you. I pleaded with her to tell me everything she knew about Paul, Ashley, Patrick and whoever else she thought could help throw light on this issue."

"What was her response?"

"She was terribly shaken by the news of your attack and asked if she could meet with you. When I told her it wouldn't be possible, she insisted you needed to be present before she could reveal anything further to me."

"Then…?"

"Would you consider meeting with her?"

"My life may depend on it so why not?"

"Okay, great. Should we do nine o'clock this morning?"

"Will Ashley be there?"

"No, Ashley was taken by child protective services a few days ago."

"Oh! That poor child. He deserves to be with his mother."

"But his mother could be a murderer."

-

The Evans' home was Edwardian and set back from the road on an acre of wooded land. Ivys and honeysuckle, supported with a metal framework crowded the east end of the wall and covered the windows facing the road. A thicket of shrubs lined the entrance to the house, and a rose garden nestled on the Westside under a set of open windows. Phina, wild with anticipation, sighed and fanned herself with her hand as Detective Sommers pressed the doorbell. The unusual downpour the night before did nothing to cool the late August air but left a sweet aroma.

Melissa, a tall brunette with streaks of silver hair and porcelain white skin opened the door a few minutes after Detective Sommers pressed the bell for the second time. She was in linen pants and a matching top. Phina was stunned by her attractiveness.

"Welcome to my home," Melissa said in an accent Phina couldn't quite place before ushering them in. The living room was so sparse and the furniture pieces so mismatched it was obvious they were just thrown together.

"Thank you," Phina responded, wondering if Melissa was Patrick's mistress. "Is that what she wants to tell me?" Phina thought. "Could she be Ashley's real mother?"

After they were seated, Phina looked around the room and later returned her gaze to Detective Sommers who sat silently, nodding and fiddling with his notebook.

"Thank you, Mrs. Evans," Detective Sommers finally said after everyone was settled. "You told me last night that you wouldn't speak with me unless we had Lady Campbell present."

Melissa nodded with a smile. "I called you sometime," she said, turning to the side to face Phina. "That was when Paul and I first moved here. I wanted you to meet me at a café in… I don't remember the name, but I had friends there." She spoke slowly.

"Wait! Was this soon after Patrick died?" Phina asked.

"Yes. After Lord Campbell passed," Melissa said.

"Oh, so you're the woman that called me. I've been searching for you," Phina said in an accusatory tone. "Lombardi and his men even accused me of lying about that call ever happening. By the time I hired Detective Sommers, the phone company had erased that month's records so we couldn't even follow that lead."

Melissa shook her head and grimaced. "I doubt they would have been able to trace me even if they checked the records earlier. I made the call from a public phone. I had no idea you were looking for me. I mean…" She stopped mid-sentence to scratch her cheek with a well-manicured index finger. "I know that I skipped out on you but I had a very good reason for doing so. Paul was being threatened."

"By whom?" Phina asked. She noticed Detective Sommers scribbling at a fast pace on his notepad.

Melissa shook her head slowly. "I don't know. I'm sure the same people that killed him. The police say it's not suicide like I was tricked to believe. I knew it couldn't be suicide. Paul was into shady dealings but he didn't have a sad bone in his body. He was always planning the next big project. Tell me, how could such a person take his own life?" She stopped and sobbed into her handkerchief. After a deep sigh, she raised one hand. "I'm in fear of my life now, Lady Campbell."

"Why?" Phina asked, her voice devoid of emotion.

"Why not? Your PI told me what happened last night at Hazel House." She raised her face and stared at Phina with big round eyes. "Aren't you afraid?"

Phina nodded once. "I am. That's why I'm here. What do you know?"

"No more than I knew a year ago."

"So, what was it you wanted to see me about?" Phina asked with the same steely tone.

An awkward silence passed, during which Detective Sommers put a dash beside mystery caller on his list and wrote *Melissa Evans* beside it.

"Paul was acting funny, and we'd just been newly married. Beyond funny, he was acting nervous. Some powerful people were threatening him. They said it was very important. I was scared and the only person I had contact with at the time was Lord Campbell – your late husband. I knew he was the boy's father but the way he and Paul were acting, it was as though somebody was after them. I wanted to leave Paul and run away. That's when I called you."

"Then why didn't you follow through with your plan?"

Melissa looked away for a brief moment. "I wanted to tell you about Lord Campbell because I thought that might save Paul... free him."

Phina sighed in exasperation. "Why did you change your mind? For almost a whole year, I wondered what you had wanted to tell me and what might have happened to you." Phina tried to hide the annoyance in her voice.

"Paul found out what I was up to before I could meet you that day. He pleaded with me and convinced me there was a lot of money in it for us. He insisted we were innocent of any crime, and they paid for this house," she said, waving her hand slowly across the room. "And the checks, those came every month."

"Do you know who else Paul was working with?" Detective Sommers asked.

Melissa shook her head. "The only person I ever met was Lord Campbell. I took care of the boy like it was mine. No, Paul took care of him, mostly. I didn't mind it. Ashley is beautiful."

Phina sighed, her heart pounding in her chest. As Detective Sommers queried Melissa, she shook her head, convinced she was hiding something. How could she trust a woman like Melissa? She'd already deceived her once before and she did not believe her reason for backing out on their meeting. In her mind, she'd wanted a conquest – possibly to blackmail her and another victim simultaneously but realized it would be no good. Springing out of her reverie, Phina asked, "Do you have any idea who Ashley's Mother is?"

Melissa shook her head. "No idea. I know the hospital he was born. That can help you find the mother."

"I asked you the same question the last time I was here, but you said you didn't know," Detective Sommers scowled.

"Paul was here. I was forbidden to reveal that information. Ashley was born at a private hospital just outside the city. We took him there for his vaccinations. I'll get the name and address for you. I have it written somewhere," she said, rising from her seat.

After Melissa exited the room through an adjoining door, Phina stood up to look at the pictures on the stone mantelpiece above the fireplace. One picture caught her eye. It was a picture of young Melissa and a young man that looked awfully familiar. As she examined the photo, she was startled when Melissa walked behind her. "That was me and Paul. Many years ago when he still had hair," Melissa said.

"Paul looks terribly familiar. I could swear I've met him before," Phina responded.

Melissa shook her head. "I don't know. We moved here a couple of years ago. I'm not sure where you would have met him."

"I now recall," Phina squealed. "He's the spitting image of Geoffrey."

Detective Sommers stopped his scribbling, stood up and walked with long strides towards the fireplace. Phina handed him the picture frame with the photo. He scrutinized the picture with care. "This is definitely a much younger image of your Paul," he said, looking at Melissa. "Does he go by another name by any chance?"

Melissa shook her head. "I only know him as Paul," she muttered and looked away.

Phina took the frame from Detective Sommers and gazed at the picture again.

"Do you have a more recent photo of him?" she asked.

Melissa thought for a second before responding. "We hardly took any photographs. Our wedding pictures are in my mother's house in Wales. I don't have other pictures on me. Paul was very squeamish about such things."

"How soon can you get to your mother's?" Detective Sommers asked.

Melissa shrugged and handed a note to Detective Sommers. "I don't know. I haven't been there since after her funeral."

"St Joseph's hospital?" Detective Sommers said, staring at the note he'd just received. "His middle name is Bernard?"

"Yes, it is," Melissa said.

"Can I see?" Phina asked, taking the note from Detective Sommers. "Ashley Bernard Campbell... ABC. Are those Ashley's initials?"

Melissa looked from one person to the next. "I suppose so."

"Does the number 682 mean anything to you?" Phina asked, looking at Melissa, the note dangling from her hand.

"I'm not sure what you're asking." Melissa said with a grimace before settling in her seat.

"Never mind," Phina responded, eyeing her surreptitiously.

-

"Now we know who the mystery caller is." Detective Sommers said to Phina after they left The Evans' home.

Phina, deep in thought, managed to nod. "Work with her to get those recent pictures. I'm pretty sure that was Geoffrey from the store some years back. I wonder if he was working for Patrick also," she muttered.

"Who is this Geoffrey?" Detective Sommers asked in an exasperated tone.

"He leaked information about my company to the Inquirer over a year ago. I'm sorry; I should have told you about him. Now I know why we couldn't find him. Geoffrey was a pseudonym."

"Everything, even the minutest detail could be relevant to this investigation. Can we get more information on Geoffrey from Human Resources?"

"I'm not sure. We can try. I'm wondering what he had to do with Patrick's murder though," Phina said.

"Your HR must have something that could help us confirm his identity," Detective Sommers reiterated.

"At the time, HR had no forwarding address for him and the one he provided when he was hired was nonexistent. That was a long time ago. I still can't believe Paul was Geoffrey," Phina said, shaking her head incredulously.

"Did you ever find out who he was working for?"

"Yes. He was gathering information for Lady Thompson regarding my business affairs with Isabel Hartier. Lady Thompson was involved in a share sale transaction with my husband and could not bear the value of Ophinas shares being devalued, so she sent Geoffrey to be her eyes and ears in the organization."

"A recent picture will help to confirm if we're referring to the same person. It will make my work a lot easier if I don't have to work off an old picture that was taken when Paul – or is it Geoffrey – was a decade younger."

Phina shook her head.

"I don't know if there will be anything. I suggest you follow up with Melissa to get a recent picture from her mother's stack. That could be our best bet. I'll still ask HR to cover that base but I'm positive that's him. Do you think he could have murdered Patrick?"

Detective Sommers shrugged. "I'm still pondering his connection to Lady Thompson. Did you end up confronting her about the issue?"

"No. We all thought Geoffrey was a nuisance – a spy Lady Thompson had used to fish out information about our organization. He took things a step further by selling the information to the Inquirer in exchange for money and causing a lot of embarrassment for me and Ophinas. I don't recall ever speaking to her about that particular issue.

278 - OBY ALIGWEKWE

I had bigger fish to fry, what with Patrick selling off my shares to her and subsequently getting murdered."

"What about the number 682?" Detective Sommers asked.

"What about it? Oh! They're the numbers on a charm bracelet I found in Patrick's drawer after he first passed," she answered nonchalantly.

"Why didn't you mention this earlier? If my assumption is right, the bracelet didn't belong to Patrick, so why did you withhold that piece of evidence?" Detective Sommers struggled to hide his annoyance albeit unsuccessfully.

"I completely forgot about it until the other day when I saw Brigitte wearing it. The first time I saw it, I was so distraught by the letter that nothing else mattered. Hearing you mention that Ashley's second name was Bernard, reminded me of the ABC charms on the bracelet. ABC... Ashley Bernard Campbell. Makes sense?" she asked, squinting her eyes.

"Where is this bracelet?"

"Right here." Phina dug her hand into the bottom of her purse and pulled out the charm bracelet. "Here it is."

Detective Sommers took the bracelet and examined it. "682... ABC. Hmm... then what do you suppose 682 means?"

Phina shrugged and raised her hands mid-air. "I don't know. Can't you find out?"

-

Phina didn't know which was worse, the numbing fear that came with the knowledge that the killer had stricken again or the fury that enveloped her knowing that she had been deceived for many years. As the chauffeur drove through the tree-lined streets, she pulled out her new mobile phone and dialed the office to speak with the Chief of Human Resources. Unable to reach her, she left a voicemail with a request for an urgent meeting at her office. Soon after Phina sat down

on her desk, she heard a knock on her door. A second later, Danielle –
a forty-ish Cameroonian woman who Phina had hired as a replacement
after the share sale scandal – walked in.

"I need information on Geoffrey," Phina said after Danielle sat
opposite her on the desk.

"Are we talking about the Geoffrey that jumped ship?"

"Yes. That same Geoffrey."

"I remember we tried to reach him but his address was invalid."

"That's right. I was hoping we will have a picture of him on file.
Can you check?"

Danielle cocked her head to the side and poked her index finger
into the center of her head. Phina watched as her wig swallowed most
of the finger. "I'll look into it right away," she said, as she withdrew her
finger from her hair.

"Thank you."

As she watched Danielle leave, Phina feared she may have just
sent her on a wild goose chase. She wasn't surprised when Danielle
returned to her office thirty minutes later.

"Geoffrey's file is nowhere to be found," she said, wide-eyed and
confused.

"I half-expected that. Thank you. We'll look for another way to
get the information we need."

Phina knew only one way to get information on Geoffrey, but it
was going to require dredging up old wounds. Still, she threw all
caution to the wind and made that dreaded phone call to Lady
Thompson. When no one answered, she left a message asking her to
call back as soon as possible.

-

At the end of a long day – three new clients, a dance recital and a road
mishap – Victoria pulled up to Hazel House and rang the doorbell.
While she waited, she battled with her feelings about everything that

had occurred since Patrick's passing. She loved Hazel House but at that moment, everything about it filled her with dread. Her brother's death and the recent attack on Phina in a place she was supposed to feel safest left her no choice but to bridge the divide between them. It was time to reveal every detail she felt could help in piecing the puzzle together.

Phina hugged Victoria the moment she walked into the library. She had been waiting anxiously for Victoria for about half an hour after she received an erratic phone call from her. Phina noted that Victoria's eyes were filled with tears after they released each other from their hug.

"What is it you wanted to tell me?" Phina asked, staring into her eyes.

"Nothing," Victoria laughed. "Can we go to your room? I don't feel like sitting up in the library."

"Absolutely." Phina was nervous and wondered why Victoria looked so upset.

"How are you doing? I Hope you're not bruised from the attack," Victoria said as they headed to Phina's bedroom.

"Physically, no. Psychologically, severely."

Victoria swallowed hard. "I'm so sorry I couldn't come earlier. I…"

"You're here now. Are you ok?"

"I am. It's you and Brigitte I'm worried about. There's something you need to know. I don't know if it's even remotely related to Patrick's murder or the attack but at this point, I think it's important for me to be forthright with everything I know."

"Go on."

"It's about Patrick. When you asked me when he first died if I knew about an affair, I didn't want to get involved because it was more a night of passion than an affair."

"Does this have anything to do with the baby fiasco?" Phina asked, pursing her lips and arching her brows.

Victoria sighed heavily and sat beside Phina on the bed. "You've found out about the baby?" she asked.

Phina scoffed. "I have been doing a little digging on my own, and I've found a whole host of things," she announced with a smug look on her face. "So you knew about the baby?" The smug look slowly turned to one of disappointment.

Victoria bit her lips so hard, they almost bled. "I did, but I couldn't say anything before now. I'm so sorry," she said, sighing and grabbing Phina's hands while looking deep into her eyes. "If it's any consolation, I know for a fact that Lady Thompson seduced him and not the other way around. Patrick told me so himself."

Phina blinked and stared at Victoria before pulling her hands away.

"What did you say?" Phina asked.

Victoria stared in surprise and eased back.

"You didn't know?"

"Know what exactly?"

"The baby is Lady Thompson's."

Phina sat in silence for a minute. Her heart beat wildly as she punched her fists on her thighs before rising from the bed. Next, she tore the buttons off the beautiful Yves St Laurent blouse Isabel had gifted to her and walked towards the whiskey cabinet while Victoria looked on. She poured herself a glass and headed to the bathroom, littering her path with her clothing. Victoria tiptoed behind her. In the bathroom, Phina walked to the tub and placed her glass of whiskey on its edge before entering inside, almost tripping as she went in. She crouched forward to turn on the tap and then eased back. Victoria sat on the edge, facing her. With two fingers, she checked the temperature of the running water and adjusted it a little before grabbing the shower gel and pouring it all over the tub, trying hard to avoid spilling any on Phina. The two ladies sat in silence and when the water reached the level of Phina's breasts, Victoria turned off the tap and flicked the water back and forth until foam covered the tub.

"Babe," Victoria whispered, breaking the silence. "I'm sorry I haven't been there for you."

Phina grunted and stared in the direction of the door.

"I'm sorry," Victoria repeated, angling her body to figure out what Phina was looking at and returning her gaze two seconds later. "I have been looking for an opportunity to tell you, but when I found out about you and Nduka, I was so upset that I decided to mind my business. After you convinced me you and Nduka never dated while Patrick was alive, I decided I had to tell you, but it had to be at the right time."

"When did this rubbish start?" Phina asked, shaking her head.

"Patrick told me Lady Thompson was obsessed with him. She divorced her husband to prove to Patrick how much she loved him. She was always jealous of you both." Victoria waited to see if what she had revealed so far had sunk in before continuing. "Do you remember the story Patrick told us several years ago about the party at Lady Thompson's house when they were kids?"

"Who can forget such a ridiculous story?" Phina said with disdain.

"It didn't sound that ridiculous at the time. Anyway, the incident at the ball really occurred, but he never revealed what he had in common with Lady Thompson. They became lovers years later and broke up long before Patrick met you, but Lady Thompson's obsession never went away."

"Even after she got married? So did Patrick continue seeing her?"

Victoria shook her head.

"No, he didn't. After she divorced her husband, she fought tooth and nail to get back with Patrick. She kept pestering him. Patrick loved you. He worshipped the ground you walk on. He made a mistake that one night. Lady Thompson was persistent."

"Persistent? How dare you defend him?" Phina cried, glaring viciously at Victoria. "What about freedom of choice and the consequences that certainly, without exception follow whichever path we take? Huh? …What about that? What shocks me the most is that you knew about his affair and the baby all along and you did nothing."

Tears streamed down Victoria's face.

"He promised me he would tell you," she said. "How could he have known it would be too late for him?"

"But why didn't you come forward since?"

"I'm sorry. There was so much going on. I thought…"

"Yeah yeah…you thought I was having an affair with Nduka," Phina retorted moving her head from side to side. "That doesn't justify anything,"

"That's not what I was going to say. I wanted to say that I would have told you if Patrick didn't tell you by Christmas that year but then he died."

"I don't believe you," Phina said, glaring at her. "Yeah maybe you wanted to tell me after you found out your niece was in danger, but you wouldn't have told me if the attack didn't happen. Am I right?"

Victoria sighed and got up from the edge of the tub. She grabbed a towel from the rack and brought it to Phina.

"Please come out of that tub before you fall sick."

"Does the number 682 mean anything to you?" Phina asked.

Victoria hummed and raised her brows. An uneasy feeling seemed to have enveloped her.

"I found a charm bracelet with the letters ABC – Ashley's initials," Phina continued. "It also had the letters 682. Do those numbers mean anything to you?"

Victoria was silent for a few more moments before she responded, "Ashley was born in June 1982. I know the bracelet you're referring to. Lady Thompson made a pair of them and gave one to Patrick. She wears it sometimes. I'm surprised Patrick kept his."

Phina's face was laden with emotion. "I found it hidden behind his drawer."

Phina phoned Detective Sommers after Victoria left.

"Now what do you think?" she asked after she told him the entire story. "Could Lady Thompson have killed him?"

Detective Sommers paused for a second. "If she was so obsessed with Lord Campbell that she had to divorce her husband to be with him, then she wouldn't bat an eye murdering him if he refuses to be with her. Jealousy is a very strong motive. On the other hand, since they have a child together, how can the prosecution convince any judge that she was truly obsessed?"

"That's your job to find out," Phina said in a curt tone.

"Calm down, Lady Campbell."

"I am calm," Phina almost yelled. "It seems the whole world knew about their indiscretion but me. How calm do you want me to be? Her ex-husband approved of placing the baby with the guardian because he wouldn't hear of raising another man's illegitimate child. They all knew except me…" She stopped when she heard a knock on her door. "Who is it?" she yelled.

"Isabel. Just checking if you're ok."

"I'll call you back," Phina said to Detective Sommers and hung up the phone. She had completely forgotten Isabel and Simon were waiting for her.

Isabel walked into the room in her sleeping robe. She saw the pieces of clothing that littered the floor and tip-toed over them to get to where Phina was sitting on the writing desk, sobbing.

"I wanted to make sure you're ok. What happened with Victoria?" Isabel asked after she saw Phina's tear-filled eyes.

Phina sighed and tried to speak, but the words could not form in her mouth. Isabel placed a hand on her shoulder to calm her.

"Lady Thompson," she muttered shaking her head. "It was Lady Thompson all along. The baby is hers and Patrick's."

"How could – How could she?" Isabel said, shaking her head. "She was a friend of the family."

"Yeah, so I thought."

Isabel, heart pounding, grabbed Phina by the shoulders. "Oh no," she moaned. "And Victoria knew all along? Do you think Lady Thompson could have murdered Patrick?" she asked with wild anticipation.

"I have no doubt in my mind." Phina's tone was emphatic.

"I'm so sorry, darling."

Phina shook her head slowly. "Everyone knew but me. I feel like such a fool."

"You're not a fool. He was the fool."

25

THE PUZZLE

ISABEL and Simon left for New York during the last week of August. It had been an unusually unpredictable summer. The weather had been erratic, and hotter than usual. Detective Sommers was happy with the progress of the investigation but felt that one thing – an interview with Lady Thompson – was needed to fit all the pieces of the puzzle together. The only option he felt he had for getting one at that point was through Lombardi and his team. While he pursued that possibility, he continued to search for information on the numbered account in Switzerland where the ten-million-pound transfer was made. He got the break he was looking for when the police department notified him that Paul Evans' death had been ruled a homicide, the second part in a double murder case of which Patrick's was the first. Paul's death provided Lombardi and his team the justification they needed to get authority to force the Swiss bank to reveal details of the large transfer.

Two weeks later, Lombardi invited Detective Sommers to the Metropolitan Police Headquarters and pushed a piece of paper across the table after they were seated.

"Here you go," Lombardi said, watching Detective Sommers' expression.

Detective Sommers peered at the paper with Paul Evans scribbled on it. "Paul Evans? What about him?"

"That's your man. He's the owner of the Swiss account," Lombardi said in a haughty tone.

Detective Sommers eased back in his seat and stared at Lombardi.

"This is one of the trickiest cases I've ever encountered."

"Why do you say so?"

"Innumerable reasons. I can't begin to list them," Detective Sommers responded, leaning forward. "I got a picture of an older Paul Evans from his wife. Paul Evans and Geoffrey Sellers are one and the same person. Lady Campbell helped confirm this."

"So…" Lombardi began to say before he was interrupted by his Partner, Dawson, who walked in with a folder on his hand.

"The dummy accounts belong to Lady Iris Thompson," Dawson said with a smirk.

"I knew it," Detective Sommers said, thumping his fist on the table. "Now, there's no reason whatsoever to delay an interrogation."

Lombardi shifted uncomfortably in his seat. "The bigger issue is the ten million pounds transferred to Paul Evans," he said. "The value of the shares was at most five million pounds. They lost most of their value during the recession. I doubt Lady Thompson killed both men for such a meager amount. Do you know how much she's worth?" he concluded, glaring at Detective Sommers.

Detective Sommers stood up in frustration and then sat back down. "At least bring her in for questioning. She is the common link in both cases," he said, flailing his arms. "She was Patrick Campbell's lover and the baby – their baby – lived with Paul Evans his entire life. The same Paul Evans that turns out to be the guy she hired under the pseudonym, Geoffrey. What more do you want?" he concluded in a stiff tone.

"A strong motive," Lombardi groaned.

"I'm sure you can find one if you look a little deeper," Detective Sommers barked in return. "Have you forgotten that Lady Campbell was attacked in her own sanctuary? Don't create further embarrassment for your department. We have no time to waste here. Start by finding out where Lady Thompson was the night Patrick was murdered. Not that it matters much because I'm not suggesting she would have done it without help, but at least start with her alibi."

"Get that file," Lombardi said to Dawson, giving Detective Sommers a side-eye.

"Which file?" Dawson asked.

"Patrick Campbell."

Dawson left and returned two minutes later with a file for Lombardi.

"Have you asked if Paul Evans left a will and if so, who stands to benefit from his estate?" Detective Sommers continued while Lombardi examined the file.

Lombardi ignored Detective Sommers and shifted his gaze from the file to Dawson. "Place a call to Lady Thompson," he said, poking the file with his index finger. "Ask if she will be home this evening. We would like to speak with her."

Detective Sommers sighed in triumph. "Excellent. And don't forget that a woman was seen leaving the hotel room that night."

"Yeah," Lombardi said, waving his hand. "The image was unidentifiable. We have looked at it a thousand times. There's no way to tell who she is. And did you not say a minute ago she couldn't have murdered him without help?"

"Yeah... yeah. Any clue on who may have attacked Lady Campbell?" Detective Sommers asked.

"No, Detective," Lombardi said, shaking his head. "There is no single proof that anyone was there that night besides the people in the house with her. Our men checked the entire estate and patrolled there for a whole week. I had to pull them out to protect the other beautiful people in the city. The only trace of an external visitor besides her friends from New York was Blake Caldwell and even he left much earlier that evening."

"Well, let me know how your discussion with Lady Thompson goes."

Something else was bothering Superintendent Lombardi, something he was too embarrassed to reveal right away to Detective Sommers. When he looked at Patrick's file while the detective demanded that he bring in Lady Thompson for questioning, he noticed something he'd completely overlooked until then. Soon after Patrick died, someone had called the police department to inform the officer in charge that Lady Campbell had been involved in an extra-marital affair. The call was traced to Lady Thompson at the time and information regarding it was included as an addendum to the report. According to the report, the caller, who had asked to remain anonymous stated that Patrick's sister, Victoria had informed her of the said affair and that there was a letter to prove it. Another attachment to the report showed that the letter which was received at the police department two days after that call was made prompted Phina and Nduka's arrest.

It didn't take long for Lombardi to put two and two together, but his pride prevented him from revealing what he found to Detective

Sommers. Instead, when he looked up and saw Dawson standing before him, he asked, "Were you able to reach her on the phone?"

"Yes, but she said she'll be traveling early tomorrow morning and wouldn't be able to entertain visitors this evening."

"We'll pay her a surprise visit then," Lombardi smirked.

"Are you going to tell me what changed your mind so quickly?" Detective Sommers demanded.

Lombardi hesitated at first before facing him and recounting what he saw in the files.

"I'm not surprised," Detective Sommers declared. "Lady Thompson, I gather, has had one sole purpose for years; to destroy my client's union with Lord Campbell. She was obsessed with him. When he refused to budge, she decided that the next best thing was to destroy Phina by first stealing her company and then her freedom. There's your new prime suspect."

"It seems like it," responded Lombardi. "But I still can't get over the ten million pounds Patrick transferred to Paul Evans. It reeks of blackmail and to me, seems like a more plausible motive than jealousy."

Detective Sommers stood up and paced the room. "If you go with the blackmail theory, it means that Paul Evans killed Patrick and then took his own life, but why would he kill someone who was supplying him money? Should it not have been the other way round? Also, we've all determined Paul didn't kill himself. I'm certain the same person snuffed both men. Lady Thompson was obsessed with the Campbells. An obsession can make a person fantasize about killing the object of their affection if their love is not reciprocated," Detective Sommers said, looking intently at Lombardi. "As for Paul Evans, he may just be a casualty."

"We'll figure all that out tonight," Lombardi responded.

Superintendent Lombardi sat across from Lady Thompson in the interrogation room as she tapped her long fingernails on the table in front of her. She hadn't asked for a lawyer, at least not yet.

"So… that was a lot of effort creating all those dummy accounts just to conceal the share transfers," Lombardi said to a demure Lady Thompson. He couldn't decide if she was nervous or just plain stubborn, but he was absolutely convinced of her sense of entitlement.

"What offense am I charged with?" she asked after a while.

"Murder!"

"Of whom?"

"Patrick Campbell and Paul Evans," Lombardi answered. He recalled having recounted the charges when she was arrested at her home in Kensington that evening.

"I need to speak with my lawyer."

"By all means, my partner will lead you to the phone."

Dawson led her to a hallway and waited while she used the phone. When he brought her back to the interrogation room, he noticed her attitude had changed. She returned to her seat, a little more genial.

"It was my money," she said. "He was just paying it back in shares because he ran out of cash. It wasn't even enough to pay all he owed me."

"How much did he owe you?"

"Five times what he's been able to pay and don't forget that I had his child. If he wasn't going to claim it, then he had to pay for it somehow. He had no other choice. I'll be damned if you even remotely think there was something wrong with that. In legal terms, it's called child support not blackmail as I'm sure you're assuming."

Lombardi stared at her for a minute before speaking. "It's my understanding that Lord Campbell wanted to reveal his indiscretion and come clean to his wife and you couldn't bear the fact that he would owe you nothing after it all came out to the open. Besides, it would cause you some embarrassment."

"That's untrue. He wanted to keep Ashley hidden more than I even cared," she protested, shaking her head vehemently.

"What about Paul Evans? What is your connection to him?"

"None," Lady Thompson said, acting demure once again.

"But you chose him to take care of your baby and many years ago you hired him under the alias Geoffrey. Do you still insist you have no connection?"

"Patrick hired him and made me take the fall for him when he needed to snoop on his wife and I did that willingly. I had nothing to lose."

"But you had everything to gain. You hated Phina Campbell." Lombardi said, staring at her and hoping for any expression at all. When he found none, he continued. "Where were you the night Patrick was murdered?"

"I was out of town. Valencia."

"Do you have an alibi?"

"I was at a dinner with new friends."

"What about the day Paul Evans was murdered?"

"I was at home."

"Can anyone vouch for that?"

"No, I was alone. But it's ridiculous that you think I killed both men. I didn't kill Patrick. Phina Campbell killed him, and you idiots let her get away with it. As for Paul Evans, I hardly knew the man."

"Be careful not to insult a police officer," Lombardi warned.

Lady Thompson ignored his caution and continued.

"She charmed you and that's why she's running around free as a bird."

"How do you know she killed him?"

"Because she was having an affair," Lady Thompson stated brusquely.

"Someone, no, you," Lombardi said pointing in her direction, "delivered a note to the police station after Patrick died. This helped us tie the murder to his wife. Later, when it was discovered that she was not actually cheating on her husband, and we realized we had been working with a false motive, we dropped the case against her. It seems to me you wanted to divert attention from yourself to make us believe Lady Campbell was the killer. You framed Lady Campbell."

"She wanted to be with her boyfriend. She was a mess." Lady Thompson was yelling. "They didn't try to keep it a secret. I warned Patrick that she wasn't good for him but he didn't listen. I promised him I'd take care of him. I loved him, but I could never get him to love me back."

Lombardi glanced toward the two-way mirror, gave a slight nod and backed away from her. "Lady Thompson, we're charging you with the murder of Patrick Campbell," he said.

"Why?" she shrieked.

"You'll hear from the Magistrate." Lombardi glanced at the door as his deputy walked in with handcuffs. "Take her away."

"Rubbish, you can't charge me for a crime I didn't commit. I'll sue you, I'll sue the police department, and I'll sue your entire family. You'll keep paying for generations." She was screaming at the top of her voice.

-

Lady Thompson was kept in a holding cell that night. That same day, Victoria and Jorge, on hearing about the recent developments, visited Phina with their children. They rendered a full apology for abandoning her at the time she needed them most.

"I wish I had been more upfront earlier," Victoria said.

"It's okay. Better late than never. You still came through though."

"I know, but I should never have doubted you. If only I had trusted my instincts, all these would not have happened and Patrick would probably still be alive."

"Don't beat yourself up darling," Jorge said to Victoria. "Patrick was a grown man. We all are responsible for the choices we make."

Victoria and Jorge spent the night at Hazel House. Before bed, Phina walked around the whole house with Victoria in tow and made sure all the doors and windows were locked.

-

The following morning, Blake barged through the door while they were sitting around the breakfast table. "Lady Thompson tried to kill herself last night," he said.

Phina covered her mouth with both hands.

"What?" Victoria shrieked.

Jorge waved his hand to gesture to the nanny to take the children away.

"Oh my God!" Victoria shouted, her heart beating rapidly. Jorge came behind and held her shoulders to calm her down.

"She's been restrained in a psychiatric ward," Blake continued.

"Wow… that woman is capable of anything," Phina said in an exasperated tone.

"What happened? Can someone enlighten me?" Blake pleaded.

Phina volunteered while Victoria and Jorge looked on.

"She's been blackmailing Patrick for years because of the baby and forcing him to hide it from me."

"There's a baby? Is that why they think she killed him?"

"No. It's a long story. Just before Patrick died, I think he insisted on coming out." Phina gasped for a second. "I also think she was blackmailing him. I don't have all the details. My P.I and the police detectives have more information."

"Do they have proof?" Blake asked, drawing out the last word.

Phina shrugged her shoulders. "I don't know. What I know is that all the evidence point to her. There's her connection to Paul Evans, the dummy corporations, and then the baby."

"She was obsessed with Patrick and she hated Phina," Victoria added. "She bought Patrick's Ophinas stock right under Phina's nose. My guess is she planned to own all of it and then leave him with no choice but to run off with her. I'm certain the shares transferred to the dummy corporations were meant to drain his finances. She didn't need his hush money. She just wanted to make him pay."

Phina shuddered. "I can't believe how treacherous the situation became. That Lady Thompson is such a good actress. I would never have imagined in a million years she would be capable of such betrayal."

"You've got to forgive Patrick and finally move on," Blake said as he sat down.

"I have forgiven," Phina said, glaring at Blake and pointing at her chest. "I didn't really think I had any choice. Everything occurred outside of my physical body, so I saw no sense in harboring resentment in mine."

"Patrick made a mistake through one night of passion that sent everything downhill," Victoria added with an apologetic look.

"That's what everyone wants me to believe," Phina responded, angling her head to meet Victoria's gaze. "I don't believe that for a second. In fact, I'm done listening to excuses for his behavior. At first, when I thought he was having an affair, I mourned his memory. Later, when the issue of the letter was resolved, I went into deep mourning for his death. Now, I have no strength left in me to think of Patrick."

An awkward silence followed. The air was laden with emotion, so thick one could cut it with a razor.

"Hey," Blake said, breaking the silence. "I'm happy you've moved on with your life."

"There's no doubt about that," Phina acknowledged. "I like me. No... I love me. I'm done beating myself up for things I have no control over."

"The letter," Victoria recalled, snapping her fingers. We never discovered how it got to the police."

Phina chuckled a little.

"It was Lady Thompson, but how she got it from my room remains a mystery until today. I wouldn't be surprised if she knows the person that attacked me."

"Any news of who that could be?" Blake asked.

"None yet. The only thing I know is that it had to have been a male because I felt strong biceps. He also had this citrusy sweet smelling scent about him, but I couldn't tell anymore because I passed out before I could see who it was.

26

THE HEARING

LADY Thompson pleaded not guilty at the preliminary hearing. Her attorney, Dean Shaw - from the top law firm, Bonam, Styles, and Shaw - fought tooth and nail to prevent her case from going to trial. Dean had handled several high-profile cases in the past and won them easily. Iris Thompson's case presented a challenge to him. She was up against other prominent members of the society who had solid backing from important personalities that included Lord Macpherson and Blake Caldwell of the House of Lords. The news that his client had attempted suicide in her cell pointed Dean to the perfect opportunity to exonerate her.

On the day of her hearing, Lady Thompson and her lawyer first held a private meeting at the hospital before they appeared in court. Lady Thompson insisted she hadn't tried to kill herself and claimed that someone had covered her mouth and nose with a piece of cloth that smelt like wood varnish and rendered her unconscious. Had the guard not arrived soon after, she would have been dead within seconds. It was after she was resuscitated that she heard there had been a noose around her neck. She also denied playing any role in Patrick's murder but admitted that she hated Phina and always wanted to punish her. Convincing Patrick to sell his Ophinas' stock was one way she had achieved that. When she insinuated that her cell attack was orchestrated by Phina, her lawyer informed her that her habit of voicing her feelings about Phina was the main reason she became a prime suspect in Patrick's murder. He cautioned her to avoid repeating how much she hated Phina Campbell as that would only worsen her situation.

-

At the hearing, McCracken presented the case against Lady Thompson. Afterwards, she presented two witnesses who claimed they had knowledge of her obsessive relationship with Patrick Campbell. When Dean Shaw took the floor, he tried to convince the Magistrate of his client's innocence and pleaded for her to be granted bail. At first, the Magistrate declined on grounds that the crimes she was accused of were heinous. She also resented that Lady Thompson had tried to escape punishment by attempting to end her life in the holding cell.

"Your honor," Dean protested. "My client insists that she did not try to commit suicide."

"Did I overlook something?" the Magistrate asked, taking another look at the papers before her. "She was found unconscious in her cell with a rope around her neck. How do you explain that?"

"Your honor, my client maintains that someone tried to smother her. Her attacker staged the scene to look like a suicide."

"Do you have proof to support your statement?"

"I don't your honor but the police department should have assigned a detective to look into the matter. As far as my client's health history goes, there is nothing that proves susceptibility to such behavior. She doesn't have a history of mental or psychological problems."

"Her Alibi," the Magistrate interjected. "She has not been able to establish it."

"Your honor, she was in Valencia with friends."

"Why haven't any of those friends come forward to exonerate her?"

"They were acquaintances she just met, and we're still working on obtaining the information we need. My client almost died under arrest and has been in the hospital for the past two days. Please grant her bail so she can return to the safety of her home until her case is decided."

The Magistrate glared at Dean Shaw for five seconds and then looked down at the pile of papers on her table.

"I can't decide with the facts before me if there is enough evidence to put you on trial," the Magistrate said, looking in Lady Thompson's direction. "Also, because I don't think you pose a flight risk, I'm going to adjourn the hearing for a week and allow bail while I wait for your counsel to gather sufficient evidence to support your case."

A rumble spread across the courtroom.

"Thank you, your honor," Dean Shaw said.

"As a condition for her bail, Lady Iris Thompson is to remain in the UK until her trial. She is to stay at least three hundred feet from the deceased's families and their friends," the Magistrate concluded before exiting the room.

-

Detective Sommers was in the courtroom during the deposition. Something about the defense statement caught his attention. He wasn't disappointed that the Magistrate hadn't arrived at a decision to send the case to a Crown Court. Rather, he was bothered by the defendant's account of what she claimed to be an attack in her cell. It reminded him of something Phina had told him about her attack at Hazel House. She had mentioned that her attacker was definitely male and had smelt sweet and citrusy. Lady Thompson was more in tune with her surroundings during her own attack. She was able to determine that the attacker had tried to suffocate her by covering her mouth with a piece of cloth that smelt like wood varnish.

When he left the courtroom, Detective Sommers contacted his friend, a chemist who worked in anesthesiology. He had previously worked as a policeman before going into the medical field so he kept up to date on advances in chemicals and their usage for both medical and criminal purposes. Detective Sommers provided him with detailed information from both attacks and asked him for his expert advice. While he waited to get results back from his friend, he contacted Lombardi to air his suspicions.

"If we can get anything, maybe an item of clothing that Lady Thompson had on in that cell, we may be able to gather minute traces of the chemical and trace it to the unique chemical signature of some common agents," Detective Sommers suggested.

"It is true," Lombardi agreed. "Someone did attack her. The guards confirmed that her cell door was broken into. It hadn't seemed that way at first because the culprit went through great pains to reattach the lock. Our department only realized this after the hearing."

Detective Sommers was stunned for a second before responding. "That explains it then."

"I guess so," Lombardi said. "Who could have wanted her dead and why?"

"Someone who is afraid she'll speak?" Detective Sommers suggested.

At Ophinas, a few days later, the Board of Directors held an emergency board meeting. Through a unanimous vote, Lady Thompson was forced to resign as a member of the Board of the corporation. She agreed to step down quietly, without a fuss. It was a victory for Phina who for months had been thinking of ways to purge the organization of undesirable elements. Although Lady Thompson still had the second largest number of shares, she was no longer going to be directly involved in decision making for the company. This gave Phina a lot to celebrate, but on arriving at Hazel House she put her celebration on hold when she found Detective Sommers waiting for her in the drawing room.

"I'm sorry to disturb you, Lady Campbell, but I have new information on your attacker."

"Okay," Phina said as she sat to face him, her heart racing.

"We found out it's the same person that attacked Lady Thompson. In your case, you were able to get help right away, but Lady Thompson wasn't so lucky. He was almost able to finish the job."

Phina froze. Her heart raced uncontrollably.

"It was something Lady Thompson said during the preliminary hearing that helped us put two and two together," Detective Sommers continued. "She mentioned a chemical that smelt like wood varnish but couldn't describe much else about the attack except that she was certain it was a male that attacked her."

"Are you saying she didn't catch a glimpse of this person?" Phina finally said after she got over her initial shock.

"I don't think so. He must have sneaked behind her. Do you remember the scent you told me about? You mentioned a masculine, lemony," he paused to snap his fingers, "or was it a citrusy scent in your report."

"That's right," Phina responded, nodding repeatedly.

"The police took a swab of the noose from Lady Thompson's cell and found that the attacker used the chemical Sevoflurane to suffocate her. This chemical smells like wood varnish and is used in anesthesiology. Wood varnish smells a lot like lemons, hence the citrusy scent you mentioned."

Phina, wide-eyed, placed both hands on her mouth. "Oh my God," she sighed.

"That's not all. Apparently, Lady Thompson still insists she had nothing to do with either Patrick or Paul Evans' murder. The attack in her cell scared her so much that she is now pointing fingers at her partner – your partner – Chief Gambo. She swears that if anyone knows what happened to Patrick it's him."

"That's a lie. Ridiculous," Phina said, sitting up from her crouched position.

"Apparently, Lady Thompson called Chief Gambo while in detention," Detective Sommers continued. "The police records proved that to be true. She claimed that he asked her to keep his involvement in the share transaction quiet."

"Which of the share transactions?"

"Ophinas stocks. She said it was Chief Gambo's idea to acquire Patrick's share of Ophinas stock."

Phina shook her head in confusion. "I'm at a loss."

At that moment, she realized that the eerie feeling she'd had in the past few months was actually an indication that something was seriously wrong. But, she never thought in a million years that Chief Gambo could betray her.

"After Lady Thompson took Patrick's twenty percent, her total came to thirty. That still leaves you as the majority owner. However, the plan was for her to transfer the thirty to Gambo to increase his ownership to forty percent. According to Lady Thompson, that was just the first step in Chief Gambo's grand plan to eventually own the majority stake in Ophinas?"

"What?" Phina shrieked.

"He also worked behind the scenes to abort the IPO."

"This doesn't make any sense. They both supported the IPO."

"Did they really? Think about it. What was the cause of the initial rejection by the underwriters? Did you find out?"

"The consensus at the time was that it was too messy for the underwriters to be involved since I was named a prime suspect in the case. Wait, is there another reason?"

"Those two never wanted the IPO to work which is why they tried everything to ruin your reputation. The IPO was going to ruin their plan."

"I don't believe this," Phina said, grimacing wildly. "Why is Lady Thompson choosing to reveal this now?"

"I don't know. Perhaps because she's found herself in a tight corner and is looking for a way to back out of it. She's certain Chief Gambo was responsible for her attack and thinks her life is in grave danger."

"Chief is thousands of miles away in Nigeria. How could he have attacked her?" Phina asked in a raised tone.

"That's true. His immigration records show he was nowhere near here, but he could have used an assassin. I asked the police department to give my men permission to examine her cell. The task was professionally executed. It was the work of an assassin."

"What!" Phina exclaimed, wide-eyed with shock.

"The attacker would have succeeded if the guard hadn't heard Lady Thompson screaming before she became unconscious. He must have heard the guard coming and run off before he had the chance to finish her off. One more thing, Lady Thompson just heard about the attack at Hazel House. She said she's sure Chief Gambo is responsible for that too."

Phina, unable to take the news anymore stood up and paced the room, her heart thumping. "That woman is a liar."

Detective Sommers shrugged. "Until we're able to refute her claims, we should consider this an important lead. We need to keep an open mind."

"I'm certain she's lying. She's trying to come up with another ploy to destroy me. I find it strange that she's pointing fingers at Chief Gambo. If all this was true, she would have come forward before now?"

"Well, according to her, she didn't think he was capable of murder until she almost lost her own life. When she heard about your attack and the possibility that it's connected to hers, she realized the amount of danger she was in. We have sufficient proof that she didn't try to kill herself. The real killer is still out there."

"I agree that someone may have tried to kill her, but she could very well be an accomplice. It makes sense that she's being targeted so she could be silenced especially now she's under the police radar. I still don't put this beyond her. It's one thing for her to deny killing my husband, but how could she not know what happened to Paul Evans? She hired Geoffrey, and Paul and Geoffrey are one and the same person."

Detective Sommers sighed. "She insists that Patrick hired Geoffrey."

"Don't you think it's convenient that she's contradicting everyone that's turned up dead? Chief Gambo is her new target."

"The evidence she provided about Chief Gambo's involvement in the share transaction is getting checked out. Now that we have him under our radar, we'll also look for other clues surrounding him. Have you spoken to him recently?"

"Is that a good idea?" Phina asked, staring at Detective Sommers in disbelief.

"You never know what you might find, but be careful not to give anything away. If I were you, I'd gauge his reaction to any references to Patrick, the shares, and Paul Evans."

After Detective Sommers left, Phina tried to phone Chief Gambo, but soon after she dialed the country code, she called Rashid instead. That subtle move made her nervous, so she was relieved when his secretary answered.

"He's not in the office today. Who should I say called?"

"Never mind. I'll call back later."

It seemed to Phina that Lady Thompson had not revealed all she knew. The lady had confessed to hating her, so she wondered if the shocking revelations were a last-ditch attempt to destroy everything she cared about. Even though the news was devastating, she calmed knowing Detective Sommers would find out the truth in the end. Chief Gambo was her most trusted friend, partner, and potential father-in-law. If it turned out that he used Patrick's infidelity and secrets to blackmail him into forfeiting his shares of Ophinas before murdering him, she didn't know how she could go on. She was deeply in love with his son Rashid. The only good thing that came out of the situation, she thought, was discovering that Martin was not real. Her attack was wielded by a real-life human being. For a while since the assault, she had imagined that Martin had somehow taken a life form and exerted his revenge on her. She shuddered every time the thought crossed her mind.

-

A week later, Lady Thompson's case was dismissed by the Magistrate. Detective Sommers discovered evidence tying Chief Gambo to the share extortion. By then, Phina was able to deal with the betrayal but still couldn't fathom why Chief Gambo found it necessary to eliminate

Patrick. It was easy to speculate how he may have done it. Taking Lady Thompson's experience into consideration, all he needed to do was hire an assassin. Paul Evans' involvement and the huge sum of money transferred to his Swiss account remained a mystery. Something was seriously amiss, Phina thought as she sat outside on her porch watching as the grey clouds glided across the evening sky until a chilly wind forced her to retreat indoors.

27

NAILED

HEATHROW at nine o'clock was buzzing. Several flights had landed that morning. The passengers alighted from Nigeria Airways flight number 30 and lined up at customs for clearance. The shops were decorated for Christmas even though the celebration was still a month away. Holiday music and the sound of jingle bells filled the air. A gigantic Christmas tree strung with shiny, beautiful ornaments dominated the center of the passageway.

"Akin... Dimgba, how long will you be in the UK this time?" the customs agent asked Rashid as he leafed through the little green booklet in front of him."

"A few days."

"Are you here for business or pleasure?"

"Both," he chuckled, before retrieving his passport and scurrying through the hall and past baggage claims to the car waiting for him outside.

The car sped through the streets and came to a screeching halt when it arrived at its destination in Kensington. Lady Thompson had been expecting him, but the look on his face told her that things weren't as she had expected. In one swift moment, she was looking upon the face of her handsome lover and in the next; her wrists were tied together in front of her with a thick rope by the tall angry looking gentleman that crept through the shadows behind Rashid. Rashid held his index finger to his lips and then pointed to the gun on his waist. Lady Thompson looked around in panic and obeyed. She wanted to plead with him to untie her but her lips made no sound. He dragged her by the arm to the adjoining library with a fireplace and several shelves with layers of books – mostly encyclopedias and history journals. Piles and piles of paperwork lay haphazardly on a large table in the center. She wished she hadn't obeyed Rashid's command and let her staff leave for the night. There was now no way to call for help. What she thought would be a fun night of sex with her handsome young lover was turning out to be a nightmare. She glanced across the room as the light pole across the lot was casting shadows up against the walls of the library. It was as though Rashid read her mind because he released her arm for a second and raced to close the curtains before turning on the main light switch.

"Where are the papers," he asked.

"Which papers?"

"You know which ones I'm talking about," he barked.

"Over there." Lady Thompson said, shivering as she pointed at a desk in the corner.

-

Burning the papers took longer than Lady Thompson expected. She stood in front of the fireplace and watched as Rashid fed one sheet after another to the weak flame, stopping at intervals to check that each was turned completely to ash before he threw in the next.

"Untie me," Lady Thompson finally heard herself say after she recovered from her initial shock. "I could help make this faster."

Rashid shook his head and said, "No."

He couldn't trust her to do as he said. He knew the only reason she let him subdue her earlier was because she had spotted his gun.

"Do you have a plan?" she asked, twenty minutes into the paper burning exercise.

He shifted his gaze from the fire and said the same thing he'd said to her over the phone when she asked if he loved her. The exact same words, in the exact same tone. "Of course, I do."

"I don't understand you," Lady Thompson whimpered.

Again, he looked away from the flame.

"What don't you understand?"

She shook her head. "I'm dizzy," she said. "Can I sit?"

"Over there." He pointed at the seat in the corner. "Don't try anything stupid."

Lady Thompson did as she was told and watched as Rashid burned every original piece of evidence tying him to the share transactions, the ten million pounds transferred to him by Paul Evans and records that proved the true owners of the funds. When every piece of paper had been deposited and the last bits blackened to ashes, Rashid looked at her, his eyes glowing in the dark.

"Now you're going to help me get to Phina."

"Why?" Lady Thompson said in a panic. "I'm not allowed to go near her. You have a better chance of getting to her than me."

Rashid shook his head.

"I'm not asking you to show up at her place. Here," he said banging the phone on the table and handing her the handset. "Call her. Pretend you want to make peace."

"Untie me first."

Rashid hesitated at first, and then he beckoned to his companion to untie her hands. With her hands now free, Lady Thompson dialed a number. While it rang, Rashid looked at his watch and then at his companion. He seemed to have a sudden change of mind.

"Do you know what time it is?" he said to his burly friend, before grabbing the handset from Lady Thompson and replacing it. They made a quick dash for the door without saying so much as one word to her.

Meanwhile, on the other end of town, at Hazel House, Detective Sommers visited Phina to deliver new information he thought would be helpful for the investigation.

"When Lady Thompson was arrested, I assumed she was the woman that was seen leaving Patrick's room the night he was murdered," Detective Sommers said. "You may think it's preposterous, but at one point, I felt Patrick may have been asphyxiated through kinky sex play. Has that ever occurred to you?"

"No, that has never crossed my mind, but I guess anything is possible at this point," Phina said, sounding unperturbed.

"Well, I started to doubt that hypothesis when I learned that Lady Thompson's hatred was the motivation behind the share transfer and the treachery surrounding it."

"So what do you think of it now?"

"Good question," Detective Sommers said, adjusting himself in his seat. Still a little uncomfortable, he got up and folded both hands over his chest and paced the room. "If her intention all along was to punish you, then I believe what Victoria told you about Lady Thompson's obsession with Patrick and the fact that Patrick loved you and only you. Lady Thompson couldn't have been the one with Patrick that night. Ashley is the result of a one-night stand and the shares were blackmail."

Phina hummed sarcastically. "Let's leave the word 'love' out of this. Men don't cheat on women they love."

"I agree, but let's just assume that Patrick loves you, just an assumption and nothing more. In that case, then he was not with a love interest that night. I believe Chief Gambo… or an assassin, perhaps the same one that attacked you and Lady Thompson was there."

"But Chief Gambo's travel records showed he was nowhere near the country when Patrick was murdered."

"That's true, but the point I'm trying to make is that it's unlikely the person seen by the hotel staff that night was a woman. Judging by how Patrick was killed, a man was needed to subdue him. This is why I believe that the hotel staff may not be a credible witness."

"The cops in Barcelona interviewed the witness, and he maintained his stance. He saw a woman leave Patrick's room that night."

Detective Sommers shook his head vigorously.

"These two men were definitely killed by a man because of the strength required by the method used. And if that is the case, then it's either the woman that was seen leaving the room that night is of no consequence to his murder, or it was a man disguised as a woman."

"Hmm… This case is getting more frustrating by the day," Phina mumbled.

"It was most likely done by an assassin hired by Chief Gambo," Detective Sommers continued. "Now, we need to find concrete evidence that ties him to the murders before we can send out a warrant for his arrest. The only thing we have right now is Lady Thompson's word about a possible motive, but motive alone won't convict him."

-

After Detective Sommers left Hazel House that night, he phoned the hotel in Barcelona and asked to speak to the witness from the night Patrick was murdered but discovered that he'd since resigned his position at the hotel. Next, he phoned the police department and requested the facial composite of the mystery woman that was seen leaving Patrick's room that night and one was faxed to him within minutes. The sketch, although basic, looked androgynous, causing him to believe his hypothesis. Doubts about the validity of Chief's immigration records crept into his mind, so he contacted Lombardi and airport security. The airport was kept under strict surveillance and the sketch provided at all borders. Instructions were provided to review old recordings for hints of activity regarding anyone that looked remotely like Chief Gambo.

By morning, a few hours after Detective Sommers sent in the sketch, Lombardi received a call from airport security, a match had been found. A male traveling under the name Akin had been arrested. The sketch, along with distinctive physical descriptors recorded by the police in Barcelona as provided by the eyewitness as well as the instruction that the female head covering may have been used to disguise a male was used to make the arrest. Lombardi headed to the airport soon after while Detective Sommers waited patiently in his office for the results to be brought to him.

-

"How long have you been traveling with this passport?" the security official asked Rashid.

Rashid stared at him in silence.

"We're arresting you for traveling with forged documents," the official continued. "Which is your legal name?"

Rashid remained silent and glanced at his watch impatiently.

"Don't worry about that," the official said regarding his pending flight. "The police will be here shortly. You will be detained."

An image of Rashid, recorded with the video surveillance system a few weeks back, flashed on the screen. A second image showed him dragging his hand luggage and rushing to enter a plane just before takeoff.

"Was that you?" The official asked, pointing at the screen and staring at him with bespectacled eyes.

Rashid looked away.

"Don't expect me to answer any question without my lawyer present," he said.

"Save that for the police," the official responded before giving him a scornful look.

-

At the police station, a mug shot was taken. Rashid was detained and refused bail.

"His name again?" Detective Sommers asked Lombardi when he called.

"He was traveling as Akin but goes by a couple other names."

"Describe him."

"Dark, tall, looks well to do… I'll be forwarding a picture of his mug shot to your fax. Look out for it."

"Thanks. I'll need to share it with Lady Campbell."

After hours of interrogation at the police station, and a thorough search of his belongings which comprised a single hand luggage, the police found three passports on Rashid. They bore the names Akin Dimgba, Rashid Gambo and Geoffrey Sellers. Each had a different photograph but was of the same person, same eyes, and the same facial structure. Based on the dates of the stamps registered on the passports, he had used a different one on different occasions.

-

"Why the name Geoffrey?" a stunned Phina asked after Detective Sommers recanted the entire story to her along with a copy of Rashid's mug shot when he came to Hazel House in the morning.

"I don't know," Detective Sommers said, just as confused about that prospect.

Phina was shaking like a leaf, but she did the best she could to keep it under control.

"I don't understand what's going on. I thought we were on to Chief Gambo. Nothing makes sense right now," she said rather incoherently, grabbing the pit of her stomach.

"Rashid is the person we've been looking for all along."

Phina stared in shock and for the first time since Detective Sommers appeared, she felt a pang of emotion replace the hurt that had enveloped her all morning. "What about Chief? What role did he play?"

"I don't have all the facts right now."

Phina bent her head and sobbed, at first from the pain of her loss and then from relief. She had wanted to clean house, but she had no clue how much cleaning was needed. Things always worked out for her in the end, they always did. She just couldn't bring herself to believe the extent of danger she had been in and realized how stupid she had been. Humans were more dangerous than ghosts whether real or imagined.

"Do they know with absolute certainty that Rashid did it?" she asked, stepping out of her reverie.

"Video surveillance tapes at the time Patrick was murdered had already been erased but immigration records show he was here as Akin. He was also here as Akin when Paul Evans was killed."

"I saw him that week, but he was in Nigeria the day Paul Evans died. I spoke to him."

"Are you sure it was him you spoke to?"

"Pretty sure. He phoned me."

"There you go! There's no way you would have known for certain if he was calling from Nigeria."

"We hung out the night before he traveled. I saw him before he left for the airport. I was so sure he was in Nigeria."

Detective Sommers shook his head.

"His business took him all over Europe after he supposedly left London. He was back in London before he finally left for Nigeria. I have his travel records in case you need to see them," Detective Sommers said.

"Could he have attacked me then?" Phina asked, wide-eyed.

Detective Sommers shrugged his shoulders.

"Who knows? Those details will be revealed during his trial if the case does go to trial. The guy has diplomatic immunity. Did you know?"

Phina shook her head.

"I want to see him," she said in a firm tone.

"Are you sure that's a good idea? We're dealing with a hardened criminal."

"Yes, I'm sure. I'll like to find out a few things from him… ask him some important questions."

"I'm not absolutely sold on the idea, but that can be arranged."

-

With his diplomatic immunity waived, Rashid became subject to prosecution. Phina put her emotions aside and visited him at the prison where he was being held before trial. Wearing a blue prison suit, he approached the waiting room, but the moment he sighted Phina through the door, he turned on his heel and stood still.

"I don't want to see her," he said to the guard loud enough for Phina to hear.

"As you wish," the guard spoke fiercely and followed him.

"Ra…" Phina was about to call out before Rashid paused and walked towards her with the guard. She wasn't sure what changed his mind.

After he was seated, he stared at her with hostility. Phina, pretending to be unfazed, asked, "Is it true?"

"Is that why you came all the way here?"

"I wanted to hear from you. Did you kill Patrick and Paul?"

"Believe whatever the hell you want to believe." He spoke callously, deliberately and with a tone of indifference as though he didn't care what happened to him.

Phina was stunned by his aloofness. He was an entirely different person from the man she thought she knew. But since she hadn't fully deliberated on what to expect from that visit, she was prepared for anything that would give her the opportunity to make the slightest sense of the situation.

"Did Chief put you up to this?"

"Leave my father out of this," he said, glaring at her. "Do you think I'm stupid? You come here acting so self-righteous?"

Phina shook her head.

"I don't think you're stupid. I think you're evil."

"Then why are you here?"

"To see for myself…" She hissed and got up to leave.

"Wait," he said, sobering up for a moment. "Not everything was a lie."

Phina looked down at him, stunned by the sudden change in demeanor. "Which part was true?" she asked, choking on her words while she feigned a smile.

He raised his hand to speak, but the words failed him.

Phina chuckled and shook her head. "Unbelievable," she muttered under her breath and walked in the direction of the door. After a few steps, she looked back and saw him still sitting with his elbows on the table and both hands on his head.

-

Within a few days, Lady Thompson was interrogated again by Lombardi, who extracted all the pertinent pieces of information that were needed to prosecute Rashid for blackmail. He had made her burn the original documents from the transaction right before he was detained but luckily for her she always kept copies. Detective Sommers was present at the interrogation and during a late visit to Hazel House, he explained everything to Phina. Patrick had been a victim of blackmail for his infidelity and secrets. The ultimate goal for Chief Gambo and his son, Rashid was to own the company that Phina had worked so hard to build. When Patrick got tired of living a double life and threatened to come out to his wife, Chief Gambo knew that also meant revealing their role to Phina. That would mean losing the business relationship in its entirety and they could not afford to let that happen. They began to fear possible prosecution for blackmail and did everything in their power to stop Patrick from coming out to Phina. Chief had begged Lady Thompson, the middle-man in the transaction, to reason with Patrick and Patrick had refused.

"Is that why Lady Thompson blames Chief for the murders?" Phina asked.

"Yes. She claimed he was responsible for the murders because of her knowledge of his involvement in the transactions and the belief that he ordered her attack. Now, her fingers are pointing at Rashid."

"Why the sudden change?"

"Good question. She changed her mind after she heard Rashid had been two-timing both of you. You know that saying, 'Hell hath no fury like a woman scorned'."

Phina threw her head back and hissed. She heard about Rashid's love affair with Lady Thompson the night he was arrested. At first, she was shocked by his betrayal but later; she laughed at her expertise at picking the wrong men. She laughed so hard that by the time she met him in the prison, she'd forgotten they were ever romantically involved.

The laughter had ripped her of all emotion. Her memory of their prior romantic connection sent shivers down her spine. As the remnants of the shivers coursed through her body, she heard Detective Sommers.

"Lady Campbell."

"Yes," she said, bouncing out of her reverie.

"I was saying that she agreed to testify against Rashid in court," Detective Sommers continued.

"Who?"

"Lady Thompson. Are you Okay Lady Campbell?"

"Yes I am. How credible will she be in the eyes of the judge now?"

"She has hard evidence, so her credibility as a witness does not really matter. All the dubious transactions were done in Rashid's name. What she's provided so far is enough to convict him for blackmail. No judge can ignore that the fear of prosecution for blackmail is a powerful enough motive for murder. Conviction for blackmail carries with it a huge penalty, not to mention the financial losses that were sure to come from losing the business relationship. Patrick was threatening to report their indiscretions. Rashid had motive, and he had opportunity. I'm sure we can prove he murdered Patrick Campbell and Paul Evans."

"What about Chief? Where does he fit into all of this?"

"From the looks of it, your friend the Chief may have his hands clean here, of the murder at least."

"No, no, no. He's no friend. Don't forget he was plotting to undo me," she said, shaking her head vigorously.

"That's true, but I was trying to distinguish between the two crimes."

"So how do you suppose Rashid got entangled in this even to the point of murdering Patrick?"

"It's all conjecture for now, but after Chief tried to reason with Patrick without success, he sent Rashid – who lived in Dubai at the time – to visit him. Rashid had heard so much about the family and was obsessed with you."

"How? We met for the first time when I visited Nigeria."

"In his mind, he's known you forever," Detective Sommers responded in a whisper.

"God help me!"

"Rashid may have attempted to get Patrick on their side and gotten into a heavy argument with him when he refused to listen. Patrick must have turned his back to him at some point, giving Rashid the opportunity to asphyxiate him with sevoflurane and then leave him lying face down in his hotel room. Research would have told him it would look like a natural death, and although he went to great lengths to conceal all the possible clues – his identity, his itinerary, and the murder weapon – they were out in the open for all to see. None of the fingerprints at the scene matched his though, but it would have been foolhardy for him not to wipe any surfaces he had contact with before leaving."

Phina was wide-eyed with shock. "So, Rashid went prepared to kill Patrick that night."

Detective Sommers nodded in agreement.

"Yes, and he had his murder weapon with him – his weapon of choice – sevoflurane, so it was entirely premeditated. Oh, I almost forgot to mention how we came to that conclusion. Even though he refuses to confess to Patrick's murder, he admitted to attacking you in Hazel House."

"How?"

"You recall I told you he never left Europe."

"Yes..."

"Something must have triggered him because he didn't seem to have planned adequately."

Phina raised her hand to stop Detective Sommers mid-sentence.

"I recall something."

"What?"

"When he came to my office during his visit, I'm sure he overheard my conversation with Lombardi. He must have known I was getting close to the truth." She spoke breathlessly. "How did he bypass the security at Hazel House?"

"That was easy," Lombardi said.

"How? I had tightened the security."

"Remember, you told me Blake Caldwell left right before your attack?"

"Yes…"

"Well, there must have been a slight breach after Blake vacated the premises. Rashid confessed to attacking you after hours of interrogation robbed him of his faculties. I think his admission of guilt in your attack brought him to his senses because he refused to speak after that. His interrogators had hoped to get a murder confession out of him."

"Did the police torture him to get him to confess to attacking me?"

"I'm not at liberty to say. However, we're certain he killed both Patrick and Paul Evans. We're also positive he attacked Lady Thompson in her cell even though it's possible he hired an assassin for that bit. Both he and his father knew Lady Thompson and Patrick's secret and manipulated them for their own selfish purpose. Their ultimate goal was to own your entire company by first diluting your interest. In the end, it was all about money and power."

Phina shook her head in disbelief, her heart pounding heavily.

"I'm still curious about how they got the letter from Hazel House."

"After Victoria told Lady Thompson about the letter, Lady Thompson saw an opportunity to frame you. She confessed to inviting you for a meeting someday and sending someone over to steal the letter from your room. Do you recall when that may have been?"

Phina shook her head and shuddered at what she'd just heard.

"Treachery!" she cried. "It could be one of the few times I've honored her invitation but can't say exactly when. I just can't imagine that whoever she sent to steal it went unnoticed by my staff. Someone may have seen something."

"You never know. She may have been working with an insider."

"That just sent another shiver down my spine," Phina whispered before grabbing both arms in fear.

28

THE WAY OUT

CHIEF Gambo lost his position on the board of Ophinas after the old board was dissolved and a new one nominated for election by the shareholders. However, a request for him to surrender his shareholdings was denied. It was the most trying two weeks for Phina, whose main goal was to eliminate all the traitors in management. Following her lawyer's advice, she decided to steer clear and search for other means to rid both Lady Thompson and Chief Gambo of their stocks. Only then, she believed, would she be sure their evil tentacles had been ripped entirely off her business.

So much had changed but Phina felt she could finally breathe. She believed that after all the rigmarole; she finally ended up exactly where she needed to be. Victoria was now a board member of the revamped Ophinas. Working closely with her best friend brought her some comfort. It helped with the transition into her new life especially after the bloodcurdling incidents that occurred in recent months.

–

The week Ophinas kicked off and launched the home goods arm of the business, its stock climbed to a record thirty-five pounds a share, the highest it had ever been since the company went public. The results prompted a meeting of the new directors and a declaration of higher dividends for shareholders on record, along with a press release to announce the declaration.

A few days after the press release, Phina relaxed in front of the fireplace, in her favorite spot in Hazel House. As *Beverly Hills Cop* played on the television, she reminisced about the events of the past year. Her mind drifted to the pain she'd experienced, and she came to the realization that tough situations, with time, do really pass away. Her relaxing evening took a different turn when the housekeeper came into the room and handed her the cell phone she had left in the hallway. Detective Sommers was waiting at the other end of the line for her.

"Hello," Phina said.

"How are you?"

"Doing well and you?"

"Not bad. Rashid is going to be arraigned next week. The prosecutor offered him a deal for a reduced sentence if he would agree to plead guilty and reveal his cohorts."

"Did he accept?" Phina asked impatiently.

"No, but he named an odd accomplice in the blackmail."

"Really? Who?"

Detective Sommers paused for a second.

"None other than Paul Evans."

Phina chuckled with contempt. "I don't believe him at all. I'm sure he's protecting someone."

"I think so too. He claimed he assumed Paul's second identity – Geoffrey – to claim the ten million pounds in the Swiss account. I'm positive he killed Paul in pretty much the same way he killed Patrick and we're going to prove that."

"We've speculated why he killed Patrick, but his reason for killing Paul is still a mystery," Phina said in a perplexed tone.

"It's simple. Paul knew too much and was part and parcel of the blackmail. Paul Evans was too risky to keep around because he'd discovered their other crimes."

Phina shook her head in disbelief.

"So much evil!" she exclaimed. "Who would have thought?"

"What do you suppose will happen to Ashley now?" Detective Sommers asked.

Phina paused before responding breathlessly. "I have no idea. If his mother will pause and think about something else other than her own selfish needs, she may reclaim him from foster care and raise him as her own."

-

Phina looked upon the magic of Hazel House with a visitor's eye. It was rock-solid, beautiful, and enchanting. The house spread its wings across the entire landscape and was intentionally, she was certain positioned at the top of a hill. It overlooked the lake and the church to the south-west and acres of woods to the north-east. The breathtaking ecstasy she felt the first time she set her eyes on it several years back came back with a rush. The only changes to the place – taller trees, a fuller orchard, and an additional flower garden – were welcome ones. The fountain on the front lawn still spewed water from forbidden parts to startle their guests. Nightly, the butler still made his rounds of the building even though his services were mostly required inside. She heaved a sigh of relief as she watched Brigitte mount her bicycle and ride off while her nanny chased after her to keep her from falling. While she completed her daily walk around the grounds, she passed by the lake and watched the methodical process of the lights being lit in Hazel House, and a sense of euphoria overtook her.

-

With the investigation behind them, Phina focused on celebrating Christmas with her family. That year had been both magnificent and trying. She was selected as one of the most fascinating people that lived in 1984 by Farber Magazine. During her interview for the Magazine's annual issue, the reporter asked about her approach to raising Brigitte in a male-dominated world.

"Very difficult," she said with a smile so bright as though a ray of sunshine settled in her soul on that cold, sunny morning. "I'm trying to teach her that the future will be better for females, but she's still too young to understand that. She's a very intelligent girl, so I have no doubt she'll do fantastically well."

"Just like her mother!" The interviewer said, nodding fervently.

Phina chuckled lightly and raised her left index finger.

"Don't forget her father," she added. "He was a fine man."

Phina almost drifted off into a daydream as she thought about her beautiful, olive-skinned, hazel eyed six-year-old when the interviewer's voice jolted her.

"Indeed, God bless his soul."

-

Nduka was in London for Christmas and New Year. He saw Phina's interview on television and called to congratulate her. They chatted like old friends and even though she had given him an affirmative "no" in the past, she realized after she spoke with him that he still had strong feelings for her. He phoned several times over the holidays and made several attempts to meet, but she was just never able to see him. It wasn't for want of trying but for the need to ensure she had straightened her priorities.

Two days before New Year, they had an excruciatingly long and emotionally charged phone conversation where Nduka pleaded for her to take him back. In deep turmoil, she confided in Victoria.

"Invite him to our holiday in Jamaica," Victoria said.

"What?" Phina screeched, causing Victoria to almost jump off her seat. "That's a crazy suggestion. Thanks, but not in a million years."

Phina had been dreaming about their getaway, during which she would reunite with Isabel and Simon and sip margaritas by the beach at daytime and dance to calypso and reggae by night. She was already overwhelmed that Nduka had met with Blake in a pub to ask Blake to plead with her on his behalf. Blake, like the protective brother, had tried to convince Nduka that he was undeserving of her love.

"So, where's your mind at?" Victoria asked.

Phina paused for a moment before responding.

"Nduka is a gentleman, very deserving, also dashing, and worthy of some consideration but going with him would be terribly anticlimactic."

"Think about the future," Victoria rejoined.

Phina nodded in agreement.

"I have. I have braced myself to face my future."

A feeling of déjà vu crept underneath her belly as she uttered those last words. It was just a feeling, nothing she wanted to act on at the moment, so she paused a little before she announced, "I've decided that my new life, my newly found freedom, and all its glorious ramifications will fill the bill."

THE END

ACKNOWLEDGMENTS

As always, I would like to thank the Almighty God, with whom this was made possible.

To Mom and Dad, thank you for providing me with the right foundation to do this work. Mom, thank you for making me believe I could do anything I set my mind to and for always supporting my efforts. Dad, thank you for teaching me the love of reading. I read everything in your huge library, from novels to encyclopedias, history books, law books, and even your court briefs.

To Dumkele and Nnamdi, my two wonderful assistants. Thank you, Dumkele, for your detailed and comprehensive first set of reviews. Thank you, Nnamdi, for your masterfully done digital productions.

To Ofor, thank you for always multi-tasking to make sure everything goes according to plan.

To Ogo, Ogbo, Kene, and Azubuike. Thank you for reading my drafts. Your advice and feedback helped me take this story to a level that it could not have reached without you.

To Chichi and Moby. Thank you for cheering me on and always providing your unwavering support.

To my family and friends. Thanks for encouraging me in so many ways. Your support has not gone unnoticed. I truly love and appreciate you all.

ABOUT THE AUTHOR

Oby Aligwekwe is the author of NFUDU: Skirts, Ties, and Taboos. These days, she combines a professional accounting career with being a full-time writer. Her writings incorporate her favorite things: fashion; travel; business; humor; mystery, and strong female protagonists. HAZEL HOUSE is her second novel. Oby devotes time to helping the less privileged mainly through her charity Éclat Beginnings. She allocates her time between Nigeria and Canada where she lives with her husband and two children.

Twitter: @obyaligwekwe
Facebook: obyaligwekweauthor
Instagram: obyaligwekwe
www.obyaligwekwe.com

ALSO BY

OBY ALIGWEKWE

Praise for NFUDU

"*A Delicious Read*" – KC M, London, UK

"*A Heart Tugging Story*" – Juliet, Canada

"*Very educative, with lots of history interwoven with romance, and filled with suspense and crazy twists that took my breath away.*" – Chikaego, U.S

Made in the
USA
Middletown, DE